AN AMISH
FAMILY
REUNION

MARY ELLIS

HARVEST HOUSE PUBLISHERS

EUGENE, OREGON

Cover by Garborg Design Works, Savage, Minnesota

AN AMISH FAMILY REUNION
Copyright © 2012 by Mary Ellis
Published by Harvest House Publishers
Eugene, Oregon 97402
www.harvesthousepublishers.com

Library of Congress Cataloging-in-Publication Data
Ellis, Mary,
    An Amish family reunion / Mary Ellis.
        p. cm.
    ISBN 978-0-7369-4487-8 (pbk.)
    ISBN 978-0-7369-4488-5 (eBook)
    1. Amish—Fiction. 2. Family reunions—Fiction. 3. Life change events—Fiction. 4. Partnership—Fiction.
    5. Holmes County (Ohio)—Fiction. 6. New York (State)—Fiction. I. Title.

PS3626.E36A85 2012

813'.6—dc22

                                                            2011030460

Printed in the United States of America

12 13 14 15 16 17 18 19 20 / LB-NI / 10 9 8 7 6 5 4 3 2 1

We know how much God loves us, and we have put our trust in his love.
God is love, and all who live in love live in God, and God lives in them.
And as we live in God, our love grows more perfect.
So we will not be afraid on the day of judgment,
but we can face him with confidence because
we live like Jesus here in this world.

1 JOHN 4:16-17

ACKNOWLEDGMENTS

Thanks to Carol Lee Shevlin for welcoming me and providing my home away from home, Simple Pleasures Bed & Breakfast.

Thanks to Rosanna Coblentz of the Old Order Amish for her delicious recipes and expert *Deutsch* translations.

Thanks to my agent, Mary Sue Seymour, who had faith in me from the beginning; to my lovely proofreader, Mrs. Joycelyn Sullivan; to my editor, Kim Moore; and to the wonderful staff at Harvest House Publishers.

Thanks to my friends Donna, Patty, Peggy, Cheryl, Nilda, Joni, and Carol—exemplary grandmothers, every one of them. And to my own dear Grandma Eles, who loved me with her whole heart, even though she barely spoke a word of English.

And thanks be to God—all things in this world are by His hand.

THE MILLER FAMILY

Cast of Characters

*Brothers Simon and Seth Miller
married the Kline sisters, Julia and Hannah*

Simon and Julia's Family

Emma, *daughter of Simon and Julia*
    —James Davis, *husband of Emma*
    —Jamie and Sam, *sons of Emma and James*

Matthew, *son of Simon and Julia*
    —Martha (Hostetler), *wife of Matthew*
    —Noah and Mary, *son and daughter
    of Matthew and Martha*

Leah, *daughter of Simon and Julia*
    —Jonah Byler, *husband of Leah*

Henry, *son of Simon and Julia*

Seth and Hannah's Family

Phoebe, *daughter of Seth, stepdaughter of Hannah*

Ben, *son of Seth and Hannah*

ONE

Winesburg, Ohio

You would think that a person might be able to enjoy some peace and quiet on a Sunday afternoon. After all, it was the Sabbath— a day of rest. Yet Phoebe Miller found herself hiding behind a tree to escape from her family. There were just so many of them. Living next door to Aunt Julia and Uncle Simon guaranteed plenty of drop-in visits, impromptu potluck suppers, and more unsolicited advice than any seventeen-year-old girl needed. It wasn't that she didn't love her family, because she certainly did. She simply needed more alone time than most people.

Holding her breath, Phoebe stood stock-still until Uncle Simon headed into the barn in search of her father and Aunt Julia entered the house looking for her *mamm*. Hannah wasn't her mother by blood, but she had earned the title during the past twelve years of bandaging scrapes, helping with math homework, and remaining near while Phoebe suffered with the flu on long winter nights. She couldn't remember her birth mother anymore. She had been only five when an impatient driver in a fast-moving truck decided to pass on a blind curve. It didn't hurt much anymore. She had Hannah, her *daed*, and her little brother to love. They were all she needed…except, perhaps, for a little personal solitude.

Phoebe sucked in her gut as ten-year-old Ben ran across the yard, chasing his dog, who was chasing a rubber ball. When the two ducked under a fence into the cornfield, she ran pell-mell in the opposite direction, clutching her box of pencils and sketch pad tightly. She dared not look back for fear some cousin would be waving frantically from the porch. This time she didn't stop to watch baby lambs nursing from their mothers or to pick a fistful of wild trilliums for her windowsill. On through the sheep pasture she ran until she reached her favorite drawing spot—an ancient stone wall constructed by long ago pioneers of Holmes County. Phoebe doubted these early settlers had been Amish. Not too many Amish men would take the time to painstakingly stack flat rocks just so to form a long fence line, not when dozens of tall trees fell over in the woods each winter that could easily be split into fence rails. And not when stampeding cows spooked by thunder, or marauding sheep needing no reason whatsoever to bolt, could knock the entire wall down within minutes. That was probably why this twenty-yard section was all that remained. But it was all Phoebe needed.

Settling comfortably on a smooth flat stone, she gazed over acres of rolling pasture, lush with thick clover and alive with honeybees and hummingbirds attracted to morning glories. Those climbing vines would entwine her if she sat too long. Beyond this pasture, where *mamm's* beloved sheep frolicked and capered like small children, lay alfalfa and cornfields, peach and apple orchards, and stately pines in the distance. Like sentinels, they guarded the property line between their farm and the westerly neighbor, while a pond and lowland bog separated them from Uncle Simon and Aunt Julia to the east.

Phoebe turned to a fresh page in her oversized tablet and selected a charcoal pencil from the box. What would she draw today? Horses nibbling on fresh green grass? Sunlight glinting off dewy treetops at dawn, while the rest of the land remained cloaked in darkness? It was well past midday, but Phoebe had witnessed the dawn enough times to remember what it looked like. Maybe their three-story bank barn with open hayloft doors against a stark backdrop of pristine, unbroken snow? Everyone loved the serenity that could be found within a winter landscape. It didn't matter that it was May—and an exceptionally warm day at that. A good artist worth her salt possessed a memory capable of retaining visual imagery until the moment she re-created those images on canvas...or in her case, on a sheet of white paper.

"I thought I would find you up here."

Phoebe practically jumped out of her skin, dropping her sketch pad and spilling her box of colored pencils, charcoals, pastel chalk, and various erasers and sharpeners. "Dad! You nearly gave me a heart attack." She fell to her knees to retrieve her supplies.

Seth Miller brushed off a spot on the wall and sat down. "You're too young for a heart attack. And I wasn't sneaking up on you. I came up the same path along the same fence that you took. You were too absorbed in your masterpiece to see me."

With her supplies safely returned to the box, she plunked down next to him, clutching the tablet like a shield.

"Nothing is even started yet. I was waiting for the perfect inspiration." She giggled, knowing how full-blown that sounded.

"Plenty of pretty scenery up here to pick from. It would be hard to narrow it down to just one thing." Seth bumped his shoulder into hers.

Phoebe sighed. "*Jah*, but nothing I haven't sketched a hundred times before."

Seth shifted his position on the wall to offer his profile. "How about me? Or am I too old and wrinkled?"

She shook her head. "You're not old, *daed*, even if you do have some serious crow's feet." She bumped his shoulder in return. "But once Uncle Simon caught me doing a portrait of cousin Emma and he scolded me. He said drawing a picture of an Amish person was no different than capturing their likeness with a camera." Phoebe then lapsed into mimicking Uncle Simon's stern voice, forgetting the person she was talking to for the moment: "'As a deacon of this district, I won't have my niece and my daughter committing such a sin.'"

Her father merely shrugged. "In that case, you could draw our old buggy horse. Now that he's been turned out to pasture, we no longer have to worry about capturing his image."

"I think I'll stick to wildflowers today." With her piece of charcoal, she pointed at clumps of purple violets, green mayapples, and elusive jack-in-the-pulpits. "Sam usually has too many flies buzzing around his head to contend with."

Seth stretched out his long legs. "I saw you hiding from your *bruder* behind that tree. Has he been pestering you? Is that why you didn't want him to follow you?" He shielded his face from the sun, deepening the wrinkles webbing his eyes.

"Oh, no. Ben's been all right. It's just that he's ten years old. He doesn't understand the concept of sitting still or remaining quiet. If I let him come with me down to the river or to the duck pond, he expects me to catch tadpoles or butterflies with him. Once he dropped a two-foot black snake at my feet and told me to draw him." Phoebe met her father's gaze. "I let him come along as seldom as possible without hurting his feelings."

"Mind if I have a look-see?" Without waiting for her answer, Seth pulled the giant pad from her grasp.

For a moment Phoebe felt a familiar wave of panic. Her art was a private collection, showcasing her limited abilities. But the moment quickly passed. She was Phoebe Miller of Winesburg, Ohio, not Michelangelo of Italy. "Sure, why not?" she said, willing herself to relax.

Seth paged through her assortment of sketches, some barely begun and others filled with vibrant color and intricate shading. "These are quite good, daughter." He paused to study a picture of a small child kneeling in prayer beside a trundle bed. With white walls and dark pine floorboards, and the girl's black prayer *kapp* and white pinafore, the drawing was a contrast of light and shadows. One could feel the presence of God in the rays of moonlight streaming through the open window.

She smiled with pleasure, leaning over his arm. "That's one of my favorites. Not bad for someone with no talent and no training, huh?"

He shook his head. "You have talent—make no mistake about that. And what kind of training does an artist need? Either a person has the gift or they don't."

"A few classes would have been nice in school. My teacher's idea of art was coloring a seasonal mimeographed page. All the trees were green and every autumn leaf either red or gold. Everyone's picture looked exactly the same."

Seth dispensed his usual *daed* look. "Plain folk have no need for individuality as long as you're known personally to God." He shut the sketch pad and handed it back to her. "But providing you get your chores done, I see no harm in capturing the beauty of nature in your pictures." He rose to his feet. "Which of the lilies of the field will my artist choose to draw today?" He waved his hand toward the multitude of flowers and weeds growing along the vine-shrouded wall. "It's going to be time for the evening meal soon. Don't be late, Phoebe. You know how your Uncle Simon hates not eating at the appointed hour." Seth started down the path and did not glance back. He didn't have to. He knew she wouldn't be late for supper, or neglect her chores, or forget to say her nightly prayers...because she never did.

Phoebe was a good girl. She had never painted her face with makeup as Emma had during her *rumschpringe*, nor taken up with an English boy with a fast green truck. Everything was well and good now that Emma and James were married, raising two little boys, and sheep farming in nearby Charm. But when they first converted to New Order, both sets of parents lost more than one good night's sleep.

And Phoebe had no desire to go into business like her cousin Leah. Running a diner with a business partner as naive as she had almost landed Leah in the county jail. Who knew not collecting sales tax to send to the State of Ohio was a crime? Phoebe shuddered remembering how long it had taken Leah to pay her share of the debt incurred by the diner. Meeting Jonah Byler had been the only good thing to come out of that fiasco. Apparently, he hadn't been looking for a wife with any business savvy.

No, Phoebe was a good girl. She helped with cooking, cleaning, and laundry, and she did her fair share of gardening, canning, and berry picking despite having no particular fondness for domestic duties. Her *mamm* and Emma had their beloved sheep, along with the spinning, dyeing, carding, and weaving that came with the woolly creatures. Both women knitted such exquisite sweaters and sofa throws that tourists would pay more than a hundred dollars for one of their creations. Leah had her pie-making cottage industry. Bakeries throughout the county clamored for Leah Byler pies. But Phoebe's heart had never thrilled over a particularly flaky piecrust or the perfect sweet-tart balance of her fruit filling. Only her art held any joy for her. Painting with acrylics from the Bargain Outlet or sketching people while they were unaware lifted Phoebe's spirits like nothing else. Not exactly a practical pastime for someone Plain, but what else could she do?

With a sigh she selected a moss-covered log for today's subject. The dark moist wood, where decay added a blackish-green hue, along with the sun-baked topside, striated and gnarly from wind and weather, would provide a stark background to delicate yellow buttercups in the foreground.

For almost an hour, feeling the warm sun on her face and a cool breeze on her neck, Phoebe surrendered to her creation. Adding a bold slash here or light shading there, the flowers on paper became almost as real as those growing near her feet. She lost herself in her work, unaware of hunger or thirst or the pesky hornet circling her head. Funny how mopping the floor, hanging laundry on the line, or slicing peaches for cobbler couldn't hold her interest like this. When she was busy with those chores, all she could think about was snitching another cookie or refilling her glass with lemonade.

Finally, as the drawing neared completion, she leaned back with a satisfied sigh. There had to be something she could do with her "gift," as her parents called it. She'd been out of school for three years, yet she seldom brought to the household income more than a few dollars from selling eggs. She'd once hung up an index card at the grocery store that announced "Artist for Hire" with her name and address at the bottom in block letters. She landed two commissions from the advertisement. One, a local farmer needed an autumn replacement for his produce market sign once peaches, organic lettuce, and berries were long gone. Phoebe created a four-foot by six-foot masterpiece showcasing colorful apples, pumpkins, butternut squash, eggplant, and Indian corn. She tried to turn down the second project. An elderly widow needed someone to actually paint the white picket fence around her vegetable patch. But, of course, her *daed* made her take the job. Painting was painting, he declared.

Packing up her supplies, she started down the well-worn path to the rambling farmhouse filled with her parents, brother, aunt, uncle, and cousins. Lately, it felt as though she'd wandered into the wrong house but the residents were too polite to tell her. How could she live surrounded by affectionate and endearing people, yet still feel utterly, completely alone?

∼

Julia stepped down from the buggy gingerly, always a little nervous to see if her legs would hold her. It had been years since her double knee-replacement surgery, yet she remained skeptical about the stainless steel substitute parts.

Simon took her arm to steady her. "Easy does it, *fraa*. Did you take your pills today?"

"*Jah*, of course, like I do every day. I'm just stiff from sitting. Run off now and find your brother. With these perfectly fine store-bought knees, we should have walked here. What's the advantage of living next door to Seth and Hannah if we must drag out the horse and buggy even in perfect weather?" Julia leaned heavily on her husband's arm despite her assertion that she could have walked half a mile through scrub forest and bog.

"I'm not running anywhere until you're planted in one of Hannah's kitchen chairs," Simon insisted. "And our old gelding needs the exercise more than we do."

"If Hannah sees you practically carrying me inside, she'll start feeding me more of her herbal cures." They paused midway to the house. "Boswellia, bromelain, yucca, turmeric, sea cucumber—do you know what those things taste like?" Julie wrinkled her nose. "I burped the other day, and it tasted like stagnant green pond water."

"How is it you know what stagnant water tastes like?" Simon clutched her tightly around the waist as they reached the porch.

"I'd rather not say what my sister was like as a teenager."

"Whatever she gives you to eat or drink, you'll take without complaint. One of these days Hannah will land on a miracle cure that will have you skipping like a schoolgirl again."

Julie gulped a deep breath and climbed the steps, clucking her tongue in disapproval. "Miracles from teas and tonics? And you—the district deacon. What's gotten into you?" She reached for the door frame to steady herself.

"All miracles come from the Lord, but He uses a wide variety of delivery methods." Simon kissed her cheek. "I'll see you at supper."

Julia waited until she stopped panting like a dog before entering her sister's large, airy kitchen. "Hannah," she called, finding the room empty.

Hannah Miller bustled into the room looking as fresh and cheery as she had ten years ago. Amazing what the lack of chronic pain did for a person's appearance and attitude. "You're alone?" she said, pulling aside the curtain. "Where are your daughters? I prepared way too much glazed ham and potato salad if the rest of your family isn't coming to eat." She left the window and carried tall glasses of iced tea to the table.

Julia smiled, lowering herself onto a chair. "Just Simon and myself, but I promise to eat ravenously. Henry will stop over later. He took the open buggy for a ride after spending hours yesterday polishing every inch with leather oil. I think he's courting some gal, but when I drop subtle hints, he turns beet red and clams up."

Hannah sat on the opposite side of the long table—a table large enough to seat the entire Miller clan. "You, subtle?" She winked one luminous green eye. "Julia, you're as subtle as a blind bull in a spring pasture. Poor Henry, being the only one left at home. What about Leah? She's not coming either?" Hannah laced her fingers over her still flat belly. "I was itching for one of her peach pies."

"No fresh peaches yet. You would know that if you left your loom and spinning wheel once in a while. And all her canned peaches are gone. Anyway, she and Jonah are staying home today, as are Emma, James, and their two boys." Julia leaned back in her chair. "I saw Ben chasing that dog of his, but where's Phoebe?" She craned her neck to scan the living room. "Let me guess. She's upstairs immortalizing the intricacies of a spider in her web instead of whacking it down with a broom."

Hannah took a long swallow of tea. "Too warm upstairs in her room. She headed to the high pasture with her tablet. Seth walked up to check on her, although she can't get lost or into any trouble up there. Still, he would prefer she stay within eyeshot of the house at all times."

"I remember when you used to hide from people. Sometimes in the woods, sometimes down by the river when you first moved here from Lancaster. Especially whenever my Simon crawled up your neck."

Hannah snorted dismissively. "I wasn't hiding from your Simon. I was plotting how to snare Seth into my web, just like Phoebe's pet spider. It wasn't easy, but I ran away from him so often he finally caught me."

The two enjoyed a chuckle. "The two Kline sisters marrying the two Miller brothers. It sure made things handy, no? Maybe that's what your Phoebe does when she wanders off by herself. She's plotting how to capture the eye of some hapless young man at the next social event. Isn't she seventeen?"

"Almost eighteen. But no, she won't go to singings. She says they make her nervous. She'll only attend work frolics and quilting parties. Not too many eligible young men attend sewing bees." Hannah finished her tea and rose to refill both glasses. "She says she has nothing in common with boys her age."

"How would she know if she never steps out from behind your skirt? Has she ever talked to boys other than to say 'Pass me the catsup?'" The words escaped Julia's mouth before she could clamp her jaw shut. She mentally winced at her bad habit of overstepping the role of big sister. Running roughshod over folks—that's how Simon referred to it.

"Phoebe's still young. She has plenty of time. People aren't marrying so early anymore, not like when we were that age." Hannah tucked a stray lock of flaxen hair under her prayer *kapp*.

Julia rubbed her fingers one at a time. "She shouldn't spend so much time alone. It's not healthy."

Hannah shot Julia a look that meant *You're treading dangerously close to thin ice.* "I realize with both of your daughters married that you have no one to needle and advise. You can always go back to me to keep your talons razor sharp."

"*Ach*, I would, but I threw my hands up years ago and declared you a hopeless case. You listen to advice as well as your sheep." Julia stared out the window where the lilac bush was in full bloom without seeing the profusion of flowers. "At least your daughter has come a long way since you started courting Seth. How long did Phoebe go without speaking a single word—eight months, a year?"

Hannah paused to consider. "Almost a year and a half. Constance's death pulled the rug out from under her feet. Seth was trying to cope with a household without his wife, along with his own grief. He was too busy and too distracted to notice a little girl in serious pain." She furrowed her forehead as memories of some very difficult months returned. "Seth wasn't spending enough time with her because he had suddenly twice as much on his plate. But how can you explain that to a five-year-old?"

"Then Phoebe watched all her *daed*'s attention being lavished on you." Julia chanced a look at her sister.

Hannah scoffed. "'Lavish' would hardly describe Seth's interest in me."

"True enough. He erected quite a wall around himself while you patiently worked with Phoebe. Eventually, she came around and started talking again, but she's still a very quiet child. No one would believe she was a Miller if she wasn't the spitting image of Seth. They would have figured Constance discovered a foundling in the parking lot of Walmart and brought her home."

Hannah's smile looked bittersweet. "Seth didn't like being told how to raise his daughter, did he, but eventually he ran out of choices and took my suggestions." She shook off the reminiscence like a dog in the rain. "Now he dotes on the girl, as much as she'll allow him, to the point of wrapping her in a cocoon. Pity the poor boys that come around when Phoebe starts courting. Seth will probably stand guard in the front room with his squirrel rifle across his chest."

"I didn't know Seth ever went hunting." Julia lifted one eyebrow.

"He doesn't. He inherited that relic of a firearm from his *daed*. Just don't tell the young men that gun hasn't been fired in twenty years." They enjoyed a good belly laugh while Hannah started pulling side dishes from the refrigerator.

To feel useful, Julia pushed herself up from the table to get plates, glasses, and silverware. Sitting too long stiffened her arthritic joints, hastening the day when she would need more replacement parts. By the time Hannah carried the platter of sliced ham to the table, in trailed Seth, Simon, Ben, and Henry. Julia blinked at her son's early appearance. "You're back from your ride already, son?"

Henry's ears reddened while he washed his hands at the sink. "I saw what I set out to see." He slunk to a chair like a stray barn cat.

Phoebe slipped into the house then, joining them just in time for silent prayer. The moment everyone lifted their bowed heads and began passing bowls of food, Henry turned to his cousin. "After we eat,

Phoebe, would you like to see my new filly?" Despite the fact he was a grown man at twenty-one, he blushed whenever he addressed females, even family members.

"Sure," she agreed, popping a gherkin into her mouth. "What's wrong with this one?"

"Hardly anything. I picked her up at the Sugarcreek auction for a song. She had a mild limp, so other buyers passed her over." He drained half his glass of milk.

Simon set down his fork, dabbing his beard with his napkin. "You bought a *lame* horse, son? What are we going to do with her if she's not fit for the buggy or pulling a plow?"

Julia and Hannah exchanged a glance. Father and son had been down this road enough times to wear grooves in the pavement.

"She's not lame, Dad. A slight limp, that's all. And she's much improved since I started applying liniment and wrapping the leg." Henry built a sandwich with home-baked rye bread, several slices of ham, and hot pepper relish.

Simon grunted, picking up his coffee cup. "Could she at least pull a pony cart to earn her keep?"

"Eventually. Maybe." Henry bit into the stack, rendering further speech impossible.

"Look at it this way—she is a filly and could turn into a fine brood mare someday." Seth interjected his two cents' worth into the conversation.

Simon's brows beetled above the bridge of his nose, focusing on his brother. "We don't have room for the horses we own now. They're already two to a stall, and my horse pasture is grazed down to nubs by July. I'll have to start feeding them oats and timothy year-round."

"Maybe I'll lease you some of our pastureland. Hannah's flock is down this year. If you're willing to pay me a fair price, that is." Seth bit the inside of his cheek to keep from laughing.

"I think it's a fine thing you're doing, nephew," said Hannah, slicing pies at the counter. "Rescuing balky horses from the auction kill pen and then retraining them for useful lives is a noble calling."

Julia watched Hannah aim her dazzling smile at Simon. After all these years, she still loved getting her brother-in-law's goat.

"*Jah*, Hannah," said Simon. "But the idea was to resell the horses at a profit and make a little income while he's doing his good deed."

"I have sold some," said Henry, after swallowing another mouthful of sandwich. "Just last month I sold that three-year-old Morgan to the bishop's son. He couldn't believe the change that had come over that horse with two years of training."

Simon rolled his eyes, pushing away his plate. "Two years for a Morgan to let someone put a saddle on his back?" His muttering was barely audible, knowing he was outnumbered by animal lovers in his brother's home. "Fine, nursemaid your new filly. Just don't turn my barn into the Miller Horse Sanctuary."

Phoebe straightened up in her chair. Small and shy, it was easy to forget she was in the room. "That has a nice ring to it." She flashed Henry a grin. "Would you like me to make you a sign to put down by the road? I could paint a stallion and mare, with a young filly in the foreground. I'm pretty good at drawing horses." She winked one warm cocoa-brown eye at him.

Some of Julia's tea slipped down her windpipe and then flew right out her nose as she gagged and coughed. The rest of the family laughed more moderately, except for her beloved husband, Simon. He simply stared at his favorite niece as though she'd grown a tail.

"*Danki* for your generous offer, Phoebe, but that won't be necessary," he said in his most patient voice. "Everyone in the county already knows the location of Henry's save-a-horse society." Simon reached for the largest slice of pie among the dessert plates.

Julia wiped her face and then left the table to blow her nose, trying to compose herself. She knew she needed to better control her drinking habits because she had a feeling it would be one long, hot summer.

TWO

Phoebe followed Henry outside once the table had been cleared. Julia insisted on helping Hannah with the dishes, granting Phoebe an unexpected reprieve from kitchen chores. She practically had to run to keep up with her cousin's long strides as he walked toward the hitching post. In the shade of a sugar maple waited his usual Standardbred horse, harnessed to his courting buggy. But Phoebe would never refer to the open two-seater in such a way unless she wished Henry to turn purple. And because he was her favorite cousin, she did everything possible to avoid embarrassing him.

"Where's your filly with a limp?" she asked. "I thought she would be tethered to the back of your buggy."

"Climb in and I'll drive you to our place. I didn't want her standing around in the sun too long. Not until that leg is fully healed." Henry freed the reins, stepped up into the buggy, and clucked his tongue to the gelding. They took off at a fast trot toward the road, even though the trip next door wouldn't take long.

"It sounded to me as though you waited for Sunday dinner to break the news to your father about the filly." Phoebe appreciated his clever forethought.

He tipped the brim of his straw hat up and grinned. "Do you take me for a dope, cousin? I knew Dad wouldn't blow his stack while in his brother's house."

She reached up to grab leaves from a low-hanging branch. "Your dad never blows his stack. He just gives that look that makes you feel mighty sorry for whatever you did."

"You must have had your windows closed the night Emma announced she was marrying an *Englischer*, or the time Leah came home to say her business partner had been arrested." Henry smiled. "As for me, he's never really lost his temper. But he could demand I stop bringing home kill pen acquisitions because the barn *is* getting overcrowded. Besides, I thought I'd give the liniment a few days to make a difference. At first I was afraid her limp might be permanent. Now I think she'll be fit as a fiddle if the leg has time to mend."

The buggy rolled down Henry's tree-lined driveway, raising a cloud of dust behind them. Seldom was the month of May dry enough to raise dust. "What do you plan to do with her?" asked Phoebe. She turned her face toward the sun, something her mother always cautioned against.

"I know just the perfect girl to give this pretty filly to."

When Henry's ears turned pink, Phoebe didn't inquire further about the future recipient of the gift. She knew he would tell her eventually, so she changed the subject. "Aunt Julia almost choked on her tea when I offered to paint you a sign."

He drove the open buggy straight into the barn so that a sudden rain shower wouldn't mar its shiny finish. "That was a good one, Phoeb, although I must admit Dad handled it well. If that suggestion had come from anyone other than you, he wouldn't have remained as calm."

She jumped down and ran out the back door, knowing his latest acquisition would be in the shady paddock. Sure enough, an adorable long-legged spotted yearling stood nibbling daintily from a stanchion of hay. One leg had been wrapped in a bandage from the ankle to the knee. "You didn't tell me she was an Appaloosa," she exclaimed, trying not to startle the filly with her exuberance. Phoebe loved the coloration of large mocha patches against a cream-colored coat. It reminded her of chocolate Kisses slowly melting in a mug of warm milk. "They're my favorites!"

Henry joined her at the paddock, lifting his boot heel to the lowest rail. "I didn't get a chance to at dinner, not after you asked what was wrong with her. If I thought you would like your own horse, she would be yours. But I know you're not big on driving a pony cart, and you'd never ride a saddled horse the way Emma did if your life depended on it."

"That's true. This is close enough for me. But she is beautiful, no doubt about it. Good luck with her rehabilitation." Phoebe swatted a pesky mosquito, the first she'd seen this season.

"Oh, before I forget, take a look at this. My...friend gave these to me to think about." Henry pulled two folded papers from his pants pocket for her.

She unfolded the mimeographed sheet first and read aloud. "Bus trip to Niagara Falls, New York. See the famous Canadian Horseshoe Falls, ride the *Maid of the Mist* on the Niagara River, walk through Cave of the Winds to reach the base of the American Falls, plus many more attractions. Bus fare, two nights' hotel accommodations, breakfast and dinner included. Chaperoned." Phoebe glanced at the small-print details toward the bottom and peered up at him. "Niagara Falls? I would *love* to go there. I've seen pictures hanging on the wall in that tourist gift shop in Berlin."

"It's just for Amish kids on *rumschpringe*. Not a bad price either." Henry tapped the cost of the trip with his index finger.

The amount sounded like an enormous outlay of money, but she wasn't deterred. The trip's appeal grew by leaps and bounds with each passing moment. "Do you think there would be time to sit and sketch?"

"I don't see why not. Rebek—I mean, my friend said there's a big state park with flower gardens, a rock climbing wall, a nature center, a gigantic movie screen, and even an aquarium. Folks could wander around and choose whatever they wanted to see." Henry's enthusiasm almost rivaled her own.

Phoebe's breath caught in her throat. It sounded too good to be true. "Are you going, Henry? You and your friend?" She clutched the fliers to her chest.

His expression fell. "*Nein,* I can't go because I spent every last cent on her at the Sugar Creek auction." He gestured with his head toward the Appaloosa munching hay. "I dare not ask for a loan. Dad would only bring up my impulsive horse buying. But Rebekah Glick plans to go with her sister. You know both of them and could hang out together. The other brochure is from the state park, explaining the different attractions that are part of the package. Take the brochure and flyer to look over tonight, but make up your mind soon. The trip is in two weeks. You have only three days to get your deposit in."

"*Danki,* Henry." Impulsively, Phoebe arched on tiptoes to kiss his cheek. "I'm going home to ask Mom and Dad right now." She pivoted on the spot, tucking the papers into her apron pocket.

"Want a ride home?" asked her red-faced cousin. Even a peck on the cheek from family embarrassed him.

"Don't be silly. I'm going to run all the way. Good luck with your pretty filly, and thanks again for telling me about the trip." Her final words floated on the warm May breeze because Phoebe had disappeared around the corner of the barn, heading toward the path that connected the two farms.

She didn't, however, run as promised through the scrub vegetation surrounding the pond and bog. She walked slowly to sort out her thoughts. With only one chance to garner permission, she wanted to make sure her ducks were lined up in a row.

Phoebe located her parents on the front porch fifteen minutes later. Uncle Simon and Aunt Julia apparently had departed. Seth and Hannah were rocking in the swing like a young courting couple rather than two people no longer on the green side of forty. "Hullo, Mom and Dad. I'm glad I found you." She approached wearing her brightest smile.

"We weren't hiding from you, daughter. We're out here on plenty of warm spring nights." Seth laced his fingers behind his head. His Sunday black hat sat next to his folded coat on the swing. "What do you think of Henry's new horse?"

"She's very nice. He already has someone in mind to give her to. But I meant I'm glad you're together because I have something very important to discuss." Phoebe perched on the porch rail.

"Are you going into the horse rescue business with your cousin?" asked Hannah, her expression amused.

"Oh, no, not me, but I do wish to *go* somewhere." She slowly withdrew the flyer from her pocket. "Niagara Falls." Then, in a rush of words, she described the bus ride and the fact the price included meals and hotel accommodations, underscoring that all travelers would be Amish youths from nearby districts. She considered adding the variety of sites in the state park to pick from but thought better of it. She knew her father wouldn't like the idea of people venturing off in different directions by themselves.

Seth and Hannah stopped rocking and stared at her. If she'd mentioned she'd seen a three-headed lamb in the north pasture, their expressions couldn't have been more incredulous.

"Niagara Falls?" asked Hannah.

"You can't go there," declared Seth. The two responses had been almost simultaneous. "You need a passport to get into Canada these days, and you would have to have a photo taken for that. Out of the question." Seth gripped the arm of the swing as though he feared falling off.

"Oh, no, not Canada. Niagara Falls, New York—in the United States, so no passport will be necessary. But a person could view both falls while still in America." Her grin replastered itself to her face.

Seth shook his head as though trying to displace water from his ears after swimming. "Let me see that flyer." He barely scanned the details before shaking his head again. "That's way too much money for a two-night trip. What kind of hotel is this? A palace fit for a king and queen?"

Hannah's expression turned thoughtful as she started the swing moving again.

"Dad, that price includes round-trip bus fare, six meals, and a tourist pass that allows entry into several attractions, including a boat that goes right up to the falls. You can actually feel the spray of mist." She patted her cheeks with her fingertips as though catching the spray in Winesburg. She showed him the picture of happy tourists in bright blue raincoats experiencing it.

"I'll turn on the hose and aim it at your face," he offered.

She didn't reply, but her smile slipped a notch. "It might be two nights, but it's three full days. We leave *very* early on the first day and return late the third day, so the trip is jam-packed with sightseeing."

Seth was clearly not sharing her appreciation for good value. "I don't understand why you're so bent on this bus tip. It's a long ride. You would probably get carsick, and I'm quite sure restaurant food won't be agreeable to a picky eater like yourself." He refolded the brochure and handed it back. "And for what? To see a bunch of water rushing over a drop-off in a riverbed? You've been to waterfalls, Phoebe. This won't be any different than the ones you've already seen. Just taller."

Phoebe stared at the person sitting next to Hannah. The unfamiliar man picked the newspaper up from his lap as though the conversation had ended. "*Not any different?* It's one of the natural wonders of the world," she said, quoting from the brochure. "Folks come from all over to see it. So I imagine it's *a bit different* than the Tuscarawas River flowing through the old watermill. I would see so many interesting things I could draw once I returned home."

Seth lowered his brows, not pleased with her sarcastic tone of voice. "Be that as it may, you may visit Niagara Falls someday on your honeymoon. And under the protection of a husband, the two of you can visit the other natural wonders of the world while you're at it." He offered one final glare to punctuate his comments and then folded his paper to isolate a particular article to which he devoted his full attention.

Phoebe exhaled, realizing her mistake. She'd focused her explanation on the value of the trip rather than waylaying his fear for her safety. "Dad, chaperones will be coming with us. I'll be under their supervision the entire time. I'm sure they won't let anybody out of sight for a minute."

He lowered the newspaper, acting surprised to still see her there. "That's all well and good, but the answer is still no. It's too far away and too expensive, Phoebe. Besides, you seem to find plenty of suitable art subjects around the farm."

"I'm tired of drawing the same old house, the same old barn, and the same dumb farm animals that I have for years! I would love to see something *new* instead of the boring scenery between here and downtown Winesburg." Unbidden tears rushed to her eyes.

"I didn't realize our *dumb old farm* was so tiresome to you, daughter. Perhaps one day you will see the world, but that day won't be—" he glanced down at the flyer in his lap—"two weeks from Monday." Seth's tone could have frozen the water in their pond in July. Then he slapped his knee with the paper, stood, and stomped down the front steps.

He disappeared around the house, leaving Phoebe feeling awful. She hadn't meant to disparage her home, but she'd lost her temper. Tears ran down her face. When she glanced up, Hannah was opening her arms. Phoebe sat down in her father's vacated spot and snuggled into Hannah's side. "I didn't mean that, *mamm*. I love our farm."

"Of course you do." Hannah's arm tightened around her shoulders. "Let me go talk to him. He forgets that these are your running-around years. How can you appreciate what you have if you've never seen anything else?" She gently patted Phoebe's back.

"This is the only place I've ever had a desire to run to." Phoebe tapped the picture of Horseshoe Falls, sobbing like a child.

"Stay here and rock for a spell. You have no idea how much good a porch swing can do for a girl's heart. And I will try my best." Hannah gracefully rose to her feet and followed after her husband.

Phoebe tried to say thank you, but she only managed a strangled croak. Instead, she sat and rocked…and rocked, for close to an hour. Daylight faded. Night fell like a shroud as soon as the sun dropped behind the western hills. Fireflies blinked on and off, hovering over the fresh-mown lawn. Overhead, owls hooted from high branches as they settled down for the evening. She was about to give up and go to bed when Hannah emerged from the shadows. The look on her face required no explanation.

"He has agreed to let you attend the outing, providing you stay with the group at all times." Hannah offered a sweet smile.

Phoebe ran to her, almost knocking her mother down the steps. "*Danki, mamm.* I'm so grateful, but what about the cost? I don't have enough money saved." She squeezed Hannah as tightly as she could.

Hannah pried her arms loose to breathe. "I've enough left from selling my last load of wool to the gift shop in Sugar Creek. You'll just have to sell plenty of eggs this summer to pay me back." The two walked into the front room joined at the hip, letting the screen door slam behind them. "But let's not talk much about the trip in front of your father for a while. Give him a chance to settle into the idea."

"That won't be a problem. Thank you." Phoebe arched up on tiptoes for the second time that evening to deliver a kiss, and then she fled up the steps as though chased by a swarm of hornets.

She would be too busy planning what to pack and what art supplies she would need to sit chatting around the kitchen table. Once inside her room with the door closed, she withdrew the colorful brochure from her pocket. By lamplight she studied the grinning faces lined up at the rail of the *Maid of the Mist*, while the boat rocked precariously in turbulent waters. Soon, one of those tourists shrouded in blue plastic would be her—Phoebe Miller of Holmes County, Ohio. And that was the last mental picture she had before falling blissfully to sleep.

~

Leah Miller Byler cut salt and butter-flavored shortening into the flour until the mixture resembled coarse bread crumbs. Then she carefully added cold water and mixed, kneading with her hands until she had a soft but firm ball of dough. Dividing the dough into quarters, she then rolled each one out to exact proportions for crusts for four pies. She filled her pans, crimped the edges, broiled the crusts a few seconds to prevent shrinkage, and then baked them until golden brown.

Baking day—an all-day exercise of patience and love into which Leah threw herself wholeheartedly. Cleaning, slicing, and sweetening fruit for simple fillings like peach, apple, cherry, or blackberry, or whipping together puddings and sour cream to create complex parfaits—she was at her best. She would then top off her creations with delicate meringues or fluffy whipped cream, decorated with select berries or crystallized edible flowers. Leah's pies—twelve varieties, all original recipes—were sold throughout the county at restaurants, grocery stores, and gift shops. Folks stopped in at her former diner, now called April's Home Cooking, specifically for her desserts.

Leah loved to bake. Since getting married and selling her half of the partnership to May, April's sister, Leah could bake to her heart's content in her own kitchen. Technically, the kitchen belonged to her mother-in-law, Joanna Byler, who happily spent her days in the dairy churning out her beloved artisan cheeses. Joanna would come to the kitchen to help Leah fix meals, but the two Byler women seldom got in each other's way.

As Leah pulled from the oven the perfectly golden crusts that would soon become Peach Parfait Supreme, she heard the screen door slam.

"My goodness, are you all right? A twister must have touched down that I didn't even hear coming." Joanna Byler surveyed the room from the doorway—overflowing bowls of ripe fruit, balls of rising dough under dampened towels, trays of cooling piecrusts, and racks of finished pies, while a thin cloud of flour hung in the warm air.

"Everything is right as rain," answered Leah with a grin. "Although, I daresay, lunch will have to be served on the porch. I can't really set the table on baking day."

"No porch. It's perfect weather for the picnic table. I'll load bread, meat, and cheese into a hamper and make sandwiches outside. You grab jars of pickled veggies, plates, forks, and cups. And don't forget the pitcher of iced tea."

Sandwiches were ready to eat under the shady oak just as Jonah and his *grossdawdi* headed to the old pump house. They usually washed up there at midday to avoid disrupting either woman's work. Leah pulled her full-length apron over her head and patiently waited for her husband. Jonah. Even after four years of marriage, she still felt that ripple of excitement when she saw him coming her way.

God had shone His grace on her the day she chose *this* particular cheese maker to buy some baking supplies from. Most Old Order dairy farmers in Holmes County sold their milk to one of the large cheese houses, but Jonah had installed enough automatic milking and refrigeration equipment, run by diesel-powered generators, so that his mother could culture several varieties of specialty cheeses right here. Jonah and his mother had moved back from Wisconsin to help her parents run the farm. Milking cows, breeding heifers, and raising enough crops to feed livestock during the winter had become too much for *grossdawdi*. But it wasn't too much for Jonah, a tall man with big hands and an even larger heart. Strong and rugged, but soft-spoken, he had the prettiest blue eyes this side of the Pacific Ocean. Not that Leah had even seen the ocean. Unlike her sister, Emma, Leah was perfectly content at home, baking pies and keeping house for Jonah and his family.

"Dining in the formal dining room, are we?" called her husband, guiding his grandfather to the table. Jonah pulled off his hat and snaked a hand through his dark, nearly black hair. With his strong jaw and olive skin, he looked more like a biblical patriarch than an Amish dairy farmer, while Leah's brown hair and eyes and rather rounded figure placed her smack in the middle of ordinary. "What's for lunch, *fraa*, a standing rib roast with twice-baked potatoes? Chocolate mousse pie for dessert?" He swung his long legs under the table and reached for a cluster of grapes.

Joanna swatted his hand. "Wait to say grace." They bowed their heads for silent prayers before Joanna said to her son, "Sliced turkey with smoked cheddar sandwiches, pickled veggies, and fruit for dessert. And iced tea to drink. We have no champagne with strawberries or even ice cubes for your tea."

"Sounds perfect," he said, focusing his gaze on Leah.

She felt her cheeks grow warm while she passed the plate of sandwiches. Joanna filled plastic cups from the pitcher and set one in front of her father. When Amos reached for it with a shaky hand, his fingers knocked it over instead. "*Ach*," he mumbled. "I caught a case of the clumsies today."

Joanna wiped up the liquid with the dishtowel she kept draped over her shoulder. "No harm done, *daed*, and there's plenty more tea," she said, exchanging a meaningful glance with her son. "It's getting a bit warm today in the barn, no? I know the kitchen will be stuffy by the time Leah finishes baking."

Jonah turned toward his grandfather. "Why don't you help *mamm* with whey separation in the dairy this afternoon, *grossdawdi*? It will be much cooler in there with the fans running."

Amos scoffed. "You still got the rest of the equipment to sterilize. I might as well clean and fill the water troughs and throw down some hay bales." He took a bite of his sandwich.

Leah gritted her teeth. Poor Jonah. He tried his best to get his grandfather to not work so hard anymore. He'd gone so far as to hire three other men when his dairy herd reached two hundred head. Plenty of Amish men without farms of their own were looking for agricultural work, but Amos Burkholder had labored hard his whole life, and nobody would stick him in a porch rocker until he was ready. And how could you tell him what to do when this was his farm?

"I could really use your help with this particular batch of pepper jack," said Joanna, refilling his glass with tea. She placed a few baby beets next to his sandwich.

"Then get Esther to help you. Cheese making is woman's work. Your *mamm* will give you a hand." Amos took another bite of his sandwich, chewing slowly and painfully. Few of his back teeth remained, yet he refused to wear the partial plates made by the dentist.

Leah felt a familiar pang of sorrow. Esther Burkholder, Jonah's grandmother, had been gone for two years. Yet no matter how often they reminded *grossdawdi*, he still forgot. Since her mother's passing, Joanna had moved into the *dawdi haus* to care for her father, leaving the newlyweds alone in the big house.

After lunch, as the women repacked the hamper, Leah watched the two men walk the path to the barn—one young, tall, and strong enough to lift a calf to his shoulder; the other old, stooped, and getting frailer by the day. She whispered a prayer for protection for both of them, but especially for Amos and the gentle surrender of earthly matters along with fearless acceptance of what was to come.

～

Julia Miller spotted the mail delivery truck from her perch by the front window. It had become her habit to sew there in the late morning and watch for the mailman. Her world now revolved around an *Englischer*'s comings and goings rather than the slamming screen doors and the ongoing crisis of a shared bathroom in a big family. With Emma, Leah, and Matthew all married and living elsewhere, Julia's hectic, drama-filled days had become slower paced and far quieter.

It was the plight of every mother. Children grew up, moved away, and started their own brood. The number of family members might increase, but the amount of time spent together dwindled. She wasn't ready for this. She might be forty-seven and suffering from rheumatoid arthritis, but she didn't want to be relegated to the position of retired matriarch yet. Julia dropped the sock she was darning back into the half-empty basket. In years gone by, her sewing pile would overflow the rim. But that was no longer the case with only Simon and Henry at home.

Henry. Although he still lived there, that boy kept a low profile. He talked seldom and softly, and he moved through life with a loose-limbed grace almost without leaving footprints behind. Couldn't he at least wear out his socks more often?

Straightening her back, Julia stepped out the front door into the brilliant May sunshine. There was almost no humidity, while a breeze carried the sweet fragrance from her lilac bushes. And because the morning batch of mail contained a Willow Brook, New York, postmark, her mood improved considerably. A letter from Matthew—or, more likely, from his wife, because Julia's son never put pen to writing paper. Martha rotated between writing to her *mamm* and her mother-in-law. Then the two recipients would swap letters at the next preaching service or other social event to share the latest news of their children.

Julia leaned her weight against the mailbox and tore open the pink envelope. Knowing her daughter-in-law, Martha hadn't purchased the garish stationery. Wherever she lived, Martha befriended the greeting card merchandiser to obtain free writing supplies once a particular season or holiday had passed, those items that would otherwise end up in the dumpster. Frugal, that girl. Julia read the updates of their two children with a grandmother's dual-edged, bittersweet joy. Matthew's son and daughter were growing up fast, and Julia wasn't there to witness the precious milestones. But Martha's cheery tone soon faded as she talked about a change in Matthew's career. As Julia read the words, she also picked up the unspoken words between the lines: Martha wasn't happy about Matthew's new job, although she didn't come out and say so. How Julia wished they lived closer, so that she could see her grandchildren more often and offer a word of advice over a cup of coffee. Letters passed between many hands weren't suitable methods of communication when family members needed help.

Julia hobbled into the house as quickly as her stiff legs would carry her. She found Simon at the table, studying a list of farm commodity prices. "Oh, good, you're here." She tossed the other mail on the counter and turned on the burner beneath the coffeepot.

"Where else would I be? It's lunchtime and I'm starving. Is there any of that bean soup left?"

"*Jah, jah*, give me a minute to reheat it. Try not to faint in the meantime." Julia took the soup pot from the refrigerator, set it on the stove and turned the dial to warm it up, and then sat down opposite him. "We got a letter today from Matthew and Martha."

Simon glanced up with mild interest, waiting for the news. "And?"

"Something is not right there. Our son took a different job. He no longer trains horses at that racetrack. He was offered a trainer position at some big fancy saddlebred stable. According to Martha, those are expensive show horses for rich people." Her description dripped with ill-concealed disdain.

"*Jah*, that's *gut*." Simon surreptitiously glanced back at the current prices for corn and soybeans.

"No, not *gut* at all. They were living with their fellow Amish in a town close to the track. He either rode his horse to work or was picked up by an English employee. They would have been able to raise their *kinner* in an Old Order community similar to this one." She waved her hand in the direction of the backyard. "Matthew's new job is a great distance away. He stays in a bunkhouse for hired help and only comes home on the weekends. Martha is alone night after night, and I know she's not happy about it."

Simon peered at her over his half-moon reading glasses. "Did she say that?"

"No, no, she wouldn't, not to her husband's *mamm*, but I could tell."

He reflected for a moment. "Sometimes a man must make hard

decisions about what's best for his family. I'm sure if a job opens up closer to home, he'll jump on it. You know what a homebody he is."

She opened her mouth, but Simon stopped her with a raised palm. "In the meantime, Julia, don't start hearing voices that aren't there. Every young couple goes through an adjustment period." He lifted his newspaper in front of his face. "Those two will be fine as long as meddling relatives keep their nebby noses out of their personal business."

She crossed her arms and clucked her tongue against the roof of her mouth but didn't argue. She knew she had a nebby nose, but she also possessed a mother's well-honed intuition.

She hoped she was wrong about this particular hunch.

THREE

On the last Monday of May, Phoebe stood waiting in front of Java Joe's coffee shop in downtown Berlin with Rebekah Glick. She'd never felt like this before—she was light-headed, her stomach was queasy, and she couldn't seem to get enough air into her lungs. A doctor might diagnose car sickness, but the much-anticipated bus trip hadn't begun yet. The buggy ride before dawn with her dad had been nerve-racking. Seth had not said much—unless you counted "Stay with the group." "Don't wander off with *Englischer*s." "Don't get too close to the rail during the boat ride or too close to the Niagara River," at least a dozen times each. Other than that, he had merely grunted and chewed on a wad of gum. If she'd needed further confirmation that her father was addled by her vacation, that would have been enough. Seth Miller *never* chewed gum.

Phoebe had developed her own nervous tics. She had reached down to touch her recently purchased suitcase not less than a dozen times. It was navy blue with a long handle and rolled on wheels. She loved it. Her mother had found it at the Goodwill Store in Wooster for ten dollars and it looked brand new. Maybe someone's trip had been canceled and they decided not to reschedule. Hannah had sewn two dresses last week for her to take along. She smoothed the creases in her long black apron over the new cornflower blue one. Dad had grunted and muttered

35

about these too— *"The vain extravagance of new clothes"*—but at least the girls waiting for the bus were wearing Amish attire. As soon as their fathers were out of earshot, Rebekah told Phoebe about a *rumschpringe* trip in which the girls wore jeans, T-shirts, and flip-flops.

Dad had kissed her forehead, issued several last-minute warnings, and said goodbye, but Phoebe knew very well he hadn't left. He parked their buggy behind the German Village shopping center to watch unseen from afar. He wouldn't take his eyes off his little girl until the bus rolled out of Berlin, headed toward the Empire State. Her *daed*—how she loved him—was driving her crazy. Phoebe Miller was a grown woman, eager to see the world. His overprotectiveness was unnecessary and annoying.

"It's coming!" Rebekah's shout drew stares from passing tourists on both sides of the street.

Phoebe's stomach took another tumble. She hastily grabbed a packet of peanut butter crackers Mom had insisted upon and ate two as the bus came to a stop. If she threw up on the bus in front of kids she didn't know, she would simply die—no slip over the falls would be needed for her premature demise. Shoving the remaining crackers into her purse, she wheeled her suitcase to the curb. The driver stowed their luggage in a large compartment underneath the bus. Phoebe panicked. What if she needed something from her bag? It would be inaccessible to her.

Quickly she ticked off in her mind the things she might want: water bottle, chewing gum, hard candy, tissues, money for lunch—all were inside her purse. Just when the bus driver was about to lift her bag, Phoebe stepped forward. "One moment, please." With nimble fingers she unzipped the outer compartment and extracted a drawing tablet and pack of pencils. It wasn't her usual oversized pad she wandered around the meadow with. It was a smaller version suitable for travel. As soon as she had rezipped the case, the driver slung it into the cargo compartment along with the others. Phoebe blew out her breath with relief apparently evident on her face.

"Close call?" asked someone over her shoulder. The boys had moved up to stow their bags now that the girls were climbing into the bus.

Phoebe turned to see a tall boy with sandy-blond hair and expressive dark-brown eyes—expressive because he gazed up from under thick eyelashes and bangs much too long. Where was this boy's *mamm*? He needed to toss the hair to one side to see anything at all.

"*Jah*," she answered. One word, with no further explanation.

The blond young man stepped forward and put his suitcase—a battered duffel bag patched in several places with electrical tape—by the curb. Then he returned to her side. "Did you remember to put your name and address on the outside of your bag for easy identification? We'll stop to pick up Geauga County kids along the way, so the bus will be full by the time we arrive in New York." He peered at her from under his screen of hair.

"*Jah*." Again one word. A parrot could be trained to say more.

"And because most suitcases look alike and because these other folks will also be Amish, there's a good chance of duplicate names: Joshua Raber or Andrew Miller, for instance." He smiled rather patiently. When she offered no response, one word or otherwise, he asked softly, "And what would your name be?" He leaned closer, as though anticipating the revelation of a secret.

At that precise moment the bus window slid open and Rebekah Glick's face appeared. "Phoebe Miller! Why are you still standing there like a goose? Get on the bus so we can start the fun."

"Ah, Phoebe Miller. A name at last," he said.

Phoebe felt her five-foot-nothing height lose an inch or two, but the knowledge that Rebekah and her sister were watching from the window galvanized her into action. She hurried toward the steps, where the last travelers from Holmes County were boarding.

The verbose young man followed behind, right at her heels. "And a lovely name at that," he said, close to her ear.

She had no idea how to react to such a flagrant, unexpected

compliment, so she tripped on the first step. This wasn't an everyday occurrence—meeting a boy around her age who was a stranger to her. Most Amish youths reached courting age with at least a passing acquaintance of each other.

No one grabbed her arm to prevent her fall. Rather gracelessly she fell forward, scraping her palms on the dirty stair treads and dropping her purse.

At last the tardy young man intervened. "Wow, that's a lot of junk to carry around! Let me help you." While Phoebe brushed her hands on her apron, he picked up her purse and began retrieving items, announcing the name of each: "Sunglasses, tissues, pen, Rolaids, Jolly Ranchers, aspirin. Goodness, are you *moving* to Niagara Falls, Miss Miller?"

Phoebe's voice miraculously returned. "Give me that purse and stop making a scene!" She yanked it from his grasp. "And stop following me!" She stomped up the steps, pausing by the driver's seat.

The Amish man stood on the curb with his hands in his pockets, resembling an overlooked puppy at the dog pound. "But then how do I get on the bus?" He feigned a sincere tone of voice.

Her face grew very warm. "I meant later, during the trip." She turned and hurried down the aisle.

"Sit here," called Rebekah, tapping the back of the seat in front of her. "We can't fit three back here, so now you'll have room to spread out and draw."

Phoebe flounced down, putting her back to the window so she could talk to her friends. They were both eyeing her a little oddly.

"You hardly speak to anyone in all the years I've known you," said Rebekah. "And then you strike up a conversation with *him?*"

Phoebe had no chance to inquire what that implied because the subject of their discussion slipped onto the seat across the aisle. With forty or fifty different bench seats on the bus, he chose the one next to hers? She exhaled through her nostrils nosily.

"Don't ruffle your feathers, Miss Miller. There aren't any other seats

left except in the back, and I don't like being there due to car sickness."
He patted his black vest where his belly might be.

Phoebe craned her neck to scan the rows. True enough, the only
empty seats were singles toward the back. "Would you like some
Nabs?" she asked in a voice she didn't recognize.

"What are those?" He shook that ridiculously silky blond hair
from his eyes.

"That's what my *mamm* calls these peanut butter sandwich crackers." She produced a packet from her purse. "I don't know why. It
doesn't say 'Nabs' anywhere on the wrapper, but she says motion sickness is worse with an empty belly. So maybe you should eat a few." She
shyly extended them across the aisle.

"*Danki*, I will." He accepted the gift, ripped them open, and pro-
ceeded to devour all six while the bus pulled out of the charming but
touristy town of Berlin.

Rebekah leaned over the seat back but addressed the unfamiliar
man, not Phoebe. "That was more words than she has spoken since
Christmas. Who are you?"

Phoebe's heart nearly stopped beating. It felt as though it were
seizing up in her chest like a massive attack as she sank against the
window.

"My name's Eli Riehl. And I often affect people that way. Either
they run away fast when they see me coming or, if they stick around,
I seem to get them talking." He offered a lopsided grin to the Glicks.
"And now poor Miss Miller has nowhere to run. She's trapped like a
rat on the *Titanic*." He pivoted slightly on the seat to face her. "Eli
Riehl," he repeated. "I was hoping you would ask me my name,
but when you didn't, I figured I'd frightened you off. I'm glad your
friends aren't as shy as you and broke the ice." He winked playfully
at the sisters.

"Rebekah and Ava," said the older of the two, tapping her collar-
bone and then her sister's arm.

"I am not frightened by you and I am not shy...well, only a little bit. And what the heck is the *Titanic*?" Phoebe's words issued forth louder than expected.

People sitting nearby turned around to stare and snicker. Amish women seldom used the word "heck."

But Eli Riehl didn't seem fazed by her sudden outburst. "The *Titanic* was the largest passenger ship in the world a century ago. Very fancy, and her builders proclaimed her to be unsinkable. But on her initial voyage to the U.S. she hit an iceberg and sank to the bottom of the ocean. Most of her passengers perished because there weren't enough lifeboats for everyone on the *unsinkable* vessel." His expression turned somber out of respect.

Phoebe squinted at this person badly in need of a haircut. Amish women might never say "heck," but few Amish men would ever say "proclaimed" or "perished." She glanced back at her friends. For the moment, several horses kicking up their hooves in a spring meadow had distracted them. "Why do you talk like that, using all those fancy words?" Her question was barely a whisper, but it triggered a dazzling smile on his face.

He stood and smoothly slid onto her bench. "May I join you, Miss Miller? I don't want anyone else to overhear what I'm about to confide."

She was mortified—a boy on the girls' side? But surprisingly enough, no chaperone swooped in to separate them with a battery-powered cattle prod. Perhaps the idea of a *rumschpringe* trip did bend a few rules. "All right, but just for a spell," she murmured.

"*Danki.* I don't want too many folks to know this about me, especially no other males." He nodded his head toward those sitting on the left side of the bus. "I like words. I find them to be great fun," he whispered close to her *kapp*. "Most people keep using the same five or ten thousand tired words their whole life, completely ignoring the million or so more interesting ones. But I realize I'm fairly alone with this way of thinking. Most men seem to go out of their way to reuse the same *stupid* words."

She studied him to gauge his sincerity. "I suppose you have a point, but few people would ever worry about it. If they want extra pickles on their burger, they just say so. No sense calling them sliced-cucumbers-in-a-dill-and-vinegar-brine where you're hungry and want to eat."

His eyes bugged out with disbelief. "I have found, finally, the one person on the planet who understands me! And even better—she's Amish." Grins didn't get any bigger than his.

"But I don't understand. I said there's no need to use fancy terminology for a bunch of pickles."

He cocked his head to one side. "True enough, if we were simply having lunch at a fast-food restaurant, but I love to make up stories. So it's rather like a great pot of vegetable soup—the bigger the variety of good things you put in, the better it will taste."

She blinked. "Where are you from, Eli? Did you just move here?"

"Oh, no. I've lived in Holmes County my whole life. The Riehls have owned our farm for seven generations."

The surname did ring a bell, but Phoebe was certain she'd never seen him before. "How come we haven't met?" She thought that was a kinder way of asking, *Did you drop out of the sky from a passing flying saucer?*"

He resumed his whispered mode of conversation. "I don't go to social gatherings much. The one time I was talked into playing volleyball, I was pretty terrible. When I tried to return a serve, the ball bounced off my forehead instead." He touched a spot above his eyebrow.

Phoebe bit her cheek to keep from laughing. "Volleyball isn't as easy as it looks. I myself have never developed much expertise at the game."

He nodded, those silky bangs obscuring his piercing dark eyes. "I'm afraid it wasn't just volleyball. When I went to a Saturday softball game behind the Winesburg Library, my cousin talked me into playing centerfield. His team was short a man or he never would have asked. Anyway, a fly ball came sailing right at me. When I put up my mitt to catch it, the sun blinded me, and the ball fell right through my glove and landed at my feet. Then it took me three attempts to pick up the ball because I was so flustered. Needless to say, the other team scored an infield home run, and nobody's asked me to fill in ever since." He added an easy laugh. "Truth is, Miss Miller, I'm not much good at sports and that doesn't bother me. Although I don't admit that to my own kind." He again gestured with his head toward the left.

A dozen ideas swam through her head, but with Eli Riehl sitting so close, she could hardly place them into a sensible order. Winesburg? His ill-fated baseball debut had been in her hometown, yet she'd managed never to run into him.

"Phoebe," she said after a half-minute pause. "Please call me Phoebe."

That pulled his mouth into a smile. "So, that's why we've never officially met. I stay away from parties—I only go to barn raisings—and the singing at church services is enough singing for me. But, actually, I think I have seen you once before. It was at an auction fund-raiser. You wandered off from everybody else with a giant pad of paper. I followed you to see where you were going and what you were up to."

Just then the speakers blared with loud, raucous rock music. The driver quickly adjusted the volume down slightly, but the music rendered further conversation—or any thought process—impossible. Mrs. Stoltzfus, one of their chaperones, bustled up the aisle with a speed that belied her substantial body girth. After a short discussion with the driver, the music ceased altogether.

A little while later, after the bus had picked up the Geauga County travelers, Mrs. Stoltzfus returned to the front and clapped her hands. "Welcome, everyone," she said. "Now that we are all together, I would like you to listen to an interesting story Eli told me while waiting for the bus to arrive this morning. It supposedly is true, although parts do sound far-fetched. But, either way, I think you will enjoy hearing it."

The crowd grew quiet as Eli Riehl stood and walked up the aisle, very dignified. Several people clapped as others patted his arm, offering words of encouragement.

"Tell a good one, Eli," said one girl.

"Make up the parts you don't remember, Eli. Makes for a better story," said a boy two rows ahead. Apparently, this mysterious young man was only unknown to Phoebe Miller and anyone else who seldom left the farm except to go to church or the post office. She clapped lightly along with the crowd for want of something better to do.

Eli leaned one shoulder against a pole to prepare for bumps in the road, tugged down his black vest, and cleared his throat. Phoebe swallowed hard as a case of nerves gripped her stomach, as though she were the one addressing the tour group. Quickly, she pulled out another cracker pack. While she nibbled on Nabs, Eli launched into an intriguing tale of a middle-aged schoolmarm who had lived in the Niagara Falls region. Because she'd never married and had been a poor saver, she faced her pending retirement in a state of abject poverty. Resourceful her entire life, the woman decided to navigate the mighty Niagara River in a wooden barrel. Many had tried before but few had succeeded. Annie Edson Taylor believed her bravery in surviving the fall would bring her fame and fortune for the rest of her life. Hoping to generate an income from interviews and public speaking engagements, she alerted the local newspapers about her daring plan. That day they set up their camera tripods downstream of Horseshoe Falls, where the woman's friends were to watch for the barrel and drag it ashore. Upriver, trusted helpers drilled small air holes in the lid and then helped the sixty-three-year-old teacher, wearing a long dress and fancy hat, into the barrel. Because the schoolmarm realized this stunt could very well lead to her demise, she clutched her beloved pet—an all-black cat—in her arms for the ride. The helpers nailed down the lid and pushed the barrel off into the strong current. Bobbing and jostling, the barrel tumbled in the treacherous rapids to the brink of the falls.

Eli paused in his narration, while the silent crowd inhaled a collective breath. Phoebe, among others, thought the reckless spinster would surely be pulled out at the last moment and given a stern talking-to by her pastor or perhaps the police.

After a moment, he continued. "No one on shore suspected a human being was tucked up inside the bobbing cork. Over she went, falling hundreds of feet into the crush of waves and rocks below."

"Did the barrel bust apart into a million pieces?" called out a voice.

"Did the poor soul drown?" asked another.

"Did they ever find any remains of her body?" inquired a practical-natured sort.

Questions from the audience sang out as everyone began to clamor with their own likely scenarios. Then Eli raised his hand as though holding a patriarch's staff. The busload of normally talkative youths grew silent once again. "She lived!" he announced to thunderous applause and hoots of joy. "Miss Taylor's helpers lassoed the barrel with ropes from small boats and towed it ashore. When they pried off the lid, out leaped the teacher's cat in fine shape, only a bit perturbed, as we know cats can get. But," said Eli, roping in his audience like Miss Taylor's barrel, "the cat's fur, formerly pure black, was white as new-fallen snow, every bit of it."

"No!" cried several in unison.

"*Jah*," concluded Eli with conviction. "At least that's what the reporters said in the newspaper." He gave his vest a satisfied tug.

"But what happened to Annie?" hollered Rebekah Glick.

Eli's expression sobered. "When they helped her from the barrel, she was bruised and battered but not seriously injured." There was plentiful applause from the girls' side with a smattering from the boys'. "The sixty-three-year-old teacher had survived the one-hundred-seventy-five-foot drop over Niagara Falls in a wooden barrel—a feat many younger and stronger men could not accomplish." Applause now rose from both sides of the bus. "However, her scheme to generate a retirement income from speaking engagements never panned out. Alas, her fame soon faded, and she died forgotten and penniless in her old age."

Phoebe watched Eli place his hand over his heart upon uttering the word "alas" and felt her own pang of sorrow for a woman dead for many years. She had been enthralled by the story of Annie Taylor… and by Eli Riehl. Needless to say, she'd never met anyone so articulate and verbose. His story came alive in the mind of each who had heard it. That indeed was a rare gift. Phoebe joined with the others in a round of applause. When Eli sat down, he didn't sit with her again but slipped into a seat on the boys' side.

Mrs. Stoltzfus delivered a hands-on-hips warning about the dire fate of most who attempted to "ride the falls" lest anyone on the bus would be stupid enough to get such a notion.

Phoebe wasn't stupid enough, but her own creative fires had been stoked. She took out her pad and pencils and began illustrating Eli's tale: the teacher standing tall with her precocious black cat, the barrel riding the tumultuous currents down the river, then the barrel falling though mist and spray to the sharp rocks below, and one of Miss Taylor emerging with hat askew and badly mussed hair, clutching a pure-white cat. She sketched and shaded with frenetic glee, ignoring her travel companions. She ate lunch at the rest area picnic table without tasting her sandwich and only barely following Rebekah's chatter about new clothes. For the remainder of the way, Phoebe created pictures of Eli's narrative about a place she'd never seen. She could always change them later if need be, but his words had roused clear images in her mind.

Eli didn't speak to her again for the duration of the bus ride, but he, like his story, loomed large in Phoebe's mind. When she wasn't thinking about the adventurous schoolteacher, she was thinking about the gregarious Eli Riehl.

FOUR

Willow Brook, New York

Matthew Miller was one happy man. He leaned his head back in the comfortable cab of his foreman's late-model Ford truck. He was on his way home after a very successful workweek. Only a month on the new job, and he'd already received his first pay raise. Now he received six hundred dollars a week for easier work than he'd done at the racetrack, in addition to health care for himself, Martha, and their two children. Although, Martha was uncomfortable with the insurance card in her wallet. He had a bed in the bunkhouse and dinner each weeknight included at no charge, although the bunk was hard as nails, the blanket scratchy as a case of hives, and the chow was nothing to write home about. And writing home was something he did— every Monday night so that his wife would receive a letter while he was gone, despite the fact he usually had little news since leaving early that morning. Suppers at Rolling Meadows Stables usually consisted of chili, stew, or rolled-up tortilla concoctions because many of the workers were from south of the U.S. Matthew didn't care what filled his belly from Monday through Thursday night because he would dine on the world's best cooking on Friday nights through Monday mornings.

His Martha—the former Martha Hostetler from across the road in his beloved Winesburg. He still got chills up his spine when he thought about someone as pretty as Martha looking twice at him—tall and skinny, with carrot-colored hair and ridiculous orange freckles, even though he never worked outdoors without his wide-brimmed hat. Other men tanned to a warm brown by midsummer, but not him. Matthew's forearms would remain a semiconnected mass of freckles or, worse, scaly reddened patches of peeled skin.

God had not only brought him Martha but had since blessed them with two *bopplin* in the three years they had been married. Matthew had a son, a daughter, and a wife who could cook any gourmet chef under the table. So he no longer was the skinny man she'd married. His hard work as a horse trainer at the Sarasota racetrack and three square meals each day had added fifty pounds to his frame. Although he didn't like the separation from his family with his current job, Matthew wouldn't complain.

"Wake up, Miller. Stop daydreaming. This is your stop."

Matthew opened his eyes and glanced around. The truck was indeed idling at the end of his driveway. He scrambled to collect his duffel bag, lunch cooler, and thermos. "Thanks, Mr. Taylor," he said. "Are you sure I can't give you some money toward gas?"

"It's Pete, not Mr. Taylor. And like I told you before, I go right by your place, so I'm not taking gas money for a trip I make anyway." He grinned with a mouthful of big teeth.

"Well, thanks again. I'll see you right here Monday morning at five thirty." Matthew opened the door.

"Have a good weekend, Matty. And get plenty of rest. I'm probably turning another horse over to you. The owners have nothing but nice things to say about your work. One asked me, "What does that boy do? Stare into their eyes and hypnotize them into calming down? Or maybe whisper in their ears to convince them it's in everyone's best interest." Taylor laughed good-naturedly. "Saddlebreds aren't highstrung by nature. They are much calmer than Thoroughbreds, but every now and then you get a willful one. And then we have an uphill battle to turn that beast into something in the show ring worthy of the six figures the owner paid. So I don't care if you use Zen meditation or hypnotic trances to get your results."

Matthew nodded, but he hadn't a clue as to what his boss was talking about. It didn't matter. He had his fat paycheck in his pocket, a job he truly enjoyed, and the whole weekend before him like an unwrapped gift. "Okay, then. See ya Monday, Pete, bright-eyed and bushy-tailed." Closing the door and slinging his duffel bag over his shoulder, he hurried up his driveway toward the backyard.

Their rented house sat on a one-acre lot on the fringe of a small town in upstate New York. Many Old Order families had settled in the area, enough to form four separate districts. Their home had three bedrooms, a country kitchen, and space for a large garden. Matthew knew he would find his beautiful bride of three years tending her rows of Bibb lettuce and green beans, or picking slugs by hand from her cabbages and broccoli. She would have their two-year-old son close to her side, while their infant daughter would be slung across her chest papoose-style or dozing in her portable crib at the end of a row. Today was no exception. He spotted Martha in a long column of young tomato plants. She was bent low, setting up wire cages that would support the tomato plants as they grew and bore plump, ripe fruit.

"Hullo, *fraa*, I'm home at long last," he crowed and broke into a trot.

Martha Miller straightened her spine one vertebra at a time. It was a movement of the elderly instead of a young woman of twenty-four. Once erect, she looked like herself, except for the frown on her pretty face. "I thought you'd be home sooner than this, *ehemann*. It's nearly seven o'clock."

Mindful of where he stepped among the plants, Matthew swept her into a bear hug of an embrace. "We left five minutes after quitting time. I was packed and ready to go." He showered her face with kisses.

"Stop. You'll wake Mary and she'll start fussing again." Martha placed a firm hand against his chest and pushed him back. "My, a two-hour drive to get home from work by car? That is just ridiculous." She wiped her hands against her apron and walked gingerly down the row.

"It is far away, but you don't want to move closer to my new job. I'm sure I could find us a suitable home with room for a garden for the same rent we're paying here."

"There are no Amish families living near Rolling Meadows," she stated simply.

"No, but I could come home every night to my cheerful wife." He heard a small but distinctive chuckle even though her back was turned.

"I would be much more cheerful if you were around more to disagree with on a *timely* basis. Now I'm forced to save it up all week long." She cast half a smile over her shoulder.

"Should I look for a suitable place to rent next week?" He caught up to her and linked his arm through hers as they stepped over the low fence. The barrier was used to discourage hungry rabbits from feasting on their romaine.

Martha hesitated and then shook her head. "No, Matthew. We should live with our own kind. Our *kinner* need to grow up with other Amish children or they will become confused if constantly surrounded by *Englischer*s."

"In that case, we must deal with the long commute. With the money I can save working there, someday we'll buy our own farm near other Plain folk. And with my own horse-training business, I'll never have to leave the side of my always jolly *fraa*."

She nodded in acquiescence as they entered the house and then began setting out their dinner, keeping her eyes averted from his.

That night, Matthew got down on his knees to pray instead of saying his prayers nestled down under the covers. Then he crawled in next to Martha, who had already nodded off. He cuddled as close as he could without waking her and fell fast asleep a contented man.

~

Within a few days, Julia stopped stewing over her daughter-in-law's letter. She had spring-cleaning to complete, which wouldn't get done by worrying over her son's family. What could she do anyway, even if her intuition was correct? They were far away in New York—well beyond the reach of a *mamm's* well-intended advice. Matthew might actually listen to reason, never having been as stubborn or willful as his sister Emma.

Emma—her rebellious child—the one whose *rumschpringe* days had turned Julia's chestnut hair to dull gray by the time she married her young man. Julia decided that she would begin cleaning today in the room her daughters had shared while growing up. Inside the seldom-used guest room, Julia discovered mementos of the two sisters who'd once also shared dreams, secrets, and more than a few tears.

In the closet hung one of Leah's faded dresses, left behind because the shade of peach wasn't suitable for a married woman, and because too much of her own good cooking had rendered this size only a nostalgic memory. Julia held the worn cotton to her face to inhale the faint but distinctive scent of her daughter. She would throw the outgrown frock into her ragbag to be cut up into quilting squares.

Julia ran her dust cloth over the oak writing desk, where Leah wrote to Jonah and Emma had written to her *Englischer*, James Davis, while he'd been away at Ohio State Agricultural College. Then she headed to the girls' nightstand and matching bureaus. On a lark, she opened the bottom drawer of Emma's dresser. Emma had apparently forgotten quite a few items when she packed her bags for their honeymoon train ride to see the ocean. Emma had chosen to see the Pacific Ocean, not the much closer Atlantic. *So like my rebellious child.* Afterward she'd moved to Hollyhock Farms, owned by the Davis family of Charm. Her husband's hometown was only fourteen miles from Winesburg, but it might as well be a hundred considering how often Emma, James, and their sons came to visit.

Julia pulled out the drawer and set it on the bed to examine its contents without straining her back. The items should, no doubt, be dumped into the trash. In the streaming sunlight she spotted the blue jeans Emma had worn under her Plain dress to go horseback riding with James and his friends. She'd ridden all day long astride a thousand-pound-beast and not fallen off. Julia pressed the frayed denim to her nose to catch the fragrance of her oldest daughter. But instead she inhaled the scent of peaches! Sure enough, in the back of the drawer were containers of peach-scented shampoo, body lotion, and dusting powder, along with Cover Girl blusher and a tube of pink lip gloss. Julia squeezed a tiny bit onto her own finger to examine. It too smelled sweet. Emma had so wanted to compete with English girls, not realizing that James had fallen in love with a peaches-and-cream Amish girl who needed no enhancements to her incredible God-given beauty.

Julia took out a brochure for the Sugar Creek Swiss Festival where Emma had taken her first train ride. It had been just a short trip to Baltic and back for tourists. Was it on the train that James realized he was head over heels in love with Emma? So much so that the young man was willing to give up his fast 4 x 4 pickup truck, Levi jeans, and plaid flannel shirts forever? Their change to New Order Amish meant he could keep his farm tractor, modern harvesters, cell phone, and electricity in their home as well as in the barns. Yet driving a horse and buggy each time you wished to go anywhere had been a tough adjustment to make. Emma's change from Old Order to New had been a far easier transition. However, living initially in her pushy mother-in-law's home brought its own tribulations. Today, seeing Emma and James together with their two sons, you would think they had been born to their current lifestyle.

Her former rebel, Emma, was one happy woman.

Julia put the other mementos back in the drawer and slid it into the bureau. After returning Leah's dress to its hanger in the closet, Julia ran her dust mop quickly over the wood floors and batted down cobwebs with her broom. She took a final glance around the room and closed the door behind her.

With her heart aching, this wasn't a good day to throw junk into the trash.

Everything was how it should remain in her little girls' room…at least for now.

FIVE

Niagara Falls, New York

Phoebe Miller had never seen anything so grand—and they hadn't even reached the falls. Out the left side of the bus she viewed the Niagara River, a broad blue expanse of water dotted with seagulls bobbing on the waves, hoping for an easy lunch. Motorboats puttered to-and-fro as anglers sought the perfect spot to cast their lines. The water looked downright benign. Yet thanks to Eli's story, she knew what dangers lurked beneath the silvery calm surface.

What if a boat's engine conked out? Surely the unseen current would be too strong to paddle against, even if the vessel had oars on board. The terrified fishermen would be swept helplessly downstream. Cries for help to other boaters could go unheard. Certainly those cell phones that every *Englischer* carried wouldn't work on a rushing, turbulent river. The poor souls would be carried to the brink of the falls, where they would hover for a few seconds before dropping over the edge to their deaths, not having the protection of a barrel like Annie Taylor's.

Phoebe shuddered, trying to banish the morbid mental image. She gazed out the right-hand windows to view a cityscape of tall modern skyscrapers and many old-fashioned churches. "Buffalo," the bus driver announced jarringly. "Birthplace of buffalo wings, home of the Buffalo Zoo, the famous Buffalo Bills, and the minor league Bisons."

Not quite famous enough for a Plain artist from Holmes County to have heard of. But no matter. Viewed from the freeway, Phoebe thought the city looked exciting and somehow hospitable. As their route followed the river that connected Lake Erie to Lake Ontario, the driver shared interesting tidbits about the Peace Bridge to Canada, Grand Island, and finally the Niagara Falls region. "Look there," he said. "Do you see those tall, odd-shaped buildings sprouting in the distance?" Many rushed to the left side of the bus to get a good look. "They are in Canada, our friendly neighbor to the north."

Phoebe practically suffered whiplash trying not to miss a single landmark. Soon the bus exited the freeway and rattled down a side street, narrowed by parked cars on both sides. They pulled under the two-story canopy of their designated hotel.

"We're here," the driver called. The bus stopped so fast, Phoebe banged her nose on the seat in front of her.

Mrs. Stoltzfus exited the bus but then returned within five minutes with a middle-aged *Englischer*. She positioned herself up front with her clipboard, a bundle of white envelopes, and her I-mean-business expression. "This is our tour operator, Mr. Barnett. I will call out names in groups of four. When you hear your name, come forward and take your envelope from Mr. Barnett. Make sure *your* name is written on the envelope. Then exit the bus and go find your suitcase. Written under your name is your room number. Inside you'll find a key card to get into your room and a tourist bracelet. You can work out later who bunks with whom. Put those bracelets on your wrists snuggly. The bracelet will allow entry into each attraction one time. If you lose it, you'll be reading magazines in your room for the next two days." She paused here and narrowed her eyes. "Now listen up. Find your bag, go up to your room, leave your bag there, and then hurry back down to the bus. We have no time to unpack or lollygag. If you come down here late and the bus is gone, head back to your room…

and read a magazine." She scanned the tour group, making eye contact with suspected lollygaggers. "The rest of us will be on the *Maid of the Mist!*" She beamed then, her smile accentuating her round apple cheeks. The bus broke into thunderous applause and plentiful hoots until Mrs. Stoltzfus lifted her hand like a crossing guard.

Phoebe glanced out the window. The luggage had already been set on the sidewalk in neat rows for quick retrieval. *This tour operator knows his business.* Everyone started chatting as the first group of names was called. When she heard "Ava and Rebekah Glick, Phoebe Miller, and Mary Mast," Rebekah slapped the back of Phoebe's head as though she'd been sound asleep.

"That's us!"

Phoebe's stomach somersaulted despite having consumed a ham sandwich, chips, and an apple for lunch, along with two full packs of Nabs. She took her envelope, followed the Glick sisters off the bus, grabbed her suitcase, and then followed them inside the hotel lobby with wide-eyed wonder. Marble floors, chandeliers, fancy area rugs, leather couches grouped for easy conversations—just as *daed* had predicted—fit for a queen. Mary Mast, a small, thin Geauga County girl, looked equally intimidated, while Rebekah and Ava marched through the lobby as though perfectly at home.

"This way," said Rebekah. "Step lively. You heard what Mrs. S. said." Once they had reached the elevator and stepped inside, she pushed the button for the twelfth floor.

"How do you know which floor we're on?" asked Phoebe, inspecting the outside of the envelope. Nowhere did it indicate that information.

"Oh, Phoeb, really." Rebekah rolled her eyes. "It's room *twelve*-oh-six."

Phoebe was amazed. If her cousin Henry did marry this girl, he would never have to think another thought again. His wife would take care of figuring everything out.

Once they had reached their floor, the doors elegantly swished open and they exited the elevator like a row of little ducklings. A sign on the wall indicated their room was down the hall to the right. When they got to the door, Ava inserted her keycard in a slot until a little light turned green and then pushed down the handle to open the door. Inside the room they found two queen-sized beds, a huge TV, a sofa, an easy chair with a reading lamp, a vanity area separate from the bathroom, and a bank of windows on the far wall. Even Rebekah's mouth dropped open in shock. Ava threw herself down on one bed, acting as though making angels in fresh snow. Rebekah inspected the tiny bottles of soaps and lotions on the mirrored tray. Mary headed into the large bathroom and locked the door behind her. Doors never had locks in Amish homes. And Phoebe? She ran to the window to gaze down on the river that had captured her imagination.

After a few minutes, Mary joined her at the expanse of glass. "Wow," she enthused, with a grin.

"You're not kidding. Wow," agreed Phoebe. The two stared down on the rapids of the Niagara River. No longer placid and benign with boating vacationers, this water roiled and tumbled between sharp-cut banks with fierce intensity. Waves broke against boulders in the riverbed, sending plumes of spray high into the air. One couldn't fail to realize the river would soon reach the drop-off point.

Phoebe was mesmerized. If the entire trip entailed watching the view from this spot and nothing else, she wouldn't be disappointed. *You've been to waterfalls, Phoebe. This won't be any different than the ones you've already seen—only taller.* She couldn't help laughing at the memory.

"What's so funny?"

"I just remembered something my *daed* said." Phoebe faced her new roommate. "Ready to board the *Maid of the Mist* for the boat ride of a lifetime?"

"Sure." Mary agreed, but she looked petrified. "Mind if I hang onto you sometimes? I don't know how to swim." She whispered the words as though keeping a secret from the Glick sisters.

"Hang on all you want," said Phoebe, while thinking, *Good swimmer or not—if you fall overboard, you're a goner.*

The four girls rode the elevator down to the lobby with their tour bracelets firmly attached. All had changed into sneakers for easy walking and clutched city maps of Niagara Falls, New York. Phoebe also had her drawing tablet tucked under one arm.

Rebekah noticed it as they boarded the bus. "You can't take that along today! It'll get wet on the boat. Didn't you read about the spray of mist?"

Tiny, red-haired Mary intervened. "We'll be wearing raincoats. Phoebe's tablet can stay under that." Mary held out the picture of blue-clad people for verification.

Rebekah rolled her eyes. "Fine, but don't say you weren't warned if it gets soaked."

On the bus Phoebe and Mary sat together for the short drive to the park entrance. She almost forgot to look for Eli Riehl—almost, but not quite. She spotted his hatless head of blond hair halfway back, noticing that most of the young men had left their hats in their rooms along with their vests. And a few had even pulled their shirts loose from their trousers. And what about Mrs. Stoltzfus? Instead of correcting their wardrobe lapses to comply with the Amish *Ordnung*, she was devouring a caramel apple.

When the bus arrived at the arched walkway into the state park, Mrs. Stoltzfus walked up the aisle to dispense last-minute instructions. "We'll follow the trail through the gardens and enter the visitor center. Take the steps to the bottom level and go out the back door, and then you'll go through more gardens to the observation deck. We'll take the elevator down one hundred seventy-five feet to the river, where we will get on the *Maid of the Mist*." She peered around over her spectacles. "I want you to stay together until we're all on board. Afterward, you're on your own. You can watch the movie in the visitor center, walk the trails upriver, or board the trolley to either the aquarium or Goat Island to see Horseshoe Falls and Cave of the Winds. You have maps showing where everything is. If you lose your map, there are more available at each attraction. If you lose your bracelet, I think you *know* what you'll be doing. And don't forget the name of the hotel we're staying at."

Phoebe shivered, pressing her bracelet into her skin. This chaperone didn't act anywhere near this scary in Holmes County.

Mrs. Stoltzfus smiled now at the sea of faces, mostly eager and a few terrified. "Just meet here under this arch by six o'clock to catch the bus back to our hotel for dinner." She punctuated the word *here* with a stomp of her left foot. "That'll give you more than four hours to sightsee. But don't worry. We still have all day tomorrow to catch anything you miss today. Okay, let's go!" Without waiting for possible questions, Mrs. S. went down the bus steps.

Phoebe and Mary exchanged a laugh and quickly fell in stride with the others. As they wound their way to the boat dock, the crowd made it difficult for the group to stay together. Fortunately, their Plain clothing made it easy to find one another. Phoebe didn't know where to gaze first—the Niagara River, the flower gardens and interpretive displays, or the tourists from all over the world. Because everyone dressed in their own native costumes and talked in foreign tongues, no one looked twice at an Amish group chattering in Pennsylvania *Deutsch*. As Phoebe followed the person in front of her, sheeplike, her head swung from left to right like a pendulum.

Nothing, however, compared to the excitement of the boat trip. After boarding, Phoebe and Mary ran for spots toward the front. Covered from head-to-toe in plastic, they clung to the rail as the boat pulled away from the dock and motored through the waves. A voice over a loudspeaker announced they were approaching the American Falls. Phoebe smiled so much her face began to hurt. On both sides of the American Falls, myriad seagulls roosted on the rocks or on narrow ledges of the precipice.

"I'm here to make sure you girls don't go for a swim," shouted a voice over the roar of water. Eli wriggled in between them insistently and wrapped an arm around both sets of shoulders.

"Who are you?" asked Mary, trying unsuccessfully to shield her face from the spray.

"Eli Riehl, a friend of Phoebe's."

He seemed unconcerned that his head was already soaking wet. Although he wore a raincoat, his hood flapped down his back. The droplets of water on his suntanned cheeks made him look only more handsome, while Phoebe feared she'd assumed the appearance of a drowned rat. *A friend of Phoebe's?* That was a bit of an overstatement, but somehow having him close made her feel secure.

"My name is Mary, and I can't swim."

"With me here that won't be a problem." He smiled at her before turning his attention to Phoebe. "What do you think of the cruise so far?"

They were almost at the farthest reach of their voyage—the base of the Canadian Horseshoe Falls. Phoebe turned her face up to his, catching the spray and hearing the roar of three thousand tons of water falling every second. The stalwart *Maid of the Mist* pitched in the roll of waves, throwing Phoebe against Eli's chest. "I love it, Eli! I've never seen anything so beautiful in my entire life!" she shouted over the din as excitement swelled her heart to near bursting. The crowd behind them jostled up to get a better view.

"My sentiments exactly," he agreed but waited two seconds before focusing on the mountain of cascading water. For several minutes the ship's captain fought the strong current to remain where they were in the watery vortex. "Look there," demanded Eli close to her ear.

Her gaze followed his index finger to a rainbow, tall as a skyscraper, appearing in the mist as though heaven itself had opened a portal. "Oh, my. This keeps getting better and better." Phoebe didn't care that cold water ran down her chin and dripped inside the coat. It didn't matter that her shoes and socks were wet, or that her scalp itched from her soggy *kapp*. She had never enjoyed herself this much before.

Unfortunately, the boat eventually gunned the engines to begin the voyage back to the dock. Once conversation became possible again, Eli entertained Phoebe and Mary with trivia he'd memorized from a tourist magazine on the ride from Ohio.

Mary stared at him with wide-eyed wonder.

Phoebe found herself doing the same exact thing.

"Did you know that four of the five Great Lakes drain into the Niagara River?" he asked. "And that these lakes make up a fifth of the fresh water in the world?" Both girls shook their heads solemnly. "That's a lot of drinking water. Folks visiting here from desert countries must stand in awe."

"That's what I was doing at Horseshoe Falls," said Phoebe. "And I come from Ohio—a state with plenty of fresh water."

Mary peppered Eli with questions, which he seemed delighted to answer, while Phoebe stared at the power of nature with reverence. Only an awesome God could create something like this. But all too soon the thirty-minute boat trip was over. She would gladly have gone again if the line hadn't become twice as long.

"Whew, that was like wearing a big trash bag," Eli said, pulling his poncho over his head. He helped both girls remove their protective coverings and stuffed them all in the recycle bin. "Where to now, ladies?" he asked, looking at Phoebe.

"Let's walk out onto the observation deck," answered Mary, taking Phoebe's hand. "It'll be the closest we'll get to Canada during the vacation."

Phoebe complied, secretly rejoicing when Eli followed them into the elevator up to the street level. But once they ventured onto the extended platform, one hundred seventy-five feet above the river, she regretted her decision. They stood with nothing but air and water beneath their feet. Peering over the rail at Canada on the opposite cliff made her dizzy. She didn't even need to look down.

"Easy, Phoebe. Don't go fainting on me, not after the price we paid for this trip."

"I've had enough of this attraction," she mumbled weakly. "Apparently, I don't like heights. Who knew that living in Holmes County?"

"Hang onto me and close your eyes." Eli took her arm and practically carried her off the observation deck.

"You two go ahead. I'll catch up later," called Mary. "I want a turn with those telescoping viewers." She scampered away, unaffected by the strong breeze or the crowd jostling from all sides.

"That worked out well," he murmured, leading Phoebe back onto solid ground.

Instead of asking what he'd meant by that, she concentrated on not throwing up and ruining her afternoon. She trailed Eli, breathing deeply through her mouth. He led her to a shady grove of tall trees, where people sat resting on blankets or enjoying picnic lunches. Without asking first, he bought them each a giant soft pretzel from a passing cart. She devoured hers to settle her stomach.

"Are you up for a trolley ride over to Goat Island?" he asked as they sat on a park bench finishing their pretzels. "I'd love to see the view from Terrapin Point." Eli unfolded his park map to point out their destination.

Phoebe leaned over his arm to study the island. Indeed, Terrapin Point would be the best place to view Horseshoe Falls. "I'm ready. Let's go." Fortified from the snack, she jumped to her feet, refusing to be sick her first time away from home.

"I know a great spot to board the trolley that is less crowded than in front of the visitor center."

She didn't ask how he knew this, but his information proved to be correct. He took her hand and they ran up the walkway, through the botanical gardens, and along the trail toward the pedestrian bridge. He didn't seem affected by her, but Eli's touch had a profound impact on Phoebe. She'd never held hands with a man before—and she liked it.

On the scenic trolley they learned from the driver they could get off and on as much as they liked during a twenty-four-hour period. After squeezing into a single seat, Phoebe clutched his arm as the trolley rattled across the bridge over the upper rapids. "I don't think I'll ever get used to this much water. I wonder what the early pioneers thought when they discovered this place."

"I hope they didn't find out about the falls the hard way—in a canoe or a rowboat. Out for a nice afternoon paddle to see where it takes them and *whoosh*." Eli lifted one eyebrow wryly.

Phoebe shook her head to dispel the image. Once they exited the trolley, Phoebe and Eli ran down the hundred steps like young children to join a throng of international tourists lined up for photographs at Terrapin Point. Neither of them spoke. Both simply stared, breathing in the magic of a force beyond all but God's comprehension.

When other eager sightseers finally elbowed them from their premier positions, Eli and Phoebe chose the sidewalk leading upriver. They took turns reading aloud from the booklet describing other attractions. Phoebe placed a star by those they absolutely couldn't miss. The farther they wandered away from the falls, the thinner the crowds became. "Where are we heading?" she asked, curious but not concerned.

"Three Sisters Islands." He folded back his map to show her. "How 'bout that idea? I would love to leave three of my five sisters there."

"It's not too far away?"

"Nah, half a mile ahead. Plus, there's a trolley stop nearby to take us back." He peered at her from under his sheaf of hair.

She giggled. "Did you memorize *everything* on that map in the brochure?"

"Actually, I did. I was so excited about this trip."

Something tightened around Phoebe's heart. Here was a man unafraid to reveal himself. "Me too. I could hardly sleep at night. I was so nervous my dad would change his mind and forbid me from going."

"I'm glad he didn't. You're much more fun to hang with than the average tourist." He winked shamelessly as they started down the narrow path to the first of three bridges to Three Sisters Islands. On the third and largest of the tiny islands, they discovered a sun-baked boulder—a perfect spot to view the upper rapids.

Once they'd settled down, huddling together far from the edge, Phoebe asked in a soft voice, "What was I doing the day you followed me at the fund-raising auction?"

Eli's focus remained on the river. "Don't you remember? You walked up the hill behind the barn and sat drawing horses that were in the neighbor's pasture. I was dying to see if your drawings were any good, but then you would know I'd stalked you." He laughed easily. Nothing seemed to make this man nervous or uncomfortable.

Phoebe reflected on this as she pulled out her drawing tablet. She had tucked it into the waistband of her skirt, under her full-length apron to keep it dry. "Want to look now and judge for yourself?"

Eli met her eye and took the pad. Slowly, he perused each of the sketches contained within. Some were older works she'd completed while babysitting for her cousin's sons. Eli smiled at the antics of toddlers at play. But when he arrived at her illustrations of his story about Miss Taylor, his eyes grew very round. He stared at them, fascinated, while Phoebe held her breath.

Never had a human being's opinion mattered so much to her. She barely knew Eli Riehl, yet it seemed the rest of her life hung by the slender thread of his approval. She practically passed out waiting for him to finish. "Well?" she asked, sounding as insecure as she felt.

Eli shut the tablet. "They are...incredible, Phoebe. You have talent that's far beyond what I'd expected. I was all set to flatter you politely because I didn't want to hurt your feelings. But these? Phoebe Miller, where did you learn to draw like this?"

Phoebe gasped a bit raggedly. "Same place you learned how to spin a good yarn."

His mouth thinned into a crooked line. "Fair enough, but talking is something we pick up as *kinner*. Not too many folks learn to draw like this." Eli peered at her final rendering of a white-as-snow cat and then at the turbulent water. "I bet you'd like to draw this view, but we had better start back. My stomach tells me it's getting close to dinnertime. And my belly is more reliable than any pocket watch." He helped her up and they started back across the three narrow bridges tenuously connecting tuffs of land to the State of New York. They didn't hurry, nor did they worry when the trolley took a long time to arrive. With the excitement of new friendship, they chatted about one subject after another. And when the trolley finally completed its circuit and deposited them at the state park archway—the appointed pickup location—it took Phoebe quite a while to realize their bus was long gone. Then tears flooded her eyes, threatening to ruin her new, grown-up mystique. *What was Dad's number-one command? Don't let yourself become separated from the group.*

Eli Riehl gently lifted her trembling chin with one finger. "I didn't let you and Mary fall out and drown on the boat ride, did I?"

Unable to speak, she shook her head no.

"Then trust me when I say I won't let you miss supper our first night in New York."

Six

Leah Miller Byler had had a bad feeling all morning. She wasn't sick—far from it. Because the humidity had broken last night with the rain, she felt extra peppy. No, it was a creepy kind of feeling, like the time she ventured out to the barn looking for Jonah after dark. Suddenly, the door had swung shut behind her and all the mice decided to come out to play just when the batteries in her flashlight died. As they had that night, the little hairs on the back of her neck had stood on end since she'd woken up this morning.

Grossdawdi refused to eat his scrambled eggs at breakfast. He said he never ate eggs with "stuff chopped up and thrown in."

"Since when?" Joanna asked. "You've always loved my ham-onion-and-cheese omelets."

"No, not me. I've never touched the stuff in my life. You must be thinking of my brother." Amos Burkholder sipped his coffee black, forgetting his usual cream and two sugars.

Joanna glanced at her son, who was consuming his eggs and stack of toast with jam as though the plate might disappear at any moment. "Why don't you taste a little, *grossdawdi*?" asked Jonah. "You might find out you like them as much as your…brother does." Jonah took a swallow of coffee and cut another portion of omelet with the spatula. Holding the eggs aloft, he winked at Leah.

Since Leah had met the Byler family, she'd never heard anyone mention Amos having a brother. The poor soul probably had that disease starting with the letter *A*. She'd never heard two *Englischers* pronounce that difficult name the same way twice.

"*Nein*," argued Amos. "I just want this here bread." With a shaky hand, he lifted two slices of toast from the stack and brought one piece to his lips for a small bite.

Leah noticed that his color looked worse than ever—a dull gray instead of his usual pale white.

Amos rose unsteadily to his feet. Joanna rushed from the stove to support his arm. "Stop fawning over me, daughter. I'm a grown man, not some *boppli* you need to fuss with." Carrying his toast, Amos limped over to the row of pegs by the door. He shrugged into his chore coat, despite the temperature being already in the eighties, and settled his hat on his head.

"Give me a minute to finish breakfast and I'll head to the barn with you." Jonah took a huge forkful of eggs.

"Take your time. Finish eating while I get the milking started." Clumsily, Amos pulled open the door and walked out to the porch.

Jonah looked panic-stricken. He and his hired workers had finished milking the heifers before breakfast. Joanna placed a hand on her son's shoulder. "Eat, son. Don't gobble your food like a goat. He'll forget all about milking cows by the time he reaches the barn. He'll be fine until you get out there. You need a decent meal to see you through until lunch."

Jonah allowed Leah to refill his coffee cup and then slowed down to finish his food. When Leah returned the pot to the stove, she watched Amos make slow progress to the barn. The two forgotten slices of toast slipped from his fingers to the dusty path. His trusty dog, usually close to his heels, quickly consumed the evidence.

Watching his laborious gait, Leah's unsettled feeling ratcheted up a notch and hadn't diminished by the time she headed to the henhouse. Joanna insisted on cleaning up the kitchen alone and shooed Leah outdoors. After scattering a bucketful of feed for hungry hens, she carefully lifted those still roosting to check for eggs. She received a few ornery clucks but no pecks on the arms today from those not happy about surrendering their potential offspring. By the time she filled her basket with fresh brown eggs, her bad feeling had escalated into a sensation of dread. When a white-faced Jonah strode from the barn, not running but with a purposeful walk, it didn't surprise her in the least.

Carefully setting her basket in the grass, she ran to meet her husband. "Jonah," she murmured when she reached his side.

He gazed at her with his deep-blue eyes, soft as a robin's eggshell, and spoke in a shaky voice. "He's gone, Leah. My grandfather is dead. I went looking for him when I got to the barn. I found him sitting on a hay bale near the milking stanchions. His head was leaning against the stall wall, so I thought he was just resting." Jonah's voice broke as he glanced off toward the house. He cleared his throat before continuing. "When I touched him, I saw that his eyes were staring off into nothingness. I shook him, but I knew there was no need anymore. He had a little smile on his face, as though the last thing he saw before leaving this world and entering the next had pleased him greatly."

Leah wrapped her arms around his waist and hugged as tightly as she could. "I'm so sorry, Jonah. What can I do to help?"

He hugged her back. "He's in God's hands—the best place to be. I suppose you can take those eggs and start baking a few extra pies. Better make some extra blackberry if we still have any preserves left in the cellar. *Grossdawdi* loved to see blackberry pie on the dessert table." Jonah released her and started for the house, but not before she spotted tears in his eyes.

Leah waited a few minutes to give Jonah time with his *mamm*. When she carried her basket of eggs into the kitchen, Joanna Byler emerged from the bathroom already dressed head to toe in black. She hurried to wrap Leah in a hug. Leah broke into tears and was comforted by her mother-in-law instead of the other way around. Jonah went back into the milking parlor, where they had a business phone line, to call the sheriff and the undertaker. The undertaker would pick up Amos Burkholder, prepare his body for burial, and then return him to the Byler home for viewing.

The next few days passed in a blur. Leah and Joanna cleaned the house from top to bottom. Leah baked bread, cookies, and pies, although her heart wasn't in it. Folks dressed in black stopped by for the viewing, every one of them bringing something to eat or drink. Amish people never seemed to go anywhere empty-handed. Jonah and his mother greeted each person cordially, agreeing that Amos looked the same and thanking their visitor for yet another apple crumb cake. Leah, because a Byler by marriage, remained perfectly composed…until her own parents walked through the doorway into the crowded kitchen. Then she dissolved into an abyss of sorrow and apprehension for what was to come.

"Easy, child," murmured Julia, pulling her to the side. "Don't grieve so. It will make things worse for your husband."

"I know that, *mamm,* but I'm so afraid. I never want to lose you or *daed.*"

"You would deny us our chance at a place in paradise?" asked Julia softly. "Don't be ridiculous. When my time comes, I'll be ready to go. You just remember that. I have no fear, so you start working on getting rid of yours." Julia kissed her forehead. "Now, take me over to say goodbye to old Amos. Then you and I will share a big slice of that blackberry pie."

～

Charm, Ohio

Emma Miller Davis stood on her front wraparound porch and peered to the west. The sun's brightness nearly blinded her. Shielding her eyes from the glare, she thought she saw a lone horseback rider galloping in the distance.

That would most likely be James—her dear husband of almost seven years. How he still loved things that went fast, even if it was a Thoroughbred horse. And how she loved him. After converting to the Amish faith so they could marry, he'd sold his truck to his brother and given away his blue jeans, screen-print T-shirts, plaid flannels, and even his wristwatch. He also got rid of his video games, country music CDs, action movie DVDs, and his collection of computer software games. Their New Order sect allowed him to keep his cell phone, use the computer for farm business, have electricity in the house and outbuildings, farm with diesel tractors and harvesters, and use modern technology.

However, the sacrifices he'd made to marry her hadn't been minor. His clothing was now Plain, while his mode of transportation to visit a friend, attend church services, make bank deposits, or take his wife out to dinner in town was now a horse and buggy. And he had to learn their German dialect, Pennsylvania *Deutsch*, if he wanted to understand anything being said in church.

Emma smiled, walking slowly down the steps to their very green front lawn. The Davis family employed a farm worker whose sole job was lawn maintenance for the huge elder Davis house and their own smaller home. Their plot of land and the cost of materials had been a wedding gift from his parents, while members of their new district had donated the construction labor.

She glanced up at the semicircular balcony of their second-floor bedroom. The setting sun reflected off the French doors, making them glow like fireplace embers. She loved the house. It wasn't overly big, but with four bedrooms they would have plenty of space for more children. "Jamie," she called to her son. "Gather up your toys and put them in your wagon, along with the baby's too." James Davis IV glanced up with the aplomb of a typical four-year-old. "Why, Mommy?"

Emma bent low to lift his younger brother, Sam, from the quilt where he'd been playing with toy building blocks. "Let's see," she said, closing the distance between herself and Jamie. "It's almost time for supper, you don't want to lose any toys when it gets dark, I see your dad coming home, and because I *said so*."

It was the third reason that triggered the boy's immediate compliance. "Daddy!" he squealed, seeing James approach at full gallop. The child shoved building blocks, toy farm animals, and plastic snap-together fencing into his red wagon with both fists.

Emma settled the baby on her hip and used her other hand to block the glare.

James reined to a stop within twenty feet of his family and slid smoothly from the saddle as though a descendant of Chief Geronimo rather than a Quaker preacher from Connecticut. "Has anybody missed me?" he asked, lifting his older son high into the air and swinging him around.

Squeals of delight could be construed as an affirmative answer from little Jamie. "What about you, woman?" James placed the boy on his shoulder just as a groom appeared to take his horse. They had a small barn behind the house for their buggy horses, James' riding mount, and a pony for the boys' cart. He waited until the man walked away before buzzing her cheek with his lips.

Emma took the handle of the red wagon to drag it onto the patio. She tried to hold back her grin. "I think so…what did you say your name was again?" she asked, using a coy tone of voice.

James growled like a bear waking from winter hibernation. He set Jamie down and wrapped his arms around his wife. "Say my name ten times and give me a real kiss or I won't let you go." He tightened his grip as the baby cooed and smiled.

"Then you'll miss your favorite dinner, as I have no intention of participating in such vain foolishness." Emma struggled ineffectively. "James, stop. I need to check on the pork roast."

"Okay, that's one. I'll wait patiently until these two are fast asleep tonight to coax the other nine out of you." He wriggled his eyebrows. Then he took little Sam from her and carried him into the house.

Emma blew out her breath, waiting in the warm May sunshine

until her breathing returned to normal. How could that man make her heart race like that after more than six years of marriage? Soon she would lay the baby in his crib for a nap, wash the hands and face of her toddler, and serve a Tuesday night supper that would be no different than any other. But for one more minute, she stood gazing up into clouds lacy and white as spun cotton and counted her blessings. Despite having a mother-in-law determined to remake her in her own image, Emma Davis was one fortunate woman.

SEVEN

Niagara Falls

Eli Riehl turned out to be a man of his word—Phoebe didn't miss her first dinner in New York. While she was busy trying to find a tissue to wipe her eyes and blow her nose, Eli took her by the hand and began pulling. "Shouldn't we wait here under the arch?" she sniveled.

"No, sweet peach. That bus won't be coming back here. And I fully intend to get you back to the hotel before Mrs. Stoltzfus sends out a search party. Don't worry, except about what we're having for supper. I hope it'll be pizza or maybe burgers with spicy French fries. I love the kind that sets your mouth on fire. My mom hides the shaker of cayenne pepper from me."

While Eli chattered on, they walked down the street to the corner. At the busy intersection he stood on tiptoes scanning the traffic moving fast in both directions. When he spotted what he was looking for, he waved his arms over his head.

To Phoebe's surprise and great relief, a car slowed and then made a U-turn halfway down the block. Weaving in between other vehicles, it soon pulled up to the curb and screeched to a stop in front of them. A taxicab—right out of the blue! Eli opened the back passenger door, gave her a nudge, and followed her inside. Once he had slammed the door behind him, the cab lurched back into traffic. Phoebe clutched her drawing pad to her apron as though it were a shield of armor.

"Where to, folks?" asked the cabbie. He peered at them in his rearview mirror. He wore a dark turban and a full beard, while the car smelled as though he'd just finished eating supper.

Eli pulled the brochure of their hotel from his pocket. "Could you take us here, please?"

He barely glanced at the photo before handing it back. "Coming right up. Aren't you kids a little late for spring break?"

Phoebe tried not to breathe too deeply because the smell of fried onions was making her queasy. She had no answer for that question anyway. Eli met the cab driver's gaze in the mirror. "No, it's still spring for another three weeks, up until the twenty-first." He sounded earnest but looked confused, as did the cabbie.

Both men shrugged and focused on the heavy volume of cars. In less than ten minutes, their hotel loomed into view. The cab driver turned into the circular driveway and stopped behind a bus.

"That was our bus," cried Phoebe. "And there's our tour group." She leaned over Eli toward his window. "Look! There's Ava, Rebekah, and Mary. They're just going in now. We're not too late."

"All's well that ends well," said the cabbie. His grin revealed a gold front tooth. "That will be eight dollars, folks."

Eli extracted a ten-dollar bill from his wallet, which he passed to the front. "Thanks a lot." Opening the door, he slid out and reached for her hand.

Phoebe jumped out and whispered, "You forgot to wait for your change."

Eli winked at her. "People are expected to tip, Phoeb. Two dollars was a fair amount."

She wanted to ask how he'd learned all this during one bus ride from Ohio, but Mrs. S. gave her no chance. She bustled up with clipboard and red pen in hand.

"There you two are! What happened?" She perused them over her reading glasses to check for bloodshed or broken bones.

"We missed the bus by a hair. We spent too much time at our…attraction." Eli smiled sweetly, showing his straight teeth.

"If it had been anybody but you two, I would think you were up to no good. But not Eli Riehl or Phoebe Miller." The woman actually started laughing at the absurd notion. "Head upstairs to change clothes. We're meeting here in thirty minutes to walk to dinner. If you're late again, you'll be eating sugar and creamer packets in your room." She waltzed away to speak to the tour operator.

"While reading magazines," muttered Eli, once she was out of earshot.

At the row of elevators, Phoebe asked timidly, "What floor are you on? I'm on twelve." They stepped in as the door opened.

"Fourteen—one above yours, facing the street." He pushed both buttons.

"Two above," she corrected. "And our room faces the river."

"For some bizarre reason, there is no thirteenth floor, so just one. But you were sure lucky to get a room with a view."

Once again he'd noticed something she'd been oblivious of. *And artists are supposed to be highly observant.* A bell signaled their arrival at floor twelve. "See you downstairs in the lobby," she said nervously. They'd had the entire elevator to themselves, yet Eli stood close enough to her to count freckles.

He held the door open with his shoulder as she exited. "I hope I can see that view some time before we check out on Sunday."

Phoebe didn't look back or acknowledge she'd heard his bold comment. But the thought of blond, handsome Eli Riehl appreciating the river from her window made her feel faint. Why was he affecting her so?

Her new storytelling friend turned out to be psychic as well as observant. Down in the lobby, Mrs. Stoltzfus announced loudly enough for everyone on the block to hear: "Stay together. We're walking to Roman Garden's Pizza Shop. You'll be at tables for six. The pizza buffet is included in your package—all you can eat—but *not* the chicken wings or salads or other stuff." She glared around at suspected big eaters. "You're on your own for those, so don't try anything funny."

Phoebe ate with her roommates and two of Mary's hometown friends. She tried not to keep glancing over at Eli's table but failed miserably.

Mary noted Phoebe's distraction. "Did you two go to Goat Island? To that cave attraction?"

Phoebe swallowed her mouthful of mushroom and pepperoni. "*Jah*, we went to Goat, but not to the Cave of the Winds." She quickly took another bite of pizza to discourage further conversation.

"Why do they call it Goat Island?" asked Mary.

"Don't know." Phoebe gulped some soda.

"Is it really a giant cave with a strong breeze flowing through it?"

"Don't know." Phoebe chewed her crust industriously.

"Did you figure out how to get to the Bridal Veil Falls we saw on the map?" Mary was still nibbling her first slice.

"No, we never saw anything like that." Phoebe slurped her soft drink until she drained the glass. "Oops. I'd better get a refill." She tried to scoot her chair back, but Mary grabbed her arm.

"Wait," she demanded. For someone smaller than Phoebe, the girl had quite a grip. She peered at Eli's table and then at Phoebe. "What exactly did you two *do* over there?"

"We saw Horseshoe Falls and then walked up to Three Sisters Islands, a mile upriver. We sat on a rock watching the rapids...and talked." Her attempt to sound casual wasn't working.

"Just the two of you?" Awe gave each word special emphasis.

"*Jah*—just him, me, and about two thousand other tourists. Need more Pepsi?" Not waiting for an answer, Phoebe picked up both glasses and headed to the drink dispenser. Midway across the restaurant, she cast another glance in Eli's direction. At that precise moment, he turned in his chair and met her eye. He smiled as though he knew he'd been their topic of conversation.

Once again, he had managed to accomplish the impossible.

～

After breakfast the following day, the bus dropped them at the state park archway for another day of sightseeing. They were on their own, more or less. Of course, Mrs. Stoltzfus blocked the doorway with a short set of rules before they were allowed to disembark. "You must stay on park grounds or somewhere along the trolley route. You must stay with at least one other person from our group—no going off on your own. You are not to engage strangers in conversation other than to return a polite greeting." Her eyes shifted around the bus at the suspected friendly sorts. "You're on your own for lunch, but don't eat strange food if you have a temperamental stomach. And everyone is to meet right here, under this arch at six o'clock, for the bus ride to the hotel for dinner. No exceptions." This time she didn't gaze around at suspected dawdlers—she stared first at Phoebe and then at Eli.

"How can we know what time it is if we don't have a watch and aren't supposed to talk to *Englischers*?" asked a large boy in the back.

"You may inquire about the time and information of that nature." Mrs. Stoltzfus leaned to one side to focus on the tall boy. "Would you like to ask any more sassy questions, Jack Yoder, and chance sitting in your room with a magazine?"

There was a smattering of laughter, but not another peep from Jack.

"I'll take your silence as a no." She then stepped down to street level and allowed the group to exit. Everyone started talking, laughing, and planning their day.

A strange pang of guilt struck Phoebe. *What would my dad think about eight hours of complete freedom?* But it wasn't as though she'd lied to him, she told herself. She had no idea it would be like this.

"Let's go, Phoebe and Mary," announced Rebekah. "Ava and I are heading to the 3-D Adventure Theater. How does that sound?"

"Great!" Phoebe answered, choosing not to ask what the three D's stood for. She'd asked enough stupid questions yesterday with Eli.

Most of the Amish youths also chose the visitor center with its gift shops, giant movie screen, and endless assortment of junk food for their first destination. While waiting for the next movie showing, Phoebe saw Eli's tall blond head among the young men. Today none of them wore hats and almost all wore their Plain shirts outside their pants and suspenders. Eli stood talking and laughing with great animation while in line for the Adventure Theater.

Why do men always look like they are having more fun than women? Phoebe decided to forget about Eli for the rest of the day and have a great time with her girlfriends. After all, wasn't this her *rumschpringe?* "What are you planning to buy for souvenirs, Rebekah?" she asked. That topic lasted the entire twenty-five-minute wait for their turn to see the movie.

Mary listened to her extensive list with amazement. When Rebekah concluded and moved off to talk to others, Mary whispered to Phoebe, "Either she's in for a rude awakening at the checkout, or she's the richest Amish girl I've ever met."

"Probably more likely the first, but it costs nothing to dream big."

Suddenly, the theater doors swung inward. Phoebe felt her heart skip a beat as the crowd surged inside. All of the Plain girls sat together in two rows. She had no idea where the boys had gone, and she didn't care because the lights immediately began to dim and the story of Niagara began. On the largest movie screen she'd ever seen, the story of an unfortunate Indian princess unfolded. The girl had been ordered to marry someone as old as her granddad while she was already in love with someone else. So she devised other plans for her future. Next they learned the saga of early French explorers who discovered the falls while crossing the continent. Besides the enormous picture, the sound seemed to come from all directions, making the experience too intense for Phoebe's stomach at times.

"You'll want to pay careful attention to this next segment, Miss Miller," said a voice over her shoulder.

Phoebe jerked her head around. Despite the fact the speaker's face was hidden with an upraised map, she would recognize that voice anywhere—Eli Riehl was sitting directly behind her.

Honoring her earlier decision, she faced the screen and ignored the person tugging on a lock of hair that had escaped her *kapp*. Soon she did, indeed, identify the story developing before her in 3-D. It was the story of the schoolteacher who had ridden over the falls in a barrel in an attempt at fame and fortune.

"This is the exact story your friend told us," whispered Mary. "How did he know it before we got here?"

Mary's verbal question duplicated Phoebe's own internal one. She shrugged. "I don't know, but if I get another chance to chat with him, he has some explaining to do." However, that particular conversation would be postponed until the ride back to Ohio. For the rest of the day, the girls and half of the boys remained together in a large group. They walked the botanical gardens; browsed gift shops; toured the Nature Center and Aquarium, where they fed fish to seals; and then rode the trolley back to Goat Island for a visit to the Cave of the Winds. They had saved this attraction for last because, as on the boat ride, everyone got wet.

Eli talked mainly to his friends, while Phoebe talked to hers. But when the trolley passed the pathway to Three Sisters Islands, she experienced another odd pang—not of guilt, but of melancholy sorrow. What was wrong with her? She'd never been so affected by anyone, but knew she'd better get over it. Once they were back in Winesburg she would never see him again. During dinner that night at a delicious Chinese buffet, Phoebe made every effort to avoid Eli and his hypnotic dark eyes.

The group ate breakfast in the hotel dining room the next morning. Afterward, their chaperones announced they had exactly thirty minutes to pack up and get down to the bus for their trip home. Phoebe threw clothes into the suitcase haphazardly so she could spend her remaining time at the window.

It was a view she would never forget. So much power and energy were contained within the force of water. She stood mesmerized by the rapids, whirlpools, and ever-changing islets of trapped tree debris. God had always seemed majestic yet peaceful when she viewed the mist-shrouded meadows and rolling hills of her home. But this? This was evidence of a powerful, all-encompassing God…whom she hoped never to displease. Too bad Eli never got to see this.

"The views from our bedroom windows will never be the same after seeing this," said Rebekah, slipping an arm around Phoebe's shoulder. "Come on. You don't want to miss the bus. This would be one expensive cab ride back home."

Once their bus left the Niagara region, heading back toward Buffalo, the driver put in a Disney movie to the pass the time. Phoebe took out her pad and colored pencils, preferring to change some minor details on her drawings rather than watch a cartoon.

"Mind if I sit with Phoebe for a while?" asked Eli of Mary Mast.

"Not at all. I'll go sit with my cousin."

Before Phoebe could stop her, Mary rose from the seat and vanished.

"That was rather presumptuous of you."

"Ah, what a lovely word—presumptuous," said Eli. "But no, I presume nothing. I merely hope you will let me sit with you and maybe show me the changes you've made."

She wanted to send him away, but instead she said, "Sit, if you like." Then, as though she had no control over her hands, she gave him her tablet.

It took him no time to find the schoolteacher drawings and even less to start smiling. "Perfect! You changed Miss Taylor to match the movie." He handed back her art.

"How did you know the story before we got there? Have you been to Niagara before?"

"Nope. I read all I could before the trip in the library. You know what? I've never met anyone like you. And now that I've found you, I have a business proposition for you. Are you interested?"

She took a long pull from her water bottle while studying him closely. "A business deal? What could the two of us possibly make and sell?"

"I was thinking about a book—a children's picture book, to be exact. I could make up a story and you could create illustrations that would endear our tale in every child's heart across America." He gazed out the window at the suburban sprawl of homes. "Maybe even the world."

"Are you serious?" she asked, afraid he might be teasing.

He looked her in the eye. "I've never been so serious about anything before in my life. What do you say, Miss Miller? A joint venture of an artist and a storyteller."

She didn't need to think about it, not for a minute. "Absolutely, yes. I would love to." Phoebe would remember little about the remaining drive back to Ohio. Not the video, or the scenery of New York and Pennsylvania, or even the rest of the conversation with Eli. She could only think about one thing: She was about to become a children's book illustrator.

EIGHT

Willow Brook

Matthew recognized a bad sign when he saw one. When his fore-man dropped him off at his driveway on Friday night, his house was dark. A sole kerosene lamp burned on the kitchen table in the back of the house.

"Thanks, Pete," he called, slamming the truck door. "See ya Monday morning." Pete waved and drove home to his own family, while Matthew slung his duffel bag over his shoulder and walked up to face the music.

It wasn't as though he'd had much choice regarding his quitting time. When the owners of one of the horses he trained arrived late in the day, it was his job to present the horse and remain until everyone was satisfied. The stable's groom had handpicked tangles from the horse's tail and mane, but Matthew had to work him in the lunging ring to show off the progress that had been made since the last visit. Later, he'd tacked the horse out himself while the owners asked plenty of questions. He had a few of his own. Owners had different opinions as to how saddlebreds should be prepared for the prestigious show circuit. Because they paid very high fees for the services of Rolling Meadows Stables, it was his job to give them what they wanted, even if that meant sticking around until seven on a Friday night.

Matthew entered his home through the back door, careful not to let the screen door slam. He knew his children would be asleep by now, postponing his reunion with them until morning. "Martha?" he called in an exaggerated whisper.

After a few moments, his wife shuffled into the room. She wore a long nightgown, white socks, and an exhausted expression. She'd released her waist-length hair from its bun, and it trailed down her back in a loose plait. Despite her frown, Matthew thought she looked beautiful. "Evening, *fraa*. Sorry I'm late for supper." He hung his straw hat on a peg and went to the sink to wash.

"Late? Six-thirty or seven would be late. Supper is done and over with. I kept a bowl of stew warm for you so long that I'm sure it's not fit for hogs anymore…if we owned any hogs." She crossed her arms over her bodice. "I started supper at three o'clock. Now it's nine. That's bedtime, not the dinner hour."

Matthew considered suggesting that she start cooking at four or four-thirty, considering his schedule, but then squashed the notion. No sense stirring up a hornet's nest when their time together was short. "Since, as you mentioned, we don't own a pig, give me whatever stew you have left." He kept his voice neutral, trying not to sound angry as he poured himself a glass of cold milk.

"Do you mean to say you haven't eaten yet?" Martha sound genuinely shocked.

"That's exactly what I'm saying." He shot her a look over the refrigerator door. "I was working late tonight, Martha, not having dinner in a fancy restaurant with my boss." His neutral tone had evaporated.

She hurried to the stove and pulled a bowl from the oven with pot holders. She set it on his place mat along with some slices of homemade bread. Matthew sat down with his milk and stared into his supper. The colors and shapes of what had been potatoes, carrots, peas, onions, and beef had blended together into a greenish goo. "Good grief! How many times did you stir the pot? This looks like you put it through the butter churn."

"Quite a few times. I didn't want it to stick to the bottom of my Dutch oven."

He shrugged. "Suppose it all ends up like this in my belly anyway, but could I have a spoon instead of this fork?"

Martha brought a spoon, sat down across from him, and began to cry. "I'm sorry. I should have let it set out at room temperature. Cold would have been better than ruined. Want a sandwich instead?" Her large brown eyes were moist and shiny.

"No, this will be fine. Maybe a few pickles if we have any left." He patted her hand before she sprang to her feet.

She placed a plate of pickles on the table. "I know you like your new job at Rolling Meadows. And I understand that more money means we can save faster for a place of our own someday, but—"

Matthew interrupted, seeing a perfect opportunity to share his good news. Setting down his spoonful of mush, he extracted four twenties and a hundred dollar bill from his wallet. "You can put this into our savings account." He took another piece of bread to scoop stew.

Martha stared at the money and then picked up the hundred to study the face of Benjamin Franklin. "Isn't this the guy who invented the lightning rod? Plenty of folks' barns are still standing due to that man's ingenuity." She smiled at the cameo picture before dropping the bill atop the others.

He finished his milk in three long swallows. "*Jah*, I think so, but the important thing is I got that money this week as tips in addition to my regular paycheck." Pride bubbled up despite his better intentions. "Owners gave me those twenties just for bringing their horses out for inspection. And the owner who kept me there so late tonight? After looking at his watch he apologized and handed me a hundred dollars! I tried to refuse it, but he insisted. He said he knew I only got home on weekends and had forgotten today was Friday." He tapped the bills into a neat pile, his stew forgotten. "Summer is only beginning—the busy season for saddlebreds. Just think how many tips I might make by summer's end."

Martha's soft brown eyes hardened. "Do you ever listen to yourself, Matthew Miller? Money, money, money—it's your favorite topic of conversation these days. What would your dad say?"

"I believe he would say that a man must support his family while saving for his own farm. And maybe he'd throw in something about wives not being so all-fired-up critical of their husbands all the time."

Unfortunately, he'd spoken loud enough to wake the baby. His daughter's cries came wafting down the stairs from her second-floor bedroom.

Martha rose to her feet with dignity, although the brittle glint in her eyes was gone. "Please put your bowl in the sink when you're done, *ehemann*. I'll wash it tomorrow. I'll be upstairs."

Matthew leaned his head back and stared at the ceiling for answers. The stew had hardened into a thick plaster that could patch holes in drywall, but he didn't care. He was no longer hungry…except for a way to make his impossible-to-please wife happy.

~

Winesburg

With spring-cleaning behind her, Julia knew what she needed—an afternoon at her sister's house. Sipping coffee, eating sweets, and chewing the fat often cured what ailed a woman better than a doctor's pills or therapies. She had sent a note to Hannah early that morning that she would be coming over after lunch and to be prepared. She was in the mood to gab.

After fixing sandwiches and fresh berries in cream for Simon and Henry, Julia ate her sandwich with one eye on the wall clock.

"Are we keeping you from an important engagement, *fraa*?" asked Simon, brushing crumbs from his beard into the palm of his hand.

Henry grinned while grabbing his second turkey-and-Swiss. "I know what *ren-dez-voo* she has cooked up. I delivered her note after breakfast." He pronounced the foreign word exactly how it looked, yet Julia couldn't imagine where he'd seen it in print.

"I have a date next door with my sister. And a spice cake is in the oven. That's why I'm clock-watching." She got up to crack open the oven door for a quick peek. Satisfied, she pulled out the Bundt pan and set it on the cooling rack.

"Spice cake? You baked a spice cake while your son and I suffer with tiny strawberries that could have benefited from more time on the vine?"

"Suffer with?" Julia wrinkled her nose. "One would think a deacon wouldn't throw around that word so lightly."

Simon leaned back in his chair, his eyes twinkling. "True enough, yet I would think a good wife and mother would cut a couple slices of fresh-baked cake for her hardworking menfolk."

"A good wife might do just that, but I intend to take an intact cake next door. Goodness, Simon. It would look as though I stopped for a snack along the way." She reached for her plastic cake tote from the cupboard.

Henry winked at his father. "If you'll share your dessert, *mamm*, I'll drive you to Aunt Hannah's and come back at four to pick you up."

Julia pondered that for a moment and then reached for a knife. "Make it three thirty. I have a pot roast for supper that'll need two hours in the oven." She whacked two fat slices from the tubular cake and then shoved the ends together to form a smaller circle.

"Well done, son." Simon retucked his napkin into his shirt. "I suggest you hurry back from Seth and Hannah's."

Henry scrambled toward the door as Julia set the cake into the tote. "Be back soon, *daed*. Please don't eat both pieces."

Julia appreciated the ride to her sister's. After her son had thoughtfully helped her from the buggy, she carried her disfigured dessert up the steps to enter Hannah's kitchen. She sniffed the air like a bloodhound. "Peach cobbler?" she called.

"What a nose!" Hannah said, laughing as she delivered a baking pan to the table trivet. "The market had ripe Florida peaches on sale. I bought a half bushel since ours are still green."

Julia retrieved cups, the coffeepot, and a pitcher of milk before settling onto a tall-backed chair. "Where's Phoebe?"

"Checking on my new lambs in the high pasture. She took her tablet, so it will probably take hours to count the flock."

"And Seth?"

"Gone to the grain elevator with a load of hay."

"*Gut,* we're alone." Julia removed her spice cake from the carrier. It listed badly to one side.

Hannah studied it curiously. "What happened here?"

Julia sliced two large pieces. "Cake thieves—right here in Winesburg. The area is swarming with them, but it shouldn't affect the taste any."

Hannah sampled a forkful and smacked her lips. "Oh, this is yummy! You must give me your recipe."

"I will, if you give me some advice about my Leah." Julia tried a forkful of cake and smiled. *The sour cream did make a big difference.*

"It's a deal. How are the Bylers since the passing of Amos?"

"Joanna is planning to travel to Wisconsin to visit her sister. Jonah wants to go with her and wants Leah there too." Julia pulled over the peach cobbler and began slicing it up. "Leah thinks she should stay home to run Joanna's cheese business and keep baking."

"I thought Jonah employed several workers." Hannah took a small piece of cobbler.

"*Jah,* three. They can run the dairy fine while Jonah's gone. And check that Joanna's cheeses stay at the correct temperature for proper aging. But Leah says she must fill her pie orders."

Hannah shook her head. "This advice will be easy, dear *schwester.* Your daughter should start packing her bags. First, her place is with her husband, and he wants her in Wisconsin. Second, the county can survive a few weeks without her pies. Absence might make hearts grow fonder…and waistlines slimmer. And third, that gal needs a break from her kitchen. Sometimes Leah acts as though she's fifty-three instead of twenty-three. A change of scenery might do those two some good." She lightly patted her belly.

Julia chuckled, knowing the gesture had nothing to do with desserts. "We are in complete agreement. While my pot roast is in the oven, I'll tell her so in a letter. Henry can still deliver it tonight before he sleeps. One of those rescued horses is bound to be fast." She refilled her mug from the coffeepot. "Then I'll sleep better tonight too. That girl has been on my mind lately—ever since she started acting strange at Amos Burkholder's funeral."

NINE

Winesburg

It didn't take long for Eli Riehl to get back into the swing of things... about five hours, to be exact. One of his older sisters picked him up in downtown Berlin and brought him home. The bus from Niagara Falls dropped him off before ten o'clock, but it was well after midnight by the time their buggy rolled into the barnyard.

At five a.m., before the crow of the irritating rooster, his dad was knocking on his bedroom door. "Eli, get up, son. It's time for milking. Your vacation is over."

Indeed. Eli buried his head deeper under the pillow. Three days and two nights did not constitute a vacation. What did the *Englischers* call it—a getaway weekend? But it sure had been nice to get away... and to meet Phoebe Miller. He'd fallen asleep last night seeing her smile and hearing her soft voice in his head. Where had she been his whole life? His mom was right. He should get off the farm more often.

"Eli! Do you hear me, boy? Wake up! I'm heading out to the barn. If you're not down in five minutes, I'm sending in one of your sisters with a bucket of cold water."

He bolted up and threw off the covers. "I'm coming, *daed*. Give me a chance to dress and eat something. I'll be right out." He listened to the sound of his father's work boots clunking down the stairs. Eli washed his hands and face at his basin with a pitcher of cold water, saving a hot shower for work's end. If his sister had dumped a bucket on him, it probably wouldn't have felt any different. However, this way he denied them the pleasure of startling him. His sister Rose would find the task especially appealing. As fate would have it, Rose was at the stove when he arrived in the kitchen a few minutes later, dressed in his oldest work clothes.

"Thank goodness you're up and not sick in bed. I feared you might have caught your death gallivanting so far from home. One of those strange diseases like bird flu or mad cow disease." Rose dumped the remaining pancakes on a plate unceremoniously, and then she added five shriveled sausage links.

"I remain with the living, and a *good morning* to you, dear Rose." Eli filled the largest travel mug he could find with coffee. "I imagine a person could catch those ailments just as easily in Ohio as in New York."

She plopped his breakfast down and tossed a bag of store-bought bread on the table. "Certainly not in Holmes County."

He frowned as he withdrew a few stiff slices. "Did this come from the day-old rack? Isn't there any homemade bread left?"

"All gone, sorry. Better get up earlier if you're that picky. I bought that loaf to make stuffed chicken tonight for supper."

He did his best imitation of an angry bull facing a bright-red cape, but he wasted his efforts. Rose was already filling the sink to wash dishes and ignoring him. Eli poured maple syrup on his pancakes and began to devour the food.

"I'm so glad to see you home, little *bruder*, that I could almost hug you."

Her back was turned toward him, but the voice definitely belonged to Rose Riehl. He almost choked on a sausage. "Why would that be? Did you need someone to pin your dress pattern to, or maybe try out a new recipe for pickled herring ice cream?"

She smiled at him over her shoulder. "Did you lose your mind while at Niagara? Maybe you dropped it into the river, and it went over the falls like driftwood."

Eli grinned at the mental image. Rose might be surly at times, but she was the only one of his sisters with an imagination and a sense of humor. "Not that I recall. I tried not to lean too far over the rail."

"I'm glad to see you because now I can get back to my own work. My sewing basket overflows onto the rug. Last Friday Dad made me drive a team pulling a cutting blade in the hayfield. Then on Saturday I followed behind his baler to rake up whatever he missed into piles from sunup until sundown. I was never so tired in my entire life. Thank goodness we didn't have preaching yesterday, or I would have been snoring by the second sermon."

"That's the kind of work I do every day."

"But you're a man and you enjoy it."

Eli mopped up the syrup with a stale bread crust. "*Jah*, I'm a man, but no, I don't enjoy it. My back hurts too after a day like that. I do it because I'm a farmer."

Rose wiped her hands on a towel and then hung it up to dry. "Is that what this trip was about—checking out the English world to decide if you'll stay Amish? Because I never needed to spend two hundred dollars before I got baptized and joined the church. My *rumschpringe* consisted of buying a bicycle to ride on back roads wearing blue jeans."

She met his eye, and her earnestness nearly broke his heart. All Rose had ever wanted since that bicycle was to get married, set up her own home, and start having babies. But the right man hadn't shown up on their doorstep yet. "Rest easy, sister. I have no inclination to turn English. I plan to join the Amish church by and by. Give me some time. I like being Amish. It's tending cows and pigs that sometimes gets on my last nerve."

Rose topped off his travel mug. "An Amish man can't make a living telling stories, Eli, no matter how good he is with words." Her declaration sounded gentle and sympathetic, not cynical.

He smiled. "I know, but because our parents didn't have the

forethought to have at least one more son, my fate is sealed. I will help Dad until he retires, and then I'll assume full management of the farm. I'll be stuck here until my flesh rots into additional fertilizer for the soybeans."

Rose pulled a sour expression. "Don't talk like that. Besides, as soon as you meet a girl and fall in love, having your own farm will sound better and better."

Eli tried, but he couldn't prevent his face from turning the color of strawberry jam. He scrambled to his feet, snapping on the lid to his mug.

Rose—better known as "Eagle Eye"—didn't miss the alteration. "Are you blushing, little brother? Oh, my. Did you meet someone on the bus trip?" She closed the distance between them in three strides. "Who? Who is she?"

"Are you a barn owl, Rose?" he asked, settling his hat on his head. "Because you sure sound like one."

"You met a girl on that trip! I know it. Where does she live?" Then suddenly, her exuberance drained away. "She does live in Ohio, *jah*? And she is Amish?"

"Yes, to both questions. Stop worrying. I told you I'm not planning to jump the fence." He tried to walk out the back door, but she threw herself into his path.

"I'll bake your favorite cookies, do all your darning first, and help you with one chore if you tell me who she is." After a moment she added, "One chore, as long as it doesn't involve farm animals."

"Why are you so sure I met a young lady?" Her perceptiveness unnerved him. That's all he needed with five sisters.

"Because never in your life have you turned that shade of purple. You go around embarrassing people with your quick wit, not the other way around." She grabbed hold of his shirt. "Please tell me, Eli. I need some good news, and I won't breathe a word to anyone. This will be our little secret."

She smiled so sweetly he fell into her snare like a hapless rabbit. "I met Phoebe Miller from the other side of Winesburg. I guess one or two districts east."

Rose's expression couldn't have been more shocked. "Phoebe Miller—Leah Byler's cousin from over on Route 505? *She* went to Niagara Falls on this trip?"

"*Jah*, or at least a person claiming to be her did." Eli sighed impatiently. He needed to get to the barn before Dad became angry.

"Leah says Phoebe rarely leaves the farm except for church. She hates sewing, so she won't come to quilting bees unless she happens to be good friends with the bride-to-be." Rose's pursed lips revealed her opinion of those who disdained needlework. "She takes little interest in baking either, despite numerous attempts on Leah's part to teach her culinary skills. And she doesn't much care for shearing, spinning, or weaving wool, according to Emma Davis, Leah's sister. Of course, I can't blame Phoebe for steering clear of sheep. Have you ever noticed how dirty and smelly those creatures get in the spring?" She scrunched her face with distaste.

"Rose, much as I'd love to visit with you rather than muck out hog pens, I must get to work." He slipped around her and out the door.

"If it *is* the same Phoebe Miller, what was she doing during the drive up?"

Eli halted on the bottom step—curiosity replacing his better judgment. "She was sketching people and landscapes," he said, turning back.

"*Jah*, that's her. Leah said being an artist is the only thing that interests her younger cousin—a totally useless skill for an Amish person." Rose tapped her thin lips with a finger. "But now that I think about it, this girl sounds absolutely perfect for you, Eli." Clutching her belly, Rose giggled, making no effort to speak quietly.

So much for keeping confidences under her hat. "I'm glad I have your approval should I run into Phoebe again. And don't forget about this being our little secret." He shook his finger at her before marching off toward the barn.

Rose hollered as though using a megaphone. "Don't wait for her to get sociable. She's as much of a hermit as you. You'll have to track her down like a private detective."

He heard her uproarious laughter until the screen door slammed shut. Eli remembered a character from a magazine with a plaid hat and a huge magnifying glass. He was still chuckling when he joined his father near the horse stalls.

"Something funny, son?" Dad's tone didn't encourage agreement. "Because I didn't think it would take twenty minutes to finish a few pancakes."

"Sorry, *daed.* Rose had some questions about my trip and I couldn't break free from her."

"That trip is over with. Start cleaning the horse and pigpens, and once I finish milking the heifers you can sterilize the equipment. Then I want you to wash down the concrete floors with bleach." He sucked in a mouthful of air. "This afternoon, we'll be cutting and raking hay until sunset." Dad focused his attention on filling feed buckets with grain from a burlap sack.

"I'll get right to it." Eli grabbed his rake and the handles of the wheelbarrow.

He smelled the hogs long before he arrived at the indoor home of six sows and their broods of piglets. "Good morning, ladies. Your cleaning service is here. Ready for a little freshen-up to your accommodations?" Eli wished his sense of smell wasn't so acute as he prodded the porcine families into their outdoor pens.

Memories of a wild raging river, breathtaking waterfalls, and a beautiful dark-eyed girl began to fade away. How would the sole son of a farmer find time to play Sherlock Holmes?

~

Hancock, Wisconsin

When the bus stopped at a rest area, Leah contemplated hiding in the ladies' room until it pulled out without her. As much as she wanted to please Jonah, she hated long bus trips. All the bumps in the road jarred her kidneys, while the twists and turns upset her belly. Her mother-in-law harped that she should eat more to settle her stomach, but how could a person eat when they were already nauseated?

Jonah did the best he could. Each time they stopped he brought her a bottle of ginger ale and, finally, a package of Dramamine. He also bought her a paperback book from the spinner rack entitled *Secrets to Becoming a Better Wife*. Before her spine could stiffen, he showed her his own selection for betterment: *Secrets to Becoming a Better Husband* by the same author. "We each have our pleasure reading," he said, opening the book to chapter 1.

Leah hadn't been able to read a word. She'd kept her eyes closed for most of the trip, trying to nap, but instead she mulled over the conversation with her former business partner. April wasn't pleased about her impromptu vacation to the cheese-producing capital of America.

"What am I going to do without your pies?" she squawked. "You don't think folks stop at April's Home Cooking for my soups and sandwiches, do you?"

"You and your sister know how to bake apple, cherry, and chocolate cream," Leah insisted. "That's all you need to get by until I return home."

"Fine, run off. Have fun, but if an out-of-business sign is hanging on the diner door when you return, it will be on your conscience." April had only been half-joking. Business had been off ever since another tourist buffet had opened in town. The diner's tiny kitchen mandated an equally small menu. Even a salad bar was out of the question, and most *Englischer*s loved variety.

"Open your eyes, *fraa*. We're finally here." Jonah placed a big hand on her shoulder and gently shook her. "Welcome to Hancock."

Leah gazed out the streaky bus window and gasped. An Amish welcoming party of at least a dozen people stood on the platform. Many of them held signs proclaiming "Welcome Home, Jonah and Joanna" in both *Deutsch* and English. "Looks like word of our arrival reached Wisconsin before we did," she murmured. But Jonah was busy lifting bags from the overhead bins, looking happier than a blue heron at a fish farm. Leah followed Joanna off the bus, carrying their picnic hamper of snacks.

An effervescent crowd of young people swallowed Jonah the moment he stepped down. His old friends embraced him with hugs, slaps on the back, and snippets of news that couldn't wait. A few of their parents stepped forward to greet Joanna, including a woman whose resemblance indicated she must be her sister and their hostess. Leah remained alone on the curb, clutching her hamper like a refugee landing on American soil.

After a moment Jonah extracted himself from the group. "Andrew, Steven, everyone—this is my wife, the former Leah Miller from Holmes County, Ohio."

With all eyes focused on her, Leah wished she could have remained forgotten. *I should have lost a few pounds and sewn a new traveling dress.*

"*Welcum*, Leah," said a pretty young woman. She stepped forward to shake hands along with another equally attractive woman.

Leah nodded politely and smiled, yet due to some odd malady, her ability to speak faltered. But no matter. Jonah's cousins—four boys ranging in ages from five to thirteen—filled the ride to Jonah's aunt's house with lively chatter. Leah sat in the back of the wagon, content to watch the scenery on the way to their home for the next two weeks. One would think all farmland would look pretty much the same. Ohio's agriculture included a variety of crops besides horses, sheep, swine, and cattle, but all Leah could see of Wisconsin were grazing cows and endless acres of alfalfa to feed them. No wonder they produced so much cheese. What else could you do with so much milk?

By the time they arrived at his aunt's farm, she was exhausted, starving, and lonely for a little attention from her husband. Aunt Harriet fed them a delicious supper of chicken and dumplings with fresh vegetables and several kinds of dessert. The reunited sisters talked and talked, sipping enough tea to make them buoyant. When

Leah couldn't keep her eyes open another minute, Harriet announced, "Off with you to bed, Bylers. Tomorrow is another day."

As Leah rose gratefully to her feet, Harriet added, "Jonah will bunk with my two older boys, and I've put Joanna and Leah in the guest room." She grinned warmly, while Leah's spirits plummeted. What had she been thinking? Two weeks with her husband in their own room? With hunger satisfied and exhaustion about to be addressed, Leah realized her loneliness was only beginning. She thanked her hostess for supper and said good night before her disappointment became apparent.

"I'll carry the bags," offered Jonah, entirely too cheerful for this late at night. Halfway up the steps, Leah tripped and would have landed on her nose if not for his quick reaction. "Should I carry you, *fraa*, as if we were newlyweds?" he asked.

"*Ach*, newlyweds. We've been put in separate rooms like youngsters." Fatigue prevented appreciation of the practical arrangement.

"Absence will only make my heart grow fonder," he whispered in her ear. He set her suitcase next to one twin bed, brushed her lips with a kiss, and hurried downstairs to resume his conversation about wheat varieties with his uncle.

Leah dragged a chair to the window to say her prayers, but self-pity crept into her heart instead of thankfulness and praise. This would be a long two weeks in an unfamiliar world. Jonah had every right to enjoy visiting old friends and relatives. She shouldn't feel left out or in the way, but somehow she did. However, the loneliness she experienced crawling under Harriet's starched sheets was small potatoes compared to the loneliness she felt at the social event thrown in Jonah's honor.

On Friday his former best friend, Steven, and wife, along with several other married couples and dozens of single acquaintances, threw a potluck picnic. Jonah had talked about the upcoming event all week, trying to guess who might attend. By the time the Bylers arrived at four o'clock, volleyball and horseshoe games were already underway. Steven started a fire to roast hot dogs and marshmallows to accompany the side dishes. Jonah and Leah ate supper together, but once he finished eating he hurried back to the games with the other men. Leah discovered several of his former classmates were also professional cooks and bakers. One woman worked at a bakeshop and another in a restaurant, while a third created fancy cakes in her home the way Leah did. The women remained at the table for hours, swapping stories, sipping coffee, and sampling desserts.

When Leah didn't dare consume another morsel without fear of popping pins, she rose to her feet. "Excuse me, please. I must stretch my legs before I grow attached to this bench."

Annie, Steven's wife, also hopped up. "I'll walk with you. I can use the exercise after that dinner."

The two hadn't wandered twenty yards when Leah spotted something that chilled her blood—Jonah and a blond woman were on the porch steps, deep in conversation. They were in plain sight of everyone and not sitting improperly close, yet their familiarity unnerved Leah. Chatting and laughing, they seemed to be aware of no one else but each other. "Who is Jonah talking to?" asked Leah, hoping to keep her voice casual.

Annie squinted into the fading light. "Oh, that's Sarah Gingerich. She and Jonah courted for a while before he moved away. Folks thought they might announce an engagement, but then he met you and fell in love. So it's water under the bridge." Annie linked her arm through Leah's. "Don't worry about them. They're just catching up. Let's go look at my newborn collie pups. They are the cutest dogs in the world."

Leah complied, oohing and ahhing at the pups appropriately, except for the "don't worry" part. It might have been easier if the old flame wasn't tall and thin and beautiful. Jealousy and envy were sins. Jonah had never given her one reason to doubt his faithfulness. Yet that night, a nasty green-eyed monster reared its ugly head, taking hold of her heart with its long, razor-sharp claws.

TEN

Charm, Ohio

Emma Davis walked onto the bedroom balcony carrying the day's first cup of coffee. Although it was a long walk from the pot in the kitchen, she enjoyed the porch rocker in the early hours while her sons still slept. James had just left for work at the main office of Hollyhock Farms. He would spend most of the morning returning phone calls, updating records, checking inventories, and scheduling the workers for the day, week, month, and season ahead. He'd shown her various spreadsheets on the computer that he claimed made running an agribusiness easier, but it had looked more like a tangled ball of yarn to her. James would usually stop home to share lunch with her and the boys and then spend his afternoons on horseback, checking livestock, fences, and various work crews hired to run a large beef cattle and horse-breeding operation. And then there were Emma's sheep—the money-losing end of the business. But because sheep were what had brought them together, their flocks of Dorsets, Suffolks, and Cheviots would always have a home at Hollyhock.

James might dress Plain and drive a buggy for transportation since his conversion to New Order Amish, but his day-to-day operations had remained unchanged. Computers, cell phones, Internet and e-mail, and modern technology were accepted by their Amish sect. Emma had grown up Old Order, which still used propane appliances, kerosene lamps, and draft horses to pull farming implements.

As the sun rose high enough to burn the dew off their lush rolling lawn, Emma heard her baby awaken. Little Sam would start out whimpering like a dog, graduate to crying, and if still ignored, would begin howling like a coyote at the moon. She downed her coffee and hurried to the nursery to tend to a hungry child with a wet diaper. After changing the baby into dry clothes, she carried him into Jamie's room, where her older son was already playing with blocks. "Did you climb out of your crib again?" she asked. Jamie peered up, giggling. "We need to either install higher sides or put you in your own bed."

"Mommy, look," he ordered, but the tower of blocks shifted and fell over.

"How about some breakfast before you attempt to rebuild?"

"Cheerios," he demanded, scrambling to his feet. "With bananas." The name of the fruit sounded as though the word contained two *y*'s, but she understood just fine. He ran out his bedroom door.

"Bananas it is." Emma caught hold of his back suspenders to ensure he didn't tumble down the steps in haste. And so a normal day of motherhood for Emma Davis had begun—one filled with spilled milk, burned brownies, and scraped knees. Yet she would savor the time while her children were small for the rest of her life.

Later that day, after James returned to work and she'd put both boys down for a nap, Emma curled up on her chaise with a novel. She had checked a mystery out from the library that involved a crime-solving cat, but she hadn't reached the second chapter when Barbara Davis appeared. Her mother-in-law came roaring up the driveway in her fancy gold convertible. The woman set such store by that car! How could a God-fearing Christian woman—who conducted a Bible study in her own kitchen and regularly helped at the homeless shelter, ladies' jail, and midwife birthing clinic—spend twenty-five-thousand dollars for a car? James told her that wasn't expensive by English standards, yet the price had set Emma's head reeling.

Barbara Davis was very much an *Englischer*.

"Yoo-hoo, Emma. It's me."

Emma set down her book to meet her at the top of the steps. "Hullo, would you like coffee? I have half a pot still warm from lunch."

Barbara pushed her windblown hair back from her face. "Oh, no. No time for that. I have to get to church, and I would love for you to come with me." Her smile went from one ear to the other.

Barbara attended a big evangelical Christian church close to Sugar Creek, where most of the county's non-Amish belonged. She hadn't been thrilled with her son's conversion, yet she hadn't tried to talk him out of it either. Emma would always be grateful for her open-mindedness in that regard. "I can't today," said Emma. "The boys are both asleep. Is it another flea market fund-raiser and bake sale? Because I have a bag of discards you can take with you." Emma tried to help out with Barbara's charity efforts, whether for a local family out of work or drought victims across the globe.

"Oh, no, this is much better." Barbara was practically dancing with excitement. "Our pastor is taking a group to work in Haiti. We'll be helping to rebuild a whole village. Churches from all over Ohio will join us. Those without construction skills will be sewing, cooking, painting, and carrying supplies. Can you imagine? We will make a difference in people's lives." Her enthusiasm was hitting cloud level.

"But that horrible earthquake was almost two years ago," said Emma, rubbing the back of her neck.

"That's correct, but there is still much to be done. Most of the people live in temporary camps. Now that more roads have been fixed, we can get construction materials into new areas. We'll be building homes, churches, and a school. Families will be glad to get a permanent roof over their heads."

"You're going to Haiti? What about your job in the ER?" Emma felt as though she was the parent, trying to talk sense to a flighty teenager.

"Oh, that's the best part! Because I'm a medical professional doing humanitarian aid, the hospital will hold my position indefinitely."

Emma smiled graciously. "That's wonderful news. Your family will miss you but will be so proud of you."

Barbara reached for her hand. "I'd like you to come with me. We're not leaving for a couple of months, so you would have time to prepare. Emma, this will be the experience of a lifetime."

Emma's jaw dropped open. "Me? I couldn't possibly go with you. I have a husband and two little boys."

"Your James could eat meals at the big house with his dad. Lily has agreed to move home while I'm gone to take care of things. And as far as my grandbabies? A friend's daughter just graduated from nanny school. She's willing to donate her services for the six weeks for free, as her donation to the cause. Besides, she'll get practical experience to put down on her résumé. You can rest assured that your boys would be in good hands."

Emma shook her head. "Nanny or no, I don't think I could leave them for even one week, let alone for six."

Barbara patted her shoulder. "I understand what a sacrifice it would be to be apart from them, but these people are suffering, Emma. And we'll have the opportunity to talk about Jesus besides meeting their urgent physical needs. Some of their communities still practice voodoo. At least agree to come to one of the information meetings. There will be another one in two weeks, along with a video of the blighted area." Her pretty eyes turned downright plaintive.

"I'll come to the next meeting, but I make no other promises. Now, if you'll excuse me, I need to start something for dinner." Emma forced a weak smile.

"Bless your heart, child. I'll be in touch!" In a whirlwind, Barbara Davis jumped in her shiny car and drove away.

I am a grown woman, not a child! Yet somehow a child was exactly how her mother-in-law made her feel.

~

Winesburg

"Phoebe! Come down right now or we'll leave without you."

When Phoebe heard her father's voice, she tossed her drawing pad on the bed. Her mother had already called her once, but Phoebe had wanted to finish the portrait of Eli Riehl. If she let more time slip by, her precious memories of New York—and of the handsomest man in the world—would fade away forever. And she would need something to cry over when she was elderly, frail, and still single.

She flew down the stairs and out the door as fast as Sunday decorum allowed. Hannah, Ben, and her dad were already climbing into the buggy. "I thought you would have to take the path to Uncle Simon's," said Hannah, offering her a hand to step up.

"Nobody likes latecomers, young lady," scolded Seth. "Whatever you were doing probably wasn't suitable for the Sabbath anyway."

Pining over a man I'll never see again? Probably not. Phoebe uttered a silent prayer of confession as the Millers drove the half-mile distance to the Miller family next door for church service. As she and her family joined the throng entering Uncle Simon's outbuilding, which had been scrubbed spic-and-span, her mind played a cruel trick on her. She thought she saw the tall, blond profile of Eli Riehl duck through the doorway up ahead.

It couldn't be. The Riehls lived in another district. Phoebe shook her head as though waking from a dream. When her father and brother headed toward the left-hand benches, she and Hannah found spots on the right, midway to the front. She immediately bowed her head in prayer to be delivered from her constant self-absorption. She didn't stop praying until the congregation began the first hymn. When she opened her eyes, she met the gaze of the world's best storyteller. Eli was smiling at her from across the room, not even pretending to be singing.

Phoebe felt the barn sway as though under hurricane-force winds. Her breath escaped with the sound of a squeaky door hinge, loud enough to draw Hannah's attention. She elbowed Phoebe's side and thrust the songbook *Ausbund* under her nose. "There will be time for staring at boys later. We're here to worship."

With enough to be contrite about already, Phoebe lifted her voice in praise. And for the next three hours of sermons, Scriptures, and singing, she tried desperately not to look at him. At times, she succeeded. When the service concluded, people filed out toward the long tables where lunch would be served.

"Don't wander off," warned Hannah. "We need to help Julia bring out the food."

"Of course," said Phoebe, although *wandering off* had crossed her mind. She joined the women headed toward the house.

"*Ach*, Phoebe. I'm glad you're here since Emma and Leah aren't," said her aunt. She handed her niece a giant bowl of potato salad and bustled off. Phoebe would have asked where her cousins were, but Julia appeared disinclined to chitchat. After setting the side dish on the table, she turned and found herself nose to nose with a sweet-faced girl in her early twenties.

"You're Phoebe Miller, right? Do you know where Leah Byler is?" asked the woman.

"*Jah*, I'm Phoebe, but my aunt just told me Leah didn't come today." She smiled politely.

The woman settled her hands on her rounded hips. "My name is Rose. I live one district over. Your cousin is a friend of mine. This is our off-week for church, but my *bruder* thought it would be nice to worship at your service. So here we are."

"Welcome, Rose. Would you like to join me carrying bowls? The sooner the food is out, the sooner everyone can eat. I hope you brought your appetite."

Rose lowered her chin and stared intently into Phoebe's eyes. "How's your eyesight? Do I bear no resemblance to my brother? Folks usually say we look alike, except for the height part."

Phoebe caught her breath and then stammered incoherently. "You're Rose...Riehl?"

"In the flesh. And I know Eli's both starving and anxious to talk to you. So let's get those side dishes." Rose linked arms with Phoebe, practically dragging her into Aunt Julia's house, while Phoebe scanned the crowd for a particular face.

The next hour passed in a blur, like scenery through a speeding car window. They carried and served and fetched and then cleaned up afterward. At some point Phoebe supposed she'd eaten something, but she couldn't recall what it had been because Eli Riehl made sure he was always within sight during the meal. And the moment she pulled off her soiled apron and dropped it into the porch basket, he materialized at her side.

"Miss Miller? The hospitality of your district has been gracious and kind." Eli held his felt hat over his heart. "May I trouble you to take a walk with me? Your uncle mentioned there are sheep up in the pasture. Alas, we have only cows, horses, and pigs. I'd love to see some spring lambs."

"Certainly. The sheep are ours, next door, but the two fields share a common fence line. If you'll follow me." She started walking faster than some folks run until certain they were beyond spying eyes and ears, while Eli kept pace. Then she turned on him. "You can knock off the 'alas' stuff. It's me, Phoebe Miller. What are you doing here?" Her words flew out in a breathless rush, but he seemed to understand her perfectly.

He hopped around as though he'd stepped barefoot on a bee. "I came to see you. I knew you wouldn't miss preaching, so I asked my sister to come with me today. She knows we'd met." He imbued Rose's *knowing* with special emphasis. "Rose is a friend of your cousin Leah. So, again, I can't believe you and I never met before." He stopped bobbing around. "I feared I would never see you again."

That forthright statement matched her own earlier sentiments, but hearing it vocalized had her checking over her shoulder as though they had been caught in some naughty deed. "It's good to see you too," she whispered. "I don't have many friends, especially not with common interests."

"I had to track you down. How else could we talk about our joint project? You do still want to work on a book with me, don't you?"

Phoebe resumed marching toward the high pasture so that he might not notice that his presence made her skittish as a white-tailed fawn. "Of course I do, but I don't know how we'll manage it. It's not as though you live here." She pointed down. "While I live there." She aimed her index finger at the next pasture beyond the split rail fence. Wooly sheep grazed contentedly while their offspring frolicked and played.

"You live there?" he asked, his voice heavy with reverential awe.

"*Jah*. It's just another farm, pretty much like this one."

"No, not like this one." He slowly scanned the lush rolling acres. "That's the home of Phoebe Miller—a very special place on earth, indeed."

She blushed to the top of her head. "You and your fancy talk. I'll never get used to it. Well, there are my *mamm*'s sheep—her pride and joy. I must admit the lambs are adorable."

Eli watched two pure-white babies chase after their ewe. "It is a land filled with adorable creatures." After a long minute, he sat down on a large flat rock.

Boulders had been moved to the boundary line between farms years ago, so Phoebe chose one for her own perch. "What are your ideas, Eli?" she asked, hiding her trembling hands in her lap.

"Shall I tell you the story I've come up with so far?" He interlaced his fingers to crack his knuckles.

"Please do. Then maybe I can start some sketches later today."

Unwittingly, she found herself holding her breath as Eli wove a tender tale about an ornery cow that had nothing but contempt for other barnyard animals, until the day came when the cow desperately needed a friend. Phoebe was enchanted. Eli's story bloomed in her mind as she imagined the facial expressions she would create for animal characters in each scene.

When he finished the story, he leaped to his feet and reached for her hand. "That's all I have so far. Let's start back before you're missed. I don't want to ruin my future chances of working with you."

"There will be future meetings?" she asked stupidly.

"Of course. We must collaborate on what scenes to create for each page of my story."

"True. I just wondered where we might meet to work." As they crested the hill and the Miller house loomed into view, she pulled her hand from his grip.

"Because this is a book, I thought maybe the library? Winesburg has a nice one. Could you meet me there some afternoon?" He peered at her from under his long silky bangs.

Without a moment's hesitation to ponder practicalities, she answered, "You bet I can."

ELEVEN

Willow Brook

As workweeks go, this past one had been the pits. Two of the grooms at Rolling Meadows Stables quit to return to Mexico, so Matthew found himself tending to mundane chores besides training prestigious show horses. Not that he minded, but by Friday afternoon he was bone tired and eager to get home to his wife and children.

He said a prayer of gratitude when no owners arrived late at the stable, demanding his time and attention. He and Pete Taylor left at five o'clock on the button. Along the way he closed his eyes pretending to nap, but he wasn't sleepy. He wanted to concentrate on how to approach Martha when he got home. Last weekend had been strained, to say the least. She had accused him of being overly fond of money. And he couldn't deny that finances occupied far more thinking time in New York than they had back home. Farms were more expensive here, although the price of land was rising across the country. He decided not to mention the amount of tips he'd received during the week. He would leave the envelope of cash along with his paycheck on the counter for her to deposit in the bank. Someday, he would buy his own horse training operation. Then he could stay home with his family all the time. And that day couldn't arrive soon enough for him.

Ninety minutes later Pete pulled up in front of his tidy bungalow.

"Home, sweet home, Matty. Got any big plans for the weekend?" asked the foreman.

Matthew nodded. "Yep, I plan to play ball with my son for hours and then rock my baby girl to sleep on the porch."

"Isn't your son only two years old?" Pete's grin revealed two gold caps. "How can you play baseball with a toddler?"

"We both sit in the grass and I roll a big ball to him. He giggles and knocks it away, usually in the wrong direction. I fetch the ball, sit back down, and repeat the process. You can't believe how much his hand-eye coordination has improved." Matt pulled his bag from the backseat. "On Sunday we'll go to church and stay to socialize during lunch. When we get home, I intend to sit in my porch swing and watch the grass grow."

"Sounds just about perfect. See you Monday." Pete waved and then peeled away the moment the truck door slammed shut.

Matthew headed up the driveway wearing a silly grin. He spotted Martha on the front porch in the spot he intended to occupy on Sunday. She was feeding their daughter while his son sat on a quilt by her feet. He hoisted his duffel onto his shoulder and waved like a sightseer on a tour bus. "Hullo, Millers. I'm home at last!" He hurried toward the house.

Martha offered a wave with her free hand along with a small smile. When his son lifted his arm in greeting, Matthew's heart thudded against his chest wall. A white cast encased the boy's thin lower arm, oversized and awkward on a toddler. He sprinted to the porch, dropping his bag before climbing the steps two at a time. "What happened to Noah?' he asked, lifting his son into his arms. "Is he all right?'

"Hullo, *daed*," said Noah, snaking his good arm around his father's neck. He held his cast out with a proud grin. "Broken!" he exclaimed in *Deutsch*.

Matthew hugged him tightly, burying his face in his son's fine strawberry-blond hair that smelled of warm sunshine. "All better now?" he murmured, his voice raspy with emotion. Pain shot through his own arm and shoulders, realizing what his boy must have endured.

"*Jah, gut,*" agreed Noah, squirming to be set down. He'd grown tired of the hugging and kissing and wished to return to his toys.

Matthew placed him on the folded quilt and met the gaze of his wife. Martha's expression was a mixed stew of anger, sorrow, and guilt. Her brown eyes were red-rimmed and deeply lined. Dark purple smudges beneath her lower lashes indicated she'd slept little. "What happened?" he repeated, keeping his tone even.

Martha closed her blouse, rose, and settled the infant on her hip. "I'm putting both the *kinner* to bed. Then I'll tell you what happened while you eat your supper. As the story has waited this long, I'm sure it can wait another twenty minutes." She bent down, grabbed Noah's unencumbered arm and practically dragged him into the house.

Matthew's hands clenched into fists while he squeezed his eyes tightly shut. Anger and fear welled up in his throat like stomach acid. *My son has been hurt and no one told me? I am the boy's father, not some casual acquaintance dropping by to chew the fat after work.*

For half the time Martha was upstairs washing and dressing the children for bed, he paced the porch. He needed to burn off his disappointment with her or this trouble could easily escalate out of control. His parents hadn't raised him to be a hothead, but seeing his son's broken arm triggered a protective instinct that was hard to tamp down. Back and forth he paced like the unfortunate lion in a concrete enclosure he'd seen at the Cleveland Zoo.

Finally he entered his home somewhat better composed and sat down at the table with a glass of cold milk. Ten minutes later a pale Martha Miller crept into the room. She pulled a plate of fried chicken from the oven and potato salad from the fridge and set them near his place setting. Sliced cucumbers and tomatoes already waited on his plate. Without an ounce of appetite, he pushed his dinner away. "I'd like you to tell me what happened."

She lowered herself into a chair. "I was doing laundry with the baby in her sling. Noah was tagging after me back and forth from the wringer washer to the clothesline. The baby finally dozed off, so I decided to lay her down in the crib in the living room. Noah was playing with his blocks on the mudroom floor. I was gone for two minutes," she exclaimed, meeting his eyes briefly. "During that time, he climbed up onto the electric dryer using the stepladder that leaned against it." What little color her face had faded away. "One minute he was on the floor, the next he was atop that machine. I screamed when I walked in and saw him close to the edge." Martha's head dropped to her chest. "I startled him and he fell. His poor arm is broken in two places."

From her gasps, he suspected she was crying. A growing puddle on the oak surface soon confirmed it. "Go on. Please tell me the rest, Martha," he prodded. Guilt and shame replaced his earlier pique. Where was he when his family needed him? Almost a hundred miles away.

"I didn't know what to do," she wailed. "I put the baby back in her sling, picked up Noah, grabbed my purse, and ran next door. I was almost hysterical, but the neighbor calmed me down and drove us to the hospital." Martha glanced up. "I don't know why we must have that dryer in the mudroom! We won't ever use it or any of the other electric appliances."

Matthew peered around the room. It was an odd assortment of what they'd brought with them from Ohio and things already here. "Because this is a rental house. We can't expect our landlord to rip things out when we could move to an Amish home at any time."

She shook her head, but continued the narrative. "At the emergency room, the nurse on duty wouldn't treat Noah until I handed over that insurance card you gave me." She crossed her arms and lifted her chin.

"How did she know we had insurance? Most Amish folks don't." He couldn't understand her agitation at the ER.

"The nurse asked me while filling out a form on her clipboard. I couldn't lie, so I said we had insurance through your job, but I had no intention of using it! It's not the Amish way. I'd planned to use what we've saved for a house to pay the hospital bill." Martha was breathing hard and fighting back more tears.

"I know what is and what isn't Amish way, *fraa*," he said hoarsely. "But since you had *told* her we had insurance, an *Englischer* wouldn't understand your refusal to hand over the card." His voice hardened with her continued focus on unimportant details. "How is Noah? Will the broken arm heal properly?"

"*Jah*, they set the bone. It should mend quite well, according to the pediatrician. But he must wear that cast for six weeks and not get it wet. How can I bathe him properly and keep that…club dry?"

Matthew released an audible sigh. "Thank the Lord." He sucked in three deep gulps of air before pushing forward onto the stickier topic. "You should have asked the neighbor to call me. You have the number of Rolling Meadows along with my foreman's cell phone number."

Her brown eyes darkened. "And what would you have done, Matthew? Borrowed one of those expensive horses and ridden home bareback? No one would want to drop work to drive you all the way here. I didn't even know the name of the hospital she had taken us to until the next day." Martha sounded indignant, as though his earning a living was an expendable option.

Matthew slapped his palm down on the table. "The neighbor would have known the hospital's name. And how I got home would have been *my* problem, Martha. I am your husband and those *kinners' daed*! You had no right to keep this accident from me. I love them as much as you do and would have come home if I had to use a taxicab."

With that she dissolved into uncontrollable sobbing. Normally a woman's grief broke his heart, yet this time he couldn't offer a single word of comfort. He stomped outdoors into the cool night air to release his frustration. He gazed for some time at the star-filled sky. How did their marriage, their life, run so far off track? And what could he do to fix things?

Throughout that long night Matthew sat at his son's bedside, rocking in the chair and thinking. He dozed off and on, and by morning he had one nasty stiff neck. Noah would soon awaken with a two-and-a-half-year-old's irrepressible spirit. Matthew finally realized he couldn't solve this conundrum alone. He turned the matter over to God in a long, tear-filled prayer. Only a powerful, merciful Lord could help these two angry lost lambs find their way back to each other.

～

Winesburg

Julia rocked in her porch swing as though it were some type of onerous chore to complete. Back and forth she pumped her legs, banging the swing into the house wall without even realizing it. She didn't notice because her mind was many miles away, split in three different directions.

"Are you *trying* to knock a hole in the house, Julia?" asked Simon, stepping onto the porch. He carried cups of hot tea. "You're rattling dishes on the shelves."

She looked up, planting both feet on the porch boards. "*Mir leid*," she apologized. "I was so distracted I didn't realize the commotion I caused." She gratefully accepted the cup he offered.

Simon sat down next to her. "What has you so stymied? You haven't been your normal jovial self lately."

She laughed at his rare sarcasm. "A regular barrel of monkeys, that's me." She drank deeply and stared into the black brew. "I am so unhappy, Simon. The good weather is finally here—time for gardening, picnics, and open buggy rides, but all I can think about is how much I miss my *kinner*."

"Henry's trying to saddle a horse without getting bit for his efforts.

Should I tell him to show his face? Maybe come help you punch a hole in the siding?"

Instead of smiling at her husband's attempt to cheer her up, Julia started to cry, despite vowing not to be so weak and morose. "He's the only one left," she wailed. "My other three are far away, and who knows when they'll be back?"

Simon sobered at her utter melancholy. "What hear you from Matthew and Martha?"

"Nothing. A few lines that they are well from time to time. No details, and not a word as to when they might be coming home."

He gently put the swing in motion again. "And our Leah? I thought she and Jonah were only visiting Wisconsin for a couple weeks. She'll be back before you know it."

Julia tried to calm down. "Joanna only moved here to Ohio to help care for her aging parents, but both Burkholders have now passed on to their reward. The rest of her family lives in Wisconsin—the place Jonah still considers home, according to our daughter." She tilted back her head and closed her eyes. "What if Jonah decides they should remain in Hancock? He'd have no trouble selling that farm for a fair price. Buyers for a dairy operation would line up at his door."

Simon raked his snow-white beard with his fingers, his mood rapidly deteriorating to match hers. "Oh, my, Wisconsin is so far away to visit, especially with your arthritis. But at least Emma and James aren't going anywhere. They're four peas in a pod at Hollyhock Farms."

Julia emitted an inappropriate noise for a mature woman married to a deacon. "Charm—they might as well be on the moon. When was the last time Emma came to visit with my grandsons? Busy, busy, busy—that's the excuse she gives me every time I call her from the phone shack."

Simon raised an eyebrow. "That telephone is only to be used in emergencies. Letters are for talking to kin."

"It was an emergency. I was dying of loneliness!"

Simon could have chastised her for bald-faced exaggeration, but he didn't. "We need everybody here for a good long visit. Let's plan a family get-together. Everyone must come and stay at least two weeks or face shunning."

Julia dabbed her eyes and stared at him. In all their years of marriage, Simon had never made light of such a serious matter as excommunication from the Amish church. "Like a reunion?"

"Matthew from New York, Leah from Wisconsin, Emma from the moon—or Charm, whichever—all must come this summer for a family reunion. We'll even walk out to the barn and tell Henry. He can invite that gal he's been courting and doesn't think we know." Simon chortled with delight. "A Miller family reunion. No excuses will be accepted."

Julia threw her arms around his neck and squeezed, knocking his glasses askew. "*Danki, ehemann.* Did I ever mention that I love you very much?"

He struggled against her embrace, pushing his glasses up his nose. "*Jah, jah,* once or twice, but it's nice to hear it a third time. Now go write your letters. I'll see they go out in the early post."

Julia rose to her feet and staggered inside as though she'd consumed apple cider that had begun to ferment. Her legs had stiffened in the evening air, but there wasn't another tear shed that night...or for many nights to come.

TWELVE

A watched clock doesn't move, according to *grossmammi*. And the same could be said of a calendar under close scrutiny, according to Phoebe. When Eli selected Wednesday for their meeting at the library, she knew she would have difficulty getting through Monday and Tuesday. What was the matter with her? It was a struggle just to keep from grinning foolishly every waking moment. Never before had working on a project appealed so much. But the thought of creating illustrations for Eli's delightful children's story was the most exciting opportunity of her life—even better than visiting Niagara Falls, and that was saying a lot.

On Monday she helped her mother with laundry and ironing from sunup until time to cook supper. Then she peeled potatoes, snapped green beans, and fried a dozen pork chops without rolling her eyes once. After supper, when her little brother asked her to play a game of Parcheesi, she agreed despite the fact she could barely keep her lids open. On Tuesday she weeded and hoed the garden and then picked slugs from the cabbages, brussels sprouts, and cauliflower by hand. Under a merciless sun she tossed the slimy critters into a bucket of sudsy water without sneaking to the shade the moment Hannah was out of sight. Even though her dress stuck to her back and her legs itched from brushing against nettles, Phoebe didn't complain once about her chores. She would give her *mamm* no reason not to let her go to town Wednesday afternoon.

When the anticipated day finally arrived, she expected to awaken with a case of chicken pox or a head cold or some mysterious ailment that caused a person's hair to fall out. But she felt perfectly fine as she picked a bushel of strawberries to make into jam later in the week, and there had been a normal number of lost hairs in her brush. Hannah answered her request to visit the library with an immediate, "I don't see why not." She explained that she wanted to study books to see how realistically scenes were depicted. That was the honest truth. She just didn't mention she would be consulting those illustrations with someone else.

As Phoebe drove the open buggy into Winesburg, the weather promised an absolutely perfect June day—sunny, breezy, and warm. She spotted Eli's blond head the moment she entered the building. The Winesburg Library had no area that could be called private, but Eli sat as far from the librarian's desk as possible. He glanced up from under his sheaf of hair. It looked as though someone might have trimmed his hair, but if so they had cut off the barest minimum.

"Hi, Phoebe," he called out. "Right on time!" Smiles didn't get any friendlier than Eli Riehl's from behind his stack of children's books. "I found you examples of different types of illustrations."

"*Guder nachmittag*," she greeted in more formal *Deutsch*. "I hope you haven't been waiting long." She slipped into the opposite chair at the polished wood table. "How did you manage an afternoon away from the farm this busy time of year?"

"Not long at all. I only beat you by ten minutes." He took a quick assessment of the other patrons. "Wednesdays, after morning chores, are my time off for good behavior. You know, sort of like releasing a prison inmate to pick up litter along the highway one day a week." His left dimple deepened.

"You're no prisoner, Eli," she chastised. "You're a farmer with chores, that's all."

"*Jah*, I know. Rose told me that someday I would appreciate having the farm to care for—one day soon." Oddly, he winked at her. "I don't mind milking cows or feeding livestock. It's the aftermath of all that alfalfa and spelt that gets tiresome."

Phoebe blushed for no reason she could think of, but sitting so close to him without Mrs. Stoltzfus hovering nearby made her nervous. "How do you usually spend your Wednesday afternoons?"

He bent his head close to hers. "I usually meet my friends at the Mount Hope auction. We watch the bidding on horses, mainly to see how high the price goes when *Englischer*s jump into the action. Sometimes my friends buy new milk cows or dairy goats; other times we just hang out, but we always end up having pie in the basement cafeteria."

"My cousin makes the pies they sell there," she interjected. "Leah's a great baker."

"Rose told me about your cousin." Eli leaned back in his chair. "I'll be interested to match a face to her delicious banana cream. Is Leah anywhere near as pretty as you, Miss Miller?"

Phoebe froze with her fingers midway to the stack of books. After a quick glance around the room, she hissed, "You really shouldn't say things like that. Someone could hear you."

"It's the truth, Phoebe. Anyway, nobody's here to overhear us."

She narrowed her gaze at him. "What about the librarian? You're not exactly a quiet person."

The middle-aged English woman with a thick head of silver hair glanced up and smiled.

He ran a hand through his enviable hair. "If she heard me, she's probably thinking, 'What a beautiful little Amish gal, that one is! Why, I just want to reach out and pinch one of those dimpled cheeks.'" Eli's voice had changed to an exaggerated whisper yet remained as audible as before.

Phoebe covered her face with her hands to hide her blush and her laughter. "You're incorrigible, Eli Riehl. You love getting a girl's goat."

"Not any girl. Just you, Miss Miller." He opened the first book from the stack. "But enough flirting for one day; we have work to do. Take a look at these pictures." Turning the book around, he pushed it under her nose. "These are very sketchy and cartoonish. Undefined and rather whimsical. Well executed, but not what I had in mind for our book."

She studied the two pages and nodded, not caring for the particular style either. "I see what you mean."

Eli closed the book, tossed it aside, and opened a second. "In this one the artist created more fully-defined characters but used colors too bold and striking. The illustrations aren't any more realistic than the cartoonish ones." He shook his bangs back from his face. "Seriously, have you ever seen an orange moon or trees that shade of green? This book might give little ones nightmares."

Phoebe pulled the book closer to peruse. The colors jumped from the paper. Turning the page, she said, "Look at this—purple goats and pink horses."

"Not in my barnyard, there won't be!" Eli snapped the book shut. "That book must be for New York City kids who have never seen real farm animals."

Phoebe leaned forward with a slow smile. Never before had she felt like this—that her opinion counted on a subject that mattered deeply to her. "Then it's up to us, Eli, to create a book those city *kinner* can learn from. We'll show them the soft yellow of duck down, the tender green of new leaves, and the rich brown of a mare's shiny coat."

"Exactly. Now take a look at this one." He opened a picture book about a tiger family living in a dense tropical forest.

The pictures realistically portrayed the action of the story; at least she thought so, based on her limited knowledge of tigers and jungles. "I like these. I can draw in this style, but my assortment of artist chalk might not supply enough color."

"Start with detailed sketches of each scene. We'll worry about coloration at some point down the road."

Phoebe inhaled a deep, revitalizing breath. "All right. Tell me again the beginning of your story. I'll come up with three or four preliminary illustrations before the next time we meet." She uttered the words without considering whether or not there would be a next time.

"Perfect," he agreed, not breaking stride. "Shall we plan to meet back here in one week?" Eli cocked his head to the side. "I believe the Mount Hope auction cafeteria can survive another week without my patronage."

Phoebe swallowed down the lump of expectation and excitement that had risen in her throat. "Of course. I have no plans for next Wednesday." *Or any other Wednesday for the rest of the summer.*

He handed her a spiral notebook and pen. "Prepare to take notes, sweet peach. You're about to hear the future Newberry Award-winning story, round number two." Eli settled back and began his tale of the obnoxious cow again.

Phoebe took down his words and his suggestions as fast as she could. She might not know anything about Newberry Awards, but she knew she loved children's stories…and working with Eli. While he talked, she jotted ideas for simple sketches. He praised and encouraged her. Thus far her hobby had only generated mild interest and passive indulgence from onlookers, much like one of her mom's three-day diets.

When they were leaving the library, Eli grinned and nodded at the librarian. "Good day to you."

She smiled sweetly at him and then leaned across the counter to speak to Phoebe. "You *are* a beautiful young woman, but I would never dream of pinching a complete stranger's cheek." She offered an impish wink.

"Thank you, ma'am," murmured Phoebe, blushing to her hairline.

Eli erupted with laughter, which continued until they reached their horses.

"Like I said before, you are incorrigible!" Phoebe tugged the reins loose from the hitching post.

He bowed gallantly. "I promise to improve my atrocious manners by next week." He offered his hand as she stepped into her buggy. Before releasing her, he bent low and kissed the back of her fingers. "Go straight home, Miss Miller; do not tarry. I cannot bear the thought of another man sweeping you off your feet along the way."

She drew back her hand. "Do you talk this way at home? Like you're a character in some old-fashioned novel?"

"*Jah*, but only until my sisters start throwing things at me. Then I stop."

"I must remember that next week." Grinning, she released the brake.

"Don't forget your notes." Eli handed her the tablet.

"*Danki.*" She tucked it safely into her tote bag. "I have plenty to do between now and Wednesday. Let's hope chores won't prove too… onerous for either of us," she said, choosing a word that he would like.

"Chores will only make time pass more quickly." He held his straw hat over his heart.

"Goodbye, Eli." Phoebe shook the reins over the mare's back and clucked her tongue. Once the horse pulled onto the road, she refused to look back, especially since she couldn't stop grinning. *Instead of throwing things at him, I would like to listen to him all day.*

For half the distance home she replayed each of their verbal exchanges in her mind. But soon a troubling notion crept in to spoil her mood. Was she giddy about creating a storybook for children to read and enjoy? Or was it the handsome, charismatic Eli Riehl that sent her over the moon? Because she had better stop herself right now if it was the latter. Vague yet still painful memories of her mother returned, along with the paralyzing fear of being left behind. Constance hadn't meant to die young in an accident, and yet Phoebe had been emotionally crippled by the loss. She'd responded by slipping into muteness, a reaction only her tenderhearted stepmother, Hannah, had been able to free her from.

She'd better think twice about growing too fond of Eli Riehl.

With his abundant, carefree charm, he could be here today and gone tomorrow. He might soon tire of a shy woman who uttered such profound maxims as *"You love getting a girl's goat."* As much as she wanted to create a book that would last beyond her lifetime, she would tread carefully with her storytelling partner.

～

Hancock

The crowd that turned out to see the Bylers off at the bus station was even larger than the one that had gathered on the day they arrived. Jonah was a very popular man; his wife, not so much. Although she'd met two wives who had welcomed her warmly into their community, Leah couldn't get beyond her unchristian jealousy. It wasn't as though she didn't trust Jonah with his former flame. It was simply that the people she met in Hancock made her feel like a lone mallard duck trailing after a gaggle of Canada geese—welcome to tag along but never part of the inner circle. Leah longed for her own home and kitchen instead of being a guest of Aunt Harriet. She missed seeing her parents and Henry at preaching services, and she even missed *mamm's* well-intended advice. She missed baking pies for the restaurants and shops of Holmes County. And most of all, she missed Jonah, with his soft words and tender touch as they lay together waiting for sleep to come. Lately she'd been following him from barn to bean field as he talked with his uncle after chores were done. She was lonely for her beloved husband. She longed to spend a full day with him.

And that day had finally come. Joanna Byler stood among the waving crowd as Leah and Jonah boarded their bus for Ohio. She would remain behind with her sister for a longer visit. Leah didn't know what that boded for her farm and cheese business back home, but with Jonah's arm snug around her shoulders, she would save that concern for another day.

With pretty scenery for viewing and her self-help book for reading, Leah should have been able to relax and enjoy their first hours alone together. But once again, the rocking and swaying of the vehicle conspired to turn her gills green. Despite a full belly and ginger ale to sip, she could do nothing more than concentrate on keeping her breakfast down. A second dose of Dramamine knocked her out, and from that point until they reached Holmes County, Leah only woke up three times. She moved like a sleepwalker through the travel plazas, hanging onto Jonah and eating only a tiny portion of her meals.

"If you're not back on your feed by tomorrow, I'm calling the vet… er, the doctor."

"What?" she squeaked, jarring awake. "You're calling a vet? What on earth for?"

Jonah chuckled, hooking his thumb toward the window. "No reason, my sweet, but you should check out where we are."

Leah peered out the window to regain her bearings, immediately recognizing the Greyhound stop by the grocery store. "Apple Creek! We're almost home. Thank goodness."

"I would think you would be starving. You haven't eaten anything in twelve hours. Let me help you down and then come back for our bags." Jonah assisted her off the bus and over to a bench.

"I'm glad to be on solid ground. I've never felt so sick to my stomach in all my life." She leaned her head back and closed her eyes.

"Wait here for me. Lily Davis should be here soon to drive us home. I called her from the last rest area and estimated our arrival time."

Leah's eyes blinked open. "Emma's sister-in-law is coming for us?"

"*Jah*. It'll be safer than anyone's buggy in the middle of the night."

Leah wasn't close to James Davis' sister. Nevertheless, she could have kissed the tall English woman when she pulled up to the curb ten minutes later. And then, almost before Leah knew it, Lily was pulling to a stop in front of their home.

Their farm had never looked so good. The hired employees had mowed the lawn around the house and watered her plants.

Everything else could wait until morning. While Jonah checked on his heifers and baby calves, Leah ate four slices of buttered toast and drank two cups of tea. In the kitchen that had been Esther Burkholder's and then Joanna Byler's, she sat alone, relishing the thought that the kitchen was fully hers, at least for the next couple of weeks. Wisconsin was a fine place for those whose hearts were there, but *her* heart was here in Ohio. The million-dollar question was: Where was Jonah's heart?

When he sat down for breakfast the next morning, her husband seemed like his old self.

"Everything sorted out in the dairy barns?"

"Right as rain." He kissed Leah's cheek before settling down with his own mug. "All milk pickups were on schedule, plus we have plenty of sharp and mild cheddar ready for delivery. Mom will be pleased when she returns."

"How long will she stay at Harriet's?" she asked, placing a plate of fried eggs and bacon in front of him.

"Who knows? She was downright evasive when I asked her. She and her sister have big plans for the week. They are taking the boys to the Dells for a couple days. My mom, a tourist—can you believe it? She plans to send us a postcard." Jonah shook his head. "She sure is glad to be back home."

Leah inwardly cringed, hearing him refer to Wisconsin that way. "I understand the winters are harsher there, much snowier and colder. She wouldn't like that with her thin blood. She sleeps with socks on almost year-round."

Jonah devoured his food. "Maybe a bit colder, but I don't recall Wisconsin being much snowier."

"According to the almanac—" she began, but the sound of a car door slamming outside the window curtailed her argument.

He downed his coffee and refilled his mug. "I'll see who that is. Thanks for the vittles, *fraa*. Yours put Aunt Harriet's to shame. Now you'd better start baking. The world cannot survive without your pies for another day." He nuzzled her *kapp* with another kiss and strode out the door, mug in hand.

Fuming, Leah watched Jonah approach a well-dressed *Englischer*. The woman wore a fire-engine-red suit, red high heels, and a black wide-brimmed hat with a fake red flower attached. Her outfit gave the word "fancy" new meaning. What could she want with the Bylers? Most people who stopped to buy cheese wore sneakers and jeans. Leah watched until the two disappeared into the cavernous milking parlor. *You'd better watch where you step with those expensive shoes*, she thought, scraping her breakfast into the compost bucket. Unlike her husband, her appetite had remained behind in Hancock.

Thirty minutes later, elbow deep in baking, Leah heard a car engine roar to life and then the crunch of driveway gravel. Jonah resolved her quandary when he dashed into the house. "Leah!" he shouted. "Do you know who that woman was?" He didn't pause for guesses. "A real estate agent from Wooster. Do you know how much she thinks we could get for this farm?"

Leah blinked, speechless.

Again, he allowed no opportunity for speculation had she desired, but announced an enormous dollar amount. The bag of flour slipped from her fingers, landing with a thud on the clean sheet of parchment paper on the counter.

"Can you believe it? Wait until I tell Mom. She's not going to believe it. I think I'll write her a letter right now." He disappeared into the front room.

Leah wasn't sure if it was the shock over Jonah penning a letter or the exorbitant price mentioned by the Realtor, but something made her sick. She barely reached the bathroom when the small amount of breakfast she'd eaten made a hasty reappearance.

THIRTEEN

Emma clutched her purse in her lap and glanced over her shoulder at her smiling sons. Both boys were strapped into car seats in the backseat of Lily Davis' truck.

"Are you going to have fun at Grandma's?" asked Aunt Lily, peering at them in the rearview mirror. She received dual affirmative nods, although the baby only mimicked his brother. "I want you to tell me about it on the way home, okay, Jamie?"

The boy nodded again as Emma turned to face her sister-in-law. "Thanks for the lift to my parents'. I love being able to spend the day with my mom. She's been down in the dumps lately with two of her children out of state."

"Well, Leah's home now. I picked her and Jonah up a few nights ago. And I pass your folks' place on my way to the OSU Extension Center, Emma. I'll be lecturing all day on bovine husbandry. You might as well enjoy some free taxi service while I'm living at home for the summer."

"I must admit the drive to Winesburg by buggy seems to get longer every time."

"That's because the two of them get restless." Lily grinned at her nephews in the mirror. For the remainder of the drive, she entertained Emma with amusing tales from her life as a country vet.

"Thanks, Lily," said Emma at the Miller farm. "I'll see you later when your workshop is over."

Her sister-in-law waved goodbye as she drove away. Emma picked up Sam and took little Jamie's hand and headed toward the house. Once she and the boys stepped across the threshold, Julia scolded her with the first words from her mouth.

"Emma! Why on earth didn't you tell me you were coming?" Julia stood by the sink looking as angry as a wet hen. "I have nothing baked but whole wheat bread! Not a cookie in the house."

"Hullo, dear *mamm. Jah*, I'm tickled to see you too." Emma smiled as she set the baby's carrier on a kitchen chair.

Julia smiled at the sarcasm. "Make yourself comfortable while I rustle up some chocolate chip cookies. That is, if you can stay more than an hour. Those boys look thinner. Aren't they eating for you?" Julia limped to the cupboard and began taking out sugar, flour, and baking chips.

So like mamm. *She writes letters containing poignant pleas to come visit, and then she spends the first hour scolding.* "They eat like their father—often and in great quantities. I can't keep chewy peanut butter granola bars in the house."

"What are those?" Julia pulled the basket of brown eggs from the refrigerator.

"Exactly what the name implies, plus they're coated with chocolate. James and Jamie love them."

"They don't sound healthy. Do you not bake from scratch, daughter?"

"They are very healthy, with oats, peanuts, peanut butter, honey, and all natural ingredients. And of course I bake from scratch, but Grandma Davis got them hooked on the bars."

"Hooked?" Julia snorted as she poured glasses of milk.

Emma settled into the chair next to the baby and drew a bottle from her diaper bag. "Did you think we'd have a snack and let you watch?" she asked little Sam. She gazed into her son's blue eyes as a wave of emotion stole her breath away.

"*Vas kommed fon nawtur vare gude fur dine libe un sael,*" said Julia to Jamie as she set down his cup of milk.

The child blinked his huge eyes several times.

"Isn't your *mamm* teaching you the language of your heritage?" she asked him in *Deutsch* again.

Jamie continued to stare at his maternal grandmother without reply.

Emma leaned over and patted his arm. "*Grossmammi* told you 'What comes from nature is good for body and soul,' like your milk."

The child picked up his plastic cup and drank heartily, wiping his mouth on his sleeve.

"Then she asked you if I was teaching you any *Deutsch*," explained Emma.

Jamie grinned at Julia and nodded yes. "*Ich vill some kuchlen.*" In their Amish dialect he told her he wanted some cookies.

Julia laughed while measuring sugar into the bowl. "*Se sind ready eb un shippley si schwanszwie mol shittla con.*"

Jamie looked to Emma, who translated the words into English. "She said they'll be ready before a lamb can shake his tail twice."

Julia banged her wooden spoon against the bowl. "I don't understand, daughter, why my grandson knows so little of our language. Your New Order district speaks *Deutsch*, the same as Old Order."

Emma lifted her youngest from the car seat to set in her lap. "That's my fault. Their father's Pennsylvania German is still not great, although it is improving…slowly. We usually speak English around the table and during evening devotions. I have been teaching Jamie his prayers in English."

"No, Emma. That is not how it's done!" Color rose up Julia's neck into her pale face. "To learn *Deutsch*, they must hear it continually—not this going back and forth between the two. Once the boys start school will be soon enough for English, after they've mastered *our* language." If she cracked the eggs into the bowl any more vigorously, shells would pulverize. "If you ask me, your *ehemann* would have learned the language by now if *Deutsch* was the only language spoken in his household."

"As you pointed out, it is *his* household. But I will discuss your idea with James tonight at dinner." Emma walked to the window to rein in her temper. She knew her mother was right, but why must she approach any discussion this way? Instead of offering helpful suggestions, she still treated Emma like a child or teenager coming home late from a date during *rumschpringe*. At what age did a daughter become an adult woman in her mother's eyes? What could be pleasant afternoons often turned into a defensive parlaying between the two strong-willed Miller women.

But Emma knew one thing for certain: She *was* her mother—or rapidly turning into her. And despite *mamm*'s doggedness, there was no place on earth she would rather be than here in her warm, sweet-smelling kitchen.

~

Phoebe had become proficient at completing odious tasks without a single roll of her eyes. When she helped her mother scrub out the chicken coop, did she complain? No, and she didn't balk when the clothesline broke, sending freshly laundered sheets into the dust and dirt. As she rewashed the sheets, she contemplated her afternoon visit to the library to see her friend and business partner, Eli Riehl. During the past seven days, she'd completed five double-page illustrations, each portraying the rude cow interacting with other barnyard residents. The cow was a loathsome bully who delighted in name-calling and hurting the feelings of other animals. She verbally abused the dog, horse, pig, goat, and rabbit before she landed in trouble with no friends to call on for help. Phoebe couldn't wait to show Eli her sketches for the opening scenes, and she practically sang during morning chores.

"*Mamm*, do you remember I'm going to the library this afternoon?" she asked between bites of a bologna sandwich.

"*Jah*, but I will drive you into town."

"Why?" Phoebe sputtered, choking on the suddenly dry bread.

"Because I have a doctor's appointment and your dad needs the other buggy to go to Wilmot. That's in the opposite direction." Hannah peered at her curiously while fixing sandwiches for Ben and Seth.

"Oh...okay." Phoebe sipped some tea to wash down the sandwich. "I just didn't want you to trouble yourself unnecessarily."

"No trouble. I'll come back to the library when I'm finished at the doctor's and after I stop at Ruby's Country Store. She's running a sale on heavier-weight fabrics because they're out of season. You'll have plenty of time for whatever you plan to do there for the second week in a row." Her expression of curiosity intensified with the lifting of one eyebrow.

Phoebe sighed, knowing the time had come for full disclosure. "When you're finished with your errands, you can head for home. I'm meeting a friend there, and I'm sure he will drive me home afterward."

Hannah's head swiveled around so fast she easily could have suffered whiplash. "He? Your friend is a *boy*? Who is he?" She stopped making sandwiches and dropped into the chair next to Phoebe's.

"His name is Eli Riehl—"

"You met Robert Riehl's son? Of Riehl and Son Beef and Swine Farm? Oh, my. They have the best-tasting smoked hams in the county. My mouth starts watering just thinking about their honey-maple glaze."

Phoebe wrapped up the rest of her sandwich for later. "I suppose it's the same Riehls. I met Eli on the bus to Niagara Falls and seemed to have more in common with him than with most other people."

"Why is that? Did you develop a sudden hankering for pork chops?"

"*Mamm*, could you stop thinking about food for one moment? Eli is different than most boys. He doesn't talk endlessly about horses or baseball or fishing. He likes to make up stories as his hobby. He asked me to draw some pictures to go along with one of his favorite stories."

Hannah placed her hand over her heart. "You may have met the other matching shoe, Phoebe! Shall I buy yards of soft blue fabric and enough white lawn to make a wedding outfit? Of course, your father won't let you marry until you're at least twenty. He still sees you as his little girl—"

"Stop, please. Let's go back to discussing food. Eli and I are just friends. That's all." She picked up her tote bag and headed for the door. "Shouldn't we get going? Doctors don't like to be kept waiting. I'll get the buggy."

Her brother met Phoebe halfway to the barn with the open two-seater already hitched to the Morgan. "*Danki*, Ben," she said, taking the reins and climbing inside.

"Bring me some candy from town. Any kind will do," he said with a ten-year-old's exuberance.

Hannah climbed in a few moments later and they trotted the horse briskly all the way to Winesburg, but Phoebe still arrived at the library twenty minutes late.

Eli was sitting at the same table flanked by a high pile of books, same as before. "I had almost abandoned hope," he called the moment she entered the well-lit reading room.

The same librarian was on duty and nodded as Phoebe passed her desk. The woman mimed pinching someone's cheek when the younger woman smiled in her direction.

"My mother dropped me off. She had some errands to run and needed to come into town," said Phoebe, settling into the chair beside his.

Eli jutted out his lower lip. "How long do we have before she retrieves you? Has she just come for an ice-cream cone and then turning around?"

"Not to worry. I told her to go home without me when she finishes her appointments." She graced him with her prettiest smile.

"That's very brave to volunteer to walk. I hope you wore comfortable shoes. It's quite a distance, no?" He opened the top book to the page he had marked with a small slip of paper.

Phoebe's expression fell while her brows beetled above the bridge of her nose. "Walk? I thought surely you would offer to drive me home." Her shyness vanished with the possibility of a four-mile hike.

Eli met her eye. "You thought surely?" he asked from under his silky hair.

"I did. I hope I didn't err with my supposition."

He laughed with abandon. "I seem to be rubbing off on you. That never happens at home. And since you've made an effort to expand your vocabulary, I shall drive you home. Now, let's take a look at these examples of illustrations—all very good but all very different."

Phoebe appreciated the distraction because she didn't know how to interpret Eli. Was he teasing yet again? Or was he honestly not thrilled about adding another eight miles to his trip today? That could cause him to be late for evening chores. She'd never met anyone Amish who was as difficult to decipher as an algebra textbook.

Turning her attention to the open pages, she marveled at images of scenes that couldn't possibly take place in nature. "I can't fathom how they did this." She tapped her finger on the page. "These look like photographs, but how do you take a picture of a pig in a top hat, dancing on hind legs? Or this one, wearing a dress?"

"I was wondering the same thing." Eli leaned over the book. "But my guess is the artist scanned his or her sketches into a computer, and the software added the color and glossiness to achieve the overall effect. I know that graphic illustrators can do amazing things with the right computer program."

True to form, Phoebe stared at him with an idiotic expression on her face. "I'll have to take your word on that."

"Only for now you do. But one day I intend to show you what I'm talking about. Let's look at the other books I selected. I picked these because I believe they have all been digitally enhanced."

Her expression changed to total bafflement. "Would you speak English, please?"

"That means the artist used a computer to alter and improve the original drawings." As the two pored over several children's books, Eli pointed out various aspects he either liked or disliked. He certainly had strong opinions regarding what he was looking for.

When they finished the last volume, Phoebe lifted her tote bag onto her lap. "Would you like to see what I came up with during this past week?" Her voice had the intensity of a baby sparrow's first cheep.

"Of course I would!" Eli shoved everything out of the way while she extracted her sketch pad. With trembling fingers she opened the cover to the first drawing.

He pulled the tablet in front of him. "Wow!" he exclaimed. "This is great!" Unlike her, he could have been heard in Wooster.

"Please keep your voices down, or I'll be forced to pinch some cheeks," warned the librarian, chuckling merrily as she resumed her work.

Eli blushed as he studied all four creations: a young Amish girl talking to the mean-spirited cow, the cow stuck in river mud while the other cows abandoned her, the little girl trying to pull Bessie out, and then the girl enlisting help from the pet dog and the family rabbit. The cow had been cruel to the dog by mocking his bad breath and had humiliated the rabbit because of his protruding front teeth. Yet both animals tried to help the friendless cow in her time of need.

"These are wonderful, Phoebe. They are exactly what I was thinking of." Impulsively, Eli snaked his arm around her shoulders and hugged her. "You read my mind—a feat that's never been accomplished before in the annals of history."

A warm sensation began in the pit of her stomach and spread down to her toes. "It's your story that's *wunderbaar*," she said. "I love how you used animals to demonstrate proper Christian behavior. You're teaching children in a fun way to turn the other cheek when wronged by others."

"We're in this together, Phoebe." He placed his hand atop hers. "I hope every parent and schoolteacher will rush out to buy our book for their kids. Then behavior among Ohio children will improve dramatically—both Amish and English." Eli dropped her hand to lace his fingers together behind his head.

"*Buy* our book?" she asked, still shaky from his touch.

"Of course. That's what authors do—they make a living writing books that folks buy and enjoy." He tipped his head back to stare at the ceiling. "That sure would beat mucking hog pens for the rest of my life. I could hire someone to help Dad while I sit on the back porch making up stories."

"Where would we sell them? From a stand alongside the highway?"

Eli hooted with laughter, drawing a glance from the front desk. "No, sweet peach. These aren't cups of lemonade or bushels of fruit. They would be sold in bookstores like those in Sugar Creek, Millersburg, and Berlin. Even the grocery and hardware stores have spinner racks of books. I think tourists would love to take our book home as a souvenir." His eyes glazed to an unusual brightness.

Phoebe didn't appreciate being mocked. "You're getting way ahead of yourself, Eli Riehl. In case you haven't looked in the mirror lately, we're Amish. We don't have computers or that fancy-schmancy software you're talking about. I'll bet you don't even own a typewriter." She rolled her eyes. "What we have is one giant sketch pad and an adorable story, but that's a long way from the book rack at Lehman's." She snapped her mouth shut, not meaning to sound so negative and spiteful. She was sure her one true friend—her other matched shoe, as *mamm* called him—was about to stomp out in a huff...leaving her with a four-mile walk home.

Surprisingly, he did not. Eli didn't seem offended by her outburst. "All true, Miss Miller. I do have a habit of getting ahead of myself, but every business venture must start with a plan. And I have a few tricks up my sleeve that I'm not ready to reveal quite yet."

"Because you need to work out some glitches?"

"Exactly, but tell me, are you willing to step forward in faith with only our talents? I have a fine, low-tech steno pad and pen you can use to take notes if you wish to hear the rest of my story."

She nodded, grabbing the pad and pen. "Why not?" she said with a smile. "Maybe I'll be able to pay Ben to pick slugs off cabbages with my share of the book sales." Phoebe turned to a fresh sheet, feeling that warm sensation build again throughout her body. Could they really do this? Create a real book for children that people would buy? She didn't think so, yet knew she would enjoy every minute of their joint attempt.

An hour later Eli stacked the books they had used on the library cart and escorted her toward the door. As they passed the librarian's desk, the woman said, "Good luck, kids. I think it's a great idea. Count on me for your first sale." Phoebe nodded and smiled at her.

"Number one, we're not kids," he said as they climbed into his buggy. "And number two, I really must learn to speak quieter in that place. That *Englischer* heard every word we said." He slapped the reins on the horse's back and turned in the direction of the Miller farm.

But Phoebe barely heard anything else on the ride home. Her mind whirred with ideas for illustrations for the remaining scenes of Eli's delightful story. If he believed so strongly they could do this, then so would she. Everyone needed a dream, and with perseverance and hard work this dream might someday come true.

Fourteen

Willow Brook—Late June

The Miller family left the preaching service that Sunday in better spirits than they had known in a long while. The outpouring of concern and offers of financial help from their district overwhelmed Matthew and Martha, especially because they were still relative newcomers in their Amish community. Neither had any kin living in the area, yet members created quite a fuss when little Noah arrived with his arm in a cast and sling. Many folks reached for their wallets after lunch, wishing to help pay for the hospital or doctor. Matthew refused their offers graciously, insisting the bills had been paid. However, he didn't admit to using his employer-provided health insurance due to Martha's insistence. She said she couldn't bear the shame or potential censure from the bishop. Her husband honored her request. Things had been tenuous between the two of them since Noah's fall, with Martha often distant and distracted.

But today on the drive home, she seemed like her old self—bouncing their daughter on her lap, humming the old-fashioned hymn they'd sung during the service. Noah, wedged in between them in the buggy, enjoyed shooing flies away from the horse with the long-handled crop.

"What's for supper tonight?" asked Matthew.

"We've just left the hosting farm, where you ate more than your share not more than two hours ago." Martha's large brown eyes glowed with health and mirth. "How many pieces of fried chicken did you eat—five, six?"

"I lost count, but I got in line several times so my gluttony wouldn't be so noticeable."

"I believe it might still be a sin, but I'm no one to criticize. I couldn't leave that plate of walnut brownies alone until I'd eaten three." She shook her head, peering down. "I'll never lose this baby belly at this rate."

"You are perfect just as you are." Matthew leaned over Noah to kiss her cheek.

She grinned. "To answer your question, I made a meat loaf yesterday. So we'll have cold sandwiches today with pickles and potato salad, but not until five thirty. You must hold out until then."

Matthew clicked his tongue and the Standardbred picked up the pace. "I'll take any leftovers with me tomorrow for my lunch for a couple days with a loaf of your homemade bread. They have been serving odd dishes lately in the bunkhouse. An older man from Guatemala does the cooking, and he loves frying up a big skillet of rice and vegetables. He throws just about anything into the pan—beef, chicken, leftover pork roast, ham cubes, even sausage. The last time there were two vegetables I didn't recognize. The cook said they were artichokes and okra." He shook his head.

"You're joking, right? Sort of like a mystery rice stew?"

"I'm serious. Miguel calls it *pay-ella* and says at home he would use clams, mussels, and fish instead of meat because he lived near the ocean."

"That sounds even stranger." Martha wrinkled her nose. "How does this concoction taste?"

"Not too bad. The seasoning takes some getting used to, but Miguel will never be any match to Martha Miller." He smacked another kiss on her cheek loudly.

"Stop trying to butter me up. You still must wait until five for the meat loaf."

Matthew grinned as their buggy rolled up the drive of the rental house. The electric lines running from street pole to their home marred the view, but they couldn't do much about it. "I suppose I'll play ball with my boy if you girls don't need me for anything." His daughter now slept soundly, swaddled in a pink quilt in the crook of Martha's arm.

"I'd like to talk to you about something first, Matthew. Let me put Mary in the crib and then I'll meet you on the porch." She stepped down as soon as the buggy stopped and headed to the house, not waiting for him to unhitch the horse.

"About what?" he asked, as an uncomfortable foreboding climbed up his spine. He lifted Noah down to the lawn. "Follow your *mamm*," he ordered in *Deutsch*.

"About a letter we got this week," she called over her shoulder. "From Julia."

From his mother? Since when did a letter from home need a family sit-down? Was someone sick? Had his mother's arthritis worsened, requiring more surgery? Had something happened to Dad or Henry…or one of his sisters? These and other possibilities coursed through his mind as he rubbed down their one buggy horse and put him into the garage stall he'd built from old plywood.

A little while later he found Martha and Noah on the porch swing. She placed the boy near his toys when Matthew arrived and then drew an envelope from her apron pocket. "What is it? Has something happened in Winesburg?" He settled into the spot vacated by his son.

"Your mother wants us to come home this summer for a big family reunion. She wants all her *kinner* together again, along with their families."

He expelled his breath through his teeth. "Whew, *fraa*, you had me worried. She's just inviting us for a shindig?" He leaned back, tipping his felt hat over his face.

"Hold up there. Before you dismiss this idea out of hand, I want you to read the letter. Julia is quite upset over the fact that she seldom sees her grandchildren. They'll grow up without knowing either of their *grossmammi*s." Martha gave him the envelope.

Matthew extracted the single folded sheet. He read carefully his mother's heartfelt summons for them to come to Ohio for a visit. Martha wasn't exaggerating about *mamm*'s insistence. "She wants us all home for a full month!"

"Any less time would hardly be worth the expense of bus fare," she murmured.

"*Ach*, a month off during prime show season? The owners want me to prepare their horses before and in between shows to tweak behavior and decorum. This is the busiest time of year, not to mention I'm a fairly new employee who hasn't earned any vacation time yet."

Martha lifted her chin to meet his gaze. "You're only considering two aspects, Matt. The welfare of some overpriced fancy horses along with the money aspect—the dent in your anticipated paycheck."

Matthew stared, slack-jawed. Apparently, she'd given the matter significant thought. "Well, yes, those are the first two that came to mind. My boss may not allow me to leave, Martha. It might not be my choice."

"Everyone always has a choice, *ehemann*. We simply must be willing to accept the consequences." She focused on the lawn, where bees flitted between clover heads.

"I suppose that's true, but I worked very hard to land this job. There are not many good jobs around in my business."

She turned to face him. "What about the other considerations? That none of our parents have seen our daughter yet, while Noah only has a vague memory of his Ohio family. And—" she began, but hesitated.

Matthew put his hand over hers. "Go on. Speak your mind."

"And that I'm so lonely here. *Jah*, I've met the district wives and they're nice to me, but I long to see my parent and sisters. A month in Winesburg would do me a world of good. I might not be such a grumpy old *fraa* when we come back." Her dark eyes filled with moisture, but she held back her tears. "Will you at least ask your boss for the time off?"

Her words and tears tore through his soul. It took a remarkably short time to make up his mind. "I won't ask, Martha. I will tell Pete I must go home for a month. I'll take my chances that he will keep my job open, but I won't have my wife this unhappy for another day." He drew her into his arms. "Write to both our *mamm*s. Tell them they can expect us home by the end of July. That should give them enough time to cook and bake all my favorite foods."

Nestled against his shoulder with her face buried, Martha said quietly, "*Danki*, Matty. I love you, and not because I'm getting my way."

"I know that. I'm eager to visit my folks too, so we're both getting our way. It's high time Noah and Mary met the rest of the Millers and Hostetlers."

~

Winesburg

"Yoo-hoo." A voice carried on the warm summer air, but for a moment Julia paid no attention as she reread the short letter for the fourth time. The slam of the screen door barely registered. Only when the person swept into her kitchen did Julia glance up.

"Goodness, sister, have you gone deaf?" Hannah strode to the stove, turned on the burner beneath the coffeepot, and set a baking pan on the table.

Julia lowered the letter. "What's in the pan?"

"Cinnamon rolls. I bought a tube of white frosting at the dollar store to make them look like fancy hot cross buns from the bakery. Your daughter would be proud of me." Hannah retrieved two mugs, the sugar bowl, and the pitcher of cream.

"Which daughter?" Julia broke off one roll and licked the white vein of frosting.

"Leah, of course. What's happened to you—sunstroke?" Hannah pressed the backs of her fingers to Julia's forehead.

Julia batted her away. "I'm fine. Better than fine, actually. I got a letter today from Martha. Matthew and his family are coming to visit for a full month! They'll be here for the reunion. That husband of mine is a genius!"

Hannah grinned as she carried over the pot. "Indeed he is. When do they arrive?"

"In four weeks. Matthew needs to give his boss notice and do as much as he can with his show horses before leaving."

"He must be a very important man, your son." Hannah poured coffee in both their mugs and then stirred cream and sugar in hers.

"He's done well for himself in New York, working first at the race-track and now at that stable where rich *Englischers* board their horses for training." Julia took a large bite of her cinnamon roll and licked her lips.

"Training them to do what?"

Julia dabbed her mouth with her napkin. "I don't understand exactly. It sounds as though the owners parade their horses around a ring in front of judges. They have to lift their feet quite high and stand in a certain way to get good scores."

"Which, the people or the horses?"

"Probably both." The two sisters dissolved into giggles. "I do know they buy expensive clothes for these shows. One outfit can cost a couple thousand dollars, and they need several for the multiday shows."

Hannah stopped laughing. "Surely you misunderstood him."

"I don't think so. These are very wealthy people with money to burn in their fireplaces. I believe he was joking about the fireplace part, but you can ask him yourself when he's home in a few weeks."

Hannah set down her mug with a clatter. "With all the want and suffering in the world, these horsey folks waste money seeing who has the fancier horses and duds?"

Julia broke off another cinnamon roll. "Simmer down, *schwester*.

I'm sure they donate plenty to charity and indulge in good works during the rest of the week. They just have so much money that they can't figure out what to do with it all." She sighed wearily.

Hannah downed her mug and reached for the coffeepot. "Tonight I will thank the Lord for sparing me those kinds of problems. What's the news from Emma and the Davis clan? I know they'll come to your big reunion."

Julia narrowed her gaze and huffed. "Can you believe my *kinskind* can barely speak a word of *Deutsch*? Emma and the boys were here last week, and Jamie couldn't understand a word I said. *'Ich vill some kuchlen'*—the only thing he could do in the language of his people was ask for some cookies."

Hannah nearly choked on her mouthful of coffee and hid her face behind a dish towel.

"You find this amusing? That little boy won't be able to converse with the other children after church or during socials. He needs to learn *Deutsch* now. English can wait till down the road. This is because of his other grandmother's influence. That Barbara Davis. She's as pushy and headstrong as...as..." Julia struggled to find the best comparison.

"Who would that be, Julia?" asked Hannah, lowering the gingham towel to reveal a face fighting for composure.

"Me, okay? Headstrong as me. Are you happy?"

Hannah daintily nibbled her roll. "I'm quite happy today, but tell me how will you rectify this problem with little Jamie?"

Julia crossed her arms. "I wrote to Emma yesterday. I told her about the reunion when she visited, but I decided she needs to come with the boys and stay the full month that Matthew will be here. The cousins should get to know each other. Who knows when they'll have another chance? If Emma won't leave Charm for the month, I'm insisting that I take the boys so I can teach them *Deutsch*. I'm not taking no for an answer."

Hannah winked one of her green eyes. "This is shaping up to be an interesting summer. I don't want to miss a single moment."

FIFTEEN

The following Wednesday, when Eli sauntered into the Winesburg Library half an hour early, he found a surprise waiting for him at their designated table. Phoebe Miller sat surrounded by books and magazines, including one tome thick enough to serve as a foundation stone for a house.

"My, my, I see the early bird has caught plenty of worms already." He bowed slightly as he reached her side, tossing his hat on the adjacent chair.

"You're not the only one with ideas up your sleeve, Mr. Riehl. I decided to get a head start looking up book publishers." She grinned so widely her face began to cramp.

Eli's jaw dropped open. "You are brilliant as well as beautiful." He dragged over the largest volume as soon as he settled into a chair. "*Publishers Marketplace*," he read aloud. "The library keeps a copy of this on hand?"

Phoebe stole a glance over her shoulder. "Not normally, but the librarian was so excited about our idea that she requested some research materials be sent here from Wooster."

Eli pawed through the other publications: "*How to Get Published in Today's Market* and *The Basics of Fiction Writing*." He held up a thin paperback. "*So You Want to Become a Children's Book Author.* That should make for some interesting bedtime reading."

"I'm not sure which of them I can take home, but this large one must stay here."

"I wouldn't think the horse could pull your pony cart carrying that book."

Phoebe pulled a notebook from her tote bag. "I know I accused you of getting ahead of yourself and now look at me. But I thought I should familiarize myself with how things work in publishing."

"Making any progress?" He brushed his blond hair back from his face.

She shook her head. "I've been here for two hours. I came as soon as I finished chores, but the more I read, the more confused I become." She fought to hide her discouragement.

"That's why you have a business partner. When we put our heads together, we can scale any mountain...eventually." He leaned over close enough to bump his head against hers.

"Are you like this with everyone, Eli? So relaxed and outgoing?"

"Absolutely not. Most women scare me, but not you, sweet peach. I'm not the least bit afraid of you. Now tell me your plan of attack." He drummed his fingers on the stack of books.

"The librarian said I should jot down the name and address of twenty or so publishers of picture books. They're also called children's gift books. Not all publishers have a children's line. Then she will check on the computer to make sure the information is up to date and see if their website has additional submission guidelines. When I'm ready, she and I will do that part together."

"Great idea." His face glowed with enthusiasm.

"Then we have to put together twenty identical packets containing your story and my artwork to send out to the twenty companies. We also need to state the theme—the lesson we hope the child will learn from our book."

"And then we sit back to see who bites the worm?"

"I guess so. I haven't gotten that far with Mrs. Carter yet."

"Speaking of your artwork, are you ready to show me more of your drawings?"

"As ready as I ever will be," Phoebe pulled out her sketch pad, flipping to where she had left off last week. The next several drawings showed the goat, the rooster, the horse, and the pig attempting to pull the cow from the mud, despite having suffered humiliation from the cow's jeers and name-calling. The baby lamb, followed by the flock of sheep, mustered a team of animals to finally free the heifer from her predicament.

Eli took his time, studying each double-page drawing to absorb every minute detail. "Considering how good these are, I'd have to say you're not getting ahead of yourself. I love the progression of expressions on the Holstein's face. That little cow seems to have learned a valuable lesson about friendship."

"That will be our story's theme: Everyone needs friends, and in order to have them you must be one."

Eli tipped up her chin. "My life improved immeasurably that day in Berlin, waiting for a bus to come."

Phoebe blushed but didn't look away. "I'm rather glad we struck up a conversation." She reached out to pinch his cheek.

Eli ducked his head, embarrassed at long last. "I have news for you too. You weren't the only one not letting moss grow beneath your feet." He extracted a folded sheet from his trouser pocket and opened it for her inspection.

She read the unfamiliar name and address aloud. "Who is this woman who lives in Kidron?"

She's a Mennonite friend of Rose. She's studying landscape architecture or something like that in college, but the important part is that she has a computer with that fancy software program I told you about. She can scan your artwork and then add whatever color or special effects you would like."

"I don't know what I would like, so why don't you do the choosing?"

"I'd be happy to if that's what you prefer. She said I could experiment with just the tap of a mouse...I mean, a button. Sort of like seeing what a person would look like with a dozen different hairdos. I can't wait to take your drawings to her house."

She nodded with more assurance than she felt, but as with most things in life, she knew each journey started with a single step. "Did you tell your family about what we're doing?" she whispered.

"Only Rose, not my parents. I guess I'm closer to her than my other sisters. She was downright encouraging. I wonder why she's buttering me up?" He scratched his clean-shaven jaw.

"Could it be she just wants you to be happy?"

He pondered this and laughed. "Maybe, or she wants me to beat the carpets for her, or perhaps introduce her to everyone I know at the auction barn. At twenty-three, Rose would love to get hitched. I'm only nineteen. I have an hour or two before I need to meet the woman of my dreams."

Phoebe pulled the giant book back. "Enough of your silly talk. I'll check the fiction listings for which publishers produce children's gift books. You write down what I tell you. Time's a-wasting."

Eli straightened up and positioned his pen over a fresh page of his notebook. For the rest of the afternoon, he carefully copied the information for twenty-two publishing houses that might turn their dream into reality. When they were leaving, Phoebe returned the materials to the librarian and thanked her profusely.

"I'm happy to help," Mrs. Carter answered. "And this book on crafting children's fiction can be checked out."

"All right, I'll take it home." Phoebe handed the woman her library card to swipe.

"One day closer," she said, placing the book into a plastic sack. "See you next week."

In the parking lot Eli pumped her hand and then hurried toward his own buggy. "I just remembered I was supposed to go to the grocery store for my mom and still haven't done so. I'll see you in two weeks, Phoebe. Next week I'll drive up to Kidron on my day off." His buggy left in a flurry of dust and a scattering of back lot gravel.

Phoebe traveled home at a far more leisurely pace, content to replay everything Eli had said over in her mind. *"I have an hour or two before I need to meet the woman of my dreams."* Was he talking about her? Once again she had been stymied by his teasing and cryptic comments. But what did it matter? She wouldn't turn eighteen for several more weeks, so she had plenty of time to think about courting. Perhaps it would be a blessing if she never married, considering how much she hated cooking, cleaning, and doing laundry. Yet Eli was the only man she knew who seemed not overly concerned about a perfectly run household. She could just picture the two of them creating stories on the back porch while supper burned in the oven, laundry overflowed the hamper, and weeds overran their vegetable garden and farm fields.

Phoebe grinned at the mental image. Marriage was something she considered as seriously as traveling across the country in a hot air balloon. That is, until she met Eli. But a business partnership was very different than wedded bliss. In the Amish community, marriage was for a lifetime, while their partnership could be dissolved upon receipt of their twenty-second rejection letter. Mrs. Carter had explained about queries, rejections, and how long it usually took for publishers to make up their mind on books. The librarian also explained what agents could do for writers, but she assured Phoebe that they should be able to get their work seen without one. Only discouragement could ever steal away her dream, according to her new mentor, right before she dumped a load of research materials onto the table. Phoebe vowed never to become discouraged, no matter what the future held for her and Eli. With faith in God and in herself, how could a book that teaches children kindness and tolerance possibly fail?

That night at supper, both her parents chatted about the Miller family reunion next month. Ben named the friends he would invite, while Mom planned what she would cook ahead and store in the propane freezer, and Dad considered what advice to seek from Matthew regarding horses. As the conversation around the table continued, Phoebe retreated into her private world of ornery cows mired in river mud.

"I said, how goes the *kinner* book?" asked Seth, scraping another mound of yellow beans onto his plate.

She blinked several times. "*Gut.* I have a picture to go with each scene of the story." Her forkful of roast beef hovered in midair.

"Your mom told me you were courting Eli Riehl. I must say I was surprised, but in a good way. I know Bob Riehl from the grain elevator. He's a fine man with a practical head on his shoulders. I'm sure his son has the same good common sense."

She ate the forkful, taking time to consider her reply. "*Jah*, Eli is quite a thinker, but I wouldn't exactly describe us as courting. We're more or less partners on our little venture."

Seth met Hannah's gaze and both started smiling. "You two wouldn't be the first shy people who broke the ice with a joint project as a diversion. But I must say writing a book is a new one for me. Usually it's a shared vegetable stand or maybe partnering up to breed dogs for sale."

Phoebe stared at her father. "This isn't a diversion, *daed*. We're truly writing a book."

Seth snorted while loading his fork with potatoes. "What would you two have to write about—your weekend trip to Niagara Falls? Lots of water flying over the edge making one big splash at the bottom, day after day until the end of time? Might be a pretty site, but it would be a rather short story." He laughed heartily.

Phoebe crossed her arms, focusing on her mother. Hannah shrugged her shoulders. "I had to tell him how you two met. Your dad was curious because you seldom leave the farm. But we're both pleased as punch that you're cour—I mean, *consulting* with Eli on your drawings." Hannah smiled as she walked to the refrigerator for the pitcher of iced tea.

Phoebe swallowed hard and cleared her throat. "It's no secret how we met, but I want you both to understand we're serious about this. Our story isn't a vacation memoir. It's a children's book that illustrates good Christian behavior. We intend to send our work out to various publishers to see if one will print and distribute the book."

Now it was her parents' turn to stare. "For what purpose?" Seth asked.

"To sell, of course, to parents and grandparents like the other books in the Christian bookstore in town."

"Amish people don't write books," he stated, drawing his brows together into one bushy line.

"Actually, a few Amish people have written books with assistance from their Mennonite friends," said Hannah, refilling everyone's glasses.

Phoebe smiled with gratitude at her.

Seth quickly drank down his tea and then scrambled to his feet. "I have evening chores to do. I'll let your mother talk some sense into you, daughter. Let's go outside, Ben."

Hannah waited until the screen door slammed shut behind them. "It will be very difficult for an Amish pair to get their book published. But I don't wish to discourage you—life holds enough disappointment for all of us. So good luck, and any time you want to discuss this, I'm ready to lend an ear." Her smile held only tender patience.

"*Danki, mamm,*" she murmured. Right now, that was all Phoebe needed.

～

Midway between Winesburg and Baltic

Leah clutched her belly with one hand, while her other gripped the armrest for dear life. "I'm taking it as slowly as I safely can," said Lily Davis. "The road to Baltic is loaded with potholes."

"It's not your fault. They'll work all summer to patch these roads, finishing by fall and just in time for the winter damage to start again."

"Are you sure you don't want to see a *real* doctor? I know a woman gynecologist in Wooster who would be happy to squeeze you in."

"No, thank you," said Leah, holding her breath as Lily's truck rounded a curve. "The nurse-midwife at the Amish birthing center will be real enough for me."

"Did you use that home pregnancy kit I dropped off in your mailbox?" Lily squinted at her from under the brim of her ball cap. Leah couldn't remember ever seeing the English woman without the red OSU hat.

"*Jah*, I used it." Leah lowered her chin to stare at the floorboards. The act of urinating on a plastic stick still embarrassed her a week later, even though she'd been alone in the bathroom and had told no one the results.

Lily waited for further information as the modern brick building where Plain women went to deliver their babies appeared up ahead, but Leah remained quiet. After a moment, she asked, "Did you miss your regular monthly?"

Leah peered out the window while nodding her head. Only when the truck braked to a stop in the parking lot under a nice shady tree did she release her death grip on the armrest. "Thank you for driving me here, Lily. Are you sure you don't mind waiting during the examination? I know you're busy while you're back for the summer. I could call the hired van to take me home."

"Are you kidding? I brought my laptop to do paperwork. If you're inside for six hours, it still wouldn't be enough time for me to catch up." Lily patted Leah's hand. "Don't be afraid. It'll be only women in there. And all of them have probably been down this road many times before."

Impulsively, Leah hugged Lily and then stepped out of the vehicle. Walking the fifty-foot distance to the front door, she experienced a jolt of sheer joy. Was she actually expecting a *boppli* after four years of marriage? She had feared it wasn't in God's plan for her to become a mother. She knew Jonah wanted children very much, yet he was too gentle a man to bring up the subject. How would he take the news, if indeed there were good news to tell? As she walked inside the air-conditioned, spotlessly clean clinic, one rather selfish thought crossed her mind: *If I am pregnant, I won't have to endure any more trips back to Hancock.*

One and a half hours later, after being prodded, poked with needles, and examined internally in a rather bizarre position, Leah emerged from the birthing center with a far livelier pace. She carried a packet of papers, several brochures, and two booklets to read during the coming weeks.

Lily Davis jumped out of the driver's side. "Well? What's the news?" she yelled. Since the parking lot was empty—even the nearest cow was half a mile away—Leah hollered back, "She said, 'Yes, I am, maybe even seven weeks along!'" Leah hurried to the truck as fast as a pregnant Amish woman dared to run.

Lily followed no such rules of decorum. She met Leah halfway, wrapped both arms around her and squeezed. "Congratulations! I'm so happy for you and Jonah. Now let's get you home so you can share your good news."

Leah allowed Lily to tuck her into the passenger side solicitously, but she drew the line when Lily produced a lap blanket. "Don't be silly. It's eighty-five degrees. I won't get cold between here and Wines-burg. As a vet, you deliver babies all the time."

"Only calves, colts, and fillies. No humans, but considering how long this drive is when you're ready to deliver, you might be my first. You'd better call me the moment you start labor. Fortunately, my practice is nearby."

They tried out the sound of baby names to see how they sounded with Byler for the rest of the way home. Once they were in her driveway, Leah turned on the seat. "Thanks, Lily. Not only for the ride but for sharing my joy. Now if I can ask for one more favor—please say nothing about this to your brother."

Lily grinned. "Because James will tell Emma and that will spoil your fun." She pinched her fingertips together and drew them across her mouth. "My lips are sealed."

"I can't wait to tell Emma and Mom, but I want to wait at least another month. The midwife said that the first three months are the most dangerous in terms of miscarriages." Leah's cheeks grew warm just voicing the word.

"I'll say a prayer tonight for a smooth, safe pregnancy and every night until your little one arrives."

Leah felt emotion well up, threatening her self-control. She nodded and climbed out into the hot summer sunshine. She would have her own prayers to say that night, starting with words of gratitude for the new life growing inside her. It might be a normal, everyday occurrence, especially considering the large families within the Amish community, but it was a rare, special miracle for her.

She found Jonah in the small office where he kept track of farm operations. He tried to update his log of activities and dairy conditions on a regular basis. It was no easy task to run a grade-A milk operation using diesel-powered generators rather than electric current from the grid. He heard neither his door open, nor the fall of her footsteps. "Jonah," she said softly.

Bent over his record books, her beloved husband continued to work.

"Jonah," she said, more insistently.

He startled, dropping the pencil he'd been twirling between his fingers. "Leah, what are you doing in here?" His face filled with concern. "Is something wrong?"

"Nothing is wrong. In fact, things are…quite fine."

"A relief to hear. Why don't you rest after your errands in town while I finish up? I'll be in the house soon." He turned his focus back to the ledgers.

"I'm not tired, but I do have a question. Did you ever wonder why I was so sick on the bus ride?"

He did not glance up. "Nope. That bus rocked like a ship in high seas."

"Haven't you been curious why I haven't been eating very much?"

"I know you get irritated when your skirts no longer fit, so I assumed you were trying to lose weight. But you shouldn't. I love you just how you are."

Leah shifted her stance, stifling a sneeze. Her allergies were signaling that time mingling with cows soon would be up. "Have you ever thought about when God would bless us with children, Jonah Byler? Or do pregnant heifers occupy *all* your thinking time?" Her tone discouraged any further lack of attention.

At last Jonah dropped his pencil and turned to look fully at her. "Leah—a *boppli*?"

"*Jah*, Jonah, a *boppli*. At long last." When she spotted tears in his eyes, nothing could hold back her own as he enveloped her in his strong arms.

SIXTEEN

Charm

With the supper dishes done and her kitchen tidy, Emma strolled onto her wraparound front porch carrying two glasses of lemonade. She loved this time of day when she could sit and rock, watching James play in the yard with their sons. Her work might be finished, but something niggled at the back of her mind. And this was a good time to get it off her chest. As she watched her husband chase after the boys in the grass, Emma planned her strategy. Discussing a man's mother could be a minefield, yet her dilemma with Barbara Davis couldn't be ignored any longer.

"James, please put them in the sandbox," she called. "They can play for a while before bedtime while you sit here with me." She patted the second rocking chair, a wedding gift from his brother. "There's something I need to discuss with you."

James swept up both boys, one in each arm, and carried them to their sandbox. "You two play nice. Daddy needs to see what Mommy wants. He might be in big trouble."

Jamie giggled and clapped his hands. "Daddy's getting a spanking," he cried with great glee.

James climbed the stairs and settled down beside her. "Did you catch me drinking from the milk carton again?"

Emma bit the inside of her cheek and shook her head.

"I suppose you discovered I ate all the chocolate chips you were saving for cookies?"

"You didn't! I needed those for tomorrow," she said, shocked. "But no, that's not it."

"Surely you didn't find my private jet hidden in the woods, did you? I had it perfectly camouflaged."

She rolled her eyes. "Would you please be serious? I have a problem...with your mother."

He straightened in the rocker. "What did she do this time?" He winked affectionately.

Emma filled him in on the details of Barbara's first visit to discuss her upcoming mission trip to Haiti. Then she inhaled a deep breath and forged ahead. "She asked me to attend a meeting at her church with her pastor and so I did."

"What did you think, Em?"

"I thought what the people from the different churches will be doing is a great idea. They'll help rebuild lives of those still affected by the hurricane. Those with no particular nursing, construction, or other skills will primarily be spreading the Word of God. The people of Haiti speak French, James, which I don't know a word of. I'm still not confident with some of my English pronunciations, so my teaching wouldn't be very good. I know New Order Amish is supposed to witness to their faith, something Old Order doesn't do, but I don't want to venture into a foreign land with my limited abilities." She finished in a rush of words, practically panting for air, and began rocking in her chair with purpose.

"This decision doesn't sound tough to me." He stroked his long blond beard, the hallmark of a married Amish man.

"Easy enough for you to say, but what do I tell your mother? You know how determined she can be."

"I do, but the solution is simple. Tell her you considered her offer but decided this isn't something you wish to do. Period. You're a grown woman, Emma, and entitled to make your own decisions."

"And if she doesn't speak to me for a month?"

He angled a lopsided grin. "Do you really want me to answer that?"

"No, I suppose not, but I want her to know I'm willing to witness my faith, just not in Haiti. And I'll hold bake and rummage sales, sew things, and pack up supplies to benefit the cause. My heart goes out to those people, the same as hers."

"Then tell her exactly that. Stand firm, dear wife. We are our own family. We'll serve the Lord in our own way. Now, how about we catch some fireflies with the boys before bedtime?"

She smiled at him. "There's something else—a problem I'm having with my own *mamm*."

He threw his head back, laughing. "You're getting it from both sides? And you haven't run away from home yet?"

Emma repeated her conversation with Julia about their sons' lack of language skills, practically word-for-word.

James listened patiently until she finished. "Your mother is right. We should be talking *Deutsch* in front of them so they'll learn and so I'll improve. And I think her solution is perfect. You take the boys there for the month while Matt is home but turn them over to her care. You and Martha do all the housework and cooking while you're visiting with your brother and Dad. Julia will have plenty of time to teach her grandsons. By the time I come for the family reunion, she'll have taught them *Deutsch*—if she doesn't send them and you home in a hired van first."

Emma felt her stiff back muscles begin to relax. "How did you get to be so smart, James Davis? Was it at that fancy college?"

"By eating a handful of chocolate baking morsels every day until the bag is empty."

"In that case, tomorrow I'll buy three bags—one of them just for me."

~

Winesburg

Without a cloud in sight, the July sun began to fry the two Miller women like bacon on the griddle. Hannah and Phoebe had been hard at work all morning, picking green beans in the garden. After lunch they returned to the straight rows as soon as the dishes had been washed. Hannah wiped her brow with a sodden handkerchief, trying not to think about the bee buzzing around her head. "A couple more rows and we'll be done. Then tomorrow we'll blanch and can. I'll bet we'll be able to put up at least a hundred quarts this year." Despite her cheery tone, Hannah received nary a word in response. Phoebe, kneeling on a cushion between the rows, was concentrating on the low beans hiding behind leaves.

"How about green beans for supper? I've worked up quite a taste for them today," asked Hannah.

"Sure, *mamm*, that will be fine." Phoebe advanced her kneeling pad like a robot, but didn't look up from her work.

"That was a joke, daughter."

Phoebe peered up, wiping sweat from her eyes with a sleeve. "A joke? What do you mean?" The girl looked pale and wan, and perhaps even thinner than her usual one hundred pounds.

"Never mind." Hannah rose shakily to her feet. Her legs had stiffened in the uncomfortable position. "That's enough gardening for today. It's sweltering out here. We'll finish the last rows tomorrow."

"Tomorrow? No, please let's get this done now." Phoebe kept plucking with her small fingers with feverish determination. While Hannah watched, a bead of perspiration ran down her already streaky cheek as she added the beans to her overflowing basket.

Hannah hoisted her bushel basket to one hip. "Come on. At least let's head to the house for some cold water." She stretched out a hand.

Phoebe's expression could only be described as terrified. "But if we don't get them all picked, how will we do the canning tomorrow?"

"Will it be the end of the world if we don't finish canning?"

The young woman's face indicated it might very well be. "But I had hoped to spend most of Wednesday at the library after morning chores. Please don't drag this out so I miss my day in town."

Hannah smiled down with pity. "I haven't forgotten your date to work on the book with Eli, but we don't need to suffer heatstroke in the meantime. Come," she ordered, and again offered a hand. "If I must finish picking by myself, so be it."

Phoebe dusted off her palms and then allowed Hannah to pull her up. She hefted her basket to her almost nonexistent hipbone. "The librarian, Mrs. Carter, will help me look up addresses on her computer this week. I want to allow as much time as possible. Eli won't be there. He has...business with a Mennonite woman and will use his day off to go to Kidron. I'll see him next week."

Hannah studied her as they climbed the porch steps. An afternoon in front of a library computer screen during the best weather of the year? Her shy stepdaughter was growing up if she took this project so seriously. "I have an idea. Let's play hooky this afternoon. It's too nice a day to be cooped up. We'll hike up to the high sheep pasture. You can bring your pencils and sketch pad, and I'll bring my Bible to read. We won't come down until Ben and your dad send out a search party. What do you say? You'll still have Wednesday to go to Winesburg."

Phoebe grabbed Hannah around the waist and hugged. "I say yes, since I've seen enough green beans to last a lifetime."

Hannah needed to bread pork chops for dinner and take down a load of laundry from the line before her afternoon of leisure. She sent Phoebe on ahead with a small cooler of soft drinks and some peanut butter cookies. An hour later, she found the girl easily enough. Phoebe was perched on her favorite flat rock, close to the ancient stone wall. Her tablet and supplies lay forgotten by her feet, next to an open can of orange soda. Instead of drawing, she had taken down her bun and sat brushing out her dark waist-length hair. Despite the fact they were alone except for sheep, Hannah was momentarily shocked by her behavior. Amish women never took off their *kapp*s in public, nor let their hair fall freely.

"What are you doing?" she asked as she reached the summit. "Why are you grooming your hair *here* in the middle of the afternoon?"

Phoebe glanced up before resuming her one hundred strokes. "My scalp was hot and itchy. And I wanted to see what brushing hair felt like outdoors. Once, while I waited to be served at the ice-cream shop, I watched a shampoo commercial on the television set on the wall. A lady in a long white gown sat in the forest, brushing her hair with an absolutely joyous look on her face." Phoebe tossed the brush back into her tote bag.

"Well, what did you think?" asked Hannah, stifling a grin. "Does the outdoors make a difference?" She sat down on a boulder.

"No, not really. It feels the same as in my room. But I do like the breeze blowing through it. It's so much cooler on days like this. Why must we keep our hair hidden? I would like to wear one long braid down my back. It would still be out of the way. I get headaches with it coiled and pinned like a roll of garden hose."

Hannah chose her words with care. "A woman's hair is her crowning glory—something only her husband should see."

"Why? It seems silly to jam so much hair under our *kapps*." Phoebe hastily twisted her locks into a huge bun and pinned it to the back of her scalp.

Hannah had to admit that Phoebe had far too much "crowning glory" for so small a person, but she also knew she needed to tread carefully here. The *Ordnung* was quite specific about head coverings. "Boys are fascinated by a girl's hair. A young man could become enchanted with you and lose his ability to think clearly."

To Hannah's surprise, Phoebe burst out laughing—an unexpected response. "You're joking again, right? Like you were about the green beans? Boys seldom notice I'm in the same room with them. Eli was the first male to pay me any attention at all."

Hannah tilted her head back to catch some warm rays on her face. "I'm not joking in the least. The Bible is filled with stories of men led astray by women. Do you remember the story of David and Bathsheba?"

Phoebe nodded, yet she didn't look convinced. "But that was a long time ago."

"Some things between men and women never change." Suddenly Hannah remembered that she'd brought her small Bible. "Let's see what it says in First Corinthians. I believe it talks about hair." She ran her finger down each page until she found the passage she sought in chapter eleven. When Phoebe moved closer to share the same rock, Hannah wrapped an arm around her shoulders and began to read:

"Yes, if she refuses to wear a head covering, she should cut off all her hair! But since it's shameful for a woman to have her hair cut or her head shaved, she should wear a head covering."

Phoebe whistled through her teeth. "Hard to imagine hair would be so important to get mentioned in the Good Book, beyond rules about not being vain or prideful."

Hannah smiled and decided not to say anything more. She knew her daughter didn't need lecturing on the tenets of their faith. Both women found comfortable seats on the grass with their backs against the warm wall of rocks and their legs stretched out before them. The beauty of the high meadow soothed them after their busy morning in the garden.

After a few moments of quiet contemplation, Phoebe asked, "Was my first *mamm* pretty?"

Hannah felt a fist tighten around her heart. "I don't know, dear heart. She passed away before I met your father. I was living in Pennsylvania when your mother was alive...and you were born." She forced herself to breathe. Anything that reminded her of Phoebe's dark, silent days when she'd first met Seth Miller made her feel weak and helpless. Following Constance's tragic death, the little girl had withdrawn into a private world of grief and suffering.

"Oh, that's right. I forgot." Phoebe released a sigh. "This is one time I wish Amish folk were allowed to take pictures. Maybe just one on their wedding day, in case something happens like it did to her."

"I understand." Hannah patted her shoulder. "But your dad said

Constance looked very much like you, so that means she must have been very pretty indeed."

"*Danki, mamm.*" Phoebe turned up her face. "Do you think Eli will like my dark horsetail hair if he ever gets to see it?" She tugged her *kapp* back on.

"I'm sure he will. Only time will tell if he's the one you'll marry. People change, but God always has our best interests in mind."

Phoebe shook herself like a wet dog and scrambled to her feet. "I'm talking nonsense. It'll be a long time before I marry, if I ever do. Lots of things can happen between now and then—buggy crashes, lightning strikes, heart attacks. Once I read in the newspaper about a man who choked to death on a chicken bone in a restaurant, right in front of his family. No matter how hard they slapped him on the back, he was dead before the rescue squad arrived." She crossed her arms as though angry at someone…or something.

"When the Lord calls you home, off you go," said Hannah, for lack of anything more profound to say. "But we shouldn't dwell on grim thoughts. Place your faith and trust in God and live the most productive life you can."

"I need to concentrate on being productive with my artwork and forget about impressing Eli or anyone else." Phoebe sighed. "I'm heading back to the house. I have a book to read that the librarian loaned me, and I want to finish it by Wednesday." In a flash, she grabbed her tote bag and tablet and skipped down the path.

Hannah was left holding up the wall, wondering whether she'd made progress with her daughter…or taken two giant steps back.

SEVENTEEN

Julia swallowed another dose of pain relievers with a glass of water. With the weather hot and sunny, the inflammation in her joints had somewhat lessened, though it never completely went away. With chores done and an hour before she needed to start dinner, she contemplated how to spend an uncommon opportunity for relaxation. The sound of buggy wheels in the driveway took that decision away. Drawing back the curtain, she spotted a familiar dark navy dress worn by the more docile of her two girls—Leah.

"Leah Byler, famous baker of pies and confections renowned throughout the county, to what do I owe this rare and cherished visit?"

Her daughter stopped the open buggy by the steps and climbed down gingerly. "I missed my mother's witty sense of humor. With Joanna still in Hancock, I grew lonely for someone to tease me. Jonah is busy in the dairy, but I'm caught up with my pie orders." Rosy color bloomed across her cheeks. As usual, Leah looked the picture of good health.

"Joanna is still in Wisconsin? Who's taking care of her cheese business?"

"Let me turn my horse into the paddock. Maybe Henry will rub her down a bit as I fill you in on the details. Could you carry these pies inside?" Leah lifted a hamper from the buggy as Julia ambled down the steps.

"What kind are they—peach, chocolate cream, or Dutch apple?" Julia grabbed the handles as her stomach rumbled with anticipation.

"One of each, plus a blackberry. The first berries from my briar patch were ready to be picked." As Leah unhitched the mare, her brother Henry appeared. After a shy hello hug, he finished the job and then led the horse away to the cool shade.

Inside the house, Julia lifted the pies from the hamper and watched her daughter from the window. *Was she even a bit rounder than usual?* Maybe being an expert baker wasn't a blessing after all, but she knew better than to mention it. "Come inside," she called, swinging open the door. "I have both lemonade and iced tea."

As Leah climbed the stairs, they heard another woman's voice ring out. "What a treat. My timing to pay a social call couldn't be better." Hannah rounded the side of the house. "How are you, Leah?"

"I'm fine, Aunt Hannah."

"Stop yelling, sister, before you draw the menfolk," said Julia. Mother and daughter spoke simultaneously as they entered the house. "Then we'll have to share our good fortune." Julia pointed to the four pies lined up on the counter, one more sumptuous looking than the next.

"Oh, my goodness." Hannah placed her baking pan on the table and hurried to the pies. She leaned over each one, sniffing like a starving man at a banquet. "I want a slice of all four."

Leah pulled up the foil from the pan. "What did you bring, Aunt Hannah?" Without waiting for a reply, she extracted a cookie.

"Oatmeal-spelt raisin cookies," said Hannah, reaching for plates and glasses.

"Spelt?" asked Leah. "I thought that was used as animal feed for cows and horses."

"Not anymore, young lady. It's sweet and nutty tasting, rich in nutrients, and contains less allergen than traditional varieties of wheat. Ohio has become the largest producer of spelt in the country.

Groceries and restaurants are starting to request it for baking." Hannah glowed with pride as the other two stared at her.

"You sound exactly like Seth," Julia said, setting the pitchers of tea and lemonade on the table.

Hannah blushed prettily. "He's the one who told me. He finished harvesting and milling his first commercial crop to sell at the grain elevator."

"I hope he's not gung ho, like the year he planted corn in every available square foot of land. When the price dropped, he was almost ruined."

"Don't let *mamm* discourage Uncle Seth," interjected Leah. "If this cookie is any indication, he'll do well growing spelt. It's delicious."

Julia began slicing up the blackberry pie. "Why are the three of us discussing wheat varieties? Surely you have more interesting stories, or you wouldn't have endured the walk here in this heat." She waved her spatula at her sister before lifting three pieces onto plates.

Hannah accepted a slice of pie, poured herself a glass of tea, and sat down. "I do have a tidbit of news to share. Our Phoebe is courting."

"How wonderful! Who's the lucky fellow?" Leah helped herself to another cookie.

Julia perched one hand on her hip, looking confused. "Phoebe? That tiny, dark-haired gal who hides up in the hills whenever people come to visit? The same child who runs from boys as though they carried a dreadful plague? *That* Phoebe?" Julia lowered herself into a chair with her dessert.

"*Jah*, that Phoebe." Hannah angled Julia a stern look. "She's turning eighteen, not thirty. What's the big hurry?"

"Please, Aunt Hannah, don't let *mamm* rile you today. She's just trying to stay in practice. Now, do you know who the young man is, or is it a secret?"

Hannah tucked a stray blond lock where it belonged. "It's Eli Riehl, the son of Robert Riehl who raises the best pork and hams around. I know they're both young and neither have courted before, but I have a notion he just might be the one for her."

"Why?" Julia and Leah asked together.

"Because he's…unique in the same way she is. And you know how thinking alike goes a long way in forming relationships. I'm trying not to get too excited. Plenty of things can change when people are that young." Hannah smiled at her niece fondly. "Now tell us, Leah, do *you* have any news to share?"

Leah turned beet red and tried to hide behind her lemonade glass. "Mom asked about Joanna Byler right before you arrived. I wanted to fill her in on Byler news." She dabbed at her mouth for cookie crumbs. "Joanna is still in Wisconsin at her sister's farm. Every one of her letters raves about how wonderful it is to be back home."

"Wait until winter comes," said Julia. "We'll see if she's so excited then."

"That's just it. I don't know if my mother-in-law is ever coming back. With both her parents gone, what if she decides to move back there?" A plaintive note rang loud and clear in Leah's voice.

Julia and Hannah waited for her to continue. "And if Joanna does move?" prodded Julia. "Would she leave her cheese business to Jonah to run, besides his milk operation?"

"I don't think either of them would want that. It would be too much work. I'm afraid she'll sell the farm and move us all to Wisconsin." Two large tears slipped from beneath her dark lashes.

Julia slapped her palm down. "You can't be serious."

"I don't know this for a fact, *mamm*, but it's what I fear." Leah reached for the hanky she kept tucked up her sleeve.

"Fear is the devil's handiwork. Don't give in to it." Hannah stated the words as though reading them off a wall plaque.

"You're right, Aunt Hannah, but some days I don't know how to stop myself. I truly don't want to move, but my place will always be with my husband."

"Pray, Leah, and turn the matter over to God. In the end His will shall be done. If you must go north, you might discover it's for a very good reason."

Julia clucked her tongue. "I might be an old, crabby, selfish woman, but I can't bear the thought of another child moving away. Matthew in New York, Emma in Charm, and you in Wisconsin? What would I do with myself?"

"Drive Henry crazy?" asked Hannah, finishing off her slice of pie with a satisfied smack of her lips.

"We'll see how many jokes you crack if Phoebe marries and moves away." Julia glared at her sister over her half-moon spectacles.

Hannah nodded, mollified. "You have a point. I'm sorry, Julia. Should I slice into the apple next or the peach?"

"The apple, please, but let's forget about this for now." Leah refilled everyone's glass. "I might be upsetting both of you for nothing. Tell me, *mamm*, what's the latest news from my siblings?"

"Only that your brother arrives by the end of the month and will stay until the end of August. I can't wait to lay my eyes on their little Mary for the first time. Oh, and Noah fell and broke his arm, but the cast should be off by the time they leave New York."

"And Emma? What of my sister? I miss her so much."

"She'll be staying here the month of August with her boys. Those two might as well be *Englischer*s for how much *Deutsch* they know. I've made up my mind to change that while they're here."

Leah and Hannah exchanged a pointed glance. "You will have Matthew, Martha, Noah, Mary, Emma, Jamie, and little Sam, besides Dad and Henry, all here at the same time?" asked Leah.

"Of course. I'll make room. The cozier, the better."

Leah pondered this only a moment. "Then if it's okay with Jonah, I'm coming home too, at least for a week. I want to visit with everyone and be part of the chaos."

Julia grinned. "That's a good idea. Always room for one more."

Hannah rose to her feet. "What about me? Can I move in too? Maybe bring Phoebe and Ben along?"

Leah choked on her tea, while Julia shook her head vigorously. "Absolutely not. I must draw the line somewhere. Next door is plenty close, considering your wicked sense of humor."

The two sisters locked gazes. "Fair enough," said Hannah, "but I fully intend to make a pest of myself."

"I wouldn't have it any other way," said Julia, with a satisfied smile.

~

Eli wiped his neck with his bandanna and then tied it around his head under his hat. Sweat had been burning his eyes all morning as he restrung barbed wire between fence posts.

"What are you still doing up here?"

The voice caused him to jump half a foot into the air. Shielding his eyes from the glare, he watched his sister pick her way toward him between cow pies. "What does it look like I'm doing? I found so many breaks in the fence that it's a miracle we haven't lost half our beef herd."

"That might be a blessing, but I doubt it's a miracle." Panting for breath, Rose finally reached where he stood. "Come take a break out of the sun. You missed lunch, so I brought you something to eat and drink."

Eli didn't argue but followed his sister into the shade of a lone pine tree. Checking the ground carefully for unwanted surprises, they sat down in tall pasture grass. "*Danki* for coming all the way up here."

"You're welcome." She handed him a wet washrag for his hands. "How did it go yesterday at my friend's house in Kidron?" Rose pulled her skirt down over her ankles.

"*Gut*. Sarah let me type up my story on her computer. Then she printed out twenty-five copies in the blink of an eye. She also scanned Phoebe's illustrations into the machine and showed me what they would look like using various colors and styles—amazing! I kept saying 'I don't believe this' every five minutes. After I picked out what I liked best, she printed them in full color."

Rose laughed as she poured cold water from a thermos and handed him a sandwich. "I told you she would be happy to help. She loves working on that computer. Her family has to pry her away from the thing."

"I appreciated your setting this up for me, Rose. By the time I left her place, I had twenty-five glossy copies of Phoebe's drawings. I don't think the flowers, candy, and ham I took her were adequate payment."

"Don't worry. She'll take more when the next batch is smoked. Her family loves our honey-glazed hams."

Eli gobbled his sandwich with the same speed and table manners as one of their sows. "I didn't get home until after midnight, but it was worth it. I have the packets ready to give Phoebe when I see her next week."

Rose unwrapped a second roast beef and cheddar for him. "You and your friend are going ahead with the idea of publishing a book?"

"We're going to try, but it's as likely to happen as a snowstorm tomorrow." He accepted the sandwich with a grateful nod. He hadn't realized how hungry he was until he began eating.

"You like this girl, don't you?" Rose dug her heels into the pine needles, releasing their pungent scent.

He turned his gaze skyward, where turkey vultures soared on warm air currents. "I really do. She's the best friend I've ever had. Sometimes when I'm with her I want to start singing. How's that for ridiculous? You know how badly I sing."

Rose smiled with affection. "Then you should do more than just meet her at the library for work sessions. You should properly court her."

Eli stopped shoving food into his mouth and chewed. A moment later he asked, "What do you mean, exactly?"

"Take her for an evening buggy ride or for a picnic by the lake. Take her to a singing or some other young people's event. Make an effort to be sociable, Eli, and pay plenty of attention to her if you want to win her heart."

Because his legendary gift of gab had suddenly abandoned him, he studied the cracked leather of his boots as though they could unlock the secrets of life.

After a silent minute, Rose asked softly, "You do want to win her heart, don't you?"

Eli flushed, unable to meet her eye, but he answered without hesitation. "Oh, *jah*, more than anything I've ever wanted."

"Then court her. Don't get so caught up with this book business that you miss the forest for the trees."

He laughed and then drank half the thermos of water without stopping. After he came up for air, he said, "When did you get so knowledgeable about such subjects?" There wasn't a hint of sarcasm in his voice.

She cocked her head to one side. "At long last I have someone courting me too. I'm not telling the rest of the family yet. I met him a couple weeks ago. Dad sent me to Berlin to drop off broken harnesses to be repaired. I was a bit annoyed with the errand, but I figured I would treat myself later to a caramel latte from Java Joe's." She flashed him a wry look, her dimples deepening with amusement.

"I take it you found a better reward than an expensive cup of coffee?"

"I did. I met Andrew Weaver. He seemed to like me, and I certainly liked him. I've seen him around, of course, but never talked to him much. I thought he was standoffish, but instead he's just shy like me."

"You are many things, my dear sister, but shy ain't one of them."

"Regardless, he loves singing as much as I do. He's picking me up for the next young people's singing and..." Rose lowered her voice to a whisper. "He plans to take me to Canton one day to hear a famous choir when they come back to town. I'm not telling *mamm* and *daed* until the date gets closer."

"In a horse and buggy?" Eli asked, digging into her cooler for an apple.

"No, you goose. He plans to hire a van and driver for the evening."

"Whew, he must be rich—a rare trait for an Amish fellow." He took a hearty bite of fruit.

Rose rolled her eyes. "Not rich at all. That's just the problem—he's the youngest of five sons. Their farm has been divided up into as many pieces as it can be, so he works at the leather shop. But Andrew wants to farm." She met his gaze. "It's the same story with Ruby and her beau. They're getting pretty serious, but he can't find any land within his price range. They won't announce their engagement until his prospects for buying a farm improve. I can't see them living with his folks in an apartment above the grocery store."

"I think I might have the perfect solution for both of you if you can be patient for a while." Eli threw the apple core over his shoulder and rose to his feet. He offered his sister a hand and then added, "Thanks for lunch. It was nice of you to hike up here, but I must get back to work. Don't worry, Rose. Your secrets are safe with me."

Once on her feet, she brushed leaves and twigs from her skirt. "Remember what I told you about Phoebe. All work and no play will make you an even duller boy."

"I'll remember, and if everything goes as planned, you and Ruby might get the solution you're looking for." With that cryptic comment Eli sauntered down the fence line, already so tired he didn't notice his sister's expression. Rose Riehl stood in the tall weeds looking absolutely blissful.

EIGHTEEN

Winesburg

Not the mosquito feeding on her arm, nor the bead of perspiration running down her neck, nor even the footsteps from her approaching mother broke Phoebe Miller's concentration on a hot July day. Only when Hannah tapped her on the shoulder did she glance up.

"What are you doing?"

Phoebe frowned and gestured to the surface of the picnic table where tablets, books, and writing supplies had been spread. "What does it look like, *mamm*? I'm working outdoors now that my chores are done. My room is too hot, and I thought you might need the kitchen table for baking or spreading out dress fabric." She scratched absently at a new bug bite.

Hannah slipped onto the opposite picnic bench. "I can see that, Miss Smarty-Pants, but did you forget what day it is? I thought Wednesdays were your days to meet Eli at the library and work on your book there."

"I will see Eli today. He sent a letter saying he's picking me up at two and taking me to town. We're going to Ruby's Country Store and the ice-cream shop. Then he wants to buy me supper at that new res-taurant that just opened." Phoebe reached for her glass of water. "Is it all right if I eat dinner with him?"

"Of course it is." Hannah smiled. "This sounds a lot like a date rather than your usual work get-together."

"It does to me too. That's why I plan to take another shower before I go. I've been sweating out here, even in the shade. I don't want him to see me looking as wilted as I feel." She tried to pull her damp dress away from her back.

"A second shower—with the price of water these days? Oh, no, I don't think I could allow that." Hannah lifted her chin and folded her arms.

"But, *mamm*, our water comes from a well and the rain gutters—" She halted and glared. "You're teasing me again, *jah*? You would think I'd be used to it by now."

"I am." Hannah winked as she looked through the scattered papers and books.

"I should get up earlier in the morning and stay on my toes." Phoebe held the cool glass to her forehead. "Do you need help with anything before I go?"

"Not a thing. What are you writing there?" asked Hannah, losing interest in the other books.

"The librarian gave me a sheet of blank mailing labels. I'm print-ing as small as possible the names and addresses of the publishers we're targeting."

"Targeting? Listen to my little businesswoman."

"Trying to be one, anyway." She lifted her shoulders in a shrug. "That way they'll be ready to go. Look at these." Phoebe extracted a stack of crisp sheets from a manila folder with near reverence. "This is the letter Mrs. Carter helped me compose that we'll send along with my illustrations and Eli's story. She printed off the twenty-two copies I'll need plus three extras. Check out the addresses—each one is dif-ferent. The librarian printed out the same letter, but with a different publisher's name and address on each." Phoebe fanned out the papers for Hannah's perusal.

"Amazing what things a modern computer can do. But I hope you're not getting your hopes up too high. I heard somewhere that it's hard for an *Englischer* to publish a book, let alone a couple of Amish kids."

"We're not kids. I'm eighteen next week, and Eli will be nineteen next month." She sounded indignant.

"Sorry, I forgot. And I just sewed you a new faceless doll for your birthday present."

Phoebe winked at her mother, recognizing the jest. "That's good. We'll have a gift for Matthew's little girl when they arrive later this month. I'd better finish printing my labels and get ready. I promise not to waste too much of your *expensive* well water."

"Have fun, dear one. Just remember not to monopolize the conversation and don't talk with your mouth full of ice cream." Hannah rose gracefully and leaned over to kiss the top of Phoebe's *kapp*.

Phoebe both loved and hated these demonstrations of affection. Hannah was so openly and generously loving. What would she do if her *mamm* were taken from her? She felt more comfortable with the relationship she shared with dad—an occasional pat on the back or a feeble attempt at praise, such as "This doesn't taste as bad as it did last time" or "If you keep this up, someday you're bound to get the hang of it." As she completed her final label, she watched her stepmother stroll back to the house. The memory of her birth mother had faded over the years. Phoebe could no longer see Constance's face or hear her voice when she closed her eyes. But if Constance had lived, Phoebe knew she couldn't love her more than she loved Hannah. And that kind of heart-seizing, stomach-clenching emotion made her feel nothing but vulnerable.

Two hours later, freshly showered and in a clean dress, Phoebe was waiting on their front porch when Eli pulled his open buggy into the driveway. She'd tucked her letters and labels safely into her tote bag, along with the books she would return to the library. As soon as he turned around close to the house, she jumped down from the porch without bothering with the steps.

"Hi, Eli," she called. "I'm ready to go."

"Then climb up, sweet peach, and let's get this traveling show on the road." His face glowed with a burnished summer tan.

"Did you ever see a traveling road show?" she asked, accepting his hand.

He nodded. "I went to a circus in Wooster a few years ago. They had tigers and elephants and a man who walked the high wire. I loved it, except for the big deal they made out of the Lipizzaner Stallions. Who couldn't ride a horse bareback around the ring?"

"I can't," she said sitting as close to him as decorum allowed.

"Well, I can't either," he admitted, "but I'd bet your cousins Henry and Matthew could...probably with their eyes closed."

"They'll have that to fall back on if their careers as horse trainers don't work out."

Eli laughed, flicking the hair from his eyes. "Take a gander at how I've advanced our career." He handed her a stack of large white mailing envelopes from a cloth grocery sack. "I have the twenty-two copies of my story, plus copies of your illustrations for each scene of the book." He chewed on his lower lip.

Phoebe pulled a paper-clipped group of images from the first envelope and gasped. They were glossy with bright colors that popped, yet the story scenes had remained natural and true to life. She paged through them one at a time, stunned by the sight of her sketches turned into beautiful works of art. "These came out much nicer than I thought or dreamed they could. I love them, Eli. *Danki.*" Her single word of gratitude sounded woefully insufficient.

He ducked his head, grinning. "You're welcome. I'm glad you like the chosen effects because there were plenty to pick from. I made a few extra packets so we can each save one for our old age. We'll sit on the back porch and reminisce. 'Remember our harebrained notion to become fancy book writers?'" Eli mimicked the scratchy, hoarse tone of an elderly man as the horse clip-clopped down the road. "Those were the days."

"It's not a harebrained idea. Wait till you see what I have done during our two weeks apart." She placed his packets back into the grocery sack before taking out her manila folder. "Twenty-two letters addressed to our likeliest publishers, along with mailing labels. All we need to do is sign our names in the space here." She fanned the letters in front of his nose as a car passed them on the left.

His mouth formed a perfect letter *O* in astonishment. "I can't believe it. The letters are ready to go? Those are all publishers of children's gift books?"

"Every one of them produces the kind of story we've written." Excitement coursed through her veins like wildfire. It would take a garden hose to tamp down her enthusiasm. "I must admit that Mrs. Carter helped a lot with these. I had no idea you could print out letters with a different name and address on each one."

"I didn't either, but that's rather convenient. And what's wrong with accepting help from willing folks? No one accomplishes anything in this world totally on his own. I'm proud of you, Phoebe. Good work." Without warning, he leaned over and kissed her cheek.

Startled, she instantly scooted away from him. However, in this size of buggy, she couldn't get far. "They're just letters, Eli, hardly demanding of a kiss."

"The kiss had nothing to do with letters or labels. I kissed you because I like you and you like me." With his eyes focused on the road, he suddenly feigned alarm. "You *do* like me, don't you? Or have you been faking it all this time just to get your artwork published? Do you go home after we've been together muttering: 'That Eli Riehl. I'll be glad when this book is done and I never have to see his homely face again.'"

She burst into giggles, which alleviated her mental state. The kiss, brief as it was, had left her discombobulated. "*Jah*, I like you. And I haven't once gone home muttering I'd be happy to be rid of you. Not yet, anyway."

He wiped his brow with his forearm. "Whew, that's a relief. I've usually gotten on folks' nerves by now, so this bodes well for happily ever after."

The fluttery sensation in her gut started up again. "What do you mean by that?"

"Well, because we have plenty in common and have started a business venture together, and because the mere proximity of me doesn't make your skin crawl...I'd say there's a long-range possibility of us—you and me, in particular—forming a romantic partnership as well. So, may I consider the rest of the afternoon and evening a date—as in courting?" He peered at her, fluttering his eyelashes.

"That was a lot of words, Eli Riehl, but I believe I understood the gist." She twirled a lock of hair that had come loose from her bun.

"What say you?" He wiggled his brows.

She shrugged with great exaggeration and summoned her most ambivalent tone. "I suppose so, seeing that I'm not courting anybody else. That is, I'm happy with this arrangement until a worthier candidate presents himself." She smiled as sweetly as a cat in the cream.

"Bravo! I take my victories wherever I find them. Now, if we are as successful in our partnership and sell millions of books, how do you see us living our future life, assuming we do one day marry? Keep in mind your statements in no way obligate you to future commitments to me should your skin start to crawl any time between now and then."

"You talk as though words were on sale at the bargain outlet and you purchased every last one."

"I've heard that before, but please don't avoid the question, Miss Miller."

"I wish to always remain Amish, that's for sure. But if we were to make lots of money, I would fatten up every medical fund for each district in the county. And should we someday get hitched, I would hire another Amish woman to run my kitchen, maybe a widow with no family. I would still do the gardening because that has grown on me, but I would need time for my artwork." She almost added the words "and *kinner*," but stopped herself. The embarrassment of uttering something so personal would certainly derail her confidence. "How about you?"

He slapped the reins against the horse's rump to step up the pace. "I thought you would never ask. I would also hire someone, a farmer without his own spread, maybe two of them, to help my dad. And when my sisters marry, I'll build each one a house on our farm so their husbands can join Riehl and Son Swine and Beef, the more the merrier. Then the closest I'll come to a hog pen will be interviewing the sow for my stories...or when I sit down to ham and potato salad at Sunday dinner." He swept off his hat to run a hand through his long hair.

"You think she'll want to be in your story?" she asked, facing him on the seat.

"If it'll delay or prevent ending up on someone's table, then yes." Eli turned the buggy into the library parking lot. "You go in and return your books, but try not to dawdle. I'll wait for you here. I have something to do."

Phoebe gathered up her things and hopped down, throwing a quizzical expression over her shoulder.

The librarian, as usual, beamed when she saw Phoebe. Mrs. Carter had collected several more writing books for her to read and demanded news of their progress. Phoebe couldn't check out and leave until she had provided an update. Outside in the parking lot, the sun temporarily blinded her as she looked for Eli's buggy.

"Over here," he called. He was waiting in the shade, hard at work at something in his lap. "Ready for your signature, Miss Miller." He handed her a pen as she climbed up into the buggy.

"What?" She paused on the metal step, waiting for him to pick up the packets and envelopes spread across the seat.

"I've gone ahead and affixed the correct label to match the letter and signed my name in the correct spot. As soon as you add your John Hancock we can finish our submissions."

"Who was John Hancock?"

"It's not important right now. Start signing." He cleared a spot for her to perch and presented the first batch.

With trembling fingers she wrote "Phoebe Miller" twenty-two times above his name on the letters. Eli then inserted each finished letter into the appropriate envelope with the story and artwork and sealed it shut. After he'd tucked the final packet into the tote, he whistled through his teeth. "To the post office. We should just make it before they close." He released the brake and shook the leather reins.

The horse pulled onto the pavement before Phoebe had a chance to collect her thoughts. "Right now?" she squeaked. "Are we ready to send them off *today*?"

He offered a sideways glance. "Time and tide wait for no man…or woman. The sooner they're mailed, the sooner we'll hear something."

She didn't argue, but she couldn't shake the sudden wave of anxiety that filled her belly. As much as she wanted this, she feared the unknown territory they were entering. This wasn't like running a produce stand or breeding pups for sale. This was publishing, and they were two Amish *kids*. Her *mamm* was right about that. Shouldn't they at least have consulted their bishop first or Uncle Simon?

But within minutes the decision was taken from her. Eli marched into the post office with his wallet and grocery sack full of envelopes and sauntered out a little while later wearing a grin. "They're on their way, all twenty-two sent first class. According to the clerk, every one of them should arrive within two days." He climbed into the buggy and brushed her lips with the sweetest of kisses. "We've begun our journey, sweet peach, for better or for worse. Let's head to the restaurant. I'm starving and this is supposed to be a date, not just another work session. For the rest of today, you will witness my attempt at courting."

Phoebe's head still reeled from the second kiss and from the bold move they'd just taken. Eli didn't seem affected by either, but she had to grip the bench just to stay in place. There was a distinct possibility of either fainting or floating off into the clouds.

~

Winesburg—The Byler Dairy Farm

Days didn't get any hotter than the one Joanna Byler had chosen to return home from Wisconsin. Leah straightened her back in the vegetable garden and wiped her face with her apron. So far that morning she'd fixed breakfast, swept the floors and dusted, baked six cherry pies, and fixed sandwiches for lunch. Now, unless she picked the remaining green onions, radishes, and leaf lettuce, they would go to seed and become inedible. Jonah had instructed her to take it easy in her "delicate condition," but then who would do the housework? At least his dairy employees had taken over Joanna's responsibilities with artisan cheese production or Leah would have had to give up sleeping at night.

She blinked several times as the hired van pulled slowly up their driveway. She blinked once more as Jonah's mom stepped out of the van, looking annoyingly fresh and well rested.

"Leah, dear child, you look ready to liquefy," sang Joanna. "Come out of that hot sun and give me a hug."

Leah stepped over the low garden fence and approached her mother-in-law on shaky legs. The driver set suitcases and several plastic totes on the lawn before he accepted payment, tipped his hat, and left. She reached for one suitcase handle, but Joanna intervened. "Don't you touch that, young lady. Jonah called me from his business phone line in the barn and gave me the blessed news. He couldn't wait to tell me, and I must say I'm pleased as punch. A *gross-mammi*—I can't wait!" She threw her arms around Leah and hugged.

Leah, damp from head to toe from hard work and the humidity, felt embarrassment over her disheveled state. "If I'd known you were arriving today, I would have freshened up."

"Nonsense, it's healthy to sweat. Anyway, I wanted to surprise you. Who needs fancy preparations?" Joanna stood in her side yard, gazing around like a tourist. "Let's leave the luggage for Jonah to carry in. We'll just go inside and see what I brought back." She lifted the plastic sacks and practically skipped up the path.

Leah followed her into the house, feeling like a heifer pregnant with twins.

"Oh, my, it smells wonderful in here. Is that cherry pie?" Joanna hurried to the window ledge where the pies were cooling. "Yummy. I hope one is for tonight and not all to sell."

"Of course we can cut one." Leah slipped off her gardening gloves and washed her hands by the sink, longing to stick her head under the faucet.

Joanna retrieved the pitcher of lemonade from the fridge and poured them each a glass. "Wait until you hear what I've learned. They're doing plenty of new things up north with specialty cheeses. Everything is a spread these days, mainly soft cheeses combined with you name it: herbs, vegetables, spices, sour cream, horseradish, bacon, and even seafood. They make crab spread, lobster, and, of course, shrimp. They even combine smoked cheddar with red wine."

Leah wrinkled her nose as she sipped her drink. "That sounds terrible."

"Oh, no. I tried some on a cracker and it was quite tasty. The *Englischer*s want their cheeses spreadable to slather onto fancy crackers or scoop up with vegetables. It's not like the old days, where you had a giant wheel of cheddar, one of Swiss, and maybe an aged blue cheese. Now everything is a concoction of some sort." She grinned with delight as she dumped one bag onto the table. "I brought us plenty of samples to try."

"But you had already expanded into exotic varieties right here in Ohio," said Leah, growing defensive.

"*Jah*, true enough, but Wisconsin certainly is the cheese capital of the country with all that fresh water everywhere."

Leah struggled to her feet, finishing her drink with a noisy slurp.

"Where are you going? I can't wait to tell you about my trip to the Dells."

Leah gritted her teeth, feeling old and mulish. "I'm sorry, but I need to finish picking the garden. If your stories will keep until supper, Jonah can enjoy them as well."

"Right you are. I'll drag in my suitcases, unpack, and start a load of laundry. I should change out of this dress too. Oh, Leah, I'm happy to see you and so glad about your blessed good news." Joanna squeezed her again, leaving Leah feeling guilty about her uncharitable thoughts. But that guilt soon faded during the hours it took to pick the remaining produce in the merciless sun.

And yet, when she trudged into the house at the end of the day, the kitchen floor gleamed, fresh coffee awaited, and a savory pot of stewed chicken simmered on the stove.

"I was coming to drag you in by your *kapp* strings," said Joanna. "Enough for one day." She poured a cup of coffee and thrust it into Leah's hands. "Take this with you while you soak in a nice cool tub. Dinner won't be ready for an hour. I'm going to find my son. That man doesn't even know I'm back yet." Joanna stood with arms akimbo, looking far younger than her forty-four years.

"*Danki*," murmured Leah, accepting the mug gratefully. Once inside the deep claw-foot bathtub, she tried to dwell on the positive aspects of her mother-in-law's return: help with the housework and laundry, a female perspective for advice or venting steam, assistance scheduling the constant deliveries and pickups from running three separate home-based businesses. She wouldn't let her one small fear creep in to spoil the homecoming: What if Joanna, enthralled by her home state, sold the Winesburg farm and moved them north?

But that one small fear loomed ever larger during supper. The only time Mom Byler wasn't singing the praises of Wisconsin was when her mouth was full of dumplings. "Wait till you hear about Devil's

Lake, a state park in the Dells. They have the most incredible rock formations, cut by glaciers originally, and then by the wind and rain ever since."

"Why would they name a pretty place after the evil one?" asked Leah, picking at her creamed spinach.

"I have no idea, but they have miles of nature trails with one stunning vista after another. We saw bald eagles and listened to loons each evening while falling asleep."

"I thought a 'loon' was English slang for an insane person." Leah's petulance was beginning to show more than her pregnancy.

"Oh, no. They're sort of a black spotted duck with the most sorrowful cry."

"At least our mallards on the pond seem happy, and I hear there's a nesting pair of bald eagles over in Shreve." Leah met Jonah's gaze but glanced away quickly.

"The lakes there are so clear and deep, they are perfect mirrors of the surrounding forest and overhead sky." Joanna set down her fork to gesture with her hands.

"Deep lakes mean only one thing—cold water." Leah shivered, even though the kitchen had to be eighty degrees.

Joanna stared at her curiously. "There were lots of folks at the swimming beach who didn't seem to be suffering terribly."

Jonah patted his wife's hand. "You'll have to excuse Leah, *mamm*. I believe the Ohio Department of Tourism has hired her as their spokeswoman." Two of the Bylers enjoyed a hearty chuckle, while the newest Byler concentrated on her chicken leg.

"So tell me, what did my cousins do during your vacation?" asked Jonah.

"They hiked and climbed and fished every day. One day they rented kayaks for a trip down the river. That evening, my sister and I rented a rowboat and paddled out to the middle of the lake. It was so peaceful and quiet, we didn't want to row back." She released a nostalgic sigh.

"What did the boys do while their *mamm* was off boating?"

If Joanna took exception to Leah's rather accusatory tone, she didn't let on. "They fished from the shore and caught rainbow trout, both small and largemouth bass, walleye, and a fish called a Johnny Darter. We cleaned and fried up everything the next day for dinner." Triumph crossed her features for the briefest moment.

Leah couldn't stomach any more Wisconsin conversation. She rose to her feet. "I believe I'll start the dishes, if you two don't mind. I'm rather tired and cranky tonight, so I'd like to get them over with. Then I'll probably read for a while and go to bed early."

"Nothing doing." Joanna sprang up. "I'm yammering on as though I must tell you everything in one night. You and Jonah run along— maybe take a stroll or sit in the porch swing. These dishes are mine to do, especially since my sister spoiled me while I was visiting. The closest I came to cooking a meal was peeling potatoes. High time I came back to reality."

Leah bobbed her head in Joanna's direction as a wave of emotion robbed her ability to speak. *What is happening to me? One minute I'm mad as a hornet, and then I'm weeping over nothing. What's next— breaking into uncontrollable fits of hysterics until the EMTs arrive with a straitjacket?*

"I should finish some paperwork in the office, but how about meeting me on the porch in an hour?" Jonah flashed his silver-blue eyes at his wife.

"Okay," she answered weakly. "I think I'll walk in the apple orchard until then. There's usually a breeze through the trees at night." Leah fled the house before anyone could try to stop her or offer to tag along. She needed time alone to think and pray. She needed to rid herself of this unchristian anger and resentment and prepare for the day when Joanna announced, "I'm selling the farm. Wisconsin, here come the Bylers!"

NINETEEN

Winesburg—End of July

For the first time in years, Julia Miller wasn't remotely aware of her rheumatoid arthritis. She had been too busy for days to even think about pain or stiffness. She cleaned her house from top to bottom and enlisted Henry to make sure the yard and garden were mowed and weeded. Simon moved the living room furniture several times, often replacing it exactly where it had been before. Hannah washed the windows and bedding in all rooms and had been helping her cook and bake for a week. And Julia had finally made up her mind as to where everyone would sleep during her third cup of coffee. Now, as she watched her son and husband head toward the house for lunch, she exhaled a deeply satisfied sigh.

"What's to eat, *fraa*?" asked Simon as he entered and hung his hat on a peg by the door.

"Roast partridge with pickled snails," she said cheerfully as she carried a pot of soup to the table. She returned to the counter for a loaf of fresh-baked bread.

"Again?" teased Henry, already washing at the sink. "Didn't we just have that? I was hoping for leftover soup from last night's supper."

"In that case, I'll change the menu." Julia patted his cowlick as he sat down and bowed his head.

After a silent prayer, Simon held up his bowl for her to fill. "What was your final decision regarding where to put folks? Should Henry and I cover some hay bales in the loft with old quilts for our new sleeping accommodations?"

Julia winked at him. "You get to remain with me in our room, *ehemann*. But, Henry, I'd like you to move to the back porch while your brother and his family visit from New York. I pushed together the two twin beds for Matthew and Martha. Noah can sleep in between them, and if you two can bring down the crib from the attic and set it up, it will do for little Mary."

Henry held up his bowl. "I don't mind at all. I'll bring in the old glider. It'll be far cooler on the porch than upstairs in my room. Besides, I love listening to all those crickets and tree frogs while falling asleep."

Simon snorted. "Sometimes their racket keeps me awake. What about Emma and her boys?" He dunked his bread into the soup.

"She'll be in her old room. The second bed will be for James on the nights he can stay over. She wrote to say her sons have sleeping bags, thanks to their English grandmother, so they can sleep on the floor. I'm putting Leah in the guest room so there will be space for Jonah whenever he can leave his chores at the Byler farm."

"His *mamm* is back from Wisconsin, ain't it so?" Simon peered over his glasses.

"*Jah*, she's back, but she's busy with new cheese concoctions, according to Leah's letter, in addition to her standard orders. Her cheese business keeps growing and growing, and Leah can only help out so much because of her pie making."

Simon harrumphed, a skill he'd perfected. "Then Leah should stop selling pies for profit and bake only for her family...and her dear old *daed*, of course." His eyes twinkled with amusement. "I'm sure Jonah earns enough money selling milk and beef to pay their taxes and whatnot. Building great stores of wealth only leads to man's downfall."

"In that case, my place in heaven is fairly assured, based on the balance of my bank account." Henry tipped his bowl to scoop the last drops before pushing it across the table for a refill.

Simon scowled at his youngest offspring. "No one's place is assured, son, especially not a person who would boast so recklessly."

"*Mir leid*," he said, apologizing. Henry's cheeks flushed to match the bowl of fresh-picked strawberries in the center of the table.

Simon glared another moment to hone his point and then turned back to Julia. "So I can remain with my bride? Your sister isn't moving in for the month?"

Julia ladled Henry's bowl to the brim. "She wants to, but I'm sending her home every night. She has volunteered her guest room and Ben's room for overnight guests on the weekend the whole district is here. Matthew might have old friends who'll come from far ends of the county. I could put women in the front room on cots, and you can make space in the loft for men."

Simon stroked his beard. "And Martha's family? I'm sure her kin will arrive in droves."

Julia furrowed her forehead "The Hostetlers live across the road. I trust they'll open their house to overnight guests as well. More soup, Simon?"

"*Nein*, but I'll have some of those berries with cream."

Before she could rinse out his soup bowl, he dumped in a load of fruit. "I would have washed your bowl, but I suppose it all goes to the same place." As she walked to the refrigerator for the cream, she heard the sound of a vehicle in the side yard. "Who can that be?" she muttered, drawing back the curtain. The pitcher nearly slipped from her hand. "Oh, goodness. Henry, stop eating! Go to the attic for that crib and set it up in your room. Do it now, before you start visiting." Julia faced her menfolk. "They're here! I can't believe it, but they are here!" Heat flooded her chest as her throat swelled nearly shut.

Henry sprang from his chair and took the stairs to the second floor two at a time.

"Matthew?" asked Simon unnecessarily, pushing aside the berries.

"Matthew," said Julia, turning back to the window in a vain attempt to rein in her emotions. Her son stepped from the taxicab looking fit and trim and infinitely more mature, even though he'd been gone less than two years. He clutched the hand of his son, Noah. Watching the little boy gaze curiously at the unfamiliar surroundings led to Julia's undoing. Noah had been a babe in arms when his parents moved to New York. Julia left the kitchen window and hurried outdoors with her husband close behind.

"Easy, Julia, don't break a leg," Simon cautioned. He grabbed her arm to steady her on the steps.

Once on the gravel path, Julia ran toward the new arrivals as fast as her arthritic legs would carry her. Martha was just climbing out with her husband's assistance. She carried a pink-wrapped bundle despite the July heat and humidity. Julia recognized the pink quilt as the one she and Mary Hostetler had made with the tender love of two faraway *grossmammis*. "Little Mary?" asked Julia, an equally ridiculous question as Simon's.

"None other." Martha drew back the coverlet and handed over her sleeping daughter. "I wrapped her up because the taxi's air-conditioning was turned high enough to chatter teeth."

Julia accepted the baby with a face streaming with tears. Her attempt to control her emotions had failed miserably. The little girl sported flaming orange hair, which stood out all over her head in tufts of tight ringlets. It was the same color Matthew's had been at that age. She had very long blond eyelashes lying against her round-apple cheeks as she slumbered. Her tiny button nose was pink from the sun, while her lips were pursed into a heart-shaped bow. Mary Miller was absolutely, delightfully beautiful—God's handiwork manifest in each perfect detail.

Simon thrust his head over Julia's shoulder. "Fine-looking gal, that one is," he declared. "Good luck trying to get her back." He grinned and nodded at Martha and then strode toward his son. Matthew paid the taxi driver after the man pulled suitcases from the trunk. As the vehicle backed slowly down the drive, the two men embraced with unabashed affection. "Welcome home," murmured Simon.

"Good to be here," said Matthew. "It's been way too long." He leaned back to study his father. "Is your beard even whiter than before?"

"*Nein*. Your mind's playing tricks on you." Simon slapped his son on the back. "We didn't know the exact day of your arrival, but your *mamm's* been cooking up a storm for a week. I sure hope you've brought your appetites." He grabbed the handles of one suitcase.

"You know I have. I only eat good home-cooking on the weekends." Matthew carried a bag to where Julia fawned over Mary as though the infant was some newfangled invention.

"Matty!" A shout cut through the air as Henry bounded out the kitchen door. He leaped from the porch without bothering with the steps and ran all the way to the group. "You're a sight for sore eyes! I have a bagful of questions about a couple Standardbreds I bought." The two men half-hugged and pumped hands vigorously as though priming a well.

"Those will have to wait," ordered Simon. "They'll be here a month. Let's give him a chance to come inside and relax after the long bus ride."

"And have something to eat," added Julia. She strolled toward the house rocking the baby in the crook of her arm. "I hope you haven't spoiled your appetites by eating bus terminal food."

"Especially since *mamm* made a big pot of roast partridge with pickled snails today," Henry said cheerfully as he picked up the last piece of luggage and punched his brother's arm lightly.

Martha and Matthew exchanged an anxious glance. "What are we having?" Matthew asked.

"Fried chicken, ham sandwiches, bean soup—anything you want. Don't pay any attention to Henry. He's been out in the sun without his hat again." Julia climbed the stairs with a springier step than usual as her family followed into the house. As the others carried in bags and parcels, she turned her face toward the ceiling to utter words of gratitude for the gift of family and for keeping the ones she loved safe.

～

Matthew slipped out the back door unobserved and headed toward the barn. He was home in his beloved Holmes County, and he'd nearly forgotten how much he missed life here. He and Martha had settled in his old room, where Mary was already fast asleep in her crib. Martha entertained his mother with tales of the *kinner*, trying to fill in every detail from the last two years. Henry had taken Noah on a walk to the pond with empty jelly jars. They planned to catch a few tadpoles or frogs in the fading light and forge a new special relationship between nephew and uncle. Matthew wanted to appreciate each smell and sound on the farm where he'd grown up—the rolling pastures for cows, horses, and sheep; the fields planted in golden wheat, tasseled-eared corn, sweet-smelling timothy hay, and thick green soybeans. He gazed up at the barn, which had been rebuilt more than a dozen years ago. No one had ever determined whether an errant lightning strike or a careless smoker had started the fire, but the entire community had turned out to build a new structure so strong it would likely last the next hundred years.

Framed by the setting sun, he watched the windmill blades pumping water to a cistern high on the hill. Gravity would then bring the water to the house's bathroom and kitchen with sufficient pressure. Wherever he looked, everything was neat and tidy. Even the cornflower weeds grew in straight rows beside the chicken coop. Matthew wandered into the barn with its mixed bouquet of odors, both nice and not, feeling a surge of nostalgia. As an adult he had thrived here while working for an English horse farm and later, retraining balky horses on his own. But the offer of far more substantial paychecks had lured him away to a new community and the Monday-through-Friday world apart from his wife and children.

How much happier Martha had been during the early months of their marriage, close to her parents, sisters, and everyone else she'd grown up with.

"Things shouldn't look that different to you, son," Simon said, entering the barn and quietly breaking his reverie. "Except for the outrageous number of horses we own right now. They're all out to pasture because we don't have anywhere near enough stalls for them."

Matthew laughed, lifting his boot heel up to a hay bale. "Is my brother buying up horses from the Sugar Creek kill pen? Is that where your extra stock comes from? I guess I taught him that little trick." He felt a swell of pride that his younger brother had followed in his footsteps.

Simon glanced over his shoulder. "This is not a laughing matter. We own close to thirty horses now. That's an absurd number for an Amish farmer and deacon. Do you have any idea how much a horse eats during the winter when they can't graze the pasture?"

"I would say a bale of hay each day, plus a quantity of oats or spelt." Matthew leaned against a post, holding back his grin.

"*Jah*, well, an English horse trainer can afford such extravagance, but feeding them will send me to the poorhouse, if we still had such places these days. I can't grow that amount of hay even if Seth gives me half his crop. I'm forced to buy loads at the grain elevator while my fellow brethren scratch their heads in wonder."

"Why don't you ask Henry not to acquire more until he sells down his current stock?" suggested Matthew. "Set a target number he should work toward...say fifteen or twenty, at the most."

"The trouble is Henry doesn't seem to sell any of them. He brings them home and turns them out to pasture. With some he's had success retraining, while with others no luck at all, yet it doesn't bother him." Simon again checked to make sure they weren't being overheard. "Your brother is as hardworking as any man, but he doesn't possess a lick of business sense. He completes his farm chores and then treats his new purchases more like pets than temporary investments."

Matthew pondered how best to settle this impasse. "Does he make an income by retraining balky horses owned by others?"

"No, he hasn't for a long time. When he rehabilitates a rescued horse, he gives it away to a friend or a district family suffering hard times. Soon folks will be showing up at our door with food baskets and gifts of charity." Simon shook his head.

"Ask them to bring bales of hay instead."

"Would you please take this seriously? I need your help, son." Simon shifted his weight to his other leg and crossed his arms.

Matthew sobered. Seldom did his dad ask for advice. "I'll speak to Henry and work with him during the month I'm home with specific horses. I'll point out which ones he shouldn't have purchased, no matter how low the price, and which traits to beware of. Then I'll try to fire up his training business to generate cash. He showed great promise two years ago."

Simon looked him in the eye. "Your cousin Phoebe volunteered to paint Henry a sign to install down by the road." He drew a large rectangular shape in the air with his two index fingers. "The Miller Family Horse Sanctuary. Everyone laughed at the joke, but not Henry. He thought it was a great idea."

Matthew smiled but then held up his palm before his father could object. "I know you're concerned with the practical end of matters—horses do eat a lot. But I admire his kindness and dedication to saving beasts that would otherwise have been put down."

Simon rubbed his eyelids with his fingertips. "Loving horses is fine, but then he needs to find them new homes. Once after preaching service, I overheard someone ask Henry if he could bring his buggy horse here. It was a Standardbred, gimpy and old as those hills to the west. The young man's father had told him to put the mare down because the family lived near town on only two acres. They had no room for geriatric nags."

"And Henry told him *jah*?" asked Matthew, already knowing the answer.

"Of course. She's the ancient swayback that hangs out in the high pasture, usually with a string of wildflowers around her neck. Phoebe took a shine to the horse and brings her fruit more days than not."

Matthew bit the inside of his cheek. "I'll look for her tomorrow when I take a hike in that direction."

"You do that, son." Simon started toward the door. "And be sure to take some apples along with you." In the doorway he turned back. The streaming moonlight ringed his white head like a halo. "How about some pie? I believe we have as many varieties as a tourist smorgasbord."

"I'll be up later. Save me a piece. I'm heading down to the pond to find Henry and my son." Matthew watched his father lumber back to the house. His parents were aging—the inevitable march of time of this temporal, earthly life—and the reminder filled him with guilt and sorrow.

By moon and starlight he made his way to the water supply for livestock and the kitchen garden during periods of drought. Henry and Noah were crouched on haunches with their flashlights trained on two large glass jars. Matthew crept up slowly so as not to interrupt the scene.

"We'll take your frog and this jar of tadpoles up to the house, Noah, to show *grossdawdi* and everyone else. But tomorrow we'll bring them here and put them back in the water. The big guy might have a frog family that he would miss, plus he needs to catch flies to eat on his sticky tongue. And the tadpoles need the pond to grow into big-sized frogs."

"Okay, Henny," said Noah, mispronouncing most words containing the troublesome letter *r*. He handed Henry his flashlight and clutched the jar to his chest as though a king's treasure. "We'll bring him home in time for breakfast." His son spoke in *Deutsch* and had a bit of trouble with the name of the morning meal.

Matthew watched them rise to their feet. Henry took Noah's small hand and they started up the path. His brother had the gentlest heart in the county. No way did Matthew wish to change that. He would offer his brother practical advice to turn his business into something generating more income, but he wouldn't change the one thing that made Henry extraordinary in a world where too much cruelty and neglect still existed. Matthew stepped out of the shadows. "There you two are. Anybody need a hand carrying new pets up to the house?"

"*Daed*!" exclaimed Noah. "Look who I found."

Matthew met his brother's gaze over Noah's head and grinned. *Who indeed*, he thought.

TWENTY

Winesburg—early August

Phoebe trotted her pony faster than usual on a sunny Wednesday, even though she had plenty of time before the appointed hour to meet Eli. She looked forward to an afternoon spent at the library, surrounded by books, comfortable chairs, and happy readers. Her mom had kept her busy roasting meats and baking sweets since the arrival of cousin Matthew. One would think he and Martha had brought their entire New York district instead of only two little ones, judging by the quantity of food prepared. At least Hannah hadn't insisted she stay home today. It wasn't that Phoebe didn't like her cousin and his wife—she did very much and would enjoy visiting with them. But the heart-stopping news tucked into her tote bag wouldn't keep. She couldn't wait to show Eli and watch his face as he read the letter. "Git up there!" she commanded. The spotted pony dutifully picked up his hooves.

Despite her early arrival at the library, she saw Eli's buggy already tied to the hitching post. She'd planned to have the librarian teach her more about the computer. She'd heard that a person could set up an e-mail account at a place called "Yoo-Hoo" even if they didn't own a computer themselves. Phoebe secured her pony to the rail and ran toward the door. After greeting Mrs. Carter, she found Eli at their favorite table in the back. He appeared to be napping—but thumping her tote bag down under his nose put an end to that.

"Hullo, Phoebe," he said with a slow drawl of words. "Thought I would catch up on my beauty sleep while waiting for you. Haven't been able to get much at home since Dad's not been feeling well."

Eli did look tired. Dark circles underscored his bloodshot eyes, while his normally healthy color looked pale.

"I'm sorry, Eli. Maybe you could go to bed early tonight, but you'll not want to sleep through this."

He straightened in his chair while she pulled out the letter with great drama. After placing it face up on the table, she waited for his eyes to focus on the return address. "Great Beginnings Publishing, New York, New York," he read, looking to her for confirmation.

"Yes, it's really from them. We've received our first reply to the queries. Actually, it's not the first—we got three form letters within days of our mailing saying that they weren't accepting any new submissions at this time. Oh, and one publishing house stated they accepted proposals only from agents." She breathed in and out through her mouth, trying to calm down.

Eli sat like a statue, eyeing the envelope with apparent skepticism. "And this publisher…what reason for rejection did they give us?" he asked.

She sat and scooted her chair closer until it touched his. "Why don't you read it for yourself? Your name is on the letter, same as mine."

He picked up the envelope and extracted the single sheet as though anxious to put the task behind him. After scanning the paper, his gaze met hers. His expression remained one of disbelief. She grinned as widely as her face allowed while he began to read aloud:

Dear Miss Miller and Mr. Riehl,

It is my pleasure to inform you that I thoroughly enjoyed *Who Will Be My Friend?* Both the inspirational story line and the lovely illustrations might be just what we're

looking for to expand our line of children's gift books. I
have given your proposal to our publishing committee for
consideration. The final decision whether or not to pursue
this project rests with them, but I have passed along my
heartfelt support. At your earliest convenience, please
supply my office with a phone number where you can be
reached, along with your e-mail address.

> Yours very truly,
> Ms. Heather Duncan
> Editor in Chief

Eli tossed down the letter and sucked in a lungful of air. "Oh my
goodness gracious!" He spoke each word of exclamation louder than
the last. Then he threw his arms around Phoebe and squeezed.

"We did it, Eli! We got our foot in the door, as Mrs. Carter calls
it." Phoebe hugged him back with equal exuberance. She buried her
face against the soft cotton of his shirt, which smelled like sunshine.

He kissed the top of her head at least a dozen times. It was a good
thing they were alone in the library, because such public displays of
affection were forbidden in their Amish culture. "I can't believe they
contacted us so quickly," he said. "I thought we wouldn't hear anything for months."

"It must be a good sign."

"Or it could mean it doesn't take long to read a twenty-five-page
story. But I'm happy that the right people will at least be evaluating
it." Eli leaned back and stretched out his long legs. "Now this next
stage will probably take a while, especially since neither of us has an
e-mail account. Riehl and Son Swine and Beef has a phone line, but
we didn't put it in the letter."

Phoebe lowered her head and peered from under her lashes, using
every dramatic gesture she knew. "Don't worry about that. I supplied
Miss Heather Duncan with both a phone number and an e-mail address."

"And just how did you manage that?" His excitement seemed to slip a notch.

"I wrote to her and provided our next door neighbor's phone number. Mrs. Lee doesn't mind getting messages to us. Then I could return the editor's call as soon as possible." Phoebe folded her hands primly on the table.

"And the e-mail address? Did you use Mrs. Lee's for that too?"

"No, I used your friend's e-mail—the woman who lives in Kidron. Since she kept copies of your story and my artwork, she would be able to resend anything that the publisher might need."

Eli scratched her head. "How did you know what it was?" His tone sounded a hair above accusatory.

Phoebe's confidence faltered. "It was on one of the papers in the file folder you gave me. I didn't think she would mind since she's been so helpful up till now."

Eli's eyes turned round as an owl's. "Did you contact Sarah and ask for permission?" Upon her shaking her head, he said in a low tone, "You shouldn't have done that, Phoebe, not without securing permission first. She is Rose's friend. I don't know her that well and would prefer not to take advantage of her generosity."

Phoebe dropped her chin to her chest and focused on her skirt. "I'm sorry, Eli. I let my excitement carry me away. I wrote to Great Beginnings Publishing the same night I received their letter and mailed it the next day."

Eli tipped up her chin with a single finger. "You did mention to the editor we're both Amish, didn't you?"

"No, I saw no need for that." Phoebe fought back unbidden tears.

"I think they should be fully aware of our situation and possible... limitations." He sounded only patient and gentle. "But I shouldn't work myself up about this. There's probably little need to worry about imposing on Sarah."

"You're not angry with me?" she asked. "Because I thought we could go to supper at that restaurant you liked to celebrate the good news. They have such good food. Plus, my parents are busy at my aunt and uncle's house since my cousin is visiting from out of town. Oh, I do want you to meet Matthew while he's here, but tonight I'd—" Phoebe halted mid-sentence, realizing she was running on like a magpie.

"Whew! Are you making up for lost time during your silent years?" He threw his head back and laughed. "No, I'm not mad at you, sweet peach. But in the future, let's remember to consult each other before making big decisions, okay?"

"Agreed. I'll treat you to supper to rectify my misjudgment."

Eli ran his fingertips lightly down her cheek, as tender as the brush of a feather. "What a gracious offer, but I must decline. I need to go home early. How about a celebratory ice-cream cone instead? My treat, as a gentleman doesn't allow a lady to pay." He winked with great exaggeration.

Phoebe's breath caught in her throat from his touch. "All right, ice cream it is. Shall I follow you to the shop in my pony cart?"

"No, ride with me in my buggy, and I'll bring you back here afterward." He lifted her chin a second time. "I'm happy about the news. Make no mistake about that. We're on our way, Miss Miller. There'll be no stopping us now." He hesitated briefly, and then he leaned over and brushed her lips with a kiss.

The kiss left her speechless. They were in a public library for one thing. And a kiss didn't reflect a business partnership. It spoke of a relationship she wasn't sure she was ready for.

If someone would have asked her the next day what flavor of ice cream she had eaten or what stimulating topics they discussed on the ride to the shop, Phoebe couldn't have answered. Her mind swam with more ideas than migratory salmon facing their trek upstream in the wildest rapids.

～

The following day, when Phoebe wasn't dwelling on Eli and his spur-of-the-moment kisses, she was debating when and what she would tell her parents. Thus far she hadn't mentioned the letter from the publisher. She was usually the one to fetch mail from their roadside box, and the day of the letter's arrival had been no exception. She'd tucked it into her apron pocket as though it were a deep, dark secret, even though she'd already told her parents of their plan to submit the story. But she felt better if few people knew the status of their project, as least for now. Rejection could come any day. And licking wounds might prove easier without tons of questions or commiserations from well-intentioned loved ones.

Eli had been displeased she hadn't been up-front with the editor. And he also felt she'd overstepped her bounds with Sarah of Kidron. So Phoebe didn't wish to also anger her parents by being secretive. After all, Mrs. Lee could send for her at any time to return a phone call. Or she might need to arrange a trip to Kidron to work on additional artwork or make changes to illustrations already submitted.

But in the meantime, she needed to finish picking the blackberries before scratches completely covered her forearms and face. Hannah planned to bake a cobbler with the last of the fresh berries. Phoebe stepped back from the prickly briars to gauge the sun. Both its position over the livestock barn and her rumbling stomach signaled it was almost suppertime. She quickly topped off her bucket with a few more easy-to-reach fruit and headed toward the house, swinging her pail like a nursery rhyme character. Once she reached the kitchen, she found her mother packing food into a hamper while her father filled a jug with just-brewed tea.

"There you are," said Hannah. "I thought you'd picked your way up to Orrville, you've been gone so long."

"I did as much thinking as picking, and it slowed me down." Phoebe washed her hands and then dumped the berries into a colander to rinse and sort. The faucet blast sprayed the front of her dress and face.

"That thinking stuff is hard work," said her dad. "I tried it once or twice myself and barely got my chores done that day." He tugged on one of her *kapp* ribbons.

Hannah chuckled. "Your father's in a good mood today. He just delivered the final load of spelt to the grain elevator and earned a decent price." She set a tray of warm cornbread atop the hamper of fried chicken.

"Now that we're rich, I'm ready to take my family on vacation to any exotic locale they choose, providing it's still in Holmes County." He snapped his suspenders like a teenager. "How 'bout the flea market in Berlin?"

"You had better get bragging out of your system now. You know how your brother feels about prideful talk, even if it is in jest." Hannah perched one hand on her hip.

Phoebe wheeled around from the sink. "We're going to Uncle Simon's again for supper?" she asked, drying her hands on a towel.

Hannah turned from her boastful husband to her clueless daughter. "*Jah*, we are. I usually don't use a hamper to carry food to the table. I fried the chicken and cornbread, while your aunt made the potato salad, coleslaw, and baked pies. We'll eat outdoors in the shade. Kitchens are too hot this time of year to sit around in."

Phoebe smiled weakly. "I thought maybe you were carrying supper to our own picnic table under the willow." She slouched with disappointment.

"You will not faint if forced to be sociable, Miss Hermit. I thought you enjoyed the company of Martha Miller and her little ones."

"I do, *mamm*, very much, but I had something to discuss with you and *daed*—something I don't want to talk about in front of every other Miller."

"I see," said Hannah. Then she hollered over her shoulder, "Ben, we're ready to go. Come down right now."

Seth reached for a jar of balm from the windowsill, which served as an excellent mosquito repellent. "You're in luck, daughter, because we're walking to Simon and Julia's. It's too nice an evening to hitch up the buggy to go next door. We'll take the back path around the duck pond and through the bog." He hefted the hamper brimming with chicken. "So you'll have plenty of time to bare your soul." He opened the door with a flourish.

Phoebe lifted her shawl from the peg and grabbed her water bottle. Uncle Simon and Aunt Julia might live next door, but the back path was at least a mile long. Ben suddenly appeared right behind her. He was fully dressed, but water still dripped from his wet hair. Apparently he'd waited for the last minute to take his shower. She grabbed the pan of cornbread to carry as the foursome trooped out the door.

As soon as Ben had wandered sufficiently ahead of them, Phoebe broached the subject. "I heard from a publisher about our children's book idea. Miss Duncan, the head editor, said she liked Eli's story and my illustrations. Now it's up to her bosses if the book will get published or not."

Other than the caws of crows and the incessant drone of insects from surrounding shrubs, not a sound could be heard as they strolled along the trail. Her parents remained silent for so long, she thought perhaps neither heard a word. Finally, Hannah spoke. "That's good news. You and Eli must be quite pleased."

"I still think you should discuss this with the bishop," groused her father. "Tonight would be a fine opportunity to run this scheme by your uncle."

Phoebe paused almost as long as they had before replying. "Okay, if you think I should. I also wanted you to know I gave the publisher Mrs. Lee's phone number in case they need to speak to me." She swatted at a deerfly, seemingly unaffected by the bug balm.

"Phones are permitted only for emergencies, not to advance your little hobby." Seth didn't hide his irritation.

"The bishop allows plenty of folks to use phones for business, as long as the phone isn't inside their house."

"But you haven't asked permission of anyone, have you, Phoebe? Thus far, you and Eli have operated solely by your own counsel."

She swallowed hard, deciding not to mention the possibility of working in Kidron on a computer. "I'll talk to Uncle Simon tonight after supper, and if he advises, I'll speak to the bishop after Sunday's service."

"All right, then," said Seth, followed by another grunt.

"I don't know why you're so against the idea, *daed*. We only want to help little children with stories that contain a moral lesson. This is a Christian publisher who might be interested in our books."

"Books?" he asked, halting on the path. "As in more than one?"

Phoebe almost ran into his backside. "Probably only one unless they clamor for more, which is unlikely."

Seth might have debated the topic further, but Ben interrupted. "Look there! That red-tailed hawk is carrying a rabbit in its mouth." As the four Millers watched grimly, the rabbit slipped from the hawk's talons into the shallow water of the pond. After a splash, they heard it scamper to safety in the tall reeds.

"Oh, good," murmured Hannah. "I know hawks must eat too and bunnies wreak havoc in my garden, but I'd rather not witness survival of the fittest firsthand."

Soon Uncle Simon's barn loomed into view and Phoebe's appetite rose in leaps and bounds. "Aunt Julia is carrying out the food. We're just in time."

Ahead, Henry and Matthew carried benches and extra chairs to the long tables that had been set up in the shade. Blue-checked cloths covered the tables, while stacks of plates and bowls waited for hungry diners. A ceramic frog kept a pile of paper napkins from blowing away.

When Hannah joined Aunt Julia at the table with her hamper of fried chicken, Phoebe headed to the tall oak where Martha was pushing little Noah in the tire swing. Martha greeted her with a pleasant smile and pointed to the baby carrier near the tree trunk. "Finally asleep," she said. "That child has squalled all day."

Phoebe crept closer to peer into the carrier. Pink-faced Mary napped with the beatific expression of an angel. While Martha pushed her son in the tire, Phoebe watched the infant sleep, utterly content. Babies were such magical creatures—true gifts from God. But Phoebe's hunger pangs soon became downright distracting.

When Aunt Julia finally rang the farm bell, everyone scurried to eat. After their silent prayer, Phoebe noticed no one sat at the head of the table. "Where's Uncle Simon?" she asked, accepting the bowl of coleslaw from her cousin Henry.

"Good question," said Julia. "He went to town on district business hours ago, but I expected him home long before this."

Seth's eyebrows lifted high on his forehead. "Would you like me to look for him?"

"I wouldn't even know which direction to send you. Let's be patient. He probably started jawing and lost track of time. But there's no reason to hold up supper any longer. Folks are hungry, so let's dig in. I'll reheat his plate later."

"That's assuming there's anything left." Matthew took three pieces of chicken and was reaching for a fourth when Martha placed a hand discreetly on his arm.

Phoebe relaxed and began eating with full enjoyment. There might be no opportunity tonight for a heart-to-heart chat with her uncle.

And God, in His mysterious plan for our lives, did circumvent the dreaded conversation, but not for any reason she would have chosen. Uncle Simon returned home just as the apple pies were being sliced and handed around the table. He lumbered with weariness, looking more forlorn than Phoebe could ever recall. As Henry led off the horse and buggy, Simon washed up at the old-fashioned hand pump in the yard, usually used for filling watering cans for the garden. He approached the family with a solemn demeanor.

Julia clutched her throat as Simon slumped into a chair. "What is it? Has there been an accident?"

"No, no accident, *fraa*," he said. Silently, Hannah filled his glass with iced tea. "The bishop heard from one of Robert Riehl's daughters," continued Simon. "Bob has been taken to the Canton hospital by ambulance. Apparently his son found him in the barn, not breathing. Eli resuscitated him and started his heart beating again." Simon lifted his chin high. "He read about how to do it in some book—can you believe it? The ambulance driver said it looked like a heart attack and that young Eli saved his life." Simon shook his head and took a long swallow of tea. "Read it in a book," he repeated. "Doesn't that beat all?"

Everyone at the table started chattering with theories and conjectures…except for Phoebe. She sat looking as though she might faint, and it had nothing to do with having to be sociable.

TWENTY-ONE

Winesburg—The Byler Dairy Farm

Yoo-hoo, Leah." A musical voice wafted through the kitchen window. "Come out, come out, wherever you are."

It took Leah a long moment to match a name to the voice, during which time she frowned with annoyance. She was up to her eyelashes in flour, sugar, and shortening. There wasn't a bit of air circulating through the open windows, her overly snug dress was glued to her back with perspiration, and she hadn't a clue where her mother-in-law was. Then the identity of the cheery visitor hit her like a freight train—a sole passenger car and a red caboose, to be exact. April Lambright—her Mennonite friend and former business partner—and as it turned out, her partner in crime. Who knew running a charming diner for locals serving only breakfast and lunch would land them in so much hot water with the IRS and the Ohio Department of Taxation? Leah dropped her mixing spoon and ran out the door. "Stop peeping into my kitchen, missy, before I send for the sheriff!"

April stepped back from the window and smiled gloriously. "But isn't that exactly how you and I met?"

Leah remembered the day she spotted the dilapidated train cars. She'd nearly broken her neck trying to view the remodel work going on inside. The two friends hugged hard enough to leave both breathless and teary-eyed. "It's good to see you in person, instead of corresponding by notes passed back and forth through Tom." Although Leah still supplied the restaurant with pies, April's husband picked them up on his way home from work. The women had seldom seen each other since Leah had sold her share of the partnership to April's sister, May. Leah pulled back suddenly. "What day is it? Did you close April's Home Cooking just to pay a social call?"

"No, I closed the diner today for other reasons. But do you expect me to tell the story standing here on the porch?"

"I have a pot of coffee still warm. Come inside and take a load off."

April followed Leah into a kitchen that certainly looked to be in the throes of baking day. "What happened? Did a storm touch down at the Bylers' that missed the rest of the county?" She peered around the room, wide-eyed.

"Very funny. Now you see what it takes to create my masterpieces."

"That's why I'll stick with Sara Lee."

Leah looked around the room with an objective eye. The Byler kitchen was huge, yet some part of pie making covered every available inch of the flat surfaces. Bowls of fresh fruit and jars of canned; open bags of flour, sugar, cornmeal, and spelt; tubs of shortening, butter, and whipping cream; and spices, nuts, and spilled milk littered her work area, while a fine haze of flour hung in the humid air. She seldom baked in such disorder. "*Ach*, this is truly awful. I was so busy I hadn't noticed." She slumped into a chair. "I'm way behind on my pie orders." Weariness punctuated each one of her words.

"Never fear, April is here! And I can stay the whole day. I would love to give you a hand."

"*Danki.* You've been sent by the angels."

"We'll see if that's your opinion by the end of the day. But first, we'll have that cup of coffee while I tell you my news." April grabbed the pot and two mugs from the dish drainer. "I wanted you to be first to hear that May and I have sold the diner. We signed the final papers yesterday. It's closed for a few days, but the new owners plan to reopen by the weekend." She hesitated, allowing time for a reaction.

Leah gasped for air. "You sold it? Your dream?"

"It was my dream, but then reality set in. I've tossed and turned far too many nights worrying about making ends meet."

"But May has a good head for business, far superior to mine...or yours." Leah softened the words with a wink.

"Yes, that's true, and she has worked very hard. We both have. But first I had to pay off my share of the debt you and I incurred. Then I had to pay my sister back for bailing the restaurant out with the tax department. Once we put that behind us, we thought we would finally turn a profit. My husband hoped for help paying bills by now, instead of me causing more financial hardship for our family." Her pretty blue eyes turned wistful. "But that never happened."

"Has business fallen off? The economy is taking a while to recover."

"No, business has been good. We have our local regulars and enough tourists find us that tables are usually full from the time we're opened till closed. But the place is too small to make a profit. We can't count on the outdoor tables with our unpredictable weather. And I dare not expand hours to include dinner because I'm away from my family too much now."

Leah patted her friend's hand. Not much had changed over the past four years. The basic limitations of a train car only open four days a week until three o'clock remained the same. "And you can't raise prices because the locals can't afford to pay more until things get back to normal."

"Exactly." April sighed wearily. "Tourists will choose the buffet down the road if I don't remain a good value. The appeal of home-cooking only goes so far against all-you-can-eat." She grinned, but then her gaze on Leah turned downright appraising. "That's enough about my woes. The diner is sold, and frankly I feel a great burden is off my shoulders. Now, isn't there some news you wish to share with me? I see a change has come over you." One corner of her mouth lifted.

Leah blushed up into her scalp. "What do you mean? Have I put on weight eating up all my pie profits?" She settled her hands on her rounded belly.

"Not at all. It's your countenance that's different. Your face has the fresh tender bloom of summer roses. Is there anything you wish to share with me?" April made a rocking motion with her folded arms.

Leah slapped the tabletop. "Fresh tender blooms, my foot. It's ninety degrees in here and I feel uncomfortable in my own skin." When April continued to smile, Leah relented. "You are impossible, but *jah*, I'm expecting a *boppli*. That's part of the reason I can't keep up with chores. My stomach turns queasy from the mere crack of an egg."

After a second round of hugs and tears, April sprang to her feet. "How can I help? I'm not leaving until order has been restored to this kitchen or the baby is born, whichever comes first."

"If you have time to spare, I sure could use those walnuts cracked and hulled." She pointed at a brimming burlap sack on the floor.

"Cracking nuts—my favorite. I have lots of time before my kids get off the school bus. Let's get busy."

Several hours and multiple cups of coffee later, they had baked enough apple walnut, blueberry cheesecake, chocolate mousse, and cherry pies to fill the existing orders. After fixing lunch for Jonah and his helpers, Leah and April sat down to their own bologna with Swiss sandwiches and lemonade.

"Where's your mother-in-law? I heard Joanna had returned from Wisconsin."

Leah set down her sandwich, deciding to unburden her heart about the other troubling matter. "She has, but today she left with samples of her latest creations—peppercorn Colby and tomato-basil Gouda. She's visiting cheese and gift shops to secure new orders. As though we don't have enough work with her standing accounts." Leah didn't try to hide her bad temper.

"Those varieties sound yummy. Maybe she should hire another employee." April scooped more baby beets onto her plate from the jar.

"*Jah*, I've suggested that, but instead of doing so she gives me more of her work. Today she asked me to sterilize her whey separator while she's on the road. In my condition, that yeasty odor makes my head spin and churns my stomach. Joanna said Amish women work until they give birth, but usually not in a dairy."

"We're heading there next. I've always wanted to see what she does. I've never tasted better smoked cheddar or almond Brie than Joanna's."

"Sorry, April. That's not why I mentioned this. You've helped me enough for one day and I'm grateful. Let's just sit in the shade a spell."

"I won't leave until you at least show me the dairy, so eat up."

Familiar enough with her former partner to know the woman meant what she said, Leah took her on an abbreviated tour of the cheese-making process. "Fresh milk is stored in those coolers. That contraption is our separator, and there is our diesel-powered pasteurizer. You must heat milk to one hundred sixty degrees to kill bacteria. Then we add exennet to start the solidifying process and heat the milk again to one hundred degrees. The whey then starts to separate and drops to the bottom. We next add ingredients for the different varieties, and curds form within forty-five minutes. Then you add salt, one batch at a time. After another hour, boxes are pressed and the remaining whey is forced out. Within twelve hours you have solid cheese. Then we store it in coolers for the proper amount of time, again depending on the type. Yogurt cheese only takes three days."

"How long does cheddar take?" April's face glowed with interest.

"It's stored between three and four months."

"How do you get the holes in Swiss cheese?"

"Gas pockets form naturally during the aging process." Leah felt the uncomfortable rumble deep in her gut. "Would you excuse me? I'll meet you back at the house. Feel free to look around." She fled out the door and ran smack into Jonah.

"Easy, *fraa*. No running. What are you doing in here? I told *mamm* that because the odors make you sick I would clean the equipment. Go up to the house and rest."

"*Danki*, Jonah. Could you finish giving April a tour? She's visiting today, but I need some fresh air." Leah fled to the sweet-smelling comfort of her kitchen, feeling guilty about abandoning her friend. But if she'd stayed another minute, Jonah would have had another sterilization disaster to contend with.

~

Canton, Ohio

Eli watched his father's chest rise and fall with each life-sustaining breath. Although the man remained hooked up to IVs, monitors, and other equipment, he was now breathing on his own. The hospital had transferred him from coronary intensive care to a regular room that morning. And although he was still very weak, his father should be able to go home in another week if his improvement continued. Eli bowed his head in prayer, giving thanks to a merciful Lord. Robert Riehl would soon be able to return home to his wife, daughters, and a son who loved and depended on him. The surgeon had repaired a heart valve and inserted a stent into one artery to keep the blood flowing as it should. But the marvels of science—impressive at times though they might be—could never compare to the miracles of God.

Eli had been led to check out health magazines from the library, something he'd never done before, and to read the article about administering CPR.

He had been led to return home early that Wednesday afternoon and had found his dad lying unconscious in the barn. There still had been time to act.

Even his blood turned out to be perfect to provide a transfusion during Dad's surgery. It had been no accident that Eli was in the right place at the right time. It had been the will of God. And for His grace, he would always be grateful.

"Is he still sleeping?" Rose's voice startled him as she bent over his shoulder.

"*Jah*, the nurse said that's normal. He needs plenty of rest to recover." Eli straightened the kinks in his back, one vertebra at a time. "How did you get here?"

"My beau, Luke, hired a driver so I could see *daed*. That same driver is waiting at the main entrance to take you home. You need to sleep in a real bed for a change, instead of that chair, and take a good hot shower."

"The nurses let me shower down the hall." He winced with pain as he rubbed the sore muscles between his shoulder blades.

"What have you eaten?" A frown pulled her lips into a tight line.

"They serve decent food in the cafeteria, but the prices are about to turn me into a beggar."

"Go home, Eli. The driver is waiting for a passenger to take back to Winesburg. You've been here for days and have done all you could. Now let your sisters take turns staying with Dad until we bring him home."

Eli met her gaze. "He's going to be okay, Rose. I would have felt terrible if I hadn't gone to the barn in time." His poignant confession sounded hollow in the cold, sterile hospital room.

"*Ach*, that's ridiculous. If anything, you saved his life. There's no reason for you to feel guilty." Rose plopped down in the opposite chair, smoothing her skirt with both hands.

"He might not have had the heart attack if I'd been more help around the farm. I should have assumed more responsibility as Dad grew older instead of doing only my assigned chores. And where was I when he wasn't feeling good? Chasing pipe dreams with fellow dreamer Phoebe Miller." Eli released a sigh of shameful regret.

"You listen to me, little brother. Nothing you did or didn't do caused this. According to the doctor, Dad has coronary artery disease. It's hereditary and progressive, and it would have been fatal if not for your quick response. Mom should have changed his diet years ago to reduce his cholesterol level, and he should have been on high blood pressure medication."

Eli blinked in amazement. Rose had never shown interest in topics not directly related to the kitchen. "All this time we had a doc in the family and no one knew."

A grin lit up her face. "I've kept my mind busy reading that stack of health magazines you brought home. By the way, they're all overdue. You'll owe a big fine, and you're already bankrupt from store-bought food."

He smiled at her before standing and leaning over the bed to kiss his father's forehead. She was right. He needed to get back home. Both Rose's and their sister Ruby's beaus had been there to run operations along with help from nearby district members, but those men had their own chores to do. With his dad laid up, the farm was now his responsibility. At nineteen he was no longer a boy running off with his fishing pole to the swimming hole on a hot summer day. He was a man, and he yearned to be a man his father could be proud of.

Just as he turned to leave, his father's eyes fluttered open. "Am I still with the living?"

Eli took a moment to decipher his soft, hoarse words. "*Jah*, and you'll stay with us for a good long while."

"The Lord's not ready for you yet." Rose moved closer, her face streaming with tears. "*Guder mariye, daed*," she greeted in *Deutsch*.

"You're both here? Who's running the farm?" Deep lines crinkled around his eyes.

The two siblings chuckled. "*Mamm*. And she says hurry and get well." Eli squeezed his father's hand through the blanket.

Rose dabbed her face with a tissue. "*Mamm* was here for three days straight. She went home yesterday to bathe but will return tonight."

"So much fussing over one old hog farmer." The strangled words caught in his throat.

"You're not old, but you'll have to give up that bacon you love so much." Rose smoothed the mussed hair back from his pale face. "You're in the prime of life."

"But we are hog farmers." Eli bent low to kiss his dad's papery fore-head again as a wave of love nearly overwhelmed him. The reality of what they had almost lost hit him like a mule kick. "And I'm going home to make sure they're doing what hogs are supposed to do." He swallowed hard as he straightened.

Bob Riehl's hand rose from beneath the covers and caught Eli's sleeve. "*Danki*, son. *Danki*."

Eli nodded and left the room before he started weeping like a woman. He couldn't wait to get home to start acting like the man he was.

TWENTY-TWO

Winesburg—Mid-August

Butterflies took flight and bees darted between clover heads as Julia and two little boys strolled through the meadow. A light breeze from the south kept the bright sunshine from turning oppressive. "That is a *kuh*, Jamie. And these here are *blumen*." Julia pointed at a cow grazing near the pasture fence and then pulled up a handful of flowers. She pronounced the word again in *Deutsch* as she transferred the buttercups to her grandson's small hand. Jamie dutifully repeated what she said with a child's typical eagerness.

Emma and her two sons had been staying at the farm for ten days. They had arrived within a few days of Martha and Matthew to make the most of their month-long visit. So Julia made the most of the opportunity to teach her grandsons their native language. For an Amish child, Old Order or New, not to be fluent in the German dialect was unheard of. She wanted Jamie, the four-year-old, to have at least basic knowledge before the get-together for the whole district, or she would have to face the clucking tongues and shaking heads of her friends and quilting acquaintances. Women her age had strong opinions about maintaining their cultural heritage—opinions she agreed with.

"*Gaul*," said Jamie, pointing at one of Henry's prized acquisitions up the hill.

"That's *gut. Gaul,*" she repeated with pride.

"*Cah-cah,*" called little Sam, behind them.

With horror, Julia turned to see the eighteen-month-old clutching a cowpat between his tiny fingers.

"*Cah-cah.*" The boy repeated the word, utterly delighted with himself. The mess was smeared across the front of his shirt and trousers.

"*Jah, cah-cah,*" agreed Julia. "That word is the same in every language." She shook the animal waste from his hands. "No, Sam. Don't touch *cah-cah.*" She chose English for her admonishment to make sure there would be no misunderstanding. "Let's go to the house," she said in both languages. She picked up the toddler and walked as quickly as her arthritic legs could manage while Jamie ran and jumped like a yearling colt. What would Emma say when she saw her son? Bad *grossmammi,* probably. She laughed to herself, recalling a few of her own *kinner*' childhood exploits. Once Emma had spent an hour sitting in a tree after an ornery goat deemed her an unwanted trespasser in his pasture. Fortunately, Matthew had heard her distress calls, shooed off the goat, and helped his sister down from the branch.

Pausing at the old hand pump, she washed the boy's hands and face in case he touched something before reaching the bathroom. Inside the kitchen, Emma, Leah, and Martha were finishing breakfast dishes and starting preparations for supper. All the Millers would be at the cookout tonight. Lily Davis would bring her brother, pick up Jonah Byler along the way, and then stay to eat with James' in-laws. James and Jonah planned to remain for the weekend with their wives. Seth, Hannah, Ben, and Phoebe would appear at various times during the afternoon as chores allowed.

"What happened?" asked Emma, looking aghast. She stopped kneading bread dough to hurry toward her sons. Both boys beamed at their mother as though proud of some accomplishment.

"Don't touch him. He's fine. He just needs another bath."

"Pee-u," crowed Leah and Martha. After a few backward steps, they pinched their nostrils shut with two fingers.

"Is that what I think it is?" Emma's hand perched on one hip, while her lips twitched into a frown.

"Relax, daughter. The world will soon be right again." Julia hauled the boy toward the bathroom.

"You must have gotten rusty, *mamm*. Or you're falling down on the job," Leah called after her, smiling behind her sister-in-law. That particular daughter looked the picture of health and happiness, and she was thoroughly enjoying her visit with siblings and their offspring. The other Miller women had already deduced her joyous condition, even though Leah made no admission.

"It's no wonder I'm rusty, considering how seldom I see my *kin-skinner*," Julia called from inside the modern addition to the century-old house. While filling the tub, she stripped off the child's soiled clothes. "I would think a farm boy would know not to touch a cow-pat," Julia hollered toward the open door. Sam reached for a *kapp* ribbon with his wet hand.

"He plays in a fenced section of our yard. We don't let him run wild through the fields where cows and horses graze." In the door-way Emma crossed her arms, but her expression revealed enjoyment of the situation. "What were you three doing while we cooked and cleaned and ironed clothes?" Her dimples deepened. No doubt about it—they were her prettiest feature.

"I was teaching the boys the correct names of things. And making good progress too." Julia tested the bathwater, added a capful of bubble bath, and a few moments later turned off the faucets. After undressing Sam, she lifted him into the tub. "Even this little one has started calling me *mammi* instead of Granny. I can't believe Barbara Davis prefers that term over the others." A natural competition existed between James' mother and herself—the friendly, ongoing banter between two strong-willed women with different ideas on childrearing. Julia tied her *kapp* strings behind her neck, picked up the bar of soap, and began to scrub her small grandson.

Emma stepped over her legs to get a fresh towel from the linen closet. "Would you like me to take over? You could help Leah and visit with Martha for a while. I don't want the boys wearing you out. They're a handful." She patted her mother's shoulder.

"*Ach*, you were this age once. I'll join the women while they're napping. I only have a month with them, and I don't want to miss a moment."

Martha's son, Noah, abandoned his kitchen toys and wandered into the bathroom. He splashed around in the bubbles and soon began peeling off his clothes to join the fun. Emma laughed as she closed the door behind her. "Holler if you need help, and we'll come running."

Julia didn't need a bit of help with the boys, now or for the rest of the afternoon. She relished spending time with Noah and Mary, Jamie and Sam, although from that day on she kept everyone away from the cow pasture. While the youngest three slept on quilts under a shady maple and Jamie played with his toy farm animals, she read her Bible in a lawn chair. She sent up a prayer of gratitude. All four offspring were home. From her vantage point, she could see Matthew and Henry working difficult rescue horses in the ring. Henry appreciated his big brother's advice and assistance, while Matthew was only too happy to help. During supper last night, he'd monopolized the conversation with grand ideas to bolster Henry's business. Simon had nodded with approval half a dozen times.

Emma had come home for a one-month stay as promised. Tonight James would join his family for the weekend. She and Leah were making up for lost time with nonstop chatter. Because the two sisters belonged to different orders and lived miles apart, their visits were few and far between. Martha seemed content simply to be back in Ohio, even though she seldom got a word in edgewise with Leah and Emma around. Right after they finished cookout preparations, Martha crossed the street to spend the afternoon with her mother and sisters. Julia's primary concern was Leah. She worried too much about her pie business, Joanna's cheese production, and the future home of the Byler family.

"You seem to be handling the wild pack." Leah's voice drifted over Julia's shoulder as the subject of her musings strolled into view. "I was sent to check on and rescue you if necessary."

"Goodness, you girls treat me like an old woman. I'm fine. You shouldn't hold one little mishap against me."

"I'll never bring it up again." Leah winked and lowered herself to the quilt, careful not to disturb the sleeping children. After a minute of silent contemplation, she asked, "Are you ready for one more *kinskind*?" She focused on the infant, pulling her bonnet forward to protect the delicate skin.

"I'm so happy for you and Jonah. I'd suspected that might be the case with you." Julia reached down to pat Leah's head. "Have you told your sister and Martha yet?"

"Just now. I'd been waiting until I was further along, praying it wasn't another false alarm."

When mother and daughter locked gazes, Julia saw tears in Leah's large brown eyes. "Wise choice. No sense setting yourself up for disappointment."

"I was starting to think it wasn't meant to be. We've been married four years. I thought God had chosen not to grant my prayer."

"Sometimes He does tell us no, but often we simply must wait on His timing. We shouldn't fret in the meantime—worrying only shows God we have no faith."

Leah gazed across the lawn where men were setting up long tables for the outdoor supper. "You're referring to my anxiety about moving to Wisconsin, aren't you?"

"I am. Surrender your will and trust in Him. Once you send the problem up in prayer, let it go."

Leah nodded as though she agreed, but the set of her jaw and her clenched teeth indicated a different opinion altogether.

So much easier said than done.

～

Matthew Miller couldn't remember seeing his wife this happy in a long time. She'd spent the afternoon at home, visiting with her sisters and parents. Tomorrow night they would have supper with the Hostetler clan, because Mary Hostetler couldn't get enough of Noah and little Mary. The two *grossmammi*s fussed over the *bopplin* enough to spoil them like English youngsters, but he didn't mind. His wife had greeted him with a kiss when she returned in time for dinner. And if she was happy, Matthew was happy.

Sitting at the outdoor table, he studied his extended family with pride. Uncle Seth, Aunt Hannah, and Ben had eaten with them often since his homecoming. His cousin Phoebe apparently had a beau. A blond with hair hanging in his eyes arrived just as they sat down to eat. The young man watched Phoebe's every move from the opposite bench. She couldn't sip lemonade without drawing his attention. But if this Eli stuck around, *mamm* might take a pair of shears to those bangs.

James Davis, sitting across from Emma and his sister, Lily, made an effort to speak solely in *Deutsch*. Many of his pronunciations left much to be desired, but he'd improved since Julia had taken him to task. Leah and Jonah, reunited after a week's separation, whispered across the table like a courting couple instead of two people married several years. And his father encouraged everyone to eat more hamburgers, corn on the cob, and potato salad as though the Millers teetered on the brink of starvation. Matthew loved being home. As much as he enjoyed his new position at Rolling Meadows, no place on earth offered as much joy and love as Winesburg.

When the women stacked dishes to be carried inside, Phoebe and her mysterious Eli wandered toward the pond, deep in conversation. Seth and Ben headed home for evening chores, but they would return later for pie and coffee. Henry and Dad went to milk cows and then feed and water livestock. And Matthew was left to his thoughts and reminiscences of what might have been. After refilling his coffee mug, he strolled inside the horse barn. Overhead, barn swallows were settling down for the night in rafter nests, while swifts continued to dart through the open loft window, gobbling up bugs for supper. Matthew watched their frenetic activity with fascination. How he longed for his own barn instead of a converted garage barely large enough for one buggy horse.

"Bird-watching in barns these days, Matty?" James Davis approached with a smile and hearty handshake.

"Birds roosting in the rafters are one of my fondest memories. But these are probably the grandchildren of birds I remember from childhood. The owners of the stable where I work would faint if they saw this." He pointed at the rafter nests. "They put mesh over every possible entry point in barns for expensive horses." He settled on a hay bale with a contented sigh.

"I need to pick your brain for a while." James settled on the bale to Matthew's right. "My brother picked up a horse at auction with both great bloodlines and markings. He could be a show horse if someone had the time and patience. He's a solid-looking gelding about two years old, showing no visible signs of abuse or neglect from previous owners, but the horse won't let Kevin get anywhere near his mouth. He still balks and tries to bite him even after several weeks of gentle treatment. He'll let Kevin throw a rope around his neck and ride him bareback around the paddock, but he won't let anyone come close with a bit and bridle." James pulled up a blade of hay to chew.

Matthew needed no long period of consideration. "Even though he looks healthy, he was probably lip-twitched by a former owner. It's a lip chain people once used to break horses—very old-fashioned and banned by all breeder and trainer associations. Thank goodness, you almost never see those nasty things anymore. Ignorant owners thought you had to break a horse's spirit to train them. That sort of thinking did more harm than good. Luckily, few people still maintain that viewpoint." He shook off the depressing mental images. "Kevin's horse most likely had a painful infected lip at some point. Even though it might be healed, it's no surprise the horse won't let anyone near his mouth." Matthew shuddered while his back stiffened with anger.

"What do you think Kevin can do?" James' expression also revealed his opinion of the cruel people in the world.

"He'll have to find a whole lot of patience…and pray. It might take a long time before the horse stops fearing the bit. That's probably why the owner unloaded him at auction, despite impressive bloodlines."

James stoked his beard sagely. His was a better-trimmed version of an Old Order beard. "I'll recommend both to Kevin."

"I have a question for you, James. Do you board and train saddlebreds at your place in Charm?"

"We have bred and sold some in the past, but we don't have any now. Buyers around here are looking for Morgans, Haflingers, Standardbreds, and, of course, draft horses. We get an occasional call for Tennessee Walkers or Thoroughbreds, but saddlebreds are pretty much out of the Holmes County's price range."

Matthew puckered his lips in thought. "I remember a few English folks with deep pockets. If they were to suddenly take interest in the saddlebred show circuit, you could add a breeding program easy enough. You have the right facilities with heated barns, indoor arenas, and an outdoor show ring. You can't believe how much money could be made tapping these rich folks. They spend tens of thousands of dollars to buy their daughters a hobby. And then thousands more each month for boarding, training, and outfits for those girls to wear in shows." Matthew struggled not to sound reproachful.

James' blue eyes squinted as slanted rays through the loft window illuminated his face. "I'll pass this along to my father. He might ask our equine manager to check into potential demand in the area. But I can tell you that my New Order bishop sure wouldn't like *me* involved in such a vocation. He only likes horses that pull buggies."

They laughed like longtime friends. "It's just a suggestion. The saddlebred people pay plenty of money to board their horses at certain stables, as though whoever shovels out the wood shavings makes a difference in their point standings. And the tips for trainers and grooms…I know trainers who receive five-thousand-dollar Christmas bonuses and grooms who get twenty-dollar tips just for tacking a horse fifteen minutes."

"Money! Is that all you can talk about, Matthew Miller, even back home?"

Both men's heads snapped toward the soft-spoken but petulant voice of Martha Miller. "No, *fraa*. If you'd arrived sooner, you would have heard our lively discussion on injured horse lips." Matthew kept his tone equally controlled.

James slid effortlessly off the hay. "I'm going to look for my Emma. I need to spend time with her, while you two could use some time alone. Thanks for your advice, Matty. I'll see ya tomorrow. Good night, Martha." He tipped his battered hat brim and strode out the door.

Matthew turned his full attention on his wife. "You shouldn't speak to me like that in front of James. Save what you have to say until we're alone." He clamped down on his back teeth, trying not to frown.

Martha shifted her weight between hips, blushing to a bright shade of peach. Her freckles blended into obscurity. "*Jah*, that's how I was raised. Not to air your troubles like laundry on a Monday wash line. But I was peeved to hear you going on and on about the almighty dollar—to James Davis, no less. His family doesn't need advice on how to get rich."

A silence fell between them as he silently counted to ten. He'd only reached five before he spoke. "I wasn't doling out financial advice, Martha. We were talking about horses, so I brought up the topic of saddlebreds. Would you prefer I not talk about my job or the place where I work?" He crossed his arms too, a matching stance of defiance and annoyance. "Perhaps you could supply me with a list of approved conversation topics."

Her flush deepened to plum. "Talk about what you will, Matthew, but it's a sin to dwell so much on money."

He held her gaze for a long moment. "I thought you wanted us to buy a farm and move from that rental house. People who give no thought to finances don't buy their own property. They blow around from place to place like dead leaves in the fall. Is that what you want for our family?"

She lowered her chin to glare at the straw-strewn floor. "No, but some days I don't know what I want. I only walked out here to say the pies had been sliced, in case you wanted your first choice. Coffee's still hot too. Would you like to come up to the house?" She glanced up tentatively.

He leaned back on his elbows, exhaling his breath. "I'll be up by and by. You go in now. I want a tad more peace and quiet."

She opened her mouth to protest, but then she shut it just as quickly. Nodding her head, Martha disappeared into the growing gloom as silently as she'd arrived. And Matthew was left with a sour taste in his mouth, despite consuming an exceptionally delicious supper.

Twenty-Three

Phoebe had been so shocked by the appearance of Eli Riehl in her uncle's driveway that she nearly choked on her corn on the cob. A kernel slipped down to lodge in her windpipe that would have led to her demise had cousin Emma not whacked her hard on the back. The corn kernel flew out and hit poor Henry's shirt. That alone could have led to death-by-embarrassment if Eli had witnessed the scene. "Excuse me a minute," she said, rising to her feet. "*Mir leid*, Henry." Phoebe hurried to greet the newcomer as he tied up his horse under a shady elm.

"Good evening, Miss Miller. Any food left for a weary traveler from the western fringe of Winesburg?" Eli flashed a grin that nearly caused her knees to buckle.

"I believe we could scrape a few pots to fix another plate." She stood stock-still with her perspiring hands clasped behind her back. She longed to throw her arms around him and give him a hug, considering the ordeal he'd gone through. Eli had saved his father's life, according to reports from her uncle. He'd also taken over full duties on the farm and sent his sisters' beaus home. He must be worried and exhausted yet incredibly relieved. However, Phoebe kept her arms behind her. The Amish seldom embraced, not even close loved ones. Such a display between friends and business partners would be beyond inappropriate. "Welcome, Eli. I'm glad you came…and I'm happy to see you."

"Your cousin Leah extended an invitation to me through Rose. A rather roundabout way to hear about a cookout, but I'd take any opportunity to see you."

Mortification crept up her neck like heat rash. "I didn't think you'd be able to leave your family or I would have invited you myself. How is your father? Has his condition improved?"

Eli pulled off his hat and ran a hand through his silky blond hair. "I didn't think I'd be able to leave until the last minute. My dad came home from the hospital yesterday in a hired van. He's quite a bit stronger, with a full arsenal of medications lined up on his dresser, but he still must take it easy. At least he's home in his own bed with his wife fussing over him." Eli clutched his hat to his chest like a shield of armor. "My *mamm* got several pages of dietary dos and don'ts along with his discharge papers. It took her an hour to read the new rules."

Phoebe relaxed with Eli's cheery mood. "What did she say about that?"

"Let's see." He thought for a moment before ticking off on his fingers. "'This isn't enough food to keep a bird alive.' 'If he can't have butter, margarine, honey, jam, or peanut butter, what can a man spread on his toast?' And, 'A palm-sized serving of baked chicken or fish is what we call an appetizer.'"

She laughed as the last of her uneasiness drained away. "It's a good thing he didn't come with you. We have fried chicken, buttered corn, bacon potato salad, and chocolate cream pie for dessert."

His face brightened. "Then why are we standing around here talking? I'm so hungry the old nag pulling my buggy started to look tasty."

Phoebe punched his arm as they walked toward the table. "I know you love that horse and wouldn't eat her if you were dying of starvation."

"I do like old Bess, but she isn't the one I love." He acted as though he would punch her arm too, but then he pulled back at the last moment.

After that comment, the entire county tilted to the left under her feet. Why did he say such things? Amish men never spoke the flowery, romantic words on English greeting cards. They seldom said "I love you" to their wives, even if they felt that way down to their toes.

As they reached the table, every pair of eyes turned in their direction. Phoebe cleared her throat. "Some of you already know my friend from preaching services, but for those who don't, this is Eli Riehl."

Heads bobbed in Eli's direction while a few called out welcomes. Then everyone resumed where they'd left off in their own conversations. Eli slipped onto the bench between Matthew and Uncle Simon. While Phoebe fixed him a heaping plate, Eli joined into the men's discussions without an ounce of shyness. She set the mound of food in front of him and sat down clumsily.

"Goodness, Phoebe. Did you give me everything that was leftover?" he asked. Nevertheless, he picked up his fork and began to eat ravenously.

"You said you were hungry..." she explained, but the other conversations drowned out her reply. Phoebe took dainty bites of her dinner, more for something to do than because she was still hungry. Eli's surprise visit had given her a strange case of nerves—an ailment that seemed to hit women more often than men.

Uncle Simon waited until his newest guest had finished supper before he rose to his feet. The party soon broke up, with everyone hurrying off in different directions. Dad and Ben took the back path home to chores. Uncle Simon headed toward the cow barn to join Henry for evening milking. Jonah and James continued their discussion of the sweet corn harvest near the tire swing, while the women stacked and carried dishes to the house. Phoebe felt torn between helping them and entertaining her guest. Eli's hypnotic dark eyes locked on hers like sticky tape, making the choice rather easy.

"Would you like to walk to the pond?" she asked. "At this time of day, fish jump up to catch bugs hovering above the surface."

"I can't think of a more appealing after-dinner sight." His grin mocked and flirted simultaneously. Eli offered his elbow once beyond eyeshot, which Phoebe promptly declined.

"I can walk without tripping, but thanks for your concern. Now that your belly is full, you can finish giving me a Riehl family update. How are you coping with your father's business?"

"Dad reminds me each morning what to do when I sit with him. I eat breakfast with him in his room. Work is pretty much caught up, thanks to my sisters' suitors. They managed the farm while I stayed at the hospital. Nearby district members cut, raked, and baled our last crop of hay. Rose is good with numbers, so she is helping *mamm* keep the books and records. But now that dad is home, I've taken over all his chores."

They reached the bench near the rickety fishing dock. Phoebe sat, smoothed her skirt, and peered up, feeling uneasy. Although this had to be the most peaceful spot on Uncle Simon's farm, the air seemed to be filled with the scent of impending doom. Like an animal that could sense a coming storm, she gripped the seat to brace herself. "I hope we'll soon hear good news from the publisher. That should lift your spirits and give you something to look forward to."

His expression became a combination of disappointment and pity. "That's the other reason I came here tonight. The first was to see you, and the second was to tell you my decision." He plopped down on the bench, close to her yet still separate. "I'm not going to kid myself about writing children's books for a living. My dad needs me to step into his shoes, and that's what I need—no, I want to do. From this day forward I'm Eli Riehl, full-time swine and beef farmer of Riehl and Son Swine and Beef Farm." He spoke with conviction as his lips pulled into a forced smile.

"But what of our story? It's being considered by a publishing house right now." She stood and began to pace the dock, no longer capable of remaining immobile on the bench. This news was too unsettling to accept sitting down.

He sighed. "They will most likely say thanks, but no thanks. And in the unlikelihood they want our story, it doesn't change anything regarding my role at home."

She glared as though he'd suddenly changed into an unfamiliar creature. What happened to the happy-go-lucky man who enjoyed weaving tales guaranteed to bring a tear or a chuckle to everyone within earshot? The man who always chose the fanciest words to express himself could live contentedly turning hogs into honey-glazed hams? "But we planned to hire someone to run your *daed*'s farm from the sales profits, freeing up your time to write more books."

His face filled with compassion. "Phoebe, I researched the amount a children's book author could hope to earn using the library's computer. It isn't nearly enough to pay a farm foreman. And I can't wait to see what our books might earn, especially with a first release. My family needs my help now."

There wasn't a hint of disappointment or regret in his words, but she couldn't hold back her frustration any longer. "Well, where does your decision leave me?"

He took her hand tenderly into his. "This changes nothing between us, Phoebe. You must know I care about you. There's no reason we can't continue to court properlike. I can take you home from singings and preaching and from social events. Even a farmer takes nights off now and then." He threw his hair back from his face and set his hat back in place.

She yanked her hand back. "You're making every decision by your lonesome, aren't you? I think this changes everything."

If words could hang in the air like twinkling stars, those five certainly were doing so tonight.

He sat up straighter, his carefree slouch gone. "Was I mistaken about your feelings for me? Did I read your signs all wrong?" His poignant question joined the five words in the humid August air.

"I didn't say that. It's just that you've dropped this on me all at once. I need time to think." She stepped back when he reached for her hand again…and almost landed in Uncle Simon's pond. "No, Eli. You'll have to excuse me, but I need to sort things out before I say or listen to anything else." With that she pivoted and ran like a child frightened by thunder toward Aunt Julia's house. Past the barn she veered down the back path toward the bog, not slowing down until she reached her own home. Breathless, exhausted, and confused, Phoebe broke into childish tears of self-pity.

～

Leah crawled out of bed, trying not to disturb her slumbering husband. Despite an exhausting yet satisfying day, she couldn't sleep. But it wasn't the heat or humidity that made her toss and turn under the damp sheet. The possibility of picking up roots and resettling in a northern state frightened her. Yes, she should turn the matter over to God. And she should abandon her will to the One whose plan for His children was perfect, but good old human nature kept getting in the way.

She pulled a full-length apron over her nightgown, added a sweater and *kapp*, and crept down the steps as quietly as possible. Picking up her mother's Bible and the battery lantern from the hook, she closed the front door behind her. The porch swing beckoned with nostalgic memories of summer nights gone by. How she enjoyed being back home during the past week. As much as she loved Jonah, there was something protective and nurturing in the place where she grew up, as though she could release the breath she'd been holding for months. But immersing herself in the protective womb of her parents' love wasn't helping her face a difficult decision.

Mamm told her to turn to prayer, but what could she say that didn't sound immature and self-serving? *Dear God, please don't make me move to Wisconsin. I want to stay in Winesburg close to my mother for the rest of my life.* Considering she'd been given a fine husband along with a baby on the way, Leah shuddered at such a pathetic plea.

For several minutes she closed her eyes and cleared her mind of all thoughts—selfish or otherwise. She listened to the night sounds of frogs, crickets, and owls and breathed in the fragrance of the climbing roses from the trellis. The breeze sent a shiver up her spine as she pulled her sweat-soaked gown away from her skin. Far away a dog barked, a train whistle signaled as it approached a railroad crossing, and a rumble of thunder warned of an approaching storm. But Leah sat, limp and silent, until the pressure in her chest finally lifted. When she opened her eyes, the total darkness held no danger or mystery—it had become an extension of the Miller family cocoon.

Switching on the lantern, she opened the Bible to the book of Ruth. She sought comfort and direction from a woman who faced a far more difficult situation than she. *Don't ask me to leave you and turn back. Wherever you go, I will go; wherever you live, I will live. Your people will be my people, and your God will be my God. Wherever you die, I will die, and there I will be buried.* When Leah finished the chapter, she lowered her face into her hands. Tears dropped onto the book's worn pages, so she set it aside. Ruth demonstrated courage despite far greater tribulations than Leah faced, and she was rewarded for her faithfulness.

Any leftover shame from her self-absorption vanished. Instead, hope and a renewed sense of purpose filled her heart. Life was filled with detours and roadblocks. Wisconsin would simply become another bump in the road. Leah didn't need to pray for guidance or ask for specific direction. Her prayers had already been answered. She leaned back in the swing to enjoy the nocturnal serenade before returning to bed.

"Leah, what's wrong? Was I snoring? Don't you feel well?" An anxious Jonah Byler stepped onto the porch, letting the screen door slam behind him. "I awoke and found you gone. When you didn't return soon, I became concerned." He studied her face as though searching for clues.

Leah patted the spot beside her on the swing. "Sit, *ehemann*. All is well. I couldn't sleep. Maybe it's the heat, maybe I'm overtired, but I came downstairs so I wouldn't disturb you." She folded her hands over her protruding belly.

Jonah sat, slipping his arm around her shoulders. He tried drawing her head to his chest but she resisted.

"I've been reading the book of Ruth. And it's helped me come to a decision. If your mother sells the farm and wishes us to move to Wisconsin, I'm not going to argue. Where you go, Jonah, I will follow. We'll start a new life for ourselves in the cheese capital of the world. Those folks probably eat as much pie as Ohio folks."

Even in thin lantern light she saw his incredulity. After a moment's hesitation, he said, "My mother doesn't own the Byler dairy farm, Leah. I do. Before he died, *grossdawdi* left the business and land to me."

Darkness crowded in as she stared, blinking and confused. "Joanna doesn't own the Burkholder farm?" The query underscored her desperation to hear his statement again.

"She does not. At her suggestion, *grossdawdi* wrote a will naming me as his sole beneficiary. Mom didn't want the headache as she looked toward her golden years." He laughed. "Those were her exact words. So if you were troubled about her selling, you should have asked me sooner." He pushed one foot against the floorboards to start the swing moving.

She shook her head as though waking from a nightmare. How much stress and anxiety could she have avoided if she hadn't sat meek and quiet, stewing in her own juices? Laying her head on his shoulder, she whispered, "Truer words were never spoken. I should embroider some kind of reminder in the center of our quilt." Then a stray thought crossed her mind. "And you, Jonah? What are your plans regarding the farm? I know you enjoyed your visit home very much. Would you like to start fresh in Wisconsin someday?"

His words caressed as softly as a kiss. "If I did, I would discuss the matter with you and not let you come home from quilting to a Realtor's sign in the front yard. But no, the Burkholder farm is now Byler

Dairy. I love it here and have no desire to pull up stakes and start over. Should I ever change my mind, you would be the first to know."

Thank You, Lord. My prayers have been answered. "I wouldn't like moving away from *mamm*, not with the *boppli* on the way. I'm willing to go, but I prefer not to."

"That's understandable. Julia would chase me with a stick if I took you away since Matthew lives in New York and Emma is almost in the next county. Ohio is my home now."

Leah felt every ounce of tension fade away. "What about Joanna? She misses her sister and the rest of her family. Do you think she'll return to Hancock?"

"I can't speak for her. She does sing the praises of Wisconsin often enough—everything from the taste of their goats' milk to the taxation rate and the price of available farmland. She once asked me if I could find workers for her specialty cheese business. I assured her that with this economy, there are plenty of people looking for jobs."

Leah yawned. Fatigue had settled into every bone and muscle. "Time for bed. After your reassurance, I should sleep sound as a baby tonight."

Jonah pulled her to her feet. "No matter what my mother's choice ends up being, you and I will raise an Ohio cheese-head and not one of the more famous varieties."

The mental picture of an infant with a square block of cheddar beneath a white Amish *kapp* threw Leah into a fit of giggles. With Jonah helping her up the stairs and under the sheets, the giggles lasted until her head hit the pillow. Then she drifted into the deep, dreamless sleep of a child herself.

Twenty-Four

Emma washed and dressed as quietly as a mouse. James was in the other twin bed, and her sons were in their sleeping bags, all still asleep...and she preferred they stay that way, at least for a little while. After last night's cookout, with everyone piling into the kitchen at sunset for pie and coffee, she longed for some personal time with her *mamm* before pandemonium in the Miller household began anew.

Blessedly, when Emma reached the kitchen, Julia sat alone, sipping coffee with *The Budget* unopened on the table. She looked up with a crooked smile.

"Good morning. Is Leah still in bed?" Emma headed straight for the coffeepot.

"*Jah.* And it's a good thing too. I heard her get up during the night to go outside. Probably the heat and a kicking *boppli* kept her awake."

"I like having the kitchen to ourselves." Emma noticed the breakfast preparations before carrying her mug to the table. Julia had placed bacon in one frying pan, sausage in another, while a bowl of pancake batter waited next to the stove's drop-in griddle. She'd sliced a loaf of bread and filled a basket with fresh blueberry muffins. "Looks like you're ready for the hungry masses," said Emma. "I thought your daughters were in charge of meals, while you'd been assigned to linguistic and cultural acclimation."

"Listen to your fancy talk. That must be Barbara Davis' influence. I'm not even sure what you said." Julia grinned wryly. "Someone needs to mix up the frozen orange juice."

Emma jumped to her feet, but Julia grabbed her wrist. "Mix later. Sit with me a minute. I want to talk to my eldest daughter."

Emma blew on her coffee and added two sugars, waiting patiently for *mamm* to be *mamm*.

"I heard James telling Jonah last night about visiting the local men's prison." Julia kneaded her hands like bread dough.

"He's part of a men's group that conducts Bible studies on Saturday mornings for the inmates. They take turns, but usually once a month Barbara drives him to Wooster to participate."

Julia stared at her the way she'd done when Emma walked into the kitchen wearing lip gloss during her *rumschpringe*.

"The goal is for the men to continue attending church after their release from jail." She hoped elaboration might mitigate her mother's confusion.

Judging by Julia's expression, it hadn't. "Bible studies in English?"

"Of course in English. That's the language the men speak." Emma sipped her coffee for fortification. Grogginess wouldn't serve with this particular morning discussion.

Julia nodded. "Has he two Bibles—one to take to do Barbara's work and another for at home?"

Emma drained her mug and stood to get a refill, arranging her thoughts along the way. She wanted to tread carefully over this pond of thin ice. "It's not Barbara's work but his own, although her evangelical church performs a similar type of Christian outreach. I've explained before that New Order Amish takes the commission 'Go and make disciples of all the nations' more literally than Old Order. Our bishop encourages us to volunteer around the community, not just to other Amish families." She filled her lungs with air, knowing her mother wouldn't like the next part. "And the only Bible James possesses is in English. He uses it for personal reading and evening devotions with our family."

Julia pursed her lips into a pout. "But he agreed to learn *Deutsch* and to teach his sons by example."

"That's true. And he's made every effort to converse with the boys in the *Deutsch* spoken language. However, the Amish Bible is in High German—that's another thing altogether. He has no time to learn to read written German, besides master *Deutsch*, with all his responsibilities on the farm."

"But the Bible for New Order is the same as for Old. How does he understand the Scriptures during preaching service?"

"He gets the gist of it." Emma heaped three teaspoons of sugar into her cup and stirred.

"The *gist* of it?" repeated Julia with disdain. "As though the Savior's words were vague ideas instead of specific instructions?"

Emma bit the inside of her cheek, trying to tamp down her pique. "He takes his English Bible to service and follows along as the minister reads High German. The sermons are usually in *Deutsch* with some English words thrown in. He and the boys won't miss out on anything. Little Jamie already owns a picture book of Bible stories given to him by Barbara." Emma could have kicked herself the moment those words left her mouth.

"An English picture book?" Julia clucked her tongue like a hen at an empty grain trough.

"It's important that Jamie knows about Jesus, no matter what the language." She kept her voice soft and nonconfrontational. "The boys are learning the Amish language, thanks to your help, so they'll have no trouble during church service when they're older. And as for James? Considering how much he gave up when he left his former lifestyle and turned Amish, I believe he can be forgiven a Bible written in English."

Julia stopped clucking. "I suppose you're right, providing your bishop sees nothing wrong with English Scripture."

"He does not." Emma exhaled as the kitchen clouds began to clear. She topped off their mugs and lit burners beneath the pans of bacon and sausage. The sounds of human movement overhead drifted down the stairs. "Oh, before I forget, if you have any cast-off clothes or housewares, please set them aside for me. And if you have quilts I can sell to raise money, I would much appreciate those too. I've been spinning my poor fingers to the bone, weaving as many woolen sofa throws and lap robes as possible."

"Have the Davises fallen on hard times?"

"Oh, no, nothing like that. I've organized a fund-raiser for the first weekend of September. I must return home right after the reunion to finish preparations. I'm doing my part to raise money for a mission trip to Haiti. James' mom invited me to go—"

"Where on earth is Haiti?" interrupted Julia.

"It's half an island in the Caribbean Sea. I think it's close to Cuba. The other half is called the Dominican Republic." That explanation provided no additional clarification.

"Why is Barbara Davis going there?"

"Haiti was hit by a terrible earthquake. You probably read about it in the paper. After almost two years, the living conditions are still appalling. She'll join other workers rebuilding homes, schools, churches, and hospitals. The people still need water wells to be drilled, medical supplies, school materials—you name it. They suffered widespread poverty before the disaster hit. Christians will also have a chance to teach about a loving, merciful God while they're there." Emma smiled patiently.

"And Barbara wants *you* to go along—a little Amish gal from Holmes County? That's no place for you. It doesn't sound safe." Julia shook her head like one of Henry's balky horses.

Emma thought back on the sage advice from her beloved husband: *"We are our own family. We'll serve the Lord in our own way."* She breathed in and released the air slowly before replying. "First of all, *mamm,* I am not a little Amish gal. I'm a grown woman with children of my own. That's why I intend to tell Barbara that I won't be joining her in Haiti.

My contribution to the cause will be the money I can raise between now and then. Thank you for your concern, but I'm fully capable of thinking for myself." She smiled with as much love as she could muster.

Julia stared only for a moment. Then she rose to her feet and walked to the stove. "Good. That sets my mind at ease. And I have some quilts you could sell. I think I'll get the ladies to throw one more together. And Leah can bake pies. Folks at a fund-raiser pay plenty for homemade pies. What about birdhouses? Would Henry's handiwork bring in any money?" She began flipping sausage links while mentally tallying other goods and services she could donate.

Emma relaxed. One skirmish down, with the main battle yet to go.

～

Matthew had never felt as proud of his brother as he did that summer afternoon. Henry had sold two of his rescues, one of which had fetched a very fair amount. The men drove the farm wagon loaded with sacks of feed back from the grain elevator. After delivering the horses to their new owners, they made good use of their time and money in Mount Eaton.

"You drove a hard bargain on that Standardbred and won a great price." Matthew flapped the reins above the Percherons' backs.

"That mare will give them years of reliable service. There's not an ornery bone left in her body. The new owners understand she doesn't like to be harnessed beside another horse. Because they don't haul heavy loads, they only needed a single buggy horse. They got a good deal compared to what that mare would bring at open auction." Henry settled his hat on the back of his head to catch some direct sunlight. His orange freckles would become much brighter by tomorrow.

"And I understand your bargain basement price for the sorrel."

"That elderly couple couldn't afford much in the way of horseflesh. They only need a small horse to pull their *kinskinner's* pony cart on the back lane between two farms. No long distances or hilly roads for that old gal. The folks are real animal lovers too. I've talked to the man at socials many times. My sorrel got a fine new home after leaving the Miller Family Horse Sanctuary." Henry grinned, proud of the moniker assigned by their father.

"Nothing wrong with loving horses. You know I do too. Dad just wants your business to show some profit at the end of the year."

Henry scratched his clean-shaven jaw. "*Jah*, I know how expensive grain is when our pasture gets eaten down, but I can't leave behind horses in the kill pen that have any chance for rehabilitation."

Matthew pulled on the reins and applied the brake as the wagon picked up speed on the downside of a hill. "I understand that, Henry, but you can't keep all of them. You have to heal or retrain and then sell them. Set a limit on the herd and don't go near the Sugar Creek auction until you've sold down to that number. And you could start hiring out your services as a trainer to other folks. That could bring in cash to support the sanctuary part of your enterprise."

"I'd love to do that, but I can't be everywhere at once. Dad keeps me busy with chores besides my rehab work. I've been meaning to post fliers around town to advertise my services, but there are only so many hours in a day."

"Let's get started on those fliers tonight. No time like the present." Matthew turned into their driveway and headed toward the barn. "Why don't you unload these grain sacks and rub down the team. I'll join you in a bit. First I want to see if Martha and my *kinner* are back yet from the Hostetlers."

"Missing the little wife, are ya? That's real sweet." Henry bit back his smile.

"That woman's been gone to her *mamm*'s more than she's been home with me. I can't remember if I married a blonde or a redhead. You'll understand one of these days once you find the right gal." Matthew jumped down and began unhitching the Percherons.

"Oh, I've met her already. It's summoning enough courage to ask her out that has me flummoxed. All I've managed are a few buggy rides and small talk after singings."

"Be brave, Henry. If you can handle some of those mean-tempered nags out in the pasture, you can handle one little woman."

"Go on now," ordered his brother. "Look for your wife. I'll rub this pair down and make short work out of those feed sacks. You two are supposed to be on your second honeymoon."

Matthew dusted off his palms as he headed for the house. He and Martha never really had a first honeymoon, unless you counted the journey between Ohio and upper New York State. And he knew she surely wouldn't count that. Things had been tense since the showdown in the barn a few nights ago. He hadn't appreciated being dressed down in front of James Davis, but he had chosen not to bring it up later that night or the next day. He thought Martha would forget the matter because the harsh words had come at the end of a tiring day. But instead she'd spent almost every waking moment with her family across the street.

Matthew met up with his mother on the path to the house from the clothesline. "How was life in Mount Eaton?" she asked. "Still hopping as usual?"

"They'll need a noise ordinance soon if all that excitement keeps up." Matthew joined the ongoing joke. Only one place on earth was sleepier than Winesburg, and that was Mount Eaton.

"Where are Noah and Mary? I though you and Martha would let this gray-haired *grossmammi* have some time with those two. Mary Hostetler has been getting the larger share of that pie."

He chuckled at the way his mother turned everything into a food or barnyard comparison. But he wasn't amused by the reason for her analogy. Martha was spending too much time at her former home and his family had noticed. "I'll remind her to be evenhanded with the two *grossmammi*s." *If she's here long enough to talk to her.*

True to form, Martha wandered in midway through supper. "Good evening," she greeted, leading Noah by the hand. She had tucked Mary into the crook of her elbow.

"Pull up a chair. We have meat loaf, mashed potatoes, and fresh-sliced tomatoes." Emma angled her brightest smile at her sister-in-law.

Martha didn't meet Matthew's gaze. "*Danki*, but I ate at *mamm's*. Noah was hungry, so I thought we'd get dinner over with. Well, I'd better bathe Mary and put her down for the night. She'll fuss if I wake her up later." In a flash she dragged the children into the bathroom without another word.

Matthew glared at his second helping of supper, his appetite vanishing as quickly as his wife's backside. Leah and Emma peered in his direction, while his mother continued to frown at the closed door.

"What's Mary Hostetler cooking that's better than our meat loaf and mashed potatoes?" muttered Julia.

"Maybe she made some of that fillit-mig-non and asparagus with holiday sauce," said Simon.

"Asparagus is out of season. Canned wouldn't taste the same, holiday sauce or no." Julia's comment had been directed to her husband, but her focus remained on the bathroom door. "Noah wouldn't like that kind of nonsense food anyway."

"Noah doesn't know about your secret recipe for gravy, otherwise he would have screamed to come home." Leah patted her mother's hand.

Matthew rose to his feet and threw his napkin down on the table. "Excuse me a minute," he said, pushing back his chair.

This time Leah grabbed his arm. "Why don't you wait? Talk to her after the children are in bed."

He stared at his sister, speechless. Did everyone know about the trouble in his household? And did everyone have some marital advice to offer? "Thanks for supper, *mamm*. It was delicious." Matthew grabbed his hat from the peg and strode from his childhood home. He would go for a long ride through the woodland trails, up into the hills, and not come back until his horse was lathered and he was cooled off.

Two hours later, he rubbed down his gelding until the horse's coat shone like a show contender. Yet the hard ride had done nothing to improve his mood.

He crept into the house through the seldom-used front door to avoid his family. He didn't need any more advice. He needed a heart-to-heart with his wife. Martha was sitting by the open window in his former bedroom, brushing out her hair. Mary was asleep in the hand-made crib, while Noah snoozed on one twin bed.

She looked up when he closed the door behind him. "Where have you been?" she asked. "I didn't know where you had gone."

Matthew crossed his arms and leaned back against the door. The room grew hotter and stuffier by the minute. "I went for a ride into the hills. Where have *you* been?"

The hairbrush stopped mid-stroke through her thick mane. "What do you mean?"

"You're never here, Martha. You're always across the street with the Hostetlers."

Anger flashed in her eyes. "They're my parents and my sisters."

"And I am your husband, but you've been avoiding me since we got home."

"Your home. Your family." She stared out the window into inky darkness. Her lower lip trembled but she didn't cry.

"That's right. My parents, who would like to spend a little time with their grandchildren, if you think you can stay here for a day or two."

"No, I promised *mamm* I would help her wash windows tomorrow." Martha resumed brushing her hair as two large tears ran down her flushed face.

"*Ach!*" One word summed up his frustration as the walls of their small bedroom closed in on him. Matthew stomped out of the room, down the steps, and into the cooler night air. After considering his choices, he opted to sleep in the back porch hammock next to Henry's cot, swatting at mosquitoes while trying to find a comfortable position.

∼

"Stop scratching," ordered Hannah. "You'll spread the rash and make things worse."

"I can't help it, *mamm*. It itches." Phoebe scratched the line of red welts down her calf until they started to bleed. Both of her legs looked awful because she couldn't leave them alone.

"Where did you come in contact with poison ivy? I thought you knew what it looked like." Hannah bent to inspect her ankles without getting too close.

"I veered off the path coming home from Uncle Simon's a few nights ago. I was in a hurry and didn't watch where I stepped."

"Put on some more calamine lotion and do something to take your mind off the itch. Go get the mail, for one thing." Hannah offered her most exasperated expression. "Stop moping around the kitchen."

Phoebe complied, first with the chalky, pink ointment and then with the stroll down to the road. *Don't scratch. Don't scratch.* She chanted the words mentally until she reached the mailbox and withdrew the contents. Sorting through the stack of bills and fliers, her fingers landed on an envelope with a return address that made her stomach feel funny. Riehl and Son Swine and Beef. "Oh, my," she said, and began scratching at new bumps on her forearm. Phoebe set the other mail down in the tall weeds and tore open the letter.

Dear Phoebe,

I regret dumping everything on you all at once at your uncle's cookout. If you've had a chance to mull over what I said, I think you'll see my logic. Why would we wish to compete with money-obsessed Englischers vying for the limited number of publishing contracts? Having no easy access to computers, printers, e-mail, and a phone—things other writers take for granted—would surely doom our chances. Instead, we could sit on my front porch or yours eating ham sandwiches and waiting for cicadas to emerge from their cocoons. The quality of life lies in the small, satisfying details. In that vein, I'd like to invite you to a bonfire and s'mores roast at the Barnhart farm this Saturday. We could fondly reminisce about the mighty Niagara River or—dare I dream?— plan an equally awe-inspiring future. No pressure.

Eli had drawn a smiley face to punctuate his sentence. Anxiety gnawed at her insides, recognizing the thinly veiled meaning of his letter. She forced herself to continue reading as the itching ratcheted up a notch.

We could watch the flames dance, count the stars blazing across the heavens, or take a walk in the moonlight. Anything you like, as long as we're together. I'll take you home afterward. Get word to me if Henry isn't planning to attend and I'll pick you up too. Either way, I'm counting the days until Saturday.

Eli

Several conflicting emotions fought for control in her mind. His attention flattered her, making her feel like a sought-after woman. Yet his leap from friends and partners to friends about to plan forever scared her to the bone. Tears pricked at the backs of her eyes. She had not changed. She was still Phoebe Miller, a girl who loved solitude, horses, her artwork, and her family. But a girl who also loathed chopping onions, picking slugs off cabbages, and scrubbing the henhouse floor. She thought back to the one pig-slaughtering work bee she had attended. The sounds and smells had her running for the house. Could she ever marry a hog farmer? Could she picture herself as *any* man's wife?

Eli Riehl with his charm and flowery words could quickly snare her in his web. Nothing was quite as appealing as another person's adoration. But falling in love and getting married were the last things she wanted to do. Once babies started to arrive, she would get caught up in the grind of daily life and fade into the invisible role of an Amish wife and mother. Her time to sketch in the high pasture would vanish, along with any chance of becoming a published illustrator. All because of decisions made solely by Eli.

Phoebe grabbed the mail from the roadside weeds and marched to the house with renewed determination. Just because he had succumbed to family pressure didn't mean she would surrender her dream. After dumping the mail on the counter, she pulled pen and paper from a kitchen drawer to write a response before she lost her nerve.

> *Dear Eli,*
>
> *I understand your reason for changing your mind about our book partnership, but I'm not ready to give up on our plan. Becoming an artist is the only thing I've ever wanted. You seem to be seeking a person I am not, so I'd better skip the bonfire at Barnharts' this weekend. I have no desire to give you the wrong idea.*
>
> *Your friend,*
> *Phoebe*

A rather odd ending for so final-sounding a letter, even to her own ears.

TWENTY-FIVE

Julia drove the pony cart next door by herself. Despite several offers to take her, she knew she needed some time alone with her sister before she did or said anything else she would regret.

Hannah stared with disbelief as Julia trudged up the steps with a baking pan of misshapen muffins and a heavy heart. "You have a houseful of people, and you came here paying a social call?" she asked as she held the screen door open for her sister.

"My house is no longer full. Besides, I needed some advice, or at least a sympathetic shoulder to cry on before I muck things up more."

"Come in. The coffee is still hot. Seth and Ben are in the fields, and I sent Phoebe off to count sheep before she drove me batty. She's been following me around like a lost lamb, and she won't stop scratching her poison ivy. I can't believe you're not with your *kinskinner*."

Julia lowered herself into a kitchen chair. "Emma and her sons left for Charm this morning in a hired van. She wants to be home for a few days, but she will return next week to help me prepare for the big reunion."

"Is that what has you down in the dumps? That she took her boys home?" Hannah carried the coffeepot and two mugs to the table.

"That's barely the tip of the iceberg. She wanted to speak to her mother-in-law before more time lapsed. Barbara Davis wants Emma to accompany her on a mission trip out of the country. I fear Emma will cave in and allow herself to be talked into going someplace where there are no decent shelters, strange foods, and unclean water. And she doesn't speak the language."

Hannah's eyes rounded into saucers. "What on earth are you talking about?"

Julia recounted Emma's story, adding extra emphasis on Barbara's powers of persuasion.

"Surely Emma will hold her ground and stay home with James and the boys. She's already come up with a suitable alternative with the fund-raiser." Hannah held up a lopsided muffin for inspection. "What happened to these?"

"The oven rack was crooked. And Emma might choose to go to Haiti because of me." Julia whispered her last sentence as though afraid of the words.

"What do you mean?" Hannah hesitated with the muffin halfway to her mouth. "Why would she do that?"

"Because I've been meddling in my children's lives—telling them what they should and shouldn't do. This time my good intentions might have backfired on me." Julia felt beads of sweat form at her hairline, while her muscles ached with fatigue.

Hannah blew out a snort of air. "You've been meddling off and on for years, Julia. This is nothing new. Emma has a good head on her shoulders and would never bite off her nose to spite her face." With a grin, she bit into the muffin.

"I will pray you're right, but this isn't the only water I muddied." Julia sipped her coffee black. "I sent Leah to read Scripture when she was troubled about Joanna possibly moving the Bylers up north."

"Sounds like a good idea. That always worked for me in the past."

"She found the book of Ruth—where you go I will follow. She said she's made up her mind to be happy wherever Jonah chooses to live. She's gone back home with him for a few days too." With a shaky hand, Julia set the mug back on the table. "She might be able to find happiness in Wisconsin, but I can't bear the thought of another grandchild growing up far away." Shamefully she revealed her pitiful selfishness to her sister.

But Hannah offered no recriminations. "That would be hard for you, especially considering that Martha and Matthew must return to New York after the district get-together. I know your time with Noah and Mary has been less than adequate."

"That story is the worst of the bunch." Julia stared at her gnarled fingers.

"What do you mean?"

"Another case of my meddling." Julia gazed at the wall calendar and then out the window, unable to look at her sister. "I complained to my son that Martha was never home, that she spent too much time at the Hostetlers'. They had a bad fight afterward, and Matthew spent the night in the porch hammock. I don't think they're talking to each other yet, except for things like 'Pass the catsup' or 'Would you like more noodles?'"

"*Ach*, you probably landed on an already festering sore. Coming back home often can be tricky once you're accustomed to living on your own. Any grandmother would want time with her *kinskinner*."

Julia felt little consolation. "Simon warned me to mind my own business, but I didn't listen. He said I should let water seek its own level."

"When did he tell you this? Twenty years ago?" Hannah hooted with laughter and popped the rest of the muffin into her mouth.

"Very funny. You wouldn't be laughing if your household had been upturned."

"Actually, life is unsettled here as well." Hannah walked to the back window and peered out. "Apparently, Phoebe's had a falling-out with that young man of hers."

"That Riehl boy who came to our cookout badly in need of a haircut?" Julia reached for a muffin. "Simon said his *daed* is on the mend."

"He's the one. Phoebe had high hopes of illustrating a storybook with him because he likes to make up stories, but now she won't talk about what happened. Instead, she is scratching her arms and legs raw. Her case of poison ivy isn't getting any better. She's a mess."

"Better take her for a shot of cortisone or whatever they give these days. But if you ask me, it sounds like a case of nerves, not a rash allergy."

Hannah arched one blond eyebrow. "Stress?"

Julia swallowed hard. "There I go again—sticking in my two cents where it's not wanted."

"But it *is* wanted, and I think you might be right. If that gal ever comes down from the high pasture, she must tell me what's troubling her. She's been up there for hours. Or we're going to urgent care tomorrow for an exam and medicine. Enough is enough." Hannah dropped the curtain back into place as they heard boots stomping in the hallway.

"Hullo, Julia," greeted Seth, striding into the room. He winked impishly at his wife before opening the refrigerator. "I thought that was your pony cart in the yard. I put two fifty-pound bags of spelt behind the seat. I would have loaded more but I wasn't sure how much weight that old horse can carry." He took out the pitcher of fresh milk and poured a glass.

"What am I going to do with spelt?" asked Julia.

"It's been finely ground for baking. Hannah uses it for piecrust, bread dough, cookies—you name it. The other day she made a pizza crust from it."

Hannah smiled with affection. "I'll be using spelt flour from now until Christmas cookie time. Seth's harvest was more than anyone bargained for."

Julia remembered Seth's unsuccessful attempt to corner the corn market to make a windfall profit. "Were you unable to sell your crop to the grain broker?"

"No, nothing like that. I sold plenty and received my investment back, plus a small profit. But the yield far surpassed expectations…

and current demand at the grain elevator. I'll be giving away free bags as gifts."

"Sort of like those free samples they pass out at the grocery store on Saturdays," added Hannah. "An incentive to get folks to try and then buy in the future. Spelt is really quite tasty."

Seth ducked his head to hide a blush. "I'm going to shower before supper. Tell Simon I'll bring a few more sacks over tomorrow."

"I'll tell him." Julia struggled to her feet. "I look forward to spelt dumplings and spelt pancakes, Seth, but now I'd better start for home." She locked gazes with Hannah. "*Danki, schwester*, for not making me feel like the terrible person I am."

Hannah's grin filled her entire face. "What are sisters for?"

～

Amish farms...for as far as the eye could see in every direction. Matthew had forgotten how many hills lay between Berlin and Winesburg on his way home. He enjoyed the scenic visits more than he cared to admit. He loved it here, where the Amish weren't an exception to the rule, considered by some to be an archaic oddity. Holmes County had more Plain families than English, and what's more, both Christian sects got along well.

The fertile farm fields, the undulating acres of pasture, and a thriving tourist industry provided plentiful buyers for handmade furniture, woodcrafts, quilts, and home-canned produce. Life was good here, and he would miss the easy camaraderie he'd enjoyed at the tack shop, produce market, and auction barn. Everywhere he went men seemed to be interested in the services his brother offered. Hopefully the fliers he had passed out, hung up, or left behind with business owners would lead to new customers for Henry. As the last daylight faded into a blue-black sky, he lit his battery safety lights and stepped up the gelding's pace. His trip would take longer than anticipated, even though he'd hitched up the fastest horse in Simon's barn. Dark clouds warned of the coming thunderstorm. He could only hope that the storm in the Matthew Miller family would soon blow over.

A sole kerosene lantern burned in the doorway when he finally drove the buggy into the barn. His father sat just inside, out of the rain, puffing away on a corncob pipe. "You're smoking, *daed*?" he asked, jumping down and shaking water droplets from his poncho like a dog. In all the years he could remember, he only recalled seeing his father smoke a pipe once—the summer Aunt Hannah moved to Ohio with her flock of sheep and independent ideas. She and Simon had butted heads like ornery goats, especially when Uncle Seth began courting her, until the two finally made their peace.

"Only half a pipeful, solely to test the batch Gabe Esh has dried. Seems to me our growing season in Ohio is too short for tobacco to be a cash crop." He puffed away, not inhaling much of the smoke. "No need to mention this to your *mamm* and worry her for naught."

Matthew cross-tied the Standardbred in the center aisle to rub him down after the hilly trip from Berlin. "Well, because this will be a one-time test, I'll keep quiet." He offered a good-natured wink at the amusing role reversal, but Simon's face remained composed and somber.

"Stayed out late tonight, son. Your family's probably asleep by now."

It was then that Matthew realized his father had been waiting for him. Two statements of the obvious were precursors to a larger discussion looming like those storm clouds. "I was circulating fliers to advertise Henry's horse training services. He doesn't have much chance to get to town with all his chores." He concentrated on drawing the brush through the chestnut coat with long, even strokes.

"Always plenty of work to do on a farm." A third statement of the obvious, yet Dad continued to sit puffing on his pipe.

Matthew waited, keeping an eye on their barn cat. It was in pursuit of a mouse, and he didn't want it to startle the gelding into kicking. Overhead, the barn swallows chattered away with bedtime stories to their young fledglings. After several moments, curiosity got the better of his cautious reserve. "Something on your mind, *daed*?"

"*Jah*, I suppose there is. Not that I have any intentions of meddling in my *kinners'* affairs."

That brought a smile to Matthew's face. "Meddle away. You might not have much chance to do that after next week." He used a metal pick to work some knots from the mane and tail.

"Your *mamm* tells me there are bad feelings between you and your *fraa*. Been going on a while now. That ain't right. You shouldn't let the sun go down on your anger." Simon tilted his head up to assess the night sky. The rain had dwindled to a drizzle, while a yellow half-moon attempted to break free from a bank of clouds. "As the sun has long since set, it might be time to patch up your differences, if'n Martha's still awake, that is."

Matthew huffed out his breath, similar to the horse when the comb hit a nasty tangle. "I'm no boy anymore, Pa. I'll take care of what goes on in my household. We've endured rough patches before. This one will pass too, same as the others."

"Harrumph." Simon's grunt accompanied a knock of pipe ashes into a refuse bucket.

Matthew picked up the brush again to concentrate on the lower flanks, determined not to fall into his father's trap. But after a minute of uncomfortable, anxiety-filled silence, he couldn't keep from offering a weak defense. "It would help if Martha realized that I'm the head of the family." He jumped back as the gelding shifted nervously in the cross ties.

"Uh-huh," said Simon, as unconvincingly as humanly possible.

"It states right in the Bible that a man is head of his household and that the wife should mind him, instead of throwing up barriers and excuses at every turn in the road."

Simon braced his hands on his knees while his brows stitched together between his eyes. "I'm well aware what Scripture says about marriage in the book of First Peter. I also know that a smart *ehemann* makes decisions after listening to his wife's good counsel. What kind of husband are you?" He peered up with curious interest.

"Dad, I don't want to argue with you. The problem is that Martha doesn't like living in New York. She hates raising the children away from our families, and I doubt anything will make her happy unless I announce we're throwing in the towel and moving back to Ohio." He tossed the brush into the tack box with more force than necessary and then unhitched the horse from the ties.

"And that's how you see it? As throwing in the towel? That sounds like some sort of failure on your part." Simon lumbered slowly to his feet. Years of backbreaking labor along with his own arthritis made him move like a very old man.

Matthew led the gelding to his stall, filled the water trough from a bucket, and poured oats into the wall-mounted bin. All the while he tried to organize his conflicting thoughts and feelings. "I guess I do see it like that," he agreed, latching the door behind him. "I have a good-paying job at that saddlebred stable, one many men would drool over."

Simon's mouth twisted as though tasting sour lemons. "Does it make you feel superior to have something others may covet?"

Matthew whistled through his teeth. "I'm explaining myself poorly. Maybe that's why I can't make any headway with my wife." If he'd expected his father to disagree, he would have been disappointed. Simon nodded and stroked his beard.

Matthew walked back to his father, standing almost a head taller than the older man. "I only mean this job is my chance to make money—money we can use to buy our own farm someday. Land isn't getting any cheaper or more plentiful—not here, not in New York. I want to create something I can one day leave to Noah, something he can then leave to his son and so on. Amish farms are divvied up between too many sons, leaving too little land to farm. I want to buy English land, and this job at Rolling Meadows pays me enough to set money aside."

Simon mulled this over. "Haven't you saved anything yet?"

"*Jah*. I've been saving since we moved there."

"Prices have fallen here while you've been gone. Might be worth your time to look into things. I don't want to tell you your business, but sometimes a man must take what he's got and pray it will be enough. Stop waiting for the deal of the century." Simon walked away as one hand rubbed the small of his back. "Pick your priorities. Ask yourself what's really important in life." From the doorway he spoke without turning around. "You have a few things to think about, son. *Gut nacht.*"

Just a few? Matthew rolled his eyes and shook his head. Yet even after he was tucked up in bed, he couldn't seem to stop thinking about them until dawn finally ended his restlessness, next to a woman who only pretended to be asleep.

Twenty-Six

Phoebe slid off her favorite rock to her knees and began stuffing her tablet and pencils back into her tote bag. She'd turned her drawings into crumpled wads of paper, which would end up in the burn barrel on her way back to the house. Nothing sparked much creativity today, not *mamm*'s flock of frisky sheep, not the changing cumulous cloud formations in an azure sky, not even the majestic pair of eagles that soared on warm air currents, waiting for their next tasty prey.

Even watching the adorable lambs provided nothing more than a vague, disjointed sense of annoyance. They followed their ewes around the pasture like thoughtless…well, sheep, even though they were nibbling sweet grass more often than nursing these days. They were still drawn to their *mamm*s by an almost unbreakable bond. Yet if something happened to her ewe, a lamb could easily be introduced to another lactating sheep. The lamb would transfer her devotion to the new parent figure with no emotional trauma.

How much easier it was to live a sheep's life. Ewes certainly didn't wallow for days in self-pity over rams that left them for a prettier Dorset or Suffolk face. Phoebe laughed aloud at the sheer ridiculousness of her thoughts. And yet for all her laughter, for the first time her hike to the ancient stone wall had failed to bring her comfort.

Slinging her bag over her shoulder, she dug out her last apple to feed Henry's elderly acquisition. The swayback nag was living out her final years at Uncle Simon's, usually near the fence that separated the two farms because Phoebe loved bringing her apples and carrots. The mouth full of huge, yellowed teeth nuzzled her hand before chomping into the gift. Phoebe scratched her white-whiskered nose. "I see you still haven't made friends, old girl. And apparently, it bothers you not." The mare shook her head in complete agreement while chewing the apple. She tossed her tangled mane into the breeze as though she were a prized show horse.

When Phoebe started down the well-worn path toward home, an unsettling idea crossed her mind. *I'm no different than an orphaned lamb. Once I clung to* mamm *Constance's skirts, but now I hide behind* mamm *Hannah's.* Although the transition had been anything but smooth, considering her year spent speechless, she couldn't love Hannah more than if the woman had given birth to her.

Human relationships were as temporal as those of livestock. Friends moved away and new ones came along at the next barn raising or preaching service. If mothers could be replaced by new wives, then why did losing her first beau sting so badly? At eighteen, surely she would enjoy courting a bevy of young men before she married... provided she stopped lurking among livestock.

Eli Riehl. She'd closed the door on their friendship before realizing he was her first beau.

As the dirt path cut across the pasture and then followed the wheatfield, Phoebe marveled at the subtle changes late summer had wrought. Grasshoppers leaped before each footfall, while red-winged blackbirds cackled nosily from every scrub tree. Soybean leaves had already dried and yellowed, along with cornstalks awaiting harvest. She swatted at deerflies that feasted on arms already spotted with angry red sores. Dandelions had lost their flowery heads and turned to countless white seedlings blowing in every wisp of breeze. The drone of insects, the faraway yip of a dog, the clop-clop-clopping of a passing horse and buggy—summertime sounds that usually soothed her soul—no longer helped. Without clear reason, Phoebe felt she approached some destination without packing her suitcase. With a sigh of relief she entered an empty kitchen and headed for the refrigerator. Where was that can of pop she'd hidden from Ben?

"All present and accounted for?" asked Hannah.

Not hearing her mother's approach, she practically jumped out of her skin. "*Jah*, sixty-two Dorsets with eighteen lambs, thirty-eight Suffolks with twelve lambs. None have become lost or befallen a sorrowful fate with a predator." Phoebe straightened and tried to leave the kitchen with her orange soda.

"Wait, young lady. Sit at the table with your drink. We need to talk while I bread pork chops and you snap green beans."

Phoebe shrugged while washing at the sink, unable to assess her *mamm's* mood.

"First of all, pull up your skirt and push up your sleeves." Hannah set a colander of green beans on the table and turned to face her.

"What?" Phoebe pretended not to understand a perfectly clear command.

"You heard me. Your aunt thinks your nerves might be causing the itching."

"I got poison ivy from Aunt Julia's bog. She's well aware that it grows everywhere off the path." Phoebe dried her hands on a paper towel.

"Please do as I asked."

Phoebe lifted her skirt to reveal a string of flaming bumps on both shins. "The ointment doesn't seem to be working."

"Do your arms look like that too?"

"Not quite so bad." But just speaking on the topic caused some welts to itch furiously. Phoebe bit the side of her mouth to keep from attacking her skin with her fingernails.

"Tomorrow we'll take the buggy to the doctor in Winesburg. You need a shot of antihistamine before you scar yourself for life." Hannah carried eggs, flour, breadcrumbs, and pork chops to the table.

"What difference does it make? I never go anywhere I would be noticed."

"That's your own choosing. You're still getting the shot." Hannah cracked several eggs into a bowl and beat them until they were frothy. "Does this have something to do with your former book partner? I want to know what's bothering you, daughter."

"Eli didn't give me poison ivy, *mamm*, but I suppose he's the reason I wasn't minding the path and ran through vines."

Hannah's lifted eyebrows prodded Phoebe to continue.

"When he said he was no longer interested in being a writer, I panicked. And then I guess I gave him the idea I didn't want to be friends anymore."

Hannah dipped pork chops into flour, then into the egg mixture, and finally coated them with breadcrumbs so they would be ready for the frying pan. "He changed his mind about his vocation, so you dropped him for a friend? That doesn't sound very nice."

Phoebe would have loved to argue but couldn't. "I didn't act very nice, but Eli makes me nervous when we're together. He becomes flirty and says really sweet things. Yet when I open my mouth only stupid words come out."

Hannah smiled, but she quickly tried to hide her amusement. "That's a common occurrence when young people start to court."

"He's the one who wants to court seriously. He talks about the future and makes these big plans for us."

"And you don't feel that way about him?" Hannah peered up from her work.

"I like him a lot, but I don't want to get all dewy-eyed attached to anybody. What if something happens to him?" She whispered her words, even though they were alone in the room.

"Are you thinking about his *daed*'s heart attack?"

"Maybe. Heart disease runs in families."

Her mother looked truly sad. "My sweet girl, Eli is a young man."

"My first *mamm* was young. You said that yourself, but she still died. She left us, even though she didn't want to." Phoebe concentrated on snapping the ends off beans and then breaking them into the pot.

Hannah paused to reflect. "That's true. Sometimes even young people die. God may call someone home who by our perspective is just starting life. But His plan is perfect for each of us. Not everyone has been chosen to live a long earthly life, but He promises paradise for those who believe."

"So we're supposed to hope we don't fall in love with the wrong person—someone whose earthly time might be cut short?"

"Not exactly. You need to let God's love fill your heart first and foremost, because His love is the only love we can never lose. It must be sufficient, because in the end it's all we have. Our other relationships might be fleeting, but that doesn't mean we shouldn't form them. Look at the price you pay by living in fear, afraid to let people close."

Phoebe's head jerked up from the beans. "What do you mean?"

"The reward for fear isn't protection from pain; it's loneliness. You're miserable now because you have lost your friend."

"No, I got mad because he threw away our goal of publishing a book."

"He had to face the reality of being an Amish farmer. That's not the same as throwing away your shared dream. Maybe the two of you can find a way so he can have both."

She stared at the pile of bean tips, hoping they might offer a solution. "Do you think I behaved like a selfish child?"

"If you did it's because you're young." Hannah laughed unexpectedly, much to Phoebe's chagrin. "If people my age still make mistakes, surely you could be forgiven one selfish lapse of judgment."

"He was the only one who could see inside me, whom I felt safe with. And I know I hurt his feelings."

"Then you should apologize. But even if Eli no longer shares your dream, that doesn't mean you should abandon it."

"*Danki, mamm,*" she murmured, fighting back tears. "Somehow being a famous children's book illustrator doesn't hold much joy anymore." Several teardrops fell into the bean trimmings.

"Come here, dear girl. You're not so big that you can't by comforted by your old *mamm*." Hannah wiped her hands on a paper towel and opened her arms wide.

Phoebe sprang onto her mother's lap, just like the time her favorite lamb, Joe, had died. She buried her face against Hannah's shoulder and cried herself dry, praying she'd *never* grow too old to find comfort in her mother's arms.

～

Charm

Emma walked among her beloved flock of merino sheep, counting the number who could be shorn immediately. Because she'd hired a helper for spinning and carding, Emma wanted as much wool ready to be woven as possible by the time she returned from Winesburg. *Englischer*s would pay a very good price for handmade woolens, especially if the profits were going to a good cause. Her newest employee, Myra Sandoval, from Guatemala, had come to the United States with her husband on a temporary agriculture visa and work permit. They had since applied for citizenship with help from James. Myra's ambition and strong work ethic far made up for her less than fluent English. Occasionally the two women would scratch their heads, stymied by certain words they couldn't pantomime, but by day's end they had usually accomplished a great deal despite their language barrier.

The jangle from her cell phone startled Emma from her mental woolgathering. The small screen indicated the caller was her husband.

"Emma?" asked James. "Where are you? My mom stopped here on her way home from the hospital. She found the note you'd left on her kitchen table about returning to your *mamm*'s for another week." He let several seconds pass before adding, "She seems very eager to talk to you."

Emma grinned at the phone, even though no one could see her. If she knew Barbara Davis, the woman was pacing the length of their front porch, while the engine of her fancy convertible idled in the driveway. "Tell her I'll be right there. I'm in the north sheep pasture, but I'll be down in a few minutes." She clicked the phone shut, picked up Sam to avoid a short-legged pace, and took hold of Jamie's hand. "Let's run, son. Granny is here to see you." Except for the word "Granny," she spoke in *Deutsch* so as to identify which grandmother had come for a visit. He happily complied because he loved to run, and seldom did his English granny stop by without treats.

Emma hurried as fast as her long dress and the rocky terrain allowed. Rounding the house, she found her mother-in-law walking back and forth on the porch, still dressed in her nurse's scrubs. She set the squirming toddler down in the grass.

"Emma, Jamie, Sam!" Barbara hurried down the steps and swept Jamie into her arms. She hugged him tightly, kissed his forehead, and then swung him around. Her exuberance befitted a longer period of absence than two weeks. When Sam reached her side he raised his arms above his head.

"I hope you haven't been waiting long," said Emma. "You must be tired after a twelve-hour shift."

"I was, but it's amazing how two little imps can revitalize me." Barbara set Jamie down and picked up Sam to duplicate her efforts. "An instantaneous second wind." She hugged and kissed the child with the same enthusiasm and swung him in a wide arc. "Jamie, go look in the front seat of my car. I bought you boys some homemade whoopie pies, made by none other than your Aunt Leah. And take Sam with you." She set the toddler down.

"Did you stop at the Bylers'?" Emma climbed the steps after her mother-in-law, but she kept an eagle eye on her sons. Blessedly, the car engine wasn't running.

"No, her whoopie pies are for sale at the market in Sugar Creek. I stopped to shop on my way home. Is Leah branching out from pies into cookies?"

"Uncle Seth grew spelt this year and had some ground for baking. So she's trying new items. How about some iced tea? I made a fresh pitcher of it this afternoon."

"I can't stay, but I wanted to speak to you before you went back to your mother's. I have plenty to get ready before the reunion, as all the nearby districts will be there. Thanks for the invitation, by the way. I wrote it on the calendar." Barbara pushed a lock of silver hair behind her ear. "Tomorrow is the last informative meeting before our mission trip. Those who have returned from Haiti will give testimonials regarding progress being made. Why don't you join me? Then I can drive you and the boys straight to your parents' after we're done." She flashed a magnificent toothy smile and braced her palms on her slim hips.

Emma closed the distance between them, matching her facial expression in love and affection, if not in enthusiasm. "Thanks for being patient while I made up my mind, but I've chosen not to travel out of the country."

"But I already hired a nanny to care for the boys while you're gone. And your New Order sect permits airline travel and encourages mission outreach." She blinked several times with her head cocked to one side. "I talked to my son about this, and he said the decision was solely yours."

"Bring that bag up here, Jamie Davis," hollered Emma. "You boys may have one sweet treat each." She shook her head at the way they attacked the bakery as though starving urchins. Dinner had been barely an hour ago. She turned back to Barbara with newfound serenity and grace. What she had been praying about for days had been delivered. "Yes, and I thought over the matter long and hard before making up my mind. I don't wish to leave my family and travel to a foreign country. In fact, I never want to be far from home." She accepted the sack from Jamie's outstretched hand and then pointed at the sandbox. He ran off with Sam toddling close on his heels.

Barbara couldn't have looked more disappointed if she had practiced in front of a mirror. "I know seeing those videos of the Haitians' plight touched you deeply. I would have thought you'd be moved to help alleviate suffering. And we'll break ground for a new Christian church while we're there. A local pastor has gathered a flock, and they need a roof over their heads."

Emma met the woman's disapproval with confidence. "Those people, indeed, burdened my heart. That's why I'm weaving all the woolens I can for the fund-raiser I've organized in our district. Everyone I've talked to will contribute yard sale items and homemade crafts or food for the buffet. We'll serve a donation-per-plate supper the day of the sale. The last fund-raiser netted an average of twenty-five dollars per plateful. And I hope for at least two or three hundred folks to show up. The Grange donated their hall and yard for the event, while every newspaper in the area will post free advertising. The local furniture makers, the large jam and jelly producer, and just about every business in Wilmot, Charm, Winesburg, Berlin, Sugar Creek, Trail, or Millersburg has promised free merchandise to help raise money. The event will be the last Saturday of September, right before you leave. James and I are pledging five hundred dollars, plus we'll collect contributions from everyone we come in contact with. Your mission team needs more than able-bodied helpers—it needs cold hard cash to buy cisterns, septic systems, and construction materials, besides food, clean water, and medicine for those in dire circumstances." She finished her explanation with a slow smile. "Are you sure you won't have some iced tea?" she asked.

The woman stared as though not recognizing her. "Maybe I will have a glass before I head home." Barbara climbed the steps but didn't take her focus off Emma. "I've underestimated and, perhaps, insulted you, Emma. And for that I apologize. You are absolutely correct. A large sum of money will be needed to restore the island to even its humble circumstances before the quake. And if Christian churches want to multiply across Haiti, those funds must continue for years."

"Boys, come into the house," called Emma, holding open the door. She waited until Barbara followed Jamie and Sam inside before continuing. "I've had plenty of time to think while my mom worked on the boys' *Deutsch*. I talked to Leah, Henry, Aunt Hannah, and my dad to help spread the word about the fund-raiser." She placed her hand tentatively on Barbara's shoulder. "When you leave in October, you'll be taking plenty of Holmes County prayers and good wishes along with you, besides every dime we can scrape together between now and then."

Barbara turned and enfolded Emma in a bear hug. "Thank you, sweet daughter. I am so proud of you."

Emma hugged her back. Then she pulled away to pour their tea. At long last, there wasn't a single thing left to say.

TWENTY-SEVEN

Winesburg—Byler Dairy

H ere, taste this."
Leah opened her mouth and closed her eyes. She let the chunk sit on her tongue for a moment before chewing. The cheese's texture was firm yet still rich and creamy. Some sort of chewy dried fruit added tartness to the mild flavor. "Yum-my." She dragged out the two syllables for emphasis.

"Do you really like it? Tell the truth. Don't try to flatter me."

Leah opened her eyes. Joanna Byler waited with several other varieties lined up on her tray. She counted them aloud. "…seven, eight, nine, ten. I can't sample all these. The doctor warned me about gaining too much weight. I'm having one *boppli*, not twin hippos."

Joanna clucked dismissively. "English doctors. They have no idea how hard Amish women work around a farm. That weight will fall off in no time with a little one to tend besides keeping up with your pie orders."

"I hope you're right. What was that fruit? I loved the taste."

"Dried cranberries. Now try this one." She scooped up sample number two.

Leah nibbled from the spoon and smacked her lips. "Delicious. Those are dried blueberries, right? I like the crumbly texture. Most of the cheeses you've made with fruit have been soft and spreadable."

"Exactly." Joanna bobbed her head. "I wanted solid, aged chunks with dried fruit that can be sliced and eaten alone or crumbled over pastas and salads. A creamy consistency limits the buyer to spreading it on crackers or toast."

"Your son eats it right out of the container with a spoon, despite all my attempts to discourage the practice."

"That's my boy, never one to follow rules unless you chase him with a switch." Joanna assessed her tray. "What will be next? I have three mild white Goudas with currants, blackberries, or strawberries. I also tried out walnut smoked cheddar crumbles and parsley and chive Swiss. I made small test batches for family and friends."

"You'll have to wait for other guinea pigs." Leah pushed back from the table. "My stomach is signaling I've had enough, but I vote yes on both of the samples I tried. Where did you get the dried berries?" She reached for her bottle of antacids in the cupboard.

"*Ach*, I forgot to tell you." Joanna slapped her forehead with the palm of her hand. "While you were staying at your *mamm*'s for a few days, your friend April Lambright stopped by. After I finished giving her another tour of the dairy and explained what I wanted to experiment with, she volunteered to take me to the bulk foods store. I bought a bit of every seasoning, herb, and dried fruit or vegetable they had. It must have been nice having a Mennonite business partner, wasn't it? Someone to run errands and drive you places." She sampled one of her cheeses, jotting notes into a spiral notebook. "April said she might be able to fill in for me in the future while I'm gone."

Leah sipped a glass of water as some niggling questions swam through her head. *Why is Joanna expanding her cheese line if she's planning to leave again? Surely she wouldn't expect April to take over the business without prior experience or knowledge of the cheese-making process?*

And I will be no help whatsoever in the dairy during my pregnancy. Irritation began to build in an already upset stomach. She turned to initiate the long overdue discussion with her mother-in-law.

For a moment, Leah studied Joanna as she sat at Grandma Burkholder's oak table, trying to objectively analyze her. Her *kapp*, slightly frayed at the edges, sat askew. Her apron had been ruined long ago by stains that wouldn't budge despite repeated launderings. Her cool blue eyes looked almost crossed behind her thick eyeglasses. Leah's heart clenched with compassion as she watched the woman who had welcomed her into the household and treated her like a daughter.

"May I ask you something that's been troubling me?" Leah sat down in the opposite chair with her drink.

Joanna pulled a face. "Ugh, this walnut cheddar tastes as salty as pickle brine. I didn't notice that April put salted walnuts in the shopping cart." She took a long swig of iced tea before jotting down more notes. Then she pitched the rest of the sample into the trash. "What is it, my dear? Do you need something from the upstairs medicine cabinet?"

"No, nothing like that. I'm curious about…your plans for the future. I know you thoroughly enjoyed your visit with your sister. And that you still miss your former home up north and the rest of your kin." Leah forced herself to continue before her resolve faltered. "Jonah explained to me while at *mamm*'s that Amos left the farm to him instead of you as I had assumed." Her air sputtered out, leaving her breathless for several seconds.

Joanna fluttered her eyelashes. "I agree with everything you've said so far, but I'm not sure of your question." She lifted a strange-looking blue-green sample to peruse and then placed it back on the plate.

Just the color of the cheese turned Leah's gills a matching hue. "Do you plan to move back to Wisconsin in the near future? Because if you are, you shouldn't increase the number of special varieties. April doesn't know a thing about making cheese. She got in over her head at the diner. Not that it should be held against her forever," she added hastily. "But you can't expect me to work in the dairy with the baby coming. Jonah wants me to cut back my pie making." Leah inhaled a great gulp of air and waited for Joanna's list of excuses.

But the older woman merely stared at her. "Have you gone plum addled-brained?" she asked after a brief hesitation.

"It's a distinct possibility." Leah clutched her water glass with both hands. "I've been out in the yard without my full-brimmed bonnet."

"Do you think I would move back to Hancock with my first *kinskind* on the way? You and Jonah have been waiting and praying and waiting some more. Well, so have I. Now that I will finally become a *grossmammi*, I'm not going anywhere."

"I hoped you wouldn't." Leah sounded meek as a mouse.

"Rest easy, missy. I wouldn't leave you two—make that three—for all the milk in the cheese capital of America." She winked one blue eye. "I actually wrote to my sister that our next family visit would be right here in Winesburg." Joanna gestured with her hands to indicate the large, and at the moment, uncluttered room.

"*Danki, mamm.* That sets my heart at ease." Leah's eyes flooded with moisture. "There go my emotions! I've been crying over everything and nothing for weeks." She wiped her face with a hanky. "The other day I accidentally trampled a tomato plant in the garden and started to sob when the main stem snapped off in my fingers. I felt so guilty."

Joanna patted her arm. "Normal hormone fluctuations. I'm sure the tomato plant accepted your apology. Believe me, I know we've been stretched to the limits around here. I don't intend to increase the number of varieties of cheese, only replace some of the slower sellers."

Leah lurched as her future son or daughter kicked her in between the ribs. "I believe the littlest Byler has voiced their approval." She met her mother-in-law's gaze. "I'm glad you're staying. This is a two-woman kitchen, if ever I've seen one—first you and Esther, and now you and me."

"And I'm praying for plenty of future reinforcements," she added with a grin aimed directly at Leah's rounded belly.

~

Phoebe rolled steamed cabbage leaves around balls of seasoned meat and rice until she and her mother filled three huge roasting pans. They put shredded cabbage between the gaps and then poured enough tomato juice to cover the top layer.

"They are finished," announced Hannah. "Now we'll have plenty of pigs-in-a-blanket to feed people whenever we need them." She pulled her spotted apron over her head and washed her hands at the sink.

Phoebe did the same, but somehow she had managed to stay much cleaner. "I'm glad to help, but I thought Aunt Julia was serving hamburgers, hot dogs, and bratwursts at the weekend reunion. Why do we need all of these?" She didn't mention the cakes, cookies, and muffins they planned to bake tomorrow.

Hannah called Ben inside to carry their pans to the basement refrigerator before answering Phoebe's question. "Simon and Henry will grill for the main meal, but folks are arriving early Saturday and staying all day. Many who live far will spend the night and attend preaching on Sunday morning. Some will sleep here and others at the Hostetlers'. *You* might eat like a chickadee, but that's not commonplace in our district." She laughed with her usual abandon. "Folks will eat several times on Saturday and Sunday, beside us Millers, who will still be cleaning up come Monday."

"Aren't families bringing side dishes to share?"

"You know they will. Don't worry, dear girl. If too much food is left over, we can always send some home with guests."

"Maybe I could deliver some to the Riehls, in case they don't show up."

"They have been invited. Haven't you heard from Eli?"

"Not yet, although he probably just got my note of apology. I included a separate invitation to the reunion picnic, so he can see Matthew and Martha if for no other reason."

"I'm sure he'll come if he's able." Hannah handed the last pan of stuffed cabbages to Ben, who waited at the top of the stairs.

"Since we finished cooking and we're having leftover soup for supper, would you mind if I took the buggy to the library? There's plenty of daylight left."

Hannah's face filled with pity. "I know it's Wednesday, but I doubt Eli will show up. He has so many responsibilities on the farm—"

"That's not why I'm going. Mrs. Carter is working today, and I have an idea I'd like to discuss with her, as long as I can still have one afternoon in town a week."

"I'll mention it to your *daed*, but I think it'll be fine." Hannah's expression brightened considerably.

Within ten minutes Phoebe had changed her dress and *kapp* and was headed to Winesburg in the open buggy. No more hiding in the high pasture with the sheep and her sketch pads. She'd discovered she liked people more than she realized, children in particular. And even if she never published a single artistic creation, she didn't want to live like a scared rabbit anymore.

Worry is the handiwork of the devil. Those who have faith walk boldly.

She took her first bold step across the library threshold. "Hello, Mrs. Carter," she greeted. "How have you been?"

The bespectacled librarian's head bobbed up. "Fine, and you, Miss Miller? Where is your friend Eli? Any news yet on the book?" Once Phoebe had broken the conversation ice, the woman's questions flowed like a river.

"I'm well, thank you. Eli is tied up with chores. I sent the book proposal to the list of publishers we compiled. And I've heard back from one that it's under consideration."

Mrs. Carter clapped her hands, causing quite a racket considering their surroundings. "That's wonderful news—a step in the right direction."

Phoebe nodded in agreement. "The other day I sent the editor a letter explaining that I'm Amish." She felt a blush climb up her neck into her face. "I neglected to mention that in my proposal. I was afraid they wouldn't consider us."

"I would think that would add credibility to your farm tale."

"Maybe so. And Eli wanted no false pretenses about our ability to market the book on the Internet, besides our limited access to telephones and computers for revisions or e-mails. It might make a difference whether they want to publish the book."

"If it does, it would be their loss."

"Thank you." Phoebe wiped her sweating palms down her skirt and glanced around at the other patrons. "Actually, I had another reason for visiting today."

The librarian rose to her feet, looking puzzled. "Let's talk at a table. I need a break away from this desk anyway."

Once they sat down at the same table she'd shared with Eli, Phoebe asked the questions she rehearsed on the ride to town. "Do you still have that story time I saw advertised on a flyer? If so, do you ever let other people read to the children? And do you think I could be a reader sometime?"

Mrs. Carter leaned back in her chair. "Goodness, you said more in one mouthful than everything I've heard you say thus far."

Phoebe ducked her head. "I'm trying to break out of my shyness."

"Good progress so far. And to answer your questions—yes, we still have story hour on Friday mornings. I would love to find a volunteer to read to the kids. With budget cutbacks, I lost my part-time helper. So if you read the stories, I could use the time to shelve books or request new releases from the main branch." She drew a small notebook from her pocket. "Could your parents spare you Friday mornings instead of Wednesday afternoons?"

"Yes. I know my mother won't mind giving me a morning off. I'll get up early for chores before I leave. She wants me to mingle more with other people." Phoebe glanced at the two young Amish men who'd walked through the door, momentarily stopping her heart. Unfortunately, neither had long silky blond hair hanging in his eyes. She refocused on Mrs. Carter. "I love little kids and I love stories, so I know I would enjoy doing the story hour."

The librarian stuck out a hand to shake. "Write your name, address, and an emergency phone number in my book. If you can't come some morning, don't worry. I'll always be here to take over, but if you're agreeable, be here by ten o'clock each Friday."

Phoebe pumped hands energetically, something Amish young women seldom did. Then she remembered the big party in three days. "May I start next week instead? This Friday I must help set up for the Miller family reunion to celebrate my cousins' visit from New York."

"That will be fine. Could you bring your tablet of drawings too? I know the children would enjoy seeing your pictures. Most of them love to color."

Phoebe momentarily froze before responding. Show her artwork, her personal creations to a group of youngsters and their mothers? What if the *Englischers* started asking questions? What if they found fault with her liberal use of color for clouds, landscapes, and animals? What if they thought art a superficial pastime for an Amish gal to pursue?

With a jerk of her shoulders, similar to old Miss Bess up in Uncle Simon's high pasture, she shook off her doubts and insecurities. "I'd be happy to bring my sketch pads for whatever value they might have during story time."

"Wonderful! You'll never know if there are budding artists in the group who might be encouraged."

"Will you select the books for me?"

"You could sort through the stacks right now if you like."

Phoebe glanced at the chair once occupied by her former best friend—the man who made her feel it was okay to be different, who told her she was both talented and pretty—and felt an overpowering sting of sorrow. What if no one ever felt that way about her again?

Mrs. Carter was watching her. Before she regretted taking on a volunteer who might be a tad off-kilter, Phoebe blurted out, "I'm sorry. I just really miss Eli. We had a falling-out, and I'll probably never see him again. So if you would pick out the first books, I'd be grateful."

Where is all this true confession coming from? It is so... English.

Mrs. Carter offered a maternal smile. "No problem. I'll select the stories to start you off. But I wouldn't worry about never seeing Eli again—we live in a very small town." She laughed and, surprisingly, so did Phoebe.

"You're right about that. See you in nine days. And thank you."

All the way home Phoebe planned and schemed. She wouldn't leave life up to chance regardless how small Winesburg was. She would take the Riehl family a basket of leftover food after the last person had gone through the buffet line. She would ask—no, beg—him to take her back as a friend. And she would tell him she would love to attend social events in the future.

He didn't have to stay forever.

He could decide at any time she wasn't worth the trouble.

But in the meantime she planned to enjoy herself.

This is the day the Lord has made. And we haven't been promised any others. God's plan for her would unfold whether she were hiding behind a rock or attempting the impossible.

"Git up there." Phoebe slapped the reins over the mare's back. "I need to bake something special to take to the Riehls," she said to the horse. Cousin Leah believed the way to a man's heart was through his stomach. If that was true, it was time for the Phoebe Miller lemon cake with lemon zest icing—her one and only specialty. And she prayed that what had worked for Leah would work for her.

TWENTY-EIGHT

Winesburg—Last Saturday of August

T hank You, Lord!" Julia's exclamation guaranteed that none of the Millers still slept on the long-waited day of the reunion. She didn't need a high-paid, overdressed weatherman to tell her there would be no rain today. The sky was a clear, infinite shade of blue—as though you were looking into heaven itself. A few lacy clouds, harmless and benign, scudded by on the breeze.

Guests would soon start arriving by the buggy load, bringing food and drinks and a desire to socialize, no matter what the weather. But a rainy day forced women to cluster on porches and inside the house, while men congregated in barns and outbuildings. Still doable—country folks always found a way around bad weather—but nowhere near as enjoyable. And a house would stay cleaner with the majority of people outdoors. Groups of chairs had been set up in the shade for conversation. Paths into the cool dark woods provided opportunities for courting couples to find privacy. A clear, spring-fed pond for swimming or dangling one's feet beckoned, while horseshoe pits and volleyball awaited the athletically inclined.

Julia peered out the back window. Sure enough, Henry and Matthew were setting up the volleyball net, using a can of yellow spray paint in the short grass to mark the court's boundary lines. Serious play called for serious attention to detail. She enjoyed seeing her sons involved in relaxation for a change. The two had huddled in deep discussion for the past month, deciding how to turn Henry's save-the-horses project into a profitable enterprise. Those conversations made Simon a happy man. Lately, he'd started dropping not-so-subtle hints, such as "Have you noticed the price of oats at the elevator lately?" Or, "How can anyone charge six dollars for a box of wood shavings? The furniture makers would just throw them out if not used for bedding material." And, "Having a horse lover like Lily Davis in the family sure is a blessing. Otherwise, the bills from any other vet would have put us in the poorhouse long ago."

Julia chuckled to herself. There was no such thing as an Amish poorhouse, but her *ehemann* loved that English term just the same.

"Is everything all right?"

The female voice from over her shoulder didn't startle Julia the way it should have. She'd been expecting someone to interrupt her few minutes of peace and solitude in the kitchen, but she hadn't expected her daughter-in-law. Martha had stayed as elusive as a rabbit in a forest loaded with coyotes.

"Yes, child, everything is right as rain. Just enjoying a cup of coffee before the busy day begins."

Martha walked to the cupboard for a mug. "You haven't had a moment to yourself since Matthew and I arrived. What with Emma coming with her boys and Leah here as often as not, your house has been busier than the Greyhound station in Cleveland." She filled her cup so high she had to bend low to sip it down.

Julia waited until Martha straightened and then looked her in the eye. "Other than we could have used another bathroom, I wouldn't have changed a thing. I loved having everyone here these past weeks. I wish Emma, and especially you and Matthew, lived closer." She watched the twenty-four-year-old face crumple with misery. Martha's large, luminous eyes filled with tears that quickly overflowed and streamed down her face.

She set down the mug and ran to Julia, throwing her arms around her waist. "I'm so sorry, *mamm* Miller. I owe you a big apology. I've been horrible since I arrived." She buried her face into Julia's shoulder, sobbing like a child.

Mamm Miller? She could only remember one other time Martha referred to her as such, and that had been on her wedding day. She'd always used her given name.

"What is it, dear? What's bothering you?" Julia had a good idea what it was about, but she decided to let this rose unfold on its own.

"I've taken the *kinner* across the street every chance I got, almost every day. You've hardly spent any time at all with Mary and Noah." Her face remained obscured while the sobbing continued unchecked.

"Understandable, I suppose. The Hostetlers are your family, Martha. Your *mamm* loves her *kinskinner*." Julia allowed the charitable side of her nature to surface.

"*Jah*, that's true, but that's not the whole reason I'm never here." Martha pulled back and brought up her apron to dab and hide her face. "I hate living in New York. I'm lonely when Matthew's gone all week at that fancy horse stable. And I'm frightened that something will happen to Mary and Noah while he's gone that I won't know how to handle. Every weekend when he comes home we're so busy running errands in town, or doing chores around the house, or socializing with our new district that we have no time for each other. Before I can blink twice, it's six o'clock Monday morning and he's headed back to work." She stepped away from Julia and sank into a chair. "I want to move back to Ohio so much."

Julia glanced out the window for the whereabouts of her sons. They were both still working in the yard, building up a pile of branches for the evening bonfire and marshmallow roast. Matthew wouldn't appreciate his *fraa* pouring out her heart to his *mamm*. "Have you discussed this with him? Let him know how you feel?"

"Many times. He insists we must stay where the pay is better to save money for a down payment on a farm of our own. *Land ain't getting any cheaper or more plentiful,"* she mimed in a masculine tone of voice. She sat down at the table and slumped forward, placing her forehead on the hard wood surface. "I'd rather live in a chicken coop at my parents' or in one of yours than return to New York. Folks in our district are nice enough—it's not that—but they're not family and we're not home." The young woman began to cry again as though her heart would rend in half. Then, suddenly, she bolted upright, drying her face for a second time. "But I didn't look for you this morning to pour out my troubles. I wanted to tell you I'm sorry I took my frustrations out on you just because I was angry with Matthew. We'll be heading back to New York come Monday, and I've deprived you of your chance to spend time with your *kinskinner*. That was selfish and I'm ashamed of myself." She met and held Julia's gaze.

Julia heard the sound of little feet on the steps, signaling they soon would be interrupted. Shuffling to where the younger woman sat, she placed a hand on her shoulder. "I understand and forgive you, but I wouldn't give up hope yet. I know Simon had a heart-to-heart with Matthew a short time ago. He might have needed time alone to think matters through."

Martha's face began to clear. It was easy to see why her son fell head over heels in love with the girl—she truly was pretty with a gentle heart, despite their recent friction. "He did? About what?" Hope curtailed the river of tears.

"I don't know exactly, only that he wanted to make sure both his sons had their priorities straight."

Jamie Davis and Noah Miller bounded into the room with typical childlike exuberance. "Go wash your face, Martha, and be strong. God will make this and all things right again. I'll feed bowls of cereal to these two. We have a busy day ahead of us." She smiled at her daughter-in-law, who immediately did as instructed.

Soon the early bird buggies would arrive, mostly friends of Matthew's to help set up tables in the barn and take benches off the church wagon. Women would come to mix large batches of sun tea and lemonade, and carry the desserts and baked goods to where they would be eaten later. Her daughters would soon return from morning chores to organize keeping cold all the appropriate side dishes. But just for a few minutes, Julia scooped two bowls of oatmeal for her grandsons, and then she drew big thick hearts on the surface with Hershey's syrup. Neither boy's mother was present to witness Julia serving chocolate for breakfast. But after all…she was a *grossmammi* and planned to enjoy every single minute of it.

~

Matthew spotted his wife in the sea of women moving like ants between the house and the main outbuilding. They were hauling foam plates, cups, and baskets of plasticware, along with bowls of fruit, chips, and whatever else didn't need to be kept cold until mealtime. This would be the best chance he would have before her sisters and friends arrived to occupy every remaining minute with gossip or tales of their children's exploits. With the speed of a determined man, he ran to cut in line just before she entered the building with a platter of sliced watermelon.

"May I have a word with you, Martha?"

Either the sun had blinded her or she was shocked by his appearance. She blinked several times and stared at her husband, gape-mouthed. "*Jah*, sure. Let me set this on the table." When she returned a few moments later, her composure had not improved. "What is it? Is there something I can get for you?" She glanced nervously over her shoulder.

"I'd like you to take a stroll with me." He tucked his hands under his suspenders.

"A stroll? It's not yet noon, and I should help the other women prepare lunch." She crossed her arms, uncrossed them, and then re-crossed them as though she didn't know what to do with her appendages.

"Look around. There must be twenty ladies here, all trying to help my *mamm*. And here comes your *mamm* and sisters up the driveway now. I'd say my mother has more help than that kitchen can hold."

Martha shielded her eyes to peer toward the street, lifted her hand in a little wave, and then turned back to him. "That's true. I suppose my taking a walk won't cause any great hardship."

Matthew stuck out his elbow, an old-fashioned gesture he hadn't used since his courting days. "I have something to show you. Let's head toward the barn instead of down the drive."

"A new horse? I know I complained that my buggy mare won't mind me, but it's too expensive to haul livestock great distances."

"No, not a horse. You're stuck with that balky mare." He winked at her, knowing he'd picked an especially slow trotter for her short trips to neighborhood farms.

Martha placed her hand in the crook of his arm. "Does this have anything to do with your conversation with your *daed*?"

He jerked his chin around. "How did you know about that?" Just before they reached the barn, Matthew pulled her off the path, cutting through the yard toward the road.

"I apologized to your mother this morning. She's been deprived of seeing much of Noah and Mary while I've been across the street. I should have brought my *mamm* and sisters over to your house more."

"I haven't seen them much either, and I'm even fonder of them than her." He made sure his tone remained nonconfrontational. They had fought enough lately to last for the next ten years. "I haven't seen much of you as well, and I'm mighty fond of you too."

"Still? Even after how I've acted?"

"Still. My own behavior hasn't exactly been a model for husbands-to-be."

She peeked up from beneath her thick dark lashes. "Do you know any husbands-to-be I'm not aware of?"

"I might, but don't change the subject, *fraa*. I didn't bring you on this walk to spill the beans about my little *bruder*." The words popped out before he could stop himself. They both broke into peals of laughter.

"Henry has a gal? I thought he'd be too shy to start courting."

"He does, but you didn't hear that from me, Martha Miller." With a quick movement, he snaked his arm around her waist, pulling her to his side.

She didn't object or pull away. Instead, she plucked some tall Queen Anne's lace that grew along the way. Butterflies delicately gathered late summer nectar. "Where are we going? Should I have packed a cooler?"

They had reached the road and for several minutes talked to the people arriving in a long string of buggies. Each family asked the same questions: "How's it being back home, Matthew?" "What are those New Yorkers like? Do they talk funny?" "You still keeping to the old ways now that you work for those rich *Englischer*s?" Finally, after assurances he would catch up to each man for an update later, the last of the buggies headed up the lane.

The pair crossed the road, jumped the drainage ditch, and walked to the shade of a gnarly Osage orange tree. The spot would provide a few minutes of privacy. Matthew remembered his *grossmammi* gathering baskets of the large green pods that dropped from this tree in the autumn. She would spread them around the foundation of the house, insisting they kept spiders out of the basement and root cellar all winter. Come to think of it, he'd never seen a spider in the cellar while *grossmammi* was alive. Matthew released his wife's hand to spread his arms wide. "What do you think of this pasture?"

Martha gazed in the direction he pointed with little interest. "This old field that the Lees own? Because livestock stopped grazing it years ago, it's overgrown with sumac, poke, thistle, and blackberry briars. There's barely a blade of grass left."

"But what do you think of it? Look at how the land rolls up to those stately evergreens. There's a nice feel to this land. It's not too rocky, and the soil hasn't been worked to death."

She squinted to focus on the pines in the distance. "Those are the old Christmas trees that Mr. Lee planted hundreds of one year. He thought they would turn a quick profit so he could take his wife on a cruise to Alaska. He didn't realize how long that variety took to mature. And not many *Englischer*s want to drive this far to cut their own Christmas tree." Martha threw back her head with a laugh. "Mrs. Lee said they're helping the planet by returning the land back to forest."

He leaned his shoulder against the rough orange bark. "There are still plenty of acres that could be planted with grass. There's access to a running stream too." He bit the inside of his cheek for concentration.

She pondered this for a minute. "Are you're talking about the same stream that runs through my parents' farm? It dries up by midsummer. That's why *daed* had to find a spring and dig a pond for livestock water."

Matthew settled his hat on the back of his head. "Ah, there are springs in the area—good to know." He couldn't hide his enthusiasm any longer.

"What's the matter with you? Why are you so interested in Mr. Lee's investment acreage?"

"Because this isn't Mr. Lee's land anymore."

Comprehension registered on her face like sun coming over the eastern hills at dawn. "Whose is it?"

"It belongs to Matthew and Martha Miller, formerly of Willow Brook, New York, and soon to be once again of Winesburg, Ohio."

"You *bought* it?" The question came soft as a child's prayer.

"I had to, once I heard my brother asking *daed* questions about it."

"We had enough money?" Martha still didn't know if she could believe it.

"Enough for a decent down payment. We'll have a mortgage, but we got a good interest rate. Because the market is still down, Mr. Lee sold it at a fair price. He said he didn't want to pay taxes on fallow land any longer." He straightened away from the tree.

She ran into his arms. "Oh, Matty. That's such wonderful news!

I'm sorry what I said about the thistle and sumac. And blackberry pie is one of our favorites." She hugged him tightly.

"We could save a few patches from the scythe. Weeds and scrub brush look better when they're your own, don't they? And we get to keep all those overgrown Christmas trees."

"They do, indeed." She turned her face up to his. "We'll be across the street from your folks and right next door to mine. That is, if you let me move here with you. I wouldn't blame you if you made me stay in New York after the poor way I've treated you." She bit down on her lower lip.

"I can't think of a better person to build a house for." He brushed his lips across hers before they started walking through the tall weeds.

"You'll build us a house? What kind?"

He laughed. "Something not too big to start, but we can always add on later. I had my eye on this property before we even got hitched. It was less overgrown, but you know what? It looks better to me now than then."

"What about your job? Good jobs like yours don't come along every day. At least, not in Holmes County."

They checked traffic before sauntering across the road. "I have prospects for a new career in mind. And if need be, I could also work at Macintosh Farms. Mr. Mac said he'd take me back anytime. But let's not get ahead of ourselves. We still have a party to go to. Folks will want to chat with us, and here we are sneaking off like a courting couple." They strolled hand in hand up the Miller driveway, under oaks and maples that had weathered storms far worse than theirs.

"*Danki*, Matthew Miller," she whispered.

"I'd do just about anything to make you happy, Martha Miller."

There it was—his heart once again pinned to his shirt for her to do with what she would. But he had a notion his future was in loving hands after all.

Twenty-Nine

"Phoebe, let's go already!" Ben halted in the path ahead with an expression that could curdle milk. "If I knew you planned to dawdle like this, I would have ridden with *mamm* and *daed* in the buggy." Over his shoulder hung a canvas bag of bats and balls, an inflatable raft, and his swimming gear.

Phoebe caught up to him as quickly as she could, trying not to jostle her perfect lemon creation inside the cake tote. "I'm walking as fast as I can. Simmer down."

"Half the Miller reunion will be over by the time we get there, and we're actually Millers." He took hold of her forearm and began to drag her. "I want to swim, play volleyball, pitch horseshoes, and paddle around in my blow-up boat. This hot weather won't last forever." He swatted a mosquito as they neared the bog and eyed her container suspiciously. "Why are you carrying that? You should have packed it in the back of the buggy with the other food."

Phoebe pulled loose from his grasp. She hadn't spent forty-five minutes bathing, pinning up her hair, and ironing her clothes only to become sweated up before reaching Aunt Julia's. "This is a special cake. It's not for the buffet table."

He looked up from under his bangs. "Not for the food table? Then what are you going to do with it at the party?"

"I plan to hide it in the bushes in the shade." She swatted something nibbling on her neck.

Ben wrinkled his nose. "You finally bake something without *mamm* twisting your arm, and you're going to hide it in the bushes? If you get any stranger, *schwester*, you'll have to look for a different family." He laughed merrily and again grabbed hold of her hand.

"Ha-ha. I might be saving it for someone special, but I don't need to tell a ten-year-old all my business."

He opened his mouth to retort but noticed her expression, perhaps remembering the last time she pulled his ear or pinched his arm. As soon as Uncle Simon's three-story barn loomed into view, he stopped dragging her and took off at a trot. At the top of the rise he paused to call back, "Good luck with that person thinking your cake is as special as you do." Then Ben Miller disappeared into a sea of friendly faces.

Phoebe skirted around to find a suitable hiding place before joining her mother, cousins, and aunt in the house. She was not, however, saddled with kitchen duties.

"The Glick sisters are looking for you." Hannah blocked Phoebe's entry into the house. "Go find them. I don't think they know that many folks, and we have things handled in here." Cheery greetings from Leah, Emma, Martha, and Aunt Julia emanated from the cool interior.

Phoebe hollered back her own hellos and marched down the steps. Rebekah and Ava Glick. She hadn't visited with them since their trip to Niagara Falls. Thoughts of standing at the rail on the *Maid of the Mist*, walking to Three Sisters Islands, and then missing the bus because she and Eli couldn't stop talking drifted back, causing the bottom to drop from her belly. She shook off the memory and located the two near the garden fence. They were chatting with some of the older married ladies.

"There you are, Phoebe Miller. Late as usual! And you live the closest." Rebekah pulled Phoebe away from the other women after polite greetings. "I've brought an add-on letter from Mary Mast in Geauga County." She handed over a folded envelope. "You can read her news yourself and then add your comments at the end. You're last in the chain, so mail it back to Mary when you're done."

Phoebe tucked the letter into her apron pocket. "*Danki.* I'm glad to see both of you. I should have written since I haven't come to any get-togethers this summer." She smiled fondly at both sisters, feeling guilty she hadn't kept up her end of the friendship.

"You're forgiven as long as you promise to start coming to socials in the future. There will be all kinds of fun events soon—cornhusking, cider making, hayrides, and bonfires. You're not getting any younger." Rebekah clucked her tongue. "Besides, Ava needs another shy person to hang out with since I will soon be leaving the ranks of single gals." Rebekah snaked an arm around Ava's shoulders.

Phoebe's mouth dropped open. "Are you engaged?"

Rebekah deflated slightly. "Well, no, not exactly, but we are seriously courting. He's just very shy."

Ava grinned with smug conspiracy as Phoebe glanced from one to the other. "Who's the lucky young man? Do I know him?"

Ava burst out laughing, while Rebekah rolled her eyes. "Of course, you know him. He's your cousin Henry. You really should pull your head out of the rabbit hole every once in a while."

Phoebe joined the laughter. "I've recently come to the same conclusion."

Rebekah looped arms with both other girls. "Good to hear. I'll expect you at the next social event. Now, walk us to see your cousin, real subtle-like. Henry and I are keeping a low profile until the fall when we see the bishop for his approval."

"You, subtle?" asked Phoebe, buoyed by their infectious good spirits.

"*Jah,* hard as that is to believe."

There was no doubt about the mutual feeling of affection on the part of her cousin. Henry had been giving the little ones pony rides inside the fenced paddock when the three women wandered up like tourists at the fair. His face turned cherry red as he stared at Rebekah and only her.

"I said, 'Hey there, Henry,'" repeated Phoebe.

"Oh, hey, Phoeb, Ava." But his focus remained glued to Rebekah while he lifted little Jamie Davis from the pony's back. "You *kinner* run along to your *mamm*s. No more rides till later."

"I'll walk them back since my job here is done," offered Phoebe.

"Ava, you must stay, please, so people won't gossip." Rebekah's lush tone of voice melted over her sister like butter on the griddle.

Phoebe chuckled while herding the youngsters back to the circle of women. Rebekah and Henry—that secret would be out long before sunset. Her grin widened when she spotted folks in line for the noon meal. The sooner folks ate, the sooner she could pack a hamper for the Riehl family. So she spent the next hour wandering the Miller farm—house, barns, and shady groves—making sure no Riehls had come to the outing. Once confident that none had, she retrieved her mother's large hamper from the porch, grabbed a handful of reusable containers from Julia's cupboard, and ran out the door...and right into Eli's sister.

"Ooofff," sputtered Rose. "Where's the fire, Phoebe Miller?"

"Rose, what are you doing here?" Her tone revealed her disappointment.

"I was invited by Leah." Rose looked crestfallen.

"Forgive me. That came out wrong. I was just on my way to pack up food to take to your place because I didn't think any Riehls had come." She held up the hamper. "Is Eli with you? How did you get here?"

"Eli didn't think Leah's invitation included him. I came with my beau."

"Oh, dear." Phoebe sighed and slumped down to the porch steps.

Rose hauled her back up like a rag doll. "There are so many people here, you never noticed me in the crowd. Go ahead with your plan. You can thank me later." She pushed Phoebe down the remaining steps.

Phoebe didn't stop hurrying until her hamper overflowed with food and she'd located Lily Davis. The tall, imposing *Englischer* was sitting with her parents at one of the long tables. "May I speak with you privately?" she whispered.

Once they had moved beyond anyone's hearing, Phoebe turned around abruptly. "I know you don't know me well, Miss Davis, but if you would drive me to the opposite side of Winesburg to run an urgent errand, I would be forever in your debt."

Lily stared at the hamper that nearly pulled Phoebe's arm from its socket and then at her flushed face. "You're Phoebe, right? Emma's cousin? Is someone sick?"

"Yes, I am, and no, nobody's sick. This situation is only urgent to me personally." She transferred the basket to her other hand. "A fence needs mending, and the person lives too far away for me to get there and back in a decent amount of time by buggy."

Lily pulled keys from her pocket. "Let me tell my parents I'll be back after an errand. I love a mystery, so let's go. Meet you at my red pickup."

It was all Phoebe could do to keep from crying as she headed toward Lily's truck. She would see Eli and she would see him today. Just as Lily started the ignition, Phoebe remembered her cake. "Could you please wait one more minute?" She jumped out and ran to retrieve the yellow cake tote from the low foliage of a lilac bush.

Lily had a bird's-eye view from where she was parked. "A hidden peace offering? A cake goes a long way to mending broken fences," she said as the truck roared to life.

Phoebe nodded, but she asked the vet questions about her equine practice in Wooster to change the subject. Within an amazingly short period of time, Lily's truck turned up the lane to Riehl and Son Beef and Swine. "I could run a few errands in Berlin since we're so close, but if you prefer I stay with you, I will."

She exhaled with relief. "Thanks, but this is something I must do alone."

"Good luck then. I'll be back in an hour and will park right there." Lily pointed to the small graveled lot.

Phoebe climbed out, lugging enough food for a small nation. With a snap of her silky blond ponytail, the pretty veterinarian drove away with an *Englischer*'s penchant for speed. Phoebe trudged up the drive to her certain doom.

∼

She left the hamper in the shade, away from the barn, and found Eli herding the world's fattest hog and her brood of piglets through an opening in the barn wall. "Let's step lively into your outdoor accommodations," he said to the sow. "So I can tidy up and redecorate your indoor quarters." He wore knee-high boots and a leather apron, but he was still quite dirty.

"Hello, Eli," she said, stepping as close as possible.

When their eyes met, his held a cool assurance that belied his appearance. "Phoebe Miller, what a surprise. My companions of late have all been porcine." He bent to gently shoo a piglet through the opening to join his siblings.

She reflected for a moment. "I take it 'porcine' has something to do with pigs?"

"It has everything to do with pigs." He closed the flap door and then stepped from the pen. "Why have you come? As you can see, I'm in no condition to entertain afternoon callers." He pointed at the muck decorating his rubber boots.

She fought back a gag reflux from the odor. "I've brought food for your family from the Miller family reunion. We were all sorry you were unable to attend."

"Ah, Miss Priss is due to deliver again, so alas, my social calendar has been curtailed." Eli noticed her trying not to breathe and took pity on her. "Go to the picnic table in the shade. I'll join you there as soon as possible."

She turned and ran from the swine barn to the grove of maples, grabbing her hamper and tote along the way. After setting down her containers, she had to wait only fifteen minutes for a refreshed Eli Riehl to appear. Water still dripped from his blond hair, which had been combed straight back from his face. His sun-burnished cheekbones glowed in the afternoon sun. He wore a clean shirt, trousers, and suspenders, but only flip-flops on his feet.

He noticed what had piqued her interest. "Don't tell the bishop about my choice of footwear."

She peered up. "Your secret is safe with me."

"What's inside?" He angled his head toward the hamper.

"There's food of every possible sort, made by everyone in the district and beyond. Tell your *mamm* to keep the hamper and containers until the next social event she's able to attend."

"*Danki*, I'll tell her." What seemed like a full minute spun out before he asked, "What's in the yellow plastic carrier?"

"Humble pie," she answered without hesitation.

That made him smile as he lifted the lid. "Looks like iced lemon cake. I love lemon cake." He dabbed a finger into the frosting.

"It's humble pie because I'm here to throw myself on your mercy. You're the best friend I've ever had, and I treated you poorly when life didn't go my way. I don't know why I did, other than the fact I'm inexperienced with things romantic. Truth is, I have fewer friends than Miss Priss has party dresses, and it's my own fault. I don't deserve you, but I'd like another chance. I will try to behave the way my mothers raised me. *Jah*, I had two *mamm*s who tried their best, yet I still turned out poorly. I like you a lot, Eli Riehl, and if you'll accept this cake as a peace offering, I would love to go to a singing with you or to a social or anywhere else." Phoebe sputtered to a stop, out of air.

His mouth twitched as he tried not to laugh. "Do you ever let a shy guy get a word in edgewise?"

"Not too often, but for you I'll make an exception."

Eli grinned wide, revealing white teeth and a generous heart. "In that case, I thank you on behalf of the Riehls for the vittles. Everyone in the family will share and enjoy." Then he picked up the cake tote and clutched it to his chest. "But this cake was a gift from you to me, and I intend to eat every last delicious morsel of it myself." He winked, and once again the geothermal plate under Holmes County shifted beneath her feet.

~

Monday Morning

Julia gazed over the yard now that the last of the weekend guests had finally departed. *Not too bad,* she thought. And with her two strong sons-in-law here to help Simon, Matthew, and Henry with the tables and benches, the remaining cleanup shouldn't take too long. And both her daughters and her daughter-in-law were still here with her to divide and distribute the leftover food. She could hear the girls squabbling on the stairs now, just like in the old days. Emma emerged first and headed into the front room with her sons while Leah appeared next and joined Julia in the kitchen.

"*Guder mariye, mamm,*" greeted Leah. "That Emma! She scolds me for monopolizing the bathroom too much. Has she forgotten her old *rumschpringe* days or the condition I'm in?" She patted her tummy before heading to the fridge for her morning glass of milk.

Julia brushed a kiss across her daughter's soft cheek. "Good morning to you, dear heart. You could occasionally use the old outhouse on crowded mornings like these. Only a suggestion."

Leah pulled a sour face. "Oh, *mamm,* you can't possibly be serious."

Julia began breaking eggs into a bowl. "Will you return home with Jonah later this morning?" she asked.

"*Jah.* I need to check my pantry for staples and supplies. I've been gone so long I've forgotten what I have on hand and what I don't. To-morrow is baking day, and I'm looking forward to it. I'll have the kitchen all to myself to bake my pies and cookies."

"And here I thought you enjoyed your time home spent with me." Julia offered a wry frown.

Leah heaved herself to her feet. "I truly have," she exclaimed, hur-rying to Julia's side. "I wasn't talking about here. I was referring to be-ing alone in the Byler kitchen." She hugged her mother's waist tight enough to hurt.

Julia tried to extract herself. "Stop, I can't breathe."

Leah released her and reached for the cheese to grate for the om-elet. She made herself comfortable at the table again. "Oh, I forgot to tell you the news Jonah brought from home. Joanna hired April Lambright as her new cheese-making partner. They'll be an excel-lent match, and I won't have to set foot in the dairy again, even after the baby comes. Nor will I have to enter the animal barns. My aller-gies to dander only keep getting worse." Her smile stretched from ear to ear. "I can remain indoors with my little one and...on the porch." She winked impishly.

"Do you think you'll be able to manage the hike to the clothesline?" asked Julia with mock concern as she poured pancake mixture onto the griddle. "Or will Jonah hire a laundry maid for his princess?" She returned the wink.

"What a fine idea, *mamm*, but Jonah already rigged a pulley from porch to barn eave. I don't have to step off the porch to hang wet laun-dry." She giggled like a child.

"I tried to tell you Jonah was spoiling Leah rotten, but you wouldn't listen," announced Emma from the doorway. Her sons ran to the ta-ble to take their places.

Leah blushed prettily and smiled into her milk glass.

"Sounds to me like you might be a tad jealous, young lady," scolded Julia. "And I believe the Tenth Commandment has something to say about that."

Emma paled. "Sorry, Leah. I've no reason to be envious of anyone or anything. The Lord has been more than generous with the Davis family." She walked to where her sister sat, wrapped arms around her, and kissed the top of her *kapp*. "I'm glad Jonah treats you so well. My James spoils me more than I deserve, that's for sure."

Leah began buttering slices of bread to toast in the oven. "It'll be hard for all of us once things get back to normal. I loved having everyone close."

"Now before they eat, Sam and Jamie have something to say to their *grossmammi*," said Emma. All eyes turned to the little boys sitting patiently with folded hands, including Martha, who'd just entered the kitchen with Mary and Noah. Emma nodded her head solemnly and then in perfect *Deutsch*, the boys said, "Thank you, Grandma, for taking care of us and teaching us to speak *Deutsch*."

Everyone laughed, except for Julia, who grew teary-eyed. "*Gern gschehne*," she said, saying, "You're welcome."

Noah ran to Julia and grabbed her around the legs. He repeated the exact same phrase. Julia patted the child's head and laughed along with everyone else. And it felt good, all the way to the tips of her toes.

"When do you have to leave?" asked Emma of Martha.

"The hired van is picking us up at nine thirty. We'll catch the ten thirty bus from Canton to Cleveland. From there we'll head back to New York, but it will only be for a short while. We'll give our thirty-day notice to our landlord so he can start looking for another tenant. And I'll start organizing my household for the move back home." Her face spoke louder than any words regarding her opinion on that.

When the women clapped their hands, the children did the same. Mary thought clapping an exceptionally fun activity.

"What about Matty's job?" asked Leah.

"He must be back to work on Wednesday, but he intends to give his notice. He'll stay longer only if they can't find a suitable replacement, but he assured me everyone is replaceable."

"At work, maybe," said Julia softly.

"And regarding the rest of his plans, he wants to tell you himself, once he's fine-tuned the details."

Everyone broke into another round of applause. Mary saw no reason why people shouldn't clap off and on all the time. So for the rest of the day and for many to come, she did exactly that.

"All right then, girls," announced Julia. "Stop sitting around chit-chatting and get this breakfast done. We have folks to feed before the van arrives. Martha needs to finish packing, and then there are always more farm chores."

The younger women sprang into action. And Julia? While they worked she lifted Mary into her arms and took her *kinskinner* on a stroll into the high pasture.

No one picked up a cowpat.

Everyone spoke only their natural, native language.

And God's grace rained down on Julia's family and filled her heart to overflowing.

Thirty

Matthew knew exactly where he would find his brother after chores. He walked through his father's barn, trying to stay as quiet as possible. One of the family's cats perched atop a stall wall, slowly scanning left and right, in case a mouse crept from his hiding place.

Light poured in through the hayloft doors and through the skylights Simon had installed in the loft workroom, where Emma once spun her wool into shawls and bedspreads. These days, the space was nothing more than dusty storage now that Emma wove in an air-conditioned, dust-filtered, electric-lit studio at Hollyhock Farms. Nostalgia welled up his throat in unmanly fashion. Fortunately, he found his brother before he began sniffling like a woman. Henry was exactly where he expected him to be—in a horse stall with a fairly new purchase. "What's wrong with this one?" he asked, peering over the stall wall.

Henry kept his concentration on the poultice he was placing on the horse's eye. The one good eye watched Henry without blinking. You could smell fear in the beast's sweat oozing from every pore. Yet the animal didn't pull away from Henry's gentle touch. Amazing. With the poultice in place, Henry taped it securely with adhesive strips. Only then did he answer Matthew's question. "Infection from a scratched cornea. Lily cleared most of it up with a round of antibiotics, but he's still blind in this eye. I'm hoping the sight will return with these herbs. This is my last hope for him."

"Good luck," said Matthew, knowing no one Amish would want a buggy horse without two good eyes. Once Henry closed the stall door behind him, Matthew asked, "Do you have time to take a ride with me? I picked half a dozen apples to take to that old nag that hangs out in the sheep pasture."

"Sure," Henry readily agreed. "You want to saddle up a pair?"

"Let's ride bareback like we did when we were boys. I think we can still manage to stay astride without falling off and breaking our necks."

"Time will tell." Henry must have had misgivings because he selected two of the smallest Morgans they owned.

"Shorter distance from horse to the ground?" Matthew combed his beard with his fingers.

"You got it. Just in case." Henry attached halters and lead ropes and then both men mounted as though they still rode this way every day.

"I'm glad you're not mad that I bought the land from Mr. Lee," said Matthew as they rode side by side at an easy pace.

"Are you kidding? I'm happy you'll be living across the street. I'll know right where to come when I have a question. And I'll always have plenty of questions. I could never save enough for a down payment anyway. I knew Mr. Lee had dropped his price a few times due to the economy, so I got brave and finally asked him. My teeth nearly fell out when he told me how much he wanted."

Matthew reached up to pluck some low-hanging leaves. "Land in Holmes County is growing more dear each year. That's why I put up all those fliers for you to drum up more business."

"You sure did a lot of salesmanship at the reunion, trying to sell my services to just about anybody who crossed your path. I don't know where you learned conversation savvy. I get tongue-tied so easily."

"It develops over time from talking to folks. You usually only talk to those who neigh or whinny in response."

"That's why I'll be living with *mamm* and *daed* for a long time to come." Henry threw his head back with a belly laugh.

Matthew, however, sobered. "Dad's glad you're here and not planning on going anywhere. He's slowing down. I've watched him this past month, and he's not as spry as he used to be." The twin Morgans gingerly crossed the shallow creek bed as though afraid to get their hooves wet. "Git up there." Matthew applied his heels lightly to the horse's flanks and he trotted up the other bank.

"I told Rebekah that if she'll marry me, I'll gladly build her a little house on the property." Henry wiped a bead of sweat away with his sleeve as they paused on the next rise.

Matthew stared, surprised about his brother's candor. "What did she say?"

"Of course I'll marry you, Henry Miller. You're the sweetest man in Holmes County." He sounded incredibly like the honey-tongued Miss Glick. Both men chuckled merrily.

"You probably are." Their laughter turned to louder guffaws.

"Then she said she saw no need for me to build a house when *mamm* and *daed* have all those rooms and it was just the two of them."

"Wow, that surprises me." Matthew would have thought the lovely Rebekah the type who would insist upon her own four-bedroom abode.

"Me too." Henry swept off his hat and resettled it atop his head. "But, hey, this saves me the work of building a house."

"Don't get too excited. You can always help me build mine." They left the dusty path and entered the sheep pasture through the aluminum gate, which Henry latched behind them.

"I'll gladly help with your house, but since it's yours, I can come home when I'm tired of pounding nails and do something different."

"We'll hold a work frolic to get the main walls and roof on. I'd still love to put it up this year, maybe in November before the snow flies. Then I can work on the interior over the winter months when there's not much else to do."

"You're doing a lot of thinking and figuring. Your brain must be mighty worn out." Henry kicked his Morgan's flanks to prod her into a faster pace.

Matthew's horse took off too. Neither slowed down until they had reached the top of the high pasture. Miller land—Seth and Simon's—spread out in both directions for as far as one could see. "This is the prettiest spot on the farm. How would you like a little house up here with this view?"

Henry shielded his eyes and gazed around, despite having seen the view his entire life. "Sure is nice, but I wouldn't want a driveway this long in winter."

"You make a good point. And *daed* thinks I'm the practical one." He pulled the apples from his pocket and began tossing them to old Bess one by one.

Henry merely smiled, content with himself.

"What do you say we put our heads together on a regular basis?" Matthew turned to face him.

Henry's face lit up. "You offering what I think you're offering?"

"We partner up in the horse-training business. You'd be the main man. I don't want to take anything away from you."

"We don't need a main man. We could be equal partners! Oh, Matty. That's been my dream, but I never thought it would happen now that you've worked for the racing industry and that fancy saddlebred stable. I say *jah!*"

"I might have to work a couple days a week somewhere else. I'm hoping Mr. Mac might take me back, but just part-time. I don't want to be away from my family. I've had enough of that to last a lifetime." He stuck out his hand to seal the deal.

Henry grabbed the hand, but instead of shaking he pulled his brother into a hug...and right off his horse. Both men tumbled into the tall grass with snorts of laughter. The Morgans calmly wandered away to nibble tasty growth elsewhere.

"You would think two fancy trainers would be able to stay astride a horse!" The taunting voice drifted over the meadow from an unseen witness.

Henry jumped up and then hauled Matthew to his feet. They spotted their *mamm* on the next hillock, surrounded by four little *kinner*.

Matthew cupped his hands around his mouth. "We were trying out a special trick."

"The trick will be for *you* not to miss your bus, young man. We're heading down for breakfast."

The men mounted almost as easily as they had fallen off the Morgans and rode back to the house without pausing. They would have plenty of time to iron out details and make their plans for their partnership. Right now, it was a Miller brother favorite—time to eat.

～

Late September

"Phoebe!"

Her mother's voice from above finally pierced her consciousness. "I'm down here, in the cellar."

First her feet and then the rest of Hannah appeared on the stairs. "What are you still doing down here?" She stepped off the bottom rung.

"You told me to clean the basement, so that's what I'm doing." Phoebe tucked a sweated lock of hair beneath her *kapp*.

Hannah peered around the room with hands on hips. "Good grief. I meant dust the metal shelves so we can bring down the rest of the canned jars. There's not a cobweb in sight. This cellar has never looked so nice." Her focus fell on Phoebe. "What's come over you?"

"Nothing. I just wanted to do a good job on my chores so nothing stands in my way of attending Saturday's singing. There'll be a hayride afterward." Phoebe resumed lining up pickle jars with meticulous precision.

"I take it Eli Riehl plans to attend this event?" teased Hannah.

"I do believe he might have mentioned as much at preaching."

"Well, there's one chore you've neglected—getting the mail."

She wheeled around. "I'll stop and do it right now, *mamm*."

"No need, I already did." Hannah paused halfway up the steps. "But you might want to interrupt artistically arranging canned vegetables to read the letter that came for you." Her words floated down, disembodied, because Hannah had already disappeared. "Some odd-sounding publishing house wrote to you—New Start Publishing or Great Beginnings or something like that."

Phoebe recognized her mother's teasing voice, but it took several moments before their meaning registered. Then she flew upstairs without her feet touching the treads. In the center of the table sat the letter. She tore it open and quickly scanned the contents. Then she slid into a chair to read more carefully, one word at a time, so there would be no misunderstanding. Slumping forward, she closed her eyes and thanked the One responsible for all life's pivotal moments. "Thank You, Lord," she whispered.

"What is it, sweet girl?" asked Hannah.

Phoebe had to wait for her composure to return. "They want to publish Eli's story and my illustrations. They want to make them into a gift book, ready by next Easter." Her voice cracked, so she sucked in a deep gulp of air. "Oh, *mamm*," she continued. "I'm going to be a children's book illustrator." Then she couldn't hold back the torrent of emotion any longer. Phoebe cried like a baby when her diaper had been wet, and like a little girl when her mother had died, and now as a young woman whose first real dream was about to come true.

"I'm so very happy for you," murmured Hannah.

When Phoebe turned around, she saw that her mother was crying too. She rose to her feet and ran for an enveloping hug. "I can't wait to tell Eli. I think he'll be pleased. How will I ever last until Saturday with this news?"

"Why wait? Show him the letter now. News like this doesn't come every day." Hannah pulled away, wiped her face, and started dicing a bunch of celery.

Phoebe remained in place, dumbfounded. "I can't take the pony cart to the Riehls'. I would never get home before dark."

Hannah attacked another stalk with her paring knife. "Tell him to meet you halfway at the library, but don't tell him why."

"How could I do that? We don't have a phone." For some reason, she felt mighty stupid for an about-to-be-published person.

Hannah glanced up from chopping. "Run next door and ask to use Mrs. Lee's. The Riehls have a business line for their hams. Eli might even be the one to answer. We're allowed to make emergency phone calls, and I'd say this is an emergency."

"*Danki*," Phoebe managed to say despite the tears that had begun anew.

"Then come back and take a quick shower before you go because you're a mess. I'll have Ben hitch up the horse."

～

Within an hour, smelling sweet as lilacs thanks to scented body wash and powder, Phoebe was on her way to Winesburg. Within two and a half hours, she sat across from Eli at their private table in their favorite place on earth.

It took him several minutes to read the relatively short letter because he kept blinking his eyes.

Phoebe sat very still, giving him time to digest the news, as she had needed.

Finally, in a bizarre accent he spoke. "This is a rather interesting turn of events, isn't it, Miss Miller?"

Then he leaped to his feet and all pandemonium broke out. Eli and Phoebe jumped up and down, shouting and laughing, as Amish people were never meant to. Fortunately, the Winesburg Library had no other patrons. Mrs. Carter soon joined them, clapping and hurrahing and behaving in such un-librarian fashion that it was a wonder the library didn't lose its license.

When everyone settled down, Mrs. Carter returned to her computer monitor and the two Plain folk restored their modest demeanor. "I know you're busy with the farm," Phoebe said. "So I'll try to do as much as I can with the edits or whatever they're called to the story. I'll set up an e-mail account here at the library and take responsibility. I'm so proud of you for stepping up to help your family as well as you have."

His forehead wrinkled in puzzlement. "You didn't think being a good farmer was something I had in me? Because I assure you, I've always been part of the reason Riehl honey-glazed hams are best in the county."

Phoebe flushed with shame. "Oh, no, I didn't mean that. I always knew you'd make a great pig farmer."

"All right, then." He tugged his cuffs down. "I don't want you to think I'm just a storytelling windbag, filled with nothing but words and hot air."

She batted her eyelashes. "Oh, no, Eli. I've seen you in action with Miss Priss, standing in the worst of it, up to your ankles."

He smiled in his long, slow fashion, something she hadn't seen in a while. "Well, that's better. And I have some good news myself, sweet peach. Although I'd be hard-pressed to top your bombshell."

She leaned closer and batted her lashes once more. "Give it a shot."

"Not one, but two of my sisters have announced their engagements."

"Is Rose one of them? Give her my best wishes."

"She is, and both of their husbands-to-be want to farm, but neither have any land." His eyes practically danced in his face. "Alas, I said. How could this conundrum be solved?" Eli pressed his index finger to his lips. "So I suggested both men build their homes at the Riehl farm and join the business!"

Phoebe had never heard the word "conundrum" in her life, but she figured out the meaning through context. "What did they say?"

"They said it was a smashing idea and had hoped and prayed for exactly that." He used his hands to frame the shape of a sign. "Riehl and Son and Sons-in-Law Swine and Beef. What do you think?"

"I think I would leave the current name alone. Customers will figure out where the other two sons came from."

Eli dropped his hands to clasp hers. All posturing and emulating odd foreign voices had gone. "Do you know what this means, Phoebe? I'll have time to be a writer *and* a farmer. And my dad gets stronger every day. He fully intends to do the paperwork and keep the books. We can meet on Wednesdays to put this book to bed. And then there are Saturday nights for socials and Sundays for preaching." He shrugged. "You might get sick of seeing me so much."

"I don't think so. You are absolutely, positively not boring." She winked.

He winked back. "What will you do with your half of the advance check when it comes?"

Phoebe straightened up. "There will be no dividing up the money, Eli. It'll all go toward your father's medical bills. And any future money can bolster our community's medical fund."

He squeezed her hand. "You're a good woman, Phoebe Miller. Even if you grease yourself down, there will be no slipping away from me now."

And that was just fine with the little picture drawer from Holmes County with no other valuable skill worth mentioning.

Fresh Lemon Sheet Cake

Rosanna Coblentz

1½ cups white sugar

½ cup butter (1 stick)

2 cups cake flour

4 teaspoons baking powder

½ teaspoon salt

1 cup milk

Juice of ½ lemon

2 teaspoons lemon zest

2 eggs, well beaten

Yellow food coloring (optional)

Cream together sugar and butter. In a separate bowl, combine the cake flour, baking powder, and salt. Add the dry ingredients to the sugar and butter mixture, alternating with the milk. Then add the lemon juice and lemon zest (and food coloring, if desired). Finally, fold in the eggs.

Bake at 350 degrees for approximately 25 minutes or until a toothpick comes out clean.

Rosie's hint: This cake is great with lemon sherbet for a cool summertime treat, or you can top it with Lemon Butter Frosting.

Lemon Butter Frosting

3 tablespoons butter (softened to room temperature)

2 egg yolks

2½ cups powdered sugar

1 teaspoon lemon zest

2 tablespoons lemon juice

Cream the butter and then blend in egg yolks. Stir in remaining ingredients until smooth.

Old Fashioned Spelt-Oatmeal Raisin Cookies
Rosanna Coblentz

3 cups brown sugar

1½ cups butter (three sticks)

4 eggs, well beaten

1 cup raisins

½ cup boiling water

3 teaspoons baking soda

1¾ cups all-purpose flour

2 cups whole spelt flour

4 cups oatmeal (quick oats)

2 teaspoons cinnamon

2 teaspoons baking powder

Cream together the brown sugar, butter, and eggs. Stir in the raisins. In a cup, mix together the boiling water and baking soda and then add to the wet mixture.

In a separate bowl, combine the flours, oats, cinnamon, and baking powder. Combine the dry ingredients with the sugar and butter mixture and mix well. Drop by rounded spoonfuls on a cookie sheet about 2 to 3 inches apart and bake at 325 degrees for approximately 10 to 12 minutes.

Rosie's hint: These make great Amish whoopie pies. Just make a filling to spread on the bottom of one cookie and then put another cookie on top. Kids love them!

Whoopie Pie Filling

2 egg whites, beaten

2 cups powdered sugar

1 teaspoon vanilla

1½ cups Crisco shortening

Beat the first three ingredients together and then add 1½ cups of Crisco shortening.

DISCUSSION QUESTIONS

1. Why does Seth change his mind about his daughter's trip to Niagara Falls with a youth group?

2. Julia has struggled throughout life with debilitating rheumatoid arthritis, yet she still manages to cope without falling into depression. In what ways has her family's moving away affected her?

3. Eli Riehl is no ordinary young man. Why does his being different appeal so much to Phoebe? And how does his uniqueness make life harder for him in an Amish community?

4. Do you feel Matthew has become "overly fond" of money as his wife asserts, or is he merely being practical as a husband and father? Why can't the Amish fully distance themselves from the English world?

5. Traveling to Hancock, Wisconsin, is a disaster for Leah Byler instead of a pleasant family vacation. What factors contribute to her misery in the land of milk and cheese?

6. Emma Davis reaches a crossroads with both her mother and her mother-in-law. How are her struggles common to all married daughters, and in what ways are they unique to an Amish wife and mother?

7. Eli and Phoebe's joint project is fraught with peril for two young people. What makes it especially troublesome, in both the practical sense and in the unforeseeable future, for Amish youth?

8. How does Matthew and Martha's visit home create as many problems as it had been meant to solve within their marriage?

9. Phoebe has grown to accept and love Hannah as her mother without reservation. But still water runs deep in this quiet teenager's emotional state. What unresolved issues still remain regarding Constance's death after all these years?

10. Why has Emma been remiss in teaching her sons *Deutsch*? And how would that make things difficult for her children in their district?

11. Often it takes tragedy to trigger necessary changes within our lives. How does his father's heart attack change Eli's life—physically, emotionally, and regarding his long-range expectations?

12. How does Julia cope with a houseful of people? And how does she finally find what she's been searching for?

13. Describe Phoebe's maturation and spiritual growth throughout the story.

14. Leah Byler has made peace with her mother-in-law. What mind-set did she need to give up for that to become possible?

15. Martha Miller, at long last, is happy. In what ways has Matthew's decision benefited him as much, if not more than his wife?

ABOUT THE AUTHOR

~

Mary Ellis grew up close to the eastern Ohio Amish community, Geauga County, where her parents often took her to farmers' markets and woodworking fairs. She and her husband now live close to a large population of Amish families, where she does her research...and enjoys the simple way of life.

Discover Mary's other books, especially *Abigail's New Hope* and *A Marriage for Meghan,* at www.harvesthousepublishers.com

~

Mary loves to hear from her readers
at maryeellis@yahoo.com
or
www.maryeellis.wordpress.com

~ *Drawing by an Old Order Amish youth* ~

Can a Young Amish Widow Find Love?

After the death of her husband, Hannah Brown is determined to make a new life with her sister's family. But when she sells her farm in Lancaster County, Pennsylvania, and moves her sheep to Ohio, the wool unexpectedly begins to fly. Simon, her deacon brother-in-law, finds just about everything about Hannah vexing. So no one is more surprised than the deacon when his own brother, Seth, shows interest in the beautiful young widow.

But perhaps he has nothing to worry about. The two seem to be at cross-purposes as often as not. Hannah is willful, and Seth has an independent streak a mile wide. But much is at stake, including the heart of Seth's silent young daughter, Phoebe. Can Seth and Hannah move past their own pain to find a lasting love?

An inspirational story of trust in the God who sees our needs before we do.

What Happens When an Amish Girl's Prince Charming Is an Englischer?

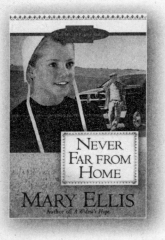

Emma Miller is on the cusp of leaving childhood behind and entering the adult world. She has finished school, started her own wool business, and longs for someone to court. When the object of her affection is a handsome English sheep farmer with a fast truck and modern methods, her deacon father, Simon, knows he has more than the farm alliance to worry about.

Emma isn't the only one with longings in Holmes County. Her mother yearns for relief from a debilitating disease, Aunt Hannah wishes for a baby, and Uncle Seth hopes he'll reap financial rewards when he undertakes a risk with his harvest. But are these the plans God has for this close-knit Amish family?

An engaging story about waiting on God for His perfect timing and discovering that dreams planted close to home can grow a lasting harvest of hope and love.

Can a Loving Amish Woman Be a Refuge for a Wounded Soul?

Leah Miller, a talented young woman in the kitchen, is living her dream come true as she invests in a newly restored diner that caters mostly to locals. Jonah Byler is a dairy farmer with a secret. Having just moved to the area, can he persuade this quiet young woman to leave her adoring fans and cook only for him? Once she discovers what he has been hiding from others, can Leah trust Jonah with her heart?

Working at the diner introduces Leah to both Amish and English patrons. Though maturing into womanhood, *rumschpringe* holds little appeal to the gentle, shy girl who has never been the center of attention before. When three Amish men vie for her attention, competing with Jonah, Leah must find a way to understand the confusing new emotions swirling around her.

A captivating story that lovingly looks at how faith in God and connection with family can fill every open, waiting heart to overflowing.

Love Blooms in Unexpected Places

As an Amish midwife, Abigail Graber loves bringing babies into the world. But when a difficult delivery takes a devastating turn, she is faced with some hard choices. Despite her best efforts, the young mother dies—but the baby is saved.

When a heartless judge confines Abigail to the county jail for her mistakes, her sister Catherine comes to the Graber farm to care for Abigail's young children while her husband, Daniel, works his fields. And for the first time Catherine meets Daniel's reclusive cousin, Isaiah, who is deaf and thought to be simpleminded by his community. She endeavors to teach him to communicate and discovers he possesses unexpected gifts and talents.

While Abigail searches for forgiveness, Catherine changes lives and, in return, finds love, something long elusive in her life. Isaiah discovers God, who cares nothing about our handicaps or limitations in His sustaining grace.

An inspirational tale of overcoming grief, maintaining faith, and finding hope in an ever-changing world.

How long will true love wait?

Meghan Yost is bright, talented, and eager to prove to her father, the bishop, that at nineteen she's mature enough to teach in an Amish school all by herself. But just as she gains confidence and assurance, a troubled student challenges her authority and an enthusiastic suitor in the headstrong Jacob Schultz challenges her patience. How can Meghan outgrow her nickname of "little goose" if she can't prove herself to be a capable adult who can stand on her own two feet?

When a series of apparent hate crimes sweep through the district, the sheriff calls in the FBI, and Special Agent Thomas Mast arrives in Wayne County carrying a secret he's hidden for years. Will he come to terms with the past and regain his relationship with God before his career hardens his heart? With more on her plate than one girl can handle, Meghan sets out to help with the investigation, and Thomas ends up working closely with the bishop, who hopes the criminals will be arrested before Meghan finds herself in love with the most inappropriate of suitors—an *Englischer*...

An engaging story of one girl's quest for independence and true love as social prejudice tests a community's faith in a simpler world.